SPYMASTER ADAGIO

Roger Bensaid

authors
online

An Authors OnLine Book

British Library Cataloguing Publication Data.
A catalogue record for this book is available from the British Library

ISBN 978-0-7552-0734-3

Authors OnLine Ltd
19 The Cinques
Gamlingay, Sandy
Bedfordshire SG19 3NU
England

This book is also available in e-book format, details of which are available at www.authorsonline.co.uk

The book is dedicated to
Kate, Chloe, Christian and Julian.

Acknowledgements and Foreword

This book was some years in the making, primarily because my English is so poor, and it would not have been published at all without the heroic editing effort of Maggie Jones who, unlike me, can tell a comma from a full stop. A second special thank you to Andrea Billen, the Authors OnLine proofreader, who brought the book together. Thank you, both.

Now I've got this first book off my chest I can get on with the sequels. I do hope the reader gets some enjoyment from an old-fashioned, cold war, soldier-spy story, with an underlying vendetta that is set to continue.

So why did I write it? Well, it's complicated. Firstly, I was serving when I wrote the middle, or part two, of the book, when it was a simple choice of go to the bar after work or create something. I chose to write and despite my poor grasp of grammar I got it done! And also in the hope it would transform me into a wordsmith.

Over the duration of the book's creation, there were many friends who helped; some were amused, some sympathetic, thank goodness, and a few somewhat bemused.

For their input and help, my thanks to Kate, Andrew, Graham, Pat, Nancy and Bob.

Roger 2014

"Get on and do it, never give up. Focus on the barriers to achieving your mission, innovate, improvise, and overcome. Just get it done!" Bob

"If it's under the bridge it's gone; only the next step counts, so step carefully." Pat

CONTENTS

Part One
THE SPYMASTERS

Part Two
THE CYPRUS AFFAIR

Part Three
THE SPYMASTER'S VENDETTA

Part One

THE SPYMASTERS

Chapter 1

SOUTH AFRICA – ZERO HOUR

Jean Saied, the mercenary leader, lay alert and tense in the brush scrubland with his men silent all around him. He knew he was beginning to show signs that he was anxious; this irritated him and he fought an uncharacteristic rising panic. He settled himself down by breathing in and out slowly until he felt calm again. A cold sweat had broken out on his forehead forming beads that ran down into his eyes stinging them. Irritably he wiped the sweat away with his forearm. His eyes still stung and he screwed them up and blinked hard to clear the mist in them.

He knew that he had to hide any outward feelings of anxiety. It would be a disaster for his men to see that he had any doubts about the task that lay ahead. As it was, the men barely tolerated him. Many of them were old enough to be his father and they had a natural distrust of the taciturn, cold-eyed Arab.

For themselves, the men felt little warmth or rapport with Saied and he knew it, just as he knew that, before the night was out, that had to change. They thought of him as a cold, calculating machine and had little confidence that if they were in trouble he would not simply dispatch any individual dispassionately in exchange for his own success or that of the mission. Nevertheless their code, such as it was, meant they would follow him. He had hired them and they had agreed to his leadership.

The men were a mixed group of whites and coloureds from a myriad of countries across the world; the team had been brigaded together for this single mission. As a body they were as good as you would find anywhere, with their freelance status as soldiers of fortune. Nevertheless most felt an unease with their Arab leader; they all knew of him but only by reputation and in many ways the men's cohesion as a team was generated by their reliance on each other rather than their leader.

Jean Saied, tanned and fit and in his early thirties, was a West Bank Arab who looked more European than Arab, save for the doe-shaped dark brown eyes and short black hair. Stocky and formidably strong for his size, he was quick in movement and thought. Jean's forays against the Israelis, as a youth, had earned him a price on his head at an early age. When the Israelis overran his family home he had to flee, working his way from Egypt down the continent of Africa. He had worked for any dissident leader who would hire him, building his reputation as a mercenary who would lead men successfully into situations where another would have hesitated.

In Angola, he was noticed by the Cuban advisers there; his leadership style when in a firefight was effective and innovative. Whilst these skills were critical to a fighter, Saied lacked other essential leadership skills in planning, logistics and administration, which the Cuban officers felt could be corrected and which would add value to his usefulness to them. They concluded that both he and they would benefit if they sent him away for leadership training where he would have the opportunity to acquire them.

They sent him to Cuba for training where they believed this rounding would give them a junior surrogate commander and a third-party dissident that they could implant into areas of interest, in effect, one step removed from them and their paymasters, the Russians, and therefore a deniable asset. On his return to Angola he had thanked his sponsors for his training and gathered knowledge, returning to the West Bank shortly afterwards to create havoc and to await a call from his masters to resume his work for them, when he hoped to continue to build himself a reputation as a quick-witted, dependable and competent commander. As the years rolled on there had been many calls from his mentors and he had always responded.

Tonight was the first time he had been in charge of a totally independent operation in a strange country he had never visited before and where there was no support or backup – no plan B.

He had been briefed well at meetings with the client, Thomas Hough, and at the first meeting, another individual had been in attendance who had said little. From the way the man acted and by the way he handled himself Saied thought he must be the sponsor and the ultimate client. For Saied, this mission should be easier than some he had undertaken but he was on his own, as he thought for the thousandth time. The men and the task were his, to win or fail. Success on the job would undoubtedly give him the reputation he needed in his shadowy world, to command his own price as a third-party operator, commanding the same privileges and remuneration as ex-British and American special forces operatives.

All Saied knew of the sponsor was that he was an exceptionally tall, gaunt individual, with steady coal-black eyes. Saied had noticed the man's left hand, which was claw-like and badly scarred. The man was, Saied had correctly surmised, a high-ranking KGB officer.

Ten minutes to go to the target. Jean gathered his three attack section leaders around him for their final briefing. Each section leader was controlling four men; his section of four, the recovery section, waited in three large inflatable Rigid Raiders just off the coast, half a kilometre away from his current position. Every section had a key task. There was no leeway for any section not carrying out its part of the mission effectively.

What was worrying him most was that immediately after the attack, he and his men must escape back across the deserted rough ground, broken only by scarred, flat, wind-blasted sandstone, palm trees and salt-dwarfed bushes. At an appointed time, an old tramp freighter would make a pass a kilometre off the coast and pick up Saied and his team. They simply could not afford to be late or they might literally miss the boat.

He watched and waited, grim-faced, as his section leaders faded away into the night and returned to their men. His head pounded but he knew that once the action started this would be displaced with the familiar adrenaline rush he always welcomed. When he was sure the section leaders and their men had advanced to their jump-off points, he and the radio operator made their way silently to the target. For the tenth time that night he checked his gun and magazines. Whilst this was a displacement activity he well knew, it was also an essential part of every soldier's drill. He worked his bolt back and forth along the slide. Confident he was ready, he slipped the safety off. Once in sight of the guardhouse at the final objective they all went to ground and made themselves as comfortable as they could. Saied watched and waited as bats whirled and swooped over them, the rustle of the palms accompanied by the pounding of the distant surf was the only constant in their dark world.

Irritants, bugs, ants, snuffling rodents and mosquitoes had to be borne in silence. A large centipede scuttled over one of Saied's hands, he watched it dispassionately as it disappeared into the darkness and then shuddered. Whatever man did this night, their insect world would not change. It would go on as it always had.

From early evening, as soon as dusk fell, filling in the twilight-lengthening shadows, his men had been infiltrating the scrubland. Their target, only half a kilometre from the beach where they had landed, was ten kilometres from the outskirts of Cape Town to its west. Their target tonight was the South African government's Computer Research Station. The research station, a solitary, three-storey, grey block slab of a building was an ugly edifice growing out of the bush lands. It was not large by many government building standards, and was completely square, 50 metres by 50 metres, flat roofed and in its own grounds. Only the front of the building had any character, with its three-storey plate glass reception area lending any aesthetic leaning to the dull grey structure. The whole of the complex was surrounded by a four metre high fence with a 100 metre clearance between the building and the fence in every direction.

In addition to the security fence was a permanent complement of ten armed guards from the South African Defence Force who rotated every 12 hours with another complement of men. Two soldiers patrolled the outside compound continuously and two manned the reception entrance, placing themselves inside the building itself. At the main entrance gate there was a substantial concrete guardroom where five other relief guards dozed in a back room.

Only the guard commander was nodding awake, his head drooping down at his desk in the small guardroom reception area. Through the window he gazed lazily at the patrolling guard that appeared in his vision every 15 minutes or so when they passed the spotlight at the guardhouse entrance. The lights in the compound were off again; an economy measure he thought to himself, or more likely nobody could be fucked to maintain them. What a shit job this was. He scratched the stubble on his chin. Halfway through the watch and as usual nothing ever happened. "Was this what I joined the Defence Force for?" cursed the commander, "Same old same old," he sighed.

A further hour on, the relief guards slept in their cots and the guard commander lolled at the desk with his view of the gate through the guardroom window blurring as his eyelids, heavy with boredom, closed more and more often now, his head lolling, until he finally let himself lean forward to rest his head on to the desk, just for a few minutes he promised himself.

To the front of the complex gate was a tarmac road. The road curved for some 100 metres through uninhabited scrubland to a minor road leading to the capital. This site is a deserted spot by any measure, so much the better for that! Saied mused as he waited in the scrub, still determinedly ignoring the biting insect life. He could, (or was it his imagination?) smell the sea to his rear on the onshore night breeze, and it was a comfort knowing that was where his escape boats bobbed up and down near the beach in the white, wave-flecked surf.

Growing all around the outside of the complex to the road in the front of the guardhouse entrance gate was a narrow but dense belt of trees planted a few metres outside the fence line. The trees, Saied knew, were an attempt by the authorities to hide the complex from casual observers but for his purpose offered excellent approach cover.

The three sections at this location consisted of an assault group with the task of eliminating the guards in the guardroom; the storm section that had been tasked with breaking into the main building complex, they then had to make their way into the secure area to steal the device they had come for; the third section had to eliminate both walking guards in the grounds and then lay down a hail of gunfire to support the assault section attacking the guardroom.

It was very dark now, nearly three in the morning, and all but silent except for the night sounds and the wind rustling through the branches and needle-like fronds of the palm trees; the night sounds broken by the occasional cough of the guards. The sounds and smells of night were not alien to Saied but still somehow foreign. The thump of a falling coconut from one of the trees close by made him start. Alert now, he strained to hear what was going on in the complex.

The guards were slack. In the scrubland, Saied smiled as he watched the guards flash their torches from time to time. They made it ridiculously easy for his men to locate them. Saied cocked his ears. He could now just discern the throb of outboard engines to seaward; the boats were controlled by his second in command who, he knew, could be relied on to ensure that the boats were there for him and that the area of the beach they would need would be free of obstructions, allowing the boats to beach and take him and his men to safety after the assault on the complex.

Saied knelt up as he received one, then two clicks on his headphones, signalling that two of his sections were inside the fence. The two clicks also confirmed that they had taken out the two walking guards with their silenced machine pistols.

The storm section responsible for neutralising the security guards in the building complex reception area were now in an assault position just out of sight of the building's glassed reception area, but nevertheless, near enough to storm the facility's glass entrance doors which barred their way. In the reception area, two guards sat talking and smoking in the visitors' soft leather chairs.

Saied toggled his throat microphone three times and received three clicks back into his earphones. His assault group had crawled to within 30 metres of the guardroom in front of the facility. They were ready for action.

They reacted immediately to the three clicks sent by Saied. They raised three Rocket Propelled Grenades and all were fired together, two rockets into the guardroom and one at the gate. As soon as the rockets exploded, the assault section dropped the launchers and picked up their machine rifles in one smooth movement launching themselves towards the gate.

The resultant destruction from the three rockets fired together at such small targets was massive. The men in the guardhouse, dead, dying or disoriented, now received a hail of fire from the section in the grounds that had dealt with the walking guards. This group only stopped firing when the assault section stormed the destroyed gates, which were still swinging lazily to the ground now made free of the wrecked hinges, and were through it.

The assault section entered the guardroom pumping bullets unremittingly until their commander cried, "Stop! Stop! Stop! I am confirming all dead." Only the security commander had reacted automatically but barely got off a few poorly aimed rounds before being cut down. With the adrenaline still pumping, their leader ordered his men to clear up any evidence that would link their presence as far as it was possible and to pack away their arsenal.

The two startled guards in the building reception area had little time to react after the rocket attack, one ran and doused the lights and the other fumbled with his rifle, panicking, finally cocking and making ready. In the darkness he saw the gleaming teeth and eyes of the storm group as they pressed against the glass entrance door. He fumbled as he pointed the AK and fired the full magazine into the group.

The security guard saw men drop flat as the glass doors exploded outwards from his burst of fire. Then the storming group of mercenaries reappeared, firing into the reception area through the shattered doorway. The guard who had failed to react after turning off the lights was shot several times as Saied's men entered the complex. The other guard ran into the building, needing cover to reload and to raise the alarm. He barged into the director's office on the ground floor where the only phone with a direct outside line was located. In a frenzy, he dialled the police while at the same time trying to thumb shells into the empty magazine of his machine gun. This is how the storm group found him. He only had time to shout, "Help!" down the phone before they scythed him down.

Jean Saied, following the storm section into the complex, appeared in the doorway of the room, taking in the position at a glance. While his men were momentarily frozen by the developing situation, he looked from the dead guard to the phone. In the ensuing silence, Saied and his men could hear policemen on the other end shouting. He quickly strode across the room, picked up the phone that was dangling on its cord from the desk and listened; on the other end a duty policeman was still shouting for information.

Saied thought quickly, "It's all right! It's all right! Sorry," he shouted back down the line, "One of the guards tripped and set off his gun accidentally. Everything is fine here except the reception area is going to need a bit of redecoration; the idiot!"

"Who are you?" the policeman was suspicious.

Saied grabbed the bloodied ID card of the dead guard, ripping it from his neck, "Lance Corporal Joseph, South African Defence Force."

"You had better get me your officer."

"Please stay on the line. My officer is sorting things out, so give me a few minutes to get him to you."

"Hurry up then," the police officer seemed to relax a little but remained impatient.

"Back in a minute, sir, stay on the line." Saied cupped the phone mouthpiece and mouthed to his radio operator to run and get the ID card of the dead guard commander. With the phone still cupped, he told the storm section commander that when his radio operator got back with the ID, he must talk to the police and convince them all was well. Curtly he handed the phone to the commander and signalled for the rest of the men to follow him deeper into the complex.

On the ground floor to the rear of the building was the strongroom. The men knew what to do. The alarm system had been their first task. They had disabled it and the line out neutralized; not a problem as they had been given the code by their client. Saied's electronics specialist in the assault team sorted out the line and alarm in seconds.

The bags they dragged in contained drills, with burning equipment and prepared explosives just in case. They worked at the task of opening the vault door, burning off the hinges and then the two locks. It was a simple steel door with a double lock securing it to the steel frame. The frame had been bolted into the stonework.

The storm section had begun the burnout of the locks when their leader, Daniel, a stocky South African black man in his early forties, returned, angry and sweating.

"Did my best, Jean," he reported, with his head on one side.

"But?" Saied questioned.

"They insisted that they send a patrol car to check that all's well and a team in the morning to take statements. I couldn't resist too much or they would have sent a squad now, and then we would be really fucked up, so I said I would receive them at the gate when they arrived; from what he said we probably have about fifteen maybe twenty minutes max before they get here."

"Hmm," grunted Saied looking at the team working on the door. "You are going to have to buy us some time, Daniel. Meet them up the track, if they see the gate they will run for it. Do what you have to but don't let them report back, unless you can persuade one of them to at least make a call to report all is well." Saied raised his eyebrows at Daniel, "Know what I mean?"

"Yes, boss, I need two men," Daniel waited.

The door to the strongroom gave way with a groan and was swung open.

Saied looked at his watch, "Wait a moment," he entered the strongroom, quickly saw what he wanted on a shelf in the middle of the room and returned to Daniel, "OK, choose two from your team. Whatever happens, you must be at the beach in..." he looked at his watch again "...thirty minutes from now, thirty-five max, or you'll be on your own, got it?"

"We'll be there," Daniel promised Saied with a grin and nodded to two of his men who were watching the exchange between the two of them. They quickly gathered their guns and utility belts and jogged off with Daniel.

Saied turned his attention back to the strongroom; he went in and collected the device in its case. He opened the case to check that the device was in it, stood looking at the contents for a moment, wondering how this laptop-sized box of tricks could be worth tonight's cost in life, never mind the funding for the operation. He shrugged, not his problem; he stuffed the device into his bergen before looking up and speaking to the other section commanders now waiting on his orders.

"We have got what we came for, you know what to do. Make sure there is nothing to link us to this site and make your way with your men back to the boats."

"Already done," said the assault section leader who had just joined him, "Reception area, outside and guardroom cleaned and cleared and all spent shells etc. collected, surfaces and phones wiped; the men have just got to collect the break-in kit used to open the strongroom and we leave."

"Good. Twenty-five minutes we leave the beach, got that?" Saied impressed on him; the man simply nodded.

Saied put the device in his bergen, secured the top and then swung the pack on to his shoulders. He collected his radio operator and left the sections to finish the clear-up and to follow him. Travelling at speed through the bush, Saied had his radio operator call up the boats to confirm the beach was secure. Five minutes later Saied and his radio operator burst out on to the palm-fringed rocky shore. His second in command, a wiry Scotsman, uncoiled himself from the side of the boat he was resting on and approached Saied.

"Any trouble, Jean?"

Saied cocked his head at the distant sound of a single gunshot in the distance, with a grin he murmured, looking down at the smaller man, "Nothing we couldn't handle, Jock, what about you?"

"Nay problem; few boys feeling a bit sick bobbing up and down on the sea but that's it, never saw a soul the whole time we've been around."

Minutes later the rest of the force arrived, running with the weapons and equipment; all were dripping with sweat from their exertions. All we need now is Daniel and his two men thought Saied and we can all get the hell out of here.

Jock immediately started to get the men and kit sorted among the boats while Saied consulted his watch once more. Daniel had only five minutes left to join them.

"Jock, two boats away as soon as you can, the other to wait five minutes for Daniel and two men." He saw Jock about to ask where Daniel was, "Tell you later. If Daniel does not turn up, the boat leaves and catches us up. Got that?"

"Done," Jock called over his shoulder.

"Second thoughts, Jock, you take the first two boats, I'll wait with the last boat."

"You sure about that?"

"Absolutely, here take the bergen and don't drop it in the sea, in it is what we came for and it has to arrive at its destination for us to get paid."

"Right, then," Jock grabbed the offered pack, swinging it on to his back. "We're away, see you later." Jock waved his two boats into the surf. Despite Jock's brash manner, he was touched that Saied had given him custody of the device and his estimation of Saied had gone up. He could lead from the front and he could delegate responsibility, skills Jock admired.

Jean Saied paced up and down on the beach; it wasn't really much of a beach, there was more sand in the hinterland than on this rocky shore, Jean thought randomly as he was pondering the next phase – handing over the device to the Russian.

Hough had simply told him that the Russian's plan was that as soon as the tramp steamer entered international waters, Saied and the device would be taken off the ship. How, Hough had not explained. Saied shrugged the tension out of his shoulders and rolled his head to loosen the muscles. Come on, come on, Daniel, where the hell are you? It was time to go. Saied listened but could hear nothing over the surf; suddenly out of the palms came three scrambling figures.

Saied ran to the boat which he and the crew moved into the waves. Daniel and his men joined them, running through the water before they all clambered on board. The driver gunned the motor, driving the boat on to the plane and skimming out to sea. By the time the boat was on the plane, Daniel had got enough of his breath back to talk to Saied.

"We bought time, boss, but it was not pretty. We blocked them a few hundred metres from the gates. There were two of them in the motor. We immobilized them immediately and worked on them. We had to kill one so the other knew we were serious."

Saied grunted and indicated that Daniel should continue, "He was scared by then, but we promised he would not be hurt if he would simply radio his control and tell them all was well; that he and his mate were going to have a look at the damage and would be back later. Control seemed to accept that and signed off."

Daniel looked at Saied, "I thought there had been enough blood spilt tonight so I tied him up and locked him in the boot of the car." Saied raised his head and was going to say something but Daniel forestalled him, "We left then, but I knew it was a mistake to leave him alive so we retraced our steps and killed him, that's why we were a delayed a bit. Sorry, boss."

Saied put his hand on the older man's shoulder. "Thank you Daniel you did well."

By now, the dark outline of the mother ship with just her running lights was looming up hard against a dark sky. The ship, the *MV Sea Jade*, was underway just enough to maintain steerage against the current. Saied's other two inflatables were already being hoisted aboard and, as Saied's own Rigid Raider was tethered to the ship, the vessel began to put on revolutions. Jock saw to the recovery and stowing of the third boat once Saied and the others were safely on board.

After cheerfully acknowledging the welcome and congratulations of his team, he reminded them that they were still a long way from home and that there remained much to do. His priority now was to speak to the captain of the vessel, Captain Ramón, to find out at what time and where they would hit international waters; a surlier Frenchman Jean had never met.

Saied and the captain worked on the charts on the bridge and agreed the coordinates for a rendezvous. In truth there had been a large degree of pre-planning and the rendezvous agreed was only a few nautical miles away from the expected meeting point.

Saied turned away from the captain in order to find a small pool of privacy on the noisy, crowded bridge to enable him to speak to his client; Saied dialled his sponsor.

The phone rang only three times before it was picked up. "Yes?" Saied thought he recognized the Russian's deep, heavily accented, voice.

"Tsygankov?" Saied wanted confirmation that the Russian was the one he had been told would be his contact for the exchange.

"Yes, it is, Saied, report please," Tsygankov answered casually.

"We have what you wanted on board."

"Good, in fact, excellent, well done. Now give me the details of the location for the transfer."

"You need to note this down; it's in the area we previously planned, near Tripp Seamount to the west of Port Nolloth Reef at 29' 43' 12' south, 13' 53' 36' east, give or take a couple of kilometres, we will be there in just under two hours from now," Jean said, giving Tsygankov the coordinates.

"Thank you, Saied, now listen carefully, you will transfer with the goods; I have a further task for you."

Saied determined to push back vehemently at this change of plan. He explained that he didn't think the men would be too happy now if he disappeared before they had been paid the other half of their fee; and he needed to see to the disposal of the kit.

"Listen, Saied, I have thought through these matters and concerns too but it is essential you come with us. In order to appease your men, I have put their money in a container on board the *Sea Jade*. It is already in the hold. The container serial number is W51098."

"About the kit?"

"Get Jock to sort it out, share the kit out or sell it; he can split the proceeds among the men."

"And what about my final payment, is that in the container too?" Saied questioned but didn't think so.

"Ah Jean, no, yours is safe with me here and you can have it after the transfer." The man's voice held a note of sympathy tinged with irony. Saied noted ruefully that Tsygankov had at least used his first name; somehow that didn't cheer him. "By the way, Jean, what is the depth of water at the rendezvous?"

Saied had noted this when he and the Sea Jade's captain had studied the charts so was able to respond immediately, "About 2,000 metres. It's just off the continental shelf."

"That will be fine. Thank you."

Puzzled, Saied cut off the call and went to find Jock and his section leaders. Once they were gathered, he gave them the container number so they could check it out, he wanted to make sure the men's money was all there and that they were being paid in full.

Saied was then able to spend the rest of his time before the rendezvous gathering his personal kit together and making time to thank his men, in groups or individually. Many of them surprised him with their thanks and promises to be happy to work with him again. After all, they had all come back without a scratch, a rare event in their uncertain world.

At six o'clock, as dawn was breaking over a rolling sea, they made the rendezvous point. Orders were shouted by the freighter captain to the crew that they were to hold the position. Whatever Saied had expected would be the vessel he would transfer to, the dark menacing silhouette of a KGB Soviet submarine would have been furthest from his thoughts.

It broke the surface a hundred metres from the *Sea Jade*, water cascading from its form, revealing a sleek black shape. The submarine was backdropped by a gentle swell on the dark cold sea. Almost immediately there was activity from the conning tower as men spilled out of it and broke out an inflatable dinghy; three men from the submarine clambered into it and rowed swiftly across to the *Sea Jade*.

Saied was leaning on the ship's rail and watched fascinated as the sea water poured off the submarine's sides as it rose out of the sea. He noticed the men sorting out the boat and others working on the deck; then two figures appeared on the bridge of the tall slim conning tower. One, who wore a high-peaked Soviet naval officer's hat, was looking through a pair of field glasses, carefully surveying the ship; the other man towered over him by a foot or more and was bare headed.

In the middle of the ocean, gulls whirled and dived and perched momentarily on the two vessels, "Scavengers, waiting for something," thought Saied, "But what?" He was puzzled and had a feeling of foreboding.

Saied gathered his bergen on to his back and clambered down a net thrown over the side into the inflatable, which was being steadied by one of the Soviet sailors. As he was rowed away from the *Sea Jade*, he waved goodbye to the men who lined the ship's rails and then turned away to look at the shortening distance between himself and the submarine.

Sea Jade was already making way and turning to the north. The plan Saied and Jock had agreed with the captain was that once the transfer had taken place, they would sail at full speed to the first harbour they could get to in Namibia, the port of Luderitz. In case of trouble they would continue north to Tombua, the first possible berth on the Congo coast. This was to be a last resort, because at Luderitz there was a small airstrip where it might be possible to charter a plane to get the men away from the immediate area of South Africa. Whatever, once the men were disembarked, the *Sea Jade* would sail north to the Gold Coast and link up with Jock later to sell off the assault kit and to settle up.

As Saied clambered up on to the submarine, he prayed that the *Sea Jade* captain would get as much distance between himself and the Russians as quickly as possible. He glanced over his shoulder and was momentarily comforted that *Sea Jade* already seemed to have gained a separation and was growing smaller with every second that passed.

Saied climbed the conning tower ladder and accepted the hand offered to him as he made the small observation platform. He looked up into the serious gaunt face and cold black eyes of Tsygankov. The captain glanced uninterestingly at Saied and returned to his field glasses trained on the *Sea Jade*. They seemed to be in no hurry to submerge. Saied's blood ran cold; they were waiting for the distance between them and the *Sea Jade* to lengthen.

They must have stood together silently for a few minutes before the captain gave orders to fire torpedoes. Saied watched in horror as the missiles ran along the surface of the sea, closing rapidly with the *Sea Jade*. There was a loud muffled double crump of a sound from the *Sea Jade* as the torpedoes struck and she slowly keeled over and sank within a minute. Saied, no stranger to violent loss of life, was appalled; the knuckles on his hands gripping the open bridge whitened in rage.

The captain gave an order in Russian and the submarine slowly nosed her way to the explosion area.

Tsygankov was studying Saied who showed no emotion or acknowledgement of the act. The act was dishonourable but he knew in his heart that this was what he had feared since boarding the *Sea Jade*. They simply had to get rid of all links to themselves.

Saied knew that the South African coastguards would have seen their ship on their radar opposite the attack site at the time of the raid and then a few hours later making its way out to sea. Eventually someone would put two and two together and a search for the *Sea Jade* would begin.

Tsygankov sensed Saied's inner turmoil, "Come, Jean, you are a realist and must have known this was inevitable, but you..." Tsygankov put his hand on Saied's shoulder, "my favoured son will live to fight another day; I need to get you to your aircraft, for you with your prize have half a world to travel to your next destination."

Saied simply nodded his acceptance of the situation but inside he burned with anger and a promise that he would avenge this atrocity.

Tsygankov took Jean's bergen and drew the device from its case, he transferred it to another pre-prepared casing. He then picked up Saied's life jacket and hooked the original device case on to it.

Saied watched Tsygankov, "Ah yes, Jean, when we get over the explosion site we add this to the debris from the ship, but with this *Sea Jade* life jacket it will float. In the likely event that the South African's trawl through what is left floating on the sea they will come to the conclusion that the device is, how they say, at the bottom of the ocean." Tsygankov bent to eyeball Saied, "Now, Jean, you and I will go below and leave the captain to clear up any necessary matters around the site of the explosion."

Saied thought of hesitating in case there were any survivors, before realizing that this was precisely why Tsygankov was getting him below.

Chapter 2

LONDON – DAY ONE

On the second floor of Number Ten Downing Street, in the rabbit warren of rooms, all was hustle and bustle as the staff sorted out the early morning business. Most doors were open and people carrying boxes, files and bundles of letters, emails and faxes, flowed along the corridors and in and out of the various offices. At the far end of the floor, one door was closed firmly as the last of three men entered. They settled themselves down to compile the prime minister's daily update on the state and progress of priority and high-profile matters in their respective areas of the intelligence services.

Sir Peter Gray of the Prime Minister's Office threw the red Secret Intelligence Service daily journal on to the small conference table, just missing the coffee pot and cups laid out for their meeting, and collapsed into a chair. He had a stinking hangover. Heavy sessions during the week were something he normally avoided like the plague and he felt his years this morning, but the PM's private secretary's three-line whip to her senior staff the night before had ended in the early hours with too much port drunk and spilt at the meeting.

Sir Peter as a norm, on this depressingly grey, misty, damp morning was in an even poorer humour than usual. He was much older than the other two men in the room, more importantly, as a Whitehall mandarin, he was very much their senior and always made that abundantly clear to them.

Rodney Brown, from a discrete cell within the Secret Intelligence Services, a project-bridging department spanning the main services of

MI6, the 'spies', and MI5, the 'counterspies', and Don Keating from the Foreign Office, looked at Peter Gray and grinned at each other. They knew from the red-rimmed eyes and knitted eyebrows that he must have had a good night and that they were about to receive the after effects.

"Good night was it, sir?" said Don, looking round the room from one gilt-framed picture to another, avoiding the man's eyes that suddenly glared in suspicion.

"Oh, yes, excellent. Got a bit of a head this morning, though," he said dismissively.

"All in the line of duty though, you know," mouthed Rodney silently.

"All in the line of duty though, you know," Peter added and Rodney and Don smiled to themselves. "Right, gentlemen, what do you have? I would like to get this over quickly today if you don't mind." Gray was all business. He thought these meetings unnecessary, the leaders of the Secret Intelligence Committee were the main source of contact and briefing for the PM and her ministers. But the PM appeared to value this odd arrangement as some sort of check on the more powerful elements of the intelligence services. He spoke in a high-pitched voice that always irritated the two men and they had often wondered how his staff and the ministers put up with him; these two had little choice.

"Coffee, Sir Peter?" asked Don pouring for himself and Rodney.

"Yes, thank you. I will take it black today, no sugar."

"We don't appear to have anything new, thank goodness, so no change," said Rodney hopefully. He spread out his hands, indicating that he had nothing new to add since yesterday's report. Rodney, fair-haired of medium height and built like a rugby wing forward, hunched over the table more in hope than expectation that his 'no change' would be accepted.

"Same here, but we could just review where we are," echoed Don pointing to the red book with one hand and pouring cream and sugar into his cup with the other.

"That simply will not do, gentlemen!" Peter Gray burst out then cradled his forehead before continuing, "Will not do at all." Both Rodney and Don sat back in their chairs. "The old PM may have accepted that but this one will not; she most certainly will not." He glared at the two men and swallowing his coffee in one gulp added, "I'll be back in half an hour and you two had better have something for the book." He stomped out of the office with his red box, leaving the door ajar.

Both men looked at each other; Rodney, the more fiery of the two, was the first to speak.

"Oh bollocks, I don't know about you, but it seems the scene is completely static. We have the routine goings-on of course but that's about it, even military intelligence is having a quiet time over there and reportedly the Argentines, although there was some traffic earlier this month, are also now seemingly in blackout mode."

Rodney was standing in for his boss, Brigadier Robinson, who headed the unique section that Rodney worked for. It had been realized in the early seventies that there were matters that fell between the home defence secret services, MI5, and the external services, MI6. A small cell had been set up by the directors of these two services under an independent government minister, responsible for them but subordinate to the central Secret Intelligence Services' steering committee on which Brigadier Robinson sat as a co-opted member as need dictated. Its remit was to fill in where neither of the other two services felt it was in their interests to be involved, politically or otherwise. This small section was also a useful tool for the prime minister of the day to play with from time to time. It was often said in joke that Robinson's small section kept the others straight. Its role developed over time into mini projects and sometimes a cold case or a task that needed focus when the busy schedule of the other two prevented them from releasing resources to the assignment. Consequently, and by natural evolution, the small department moved and worked between the two main secret services with surprising ease, mainly due to the respect and high regard in which its head, Brigadier Robinson, was held. Because of its dual role, it had been decided that Robinson's crew would report daily, separately and with the Foreign Office representative, to Sir Peter Gray who was also heavily involved with the two main branches of the secret services.

The section itself was small and deliberately so. It could use, as and when available, the full resources of the other two services. They would bid for support and intelligence through the service directors. In this way the other two knew what was going on and a bond of trust had grown between them. When Robinson's section had been set up, the byword had been 'no surprises'. The arrangement worked well. Unlike the 'no questions asked' status of the 'Ks', the day-rate men that carried out the dirty work that no particular state would admit to, Robinson's cadre of staff were accountable.

Don responded, "Just the same, nothing of interest to bother the PM with." Don was the antithesis of Rodney. He was middle-aged, tall, slim and narrow shouldered. Scratching his thinning fair hair he added, "What about a short briefing paper for Sir Peter, say, on the state of the nation for one of our less high profile fortresses but nevertheless important, especially to our American cousins, perhaps, and the perceived threat to them?"

"Risky with the mood Sir Peter is in; I don't know, what do you suggest, how about Belize? There does appear to be some unrest in the area."

"Belize, why not? It is after all the 'Jewel of the Caribbean' or was, according to the local radio station the last time I was out there; but not as far as I was concerned. Oh, never matter, it's not printable." Don was thoughtful for a moment before he consulted his watch, "Not much time."

"Look, before we do, let's just give our central controls a ring – maybe they will have something by now." Rodney picked up one of the free secure phones on the desk.

"All right, meet you back here in ten minutes." Don gathered up the red book and left. He made his way to the building's secure communications rooms where he would be able to speak to several embassies instantly.

Chapter 3

SOUTH AFRICA – DAY TWO

Since the raid on the research station had been discovered, the South African police and BOSS, the South African intelligence and security forces, had worked non-stop. This was a case that they simply must solve, not just because the raid took place so close to the heart of one of the country's premier cities, but because the device that had been stolen was so important and the political implications of it falling into the wrong hands unthinkable.

Despite the intensity of the investigation, they had so far got precisely nowhere. It was as though the raid had been the work of phantoms. Informers knew nothing. Known dissidents had been rounded up but despite threats tempered with reward, after prolonged questioning, nothing of consequence that could help had been gleaned.

Paul Vintner, the senior chief inspector in charge of the police investigation team had the feeling that they had missed something. As he sat at his desk, chin resting on his hands, staring blindly at the papers in front of him and thinking through the situation, the theory that he was beginning to favour over all others was that the job had to have had inside help and that probably the specialist team that carried out the raid had been cobbled together from outside the country.

The violence of the raid had shocked them all; it seemed unnecessarily brutal. He rationalized this in his mind by assuming the perpetrators had but a short time frame to achieve their objective and escape.

Certainly Paul and his team had tracked the criminals to the beach on the first morning and had followed up his enquiries with the coastguard who had checked back on the shipping reports, plus or minus a few hours either side of the call for help from the centre on the morning of the raid, and had come up with initially three possibilities, which they had quickly reduced to one, an old freighter, a 60 metre long motor vessel called the *Sea Jade*, a rust-bucket general cargo ship that plied its trade steaming around the coast of Africa. The problem was that the *Sea Jade* now seemed to have disappeared from the face of the earth. The owners were contacted and were as puzzled by the disappearance of their ship as were the South African police and coastguard.

What Paul did not know yet was that there was a report of debris being washed up on the beaches at Port Nolloth.

The more Paul thought through his theory around inside help, the more certain he became that he was right. He further reasoned that the only way to get a quick in was to find the person or persons that were the possible insiders. The staff had of course been interviewed and screened.

Paul was a methodical man and he knew that he had to hive off part of his team to dig deeper into the staff of the research centre. They would start from scratch if necessary, leaving nothing and no one's life not turned inside out. He would seek help to do this from his contact in BOSS, the South African Bureau of State Security.

Vintner uncoiled his long thin frame from his chair and dialled his opposite number in BOSS, "Hello, is that you Dieter? Good, Paul Vintner here. Listen, I've been going over this raid on the research centre in my mind and I believe there had to be an insider, willing or not, for them to have carried out the attack and to know exactly where to find the device."

Dieter Wolff on the other end of the phone frowned; he had come to this conclusion earlier in the investigation but had let the thought lie idle in the rush to cover the immediate fallout from the crisis.

The more he listened to Vintner, the more it made sense. Wolff asked the chief inspector to come over to BOSS headquarters in an hour's time and he would get his staff to pull out what BOSS files existed on any employees at the centre and anything that may have lead to a conflict of interest.

When Paul arrived at headquarters an hour later he found Dieter Wolff in good humour.

"I do believe we may have something of interest for us to look at. Assuming it is a one-off team, what do you need, considering that all our local activists have been virtually eliminated?" Wolff, a well built man in his middle thirties with long fair hair, for a soldier of sorts, was grinning, waiting for Paul to respond.

"You need above all a coordinator and funds," replied Vintner looking at Wolff, "Funds, lots of money – a rich man, men or an organisation?"

"Yes and no, but necessarily a clever man with a backer, perhaps a private individual, organization or even an unfriendly government, and knows there are a few who would do us harm if they could get away with it. It may not necessarily be one our activist organizations. Could be just a sympathizer, even a mischief-maker, we have plenty of those misguided fools, unfortunately. Or it could be a new group. In fact what we are saying is that it could be anyone." Wolff snorted in disgust. "Damn it, we are not getting very far are we?"

"Let's go back to first principles and take one thing at a time. Let's assume there is an inside man. What have your people turned up?" Vintner asked quietly.

Wolff smiled and indicated that Paul should take a chair, and went to the pile of files on his desk. He lifted the papers in his hand and stretched over the desk, passing them to the policeman.

"I had my people go over every employee's record at the research station, cross reference them with your police records and note where there was a match." He paused for effect, "I also had them look at other factors. For instance, if anyone had had time off recently, if anyone had been out of the country in the last year, etc."

Vintner was already leafing through the folders.

Wolff continued, "You will see we pulled twenty-five possible insiders and they are in order of suspicion, and that Mister Policeman is where you come in."

"Oh yes?" Paul said in mock annoyance.

Wolff lit a cigarette before answering, "Yes, look, Paul." Wolff stood and turned to look out of his window and then looked over his shoulder, "My money is on the top three. I'll take care of those for you and we could leave your resources to rattle through the rest of the list." Paul was not sure and he said so. To eliminate all the people on the list would take time. If they drew a blank they would have to create another list and then clear that, and so on. Dieter simply shrugged and reminded Paul of his own statement a few moments ago when he had said that they should take it one step at a time.

The careful thought processes of Paul Vintner contrasted starkly with the 'rush in' attitude of Wolff, but as a team they complemented each other and together they had had notable success in the past to prove it.

Despite their excellent working relationship, Vintner's attitude did rankle with Wolff at times; he felt constrained by the policeman's careful plodding but he took it mostly with good humour.

Wolff stubbed out his cigarette firmly, "Yeah, Paul I know what you are saying, but my money is on finding the link on that list. Now, is there anything you want me to do before the first three on the list get the once over?"

Paul grinned wryly, he could sense Dieter's frustration, "Yes, relax for five minutes and let me read through this list." He crossed his legs and began by resting the files on his knees. He began to leaf through them quickly; he knitted his dark bushy eyebrows together and from time to time blew through his teeth, another habit that amused Wolff. While Vintner read on, Wolff sat resting on the wide windowsill looking down on to the hot dusty street below. He watched the people strolling by and smiled as a large and very fat, obviously American, tourist in a floral, short-sleeved shirt and long creased khaki shorts, festooned with cameras and his waddling wife, stopped open-mouthed and aghast as a tall willowy native in just a thong, beaded headband, blanket and eight foot spear, glided majestically past. The American could not get his camera into action fast enough.

Dieter turned his attention back to Paul. He could see he was still engrossed so he lit another cigarette, leant against the window and closed his eyes, staying still and silent there until the cigarette burnt his fingers.

"Damn," he blew on the burn. "Well, Sherlock, what do you think?" Dieter was in a hurry, not just because of the urgency of the case but he knew that before long Pretoria, where his boss was based, would either be on the phone again, or worse, coming his way with a task force to take over the investigation.

"Just a minute," Paul finished making a few remarks in his notebook. "Your men have done a very good job," he beckoned to Wolff who got off the windowsill. "Look, I've changed the list a bit. I've added another name to your top three so now we have four favourites. It is two days, soon to be three, since the incident and unless we move the trail is going to get colder and colder." Wolff noticed the enthusiasm in Paul's voice.

"You think there is something there, don't you? What is it?" Dieter said hopefully, matching Paul's mood.

"Yes, perhaps, just a gut feeling at this stage, nothing more; I will give the rest of the list to my team and they can check it out. But let's pull in the top four and see what they have to say for themselves."

Dieter took the files and spreading them on his desk added, "Look Paul, we have a house on the outskirts of the city, I would rather take them there. It is one of our safe houses, admittedly, but it is completely private and self-contained and we can keep them out of the public gaze for as long as we want to."

Paul gave no reaction to the suggestion. Dieter knew he was thinking that such places had a bad name with the police because, rightly or wrongly, the story was that suspects who went into them never came out.

Wolff shrugged, "Who's the fourth man?"

"His name is Dr Michael Santos. He is an immigrant and has been here about ten years. He's worked at the centre for the last eight. He is an electronics engineer in the research lab and has worked on the device we are looking for. What is interesting is that he has had several days off, before and since the raid. Furthermore he has had several trips out of the country this year." Paul showed Dieter the file.

"Yes, he's had quite a bit of time off recently and travelled twice to Mexico, with which, despite his name, he has no connection."

"Cubans? Bit obvious, but he did have two days off, one before the raid and one the day after."

"Yeah, and to me Cubans mean Russians." Wolff was reflective, "After the raid I really thought for a moment we had returned to the problems we had in the sixties and seventies when the *Umkhonto we Sizwe* was at its height."

In the seventies when Wolff was a teenager the *Umkhonto we Sizwe* (The Spear of the Nation), a well organized guerrilla army, had terrorized South Africa. Wolff's family had perished in one of their attacks on a government installation. Since that day Wolff had systematically sought out and eliminated the guilty whenever a lead led him to a terrorist. It was no accident that he now held his powerful position within the service at such an early age; despite his outward cheerfulness, he was ruthless.

He felt very strongly that his country was an island surrounded by a cordon sanitaire of states loosely bound together only by the economic and military power of South Africa.

Anything that could jeopardize that fine balance by a loss of perceived power or ability to cope with internal security problems such as this raid worried him.

He shuddered suddenly, recovered and then continued, "Well, what do you think of the rest, the other three?"

"To be honest, Dieter, not a great deal, but you can never tell. Take Miss Christiana Ojuko for instance; sure, she's been booked once or twice for supposedly attending a nationalist speech-making and being in possession of the nationalist magazine the *Sechaba* which, as you know, is the official organ of the African National Congress here in South Africa. When we or your people pick up anybody on these occasions, just on spec, we log them on our database. There's nothing else known. True, she has had a lot of time off sick recently and was away the day before and the day after the raid, as in the case of Santos." He pointed at Dieter with his pen, "And as we deduced, the inside man on this would have to have aided that, but that's all we have."

"What about the other two?" queried Wolff.

"Of the other two, on balance I don't fancy the black for some reason but the Englishman interests me."

"Me too," Wolff was suddenly alert and looked at his partner. "Did you notice that he spent some time as a bomb disposal specialist in England? It seems strange that such a man should leave that life and go off to school again. He was three years at the London School of Economics; he then joins the Home Office for a couple of years, resigns, goes travelling, doing odd jobs and, notice his record, he has travelled to the Caribbean, Congo and Zimbabwe before he ends up here, where he joins the police as a constable then gets the job as the security and personnel manager at the centre. And he's been in post for only six months."

"It seems strange to me that such a man should end up in what would be a dead-end job."

"Yes it does," agreed Wolff.

"Just a minute," Vintner got up and went to the phone on the desk. He dialled police records. He was at the phone for a few minutes and then gently replaced the receiver. "Well, that's that; apparently he was with the squad but he fluffed a job and lost his nerve so they put him out to grass."

"I suppose that lets him out, or does it?"

"I don't know," said Paul with shrug. "Let's pull him in anyway. I've got a feeling about this man; also, he was responsible for security on the site, he may at the very least have a unique insight into the staff."

Dieter grinned; they had begun to move forward again. He always felt hemmed in mentally when an investigation began to get bogged down in detail; at least they would be following a clear course of action, the rest of his and Paul's teams could get on with the detail. Like any good investigator he knew that patient sifting of detail often brought results but that was not the part of the job he enjoyed naturally.

Paul noticed Dieter's grin, and knew by instinct what he was thinking; he just shook his head. "Better get the snatch teams organized," Dieter said. He looked at his watch, "It's now twelve and the computer centre turns out at five, so we have no more than five hours. Time enough I think."

"You are going to snatch them as they leave?"

"Yes, that way we achieve two things. One, they will have no warning and thus be very unsettled. We will also avoid a disturbance at the centre and..." Wolff remarked, "Two, we will have time to set up the safe house with the interrogation support teams."

"True. Who are we going to use to pick up the suspects, your people or mine?"

"If you don't mind," said Dieter with his head on one side, "I'd rather it was your people. I try not to compromise my people by showing their faces more than they have to."

"Yes, OK," Vintner shrugged, he knew his colleague was right. The more people Wolff could keep undercover, the better was the intelligence gathering from which they both benefited. "Let's get some lunch. It's going to be a long day and I need food."

The four were snatched one by one on their way home, well away from the centre. None of them put up any resistance when asked to get into the police cars. A separate car had been allocated to each suspect.

They were driven around randomly until darkness fell. The suspects were flustered, worried and disorientated as well as tired and hungry and were only too glad to finally be told that they had arrived.

The suspects arrived at timed five minute intervals to make sure they were not aware of the others.

The safe house was situated in a quiet sprawling suburb to the north of the city of Cape Town. As with other palatial residences in this quiet road, the house was set well back and the large private grounds surrounding it were secured by a ten foot high, whitewashed cement and pebble-dashed wall. Tall, heavily ornamented, electrically operated iron gates secured the only entrance.

The time that had elapsed driving the suspects around had not been wasted. The safe house had been occupied by Dieter's support teams who set up the control centre and prepared the rooms for interrogation. The half-dozen cells housed in the cellar were kitted out for their soon-to-be occupants. During this period, police and forensic teams had also raided and searched the suspect's homes.

On the ground floor of the house were the control room, investigation and briefing rooms, domestic living areas for the teams at rest and the canteen and kitchen. On the first floor were the interrogation rooms that were fitted with two-way mirrors and state of the art surveillance equipment. The second floor housed the team's dormitories. The house, as with its environs, was well appointed, for it would at times double as a residence for a VIP or, like tonight's business, as an interrogation centre and safe house.

As each suspect arrived they were taken to the first floor and put in a separate room, manned by two interrogators. Audio and visual feeds from the rooms were transmitted to the control room where Dieter Wolff and Paul Vintner sat and watched the screens and listened to the opening questioning of the suspects.

Change could be discerned in each suspect when after a few moments each in turn realized that they were not in the hands of the police but of another agency. If they had not been overly worried before, they were once they realized this was not simply a continuation of the police investigation.

In the operations centre Vintner and Wolff were poring over their notes while the interrogation teams started their preliminary investigations; the two chiefs would not enter the picture until the suspects were malleable. They put the papers to one side and whiled away the time discussing the case and waiting for their first break.

The break when it came was not from the interview rooms. The inspector in charge of the house searches, Bob Coveney, burst into the room, he was flushed and his normally calm eyes were wide and shining with excitement.

He was young for his rank and when he burst out, "We've got the bastard!" both the two more experienced men looked at each other not wanting to acknowledge yet that they had a lead. "No promises, no disappointments," was Paul's favourite mantra which he would quote frequently.

The inspector noticed the quizzical expressions on the faces of his two senior officers. "It's true," he said emphatically and waved two other men into the room. Each was heavily laden with boxes and files. The inspector reached into one of the boxes and pulled out a map. "See, the raid map with all the times and routes to and from the centre."

Vintner and Wolff raised their eyebrows, grinning now; could it possibly be?

Wolff let out a whoop and dived into the pile of documents, files and letters that came pouring out as the boxes were upended on to one of the free desks.

The two chiefs were soon busily examining the hoard; Wolff was his normal enthusiastic self while Vintner calmly sifted through evidence methodically sorting the items into some sort of logical order.

Inspector Coveney hung back, grinning. He was both amused and impressed as the two senior officers quickly made sense of the data his men had found. He quietly dismissed the two men he had brought with him and told them to get some food organized for everyone.

He waited good-naturedly but as time went by, with growing impatience, he could wait no longer, "He must have been mad to have kept all that stuff after the raid," he contributed to the silence. Then he went on quickly, "Surely he must have realized we would get round to investigating the staff in depth sooner or later?"

"Sooner or later perhaps, but not this soon," Wolff held up an airline ticket waving it at Bob, "He was leaving tonight, rather early hours tomorrow!"

Vintner craned his long neck so he could get a view of the ticket but at the same time continued his sorting, "Bloody hell," he exclaimed; Wolff looked at him, amused; it was not in his colleague's character to show such emotion.

"Indeed, bloody hell. One more day and we would have been too late." Wolff hunched his shoulders; they had been lucky, very lucky.

"What's the destination on the ticket?" Vintner asked, losing all interest in the paper he was looking at.

"Eventually Guatemala," said Wolff flicking through the pages of the flight document, "One way."

"What the devil would he want there?"

"Perhaps it was not his final destination?" interjected the young inspector hopefully.

"Possibly," said Wolff thoughtfully; "Good jumping-off place, he could go north to Mexico and the USA or south to South America proper."

"Or east to Belize, Miami, Cuba," snorted Vintner, "Why don't we ask him?"

Wolff laughed, "You know I had almost forgotten we had him here." He threw the ticket down, "We can look at this stuff later. Better still, Bob, would you get your men back to sort, log and catalogue this evidence into some sort of chronological order?" Coveney nodded his agreement, so Wolff, giving the inspector his thumbs up while turning to Vintner, said, "Thank you, Inspector. Right, Paul, let's get to the bastard and get him to tell us where the device is. That has to be our number one priority now." He looked at Vintner for confirmation.

"You're quite right, Dieter. The recovery of the machine is, as was, all important." He turned to the inspector, "Get the other suspects out of here, in say, six hours from now, just in case one or more of them is in cahoots with our man. That should give us enough time to make sure he was working alone, or not. Feed them and make sure they are escorted home safely with suitable apologies. Make it clear to them that this is a security operation and that if they breathe a word about tonight they will be in very hot water. To reiterate, I want you and all the rest of the team to continue to sort these documents into chronological order and everything cross-referenced as Dieter indicated. Got that?"

"No problem, sir."

"Get cracking then. If you come up with anything that relates to the location of the device or something that's useful, we want to know immediately." Dieter waved the inspector out of the room, leaving him and the duty operations room crew stirred up and ready to work.

Vintner and Wolff were buoyed by the developments but were hesitant to take the next step in case they bungled it. The next phase would not be easy. As always in these cases they had to decide which way to handle the interrogation.

Wolff voiced both their thoughts, "How do you think we should play this one? Go straight in hard or should we be more subtle and try to draw him out? Or, third option, we could, and we would be justified, break him more quickly with head screw or waterboarding."

"Under the circumstances and against my better judgment, I might go for option three, but he does still carry a British passport and there could be repercussions," Vintner cautioned.

"Then," said Wolf positively, "Let's try the second option and keep the third in reserve." He looked steadily into Vintner's eyes, "If we use the third option he may well have to meet with an accident afterwards."

"We'll see," Vintner was always surprised at the apparent callousness of his colleague at times like this. His policeman's natural inclination was to ensure that a criminal, no matter what his crime, should pay for that crime by the due process of the law. "We'll see," Vintner repeated himself, "Come on, what's the man's name again?"

"Thomas Hough, the security manager of the facility. He is the ex-soldier, UK Home Office and policeman." Wolff was looking at Vintner trying to decide if he shouldn't ask his colleague to stay out of the interrogation initially, so that he could get on with what had to be done without a representative of the establishment holding him and his men back, but Paul Vintner cut his thoughts short.

"Thomas Hough here we come," Paul picked up his notes and indicated that Wolff should lead the way to the interview room. If Wolff feared that the policeman might hold him back, the moment had passed when he should have said something. Characteristically, Wolff just shrugged, and led the way upstairs.

They passed one of Wolff's men on the stairs who confirmed that the other suspects had left the upper floor; they were down in their respective cells and were about to be fed.

They entered the interview room and received their first shock; Hough was not only an elderly, hunched, lightly coffee-coloured black man, he was tiny, barely five foot tall, but clearly strong and wiry. There had not been a photograph in the profile they had read earlier and although they had glimpsed him on the monitors they had nevertheless assumed from the man's military background that he would be white, younger, well built and with some residual military bearing.

Vintner was the first to recover, "Mr Hough?" he inquired of the interrogators. They confirmed and gave Wolff a brief rundown of what Hough had said so far, which was basically denial of any prior knowledge of the raid.

Wolff moved his head and the two interrogators left the room. They would watch developments from the control room now and be ready to pick up on the interrogation again, as and when required, or if their boss screwed up.

The room was a good size, some seven by seven metres, and

characteristic of the residence's other rooms. White walls and a wooden floor, with curtains drawn over large casement windows on two sides of the room. Except for the table up to which Vintner and Wolff had now drawn chairs and the prisoner, seated and handcuffed to a metal chair in the centre of the room on the far side of the table, the room was completely empty. The only illumination in the room was a powerful desk-mounted articulated light shining on the suspect. The prisoner squinted in an effort to make out the two new men who were now in charge of his small world. He had concluded from the way they dealt with the other two interrogators that they were senior to them.

He gave them the impression that he was not bothered; he closed his eyes wearily and made himself as comfortable as he could in the hard chair.

Wolff flicked open the file left by his staff and looked at the notes so far and at the man's general background.

The secret service man deliberately took hold of the arm of the lamp and aimed it at the ceiling. The light bounced off the whitewash and illuminated the room so that the three men could see each other in almost natural light.

Hough lifted his head and sat up in his chair. The other two became more aware of the man's lack of stature. He looked at least 60 but they knew from his file that he must be closer to 50. His eyes aged him; they were yellow, streaked with red, and his jowls were beginning to sag a little. He was relatively light skinned with a roman nose that set him apart from the local natives that both men were used to dealing with.

It took the two of them a little time to sort out in their own minds the way in which they would deal with this man. Vintner, the more inflexible and staid of the two, decided, albeit subconsciously, that the man was a middle-class black; Wolff, subconsciously, saw him only as an enemy to be ruthlessly exterminated, nevertheless he felt uncomfortable.

Hough broke the silence that had descended on the room, "Who are you, the heavy mob?" His voice was deep for such a small man, steady and cultured, but it had a contemptuous sneer to it. This sneering inflection inflamed Wolff who lashed out over the table, striking the man across the face. His heavy signet ring caught Hough on the upper lip and nose and brought a trickle of blood from the side of his mouth.

"Yes, we are, so watch your mouth," threatened Wolff.

Tears of pain moistened Hough's eyes, "You bastard Boer trash!"

Hough whispered contemptuously through clenched teeth.

Vintner saw Wolff tense up ready to strike Hough again and, had he not placed a gentle restraining hand on his arm, Wolff would have done so. Vintner kept his hand on his colleague's arm until he felt Wolff relax and then Vintner addressed Hough.

"I don't have to tell you that we, especially my colleague here, are very upset with you." Paul Vintner let the statement hang for a moment; Hough slowly raised his gaze to Vintner who continued, "We have now collected the evidence from your home that links you conclusively with the raid on the computer centre. Amongst other things were maps, plans and the airline ticket for you on the plane tonight, destination Latin America."

There was no reaction so Vintner continued, "You are in very serious trouble." Vintner looked from Wolff to Hough and then back to his notes. "It may be," Vintner said quietly, "That if you are willing to cooperate with us, help us in the recovery of the device, we could make some sort of deal."

Hough laughed and rocked in his chair, "You want me to cooperate? There is nothing you could give me."

Vintner continued quietly, "We could consider overlooking your part in this affair and simply expel you from South Africa."

Hough spat some blood from his mouth on to the floor, "You'll get nothing more from me. Now," he thrust his scrawny neck and head forward. "You bastards get me a call to the British consulate. I'm a British citizen and I'm entitled to their protection."

Wolff spoke in a quiet controlled voice, "You are entitled to nothing. You forfeited any rights when you got involved in the appalling incident at the centre. We are the only ones you can deal with. There is no one else that counts. No one else knows you are here and there is no one, at least as far as I can see, that will miss you."

Hough drew back and for the first time the men saw a flicker of fear in his eyes. Wolff followed up the attack, "I am not a patient man as you have seen, I have some serious issues with you that have to be resolved and time is running out. Either you tell us what we want or we will get the information from you in another way. You were a soldier and a policeman and you know that we will get what we want eventually. Do you really think that you can come to my country, undermine it in this way and get away with it, simply by dropping out when things go wrong?

Call your embassy? You must think we are stupid. Well? What about it?"

"How about starting with why and how you did it?" put in Vintner encouragingly. A change came over Hough. He sat upright and his eyes blazed out at them; it seemed as though he was not looking at them but through them. They felt uncomfortable with this man, he was not normal; clever he may be but there was a touch of fanaticism, even a little madness in those staring eyes.

"Maybe you're right. You see, all my life..." he began in a rumbling intense voice, "...I've been this half colour, not accepted by the whites and not trusted by the blacks. Well, that was all going to change when I had successfully concluded the deal for the device. The proceeds would have been handed over to the Brothers; I would belong at last to one side."

"You're living in a dream world," scoffed Wolff. "If you really think that putting a few thousand into the coffers of the Brothers is going to solve your problem, you're crazy," he immediately regretted the last part.

Hough looked at Wolff and smiled cunningly, "Ha, you have no idea of the value of that thing to the right buyer, have you?"

Vintner and Wolff sat back in their chairs. In training they were taught that every traitor, fanatic or madman, even once they have started, will not be able to resist telling you why they have done something and how. Paul thought that they do it either out of guilt and want to be forgiven, or because they simply want to let you know how clever they have been. They waited for Hough to spill his story. It never came. He was not typical. Over the next half hour, no matter how they tried, Hough would say nothing else. In frustration Wolff slammed his fist on the table and left. Vintner followed. Once outside Wolff let Vintner know in no uncertain terms that it was now time to try the hard way.

"Look Dieter, I know how you feel. The danger is if you start the rough stuff he may peg it before we get all we want from him. Give me another ten minutes alone with him. You go and see if the lads downstairs have come up with anything." He gave Wolff a gentle shove towards the stairs.

Wolff moved off reluctantly. "Ten minutes," said Wolff tapping his watch emphatically.

"Ten minutes. That's all I want. It will give you time to cool off too."

Wolff initially scowled at his partner then grinned suddenly and gave Vintner the finger.

"Bugger off. And knock before you come in," Paul said shaking his head from side to side in amusement at Wolff's gesture at him.

Vintner went back into the room. Hough looked up briefly, "Lost your sidekick?" Hough seemed inclined to talk again. Vintner sat quietly, still hardly breathing and let Hough ramble on. As Hough talked, Vintner apparently listened with only half an ear but he mentally noted key matters he could come back to Hough on. In the silent room Hough talked of his past and his ideals. Vintner had heard it all before but he wanted to gain the man's trust. Predictably, Hough's concept of the future was a coloured-controlled state with equality for all; the place of the whites and their position in society were, however, hazy.

Vintner let him continue for a few minutes more before he judged he could begin a conversation. He then began to draw Hough out over the affair.

"Thomas, I understand your feelings and your aims. They are not so different from others I have heard and in truth, your ideas mirror my own in some respects. But how did you do it? It must have taken a lot of money to set up such a raid. I wouldn't think the Brothers would have that sort of cash at their disposal."

"Ah, you're right of course," Hough sighed. "I had sponsors. Not from this country."

"No, not from this place; that was one of my theories; Russians, I had thought briefly. It must have taken quite some organizing," Paul said quietly.

"Russians, hmm," Hough eyed Vintner with an interest bordering on respect. "As for the organizational effort, yes, it was demanding. I had the responsibility from start to finish; big job, very satisfying," Hough smiled for the first time.

"You must have had some help; it was a complex and quite big operation."

"No, I did it all myself. It was, if you like, to be my initiation into the leadership of the Brother's organisation. My sponsor did not interfere but merely rubber-stamped and confirmed that my plan and choice of raid leader for the job was suitable and to his satisfaction."

"Therefore, I suppose now we have you as our guest, the device will never be traded, is that right?"

Hough laughed out loud and this was followed by a harsh racking cough before he spat out, "What do you take my sponsor for, a fool?

Whatever the plan, it can and will proceed without me, with some added difficulty, admittedly. Anyway I don't expect to be with you that long; they will come for me."

Vintner gazed steadily into Hough's insolent eyes and said with carefully measured tones, "You need to remember that no one knows where you are. Unless you help us and tell us what we want to know, which is simply how do we retrieve the device, I believe you will not leave this place alive." Vintner let the words penetrate Hough's consciousness for a while then added, "In a few moments my partner will be back and I will leave you with him."

Hough searched Vintner's face to see if he was bluffing. Vintner's eyes told all. Hough shifted in his chair. It was as though he was trying to come to a decision or some pact with himself. At last he shrugged his shoulders and said calmly, "If they don't come in time then I will become one of the martyrs for the cause. Maybe they will erect a statue to the man who through his efforts gave the cause enough money to enable it to take a quantum leap forward."

"Come now, that is really not in the interests of anybody, least of all yours. We have already offered you safe conduct to the border. He that fights and runs away, lives to fight another day, and all that, or so they say," Vintner smiled encouragingly.

Vintner was not dealing with an ignorant man but the apparent willingness to become a martyr over this incident didn't make sense to him although he had to admit to himself that Hough had shown a fanatical trait in his need to belong to the Brothers. He didn't have time to ponder further, Wolff knocked on the door at that moment.

Vintner excused himself to Hough and got up and left the room but not before he had seen the look of fear and apprehension that leapt into the eyes of the other man.

"Well?" asked Wolff casually as Vintner appeared.

"Nothing on the device yet, bits and pieces though; he really was the organizer, at least in the context of the raid and probably the only one, but he seems to have an immense ego that sustains him along with his paranoid need to be recognized by the 'Brothers' as he keeps referring to them, even in the face of imminent extermination. I wonder..." Paul let the last remark hang in the air and had a growing look of inspiration. He grabbed Dieter's arm, "...if that's the answer... Look Wolff, let me have another minute. You come in too."

"Come on, Paul, we'll be here all night," Wolff said, his impatience growing.

"Trust me Dieter, it might just be worth it. I have an idea I would like to try," Paul encouraged Wolff. "If I fail, it will not make any difference to your next phase of the interrogation and may help to get a little more out of him before he martyrs himself."

"Go on then, two minutes and that's your lot," Wolff said firmly and pushing the door open let Paul in before him.

Vintner took a deep breath, pushed a surprised Wolff aside and went straight for Hough. "You bastard! You've been lying to me. I thought there was some trust and empathy between us, I'm so disappointed in you; I really thought we had an understanding and we were being honest with each other like honourable men." Vintner crossed the floor coming up behind Hough who craned his neck to follow him around the room. "I've a good mind to let my colleague have you right now," Vintner was almost shouting, pointing at Wolff. A bewildered Hough did not comprehend him. He was not supposed to.

"What, what do you mean?" Hough questioned, totally confused and flushing red.

"You just told me you masterminded the whole operation. I've just learned that you are persona non grata with the Brothers. They think you are a joke and that you are just claiming the credit; they don't even know you, apart from being a nuisance."

"No, no! They are lying, you're lying!" Hough spat. "They wouldn't have the intelligence to organize a trip to a brewery."

"No, you are the one that is lying. Our informants are very reliable." Vintner spat stabbing his finger at Wolff and then at Hough and finished by smiling smugly at Hough and crossing his arms in front of him, waiting.

"It's not possible; they are lying I tell you, they had only the outline of the plan, my plan!"

"Well, they say they have the device and they are prepared to trade."

"They can't have, it's with my man Saied and they don't know where the exchange is to take place." Hough was heated; he had completely lost control of himself and laughed aloud.

Vintner thought quickly, "Well, you're wrong. They lifted the device from him as soon as he touched down in..."

Hough interrupted heatedly, "What? They couldn't have, it's too early;

the sponsor and I knew my man and the device would end up in Guatemala to see the engineer and anyway the thing has to be reconfigured for use against..." Hough blustered and then stopped. He got control of himself as quickly as he had blown up and knew he had said too much.

"Yeah, you and your supposed sponsors; tell us more. The men in the white coats will be interested in your case when I hand you over to the nuthouse if you are still alive after my friend here has finished with you," taunted Vintner looking from Hough to Wolff.

Hough folded his hands and looked away. Vintner knew they had lost him. He doubted they would get anything more from the man using the same trick again. Any confidence the man had in him was now well and truly lost.

Wolff had been watching his partner with an amused smile. The old fox had it in him after all.

Wolff watched Hough carefully and could see the prisoner had completely withdrawn into himself. Hough hung his head and his body slumped in the chair; he seemed to sense Wolff's gaze on him; he looked up once and nodded, then relaxed back on the chair; a look shrouded the man's eyes that told Wolff he was preparing himself for whatever was to come.

"He will not be going anywhere," Wolff said coldly, looking at Vintner. Vintner knew it was his dismissal. From now on Wolff would handle Hough. Wolff beckoned Vintner out of the room and on the landing instructed Vintner to hold on to Dr Michael Santos. When Paul asked why, Dieter told him, "Been thinking about the Mexico trips, what if Santos was sent to train someone how to use the device and alter it as Hough said?"

"Do you want me to interview him along those lines?"

"Not yet, I want to get all we can from Hough before we, that is, you and I, question Santos."

"Shall I let the other two go?"

"Why not, we can always get them back if we have to."

Vintner tried once more to delay the inevitable, "About Hough, are you sure we could not use drugs on him to get further information?"

Wolff shook his head. "Sorry old mate, too unreliable and time consuming. It has to be my way from now on, win or lose," Wolff's flat statement was final.

Vintner nodded his acceptance to Wolff and they both re-entered the interrogation room where they stood silently watching the diminutive man in the chair waiting for Wolff's man to arrive. There was a knock on the door and a man appeared with a wet towel. Vintner had seen the towel technique before in his service. He looked at Wolff who spread his hands at him as if to say, 'You tried, now it's for me to get the rest of the information my way.'

Vintner asked Hough once more if he would cooperate, as Wolff's man wound the wet towel round the man's head once and then started to ring the two ends of the towel together at the back of the head. Hough struggled uselessly against the towel but with his head held fast he had no leverage. The towel, now coiled together forming a screw, was twisted slowly more and more until the band on Hough's head began to tighten and the water in the towel oozed out, trickling down the man's head. He struggled weakly now, but said nothing. The man continued to screw the towel tighter and tighter until the skin around Hough's eyes was taut, his eyes bulged and his mouth formed itself into an ugly grimace. Vintner felt nauseated and left the room, wanting no further part in the proceedings. Wolff and his man were now alone with Hough.

Chapter 4

MOSCOW

Two men sat opposite each other in the large gloomy panelled office of the Director of the First Chief Directive in the headquarters of the KGB at number two, Dzerzhinsky Square.

One was the director general himself, a large white-haired, heavy-jawed peasant of a man running to fat. He was briefing his deputy, General Sergei Ivan Polyakov.

"You will be not be surprised Comrade General to learn that I have been playing in the field recently, knowing me as you do. I, uh, sponsored a little project which has now borne fruit." The director rubbed his squashed peasant nose with his spade of a hand before smiling, as he squinted at his deputy.

General Polyakov pricked up his ears. His boss was an exceptionally intelligent man and if he had taken the trouble to get involved in a little project, as he put it, it had to be important.

The Director continued blandly, "My contact in Guatemala will be in a position to arrange for the handover to us of something of great value; it apparently needs a little work but it is nearly ready for delivery." The director grinned at his subordinate, he just loved to out-engineer Sergei now and again, just to show him he was still number one. For all this, he trusted and respected his deputy over any other individual he had ever met, despite the fact that he frequently had to defend him against the other directors who saw Polyakov as a throwback to some long forgotten imperial era.

"And the contact is?" Polyakov asked.

"In the country, a good man, Major Novisti Yuri Nsenko."

Polyakov grunted. "A Department Five man, yes I know of him although I have never met him."

Department Five was the most secretive of all the KGB departments; it dealt with executive issues abroad which could end in a 'wet affair', a liquidation.

"Well Sergei, I want you to arrange the exchange personally." It was an order although the director made it sound like a request.

"Of course sir, it will be a pleasure," his deputy swept his hand in front of him and leant forward in his chair.

The director chuckled; his deputy always reminded him of a French cavalier, the most chivalrous of men. Whilst he, the director, had taken years to cultivate his image as a man of the people, a man who had come from humble stock, his deputy seemed to get away with his aristocratic manners and was accepted by all as though he was the local feudal squire, except, the director thought, by his fellow directors who, he sensed, felt threatened.

"You should know a little of the background. I used one of my old soldier comrades to head up the task, Colonel Tsygankov. You know him of course."

It wasn't a question; of course Sergei knew him, as the Spymaster. Tsygankov was as ruthless a man as you would ever wish to meet. Sergei thought of him as the only truly amoral man he had ever known and probably one of the tallest officers in the KBG. He was surprised at the director general's choice, as Tsygankov had been demoted and disgraced after he failed to stop the West getting its hands on a list of Soviet agents in July, or was it August, of 1974? Whatever, the Americans, he now recalled randomly, in 1975 called it their 'year of the spies' as they rolled up cell after cell of Soviet spies courtesy of the list. He shivered involuntarily.

The shiver didn't go unnoticed by the director, "Someone just walk over your grave, Sergei?" The director continued without waiting for his deputy to comment, "He used intermediaries. There were two principal third parties involved. One, a disgruntled security manager of a South African research institution, a half-caste idealist called Thomas Hough, who brought this matter to the notice of Major Nsenko, and a mercenary leader called Jean Saied and his men, now lost to this earth, at least his team of freedom soldiers are. We needed Saied for other work so he was spared. Saied is now in or just arriving in Guatemala; Hough has disappeared, so I have to assume that he has been picked up and will have given what information he has to whoever has him, which is not a lot, but damage limitation has to be considered. You should leave that to Tsygankov."

"Nevertheless, did Hough know that the KGB were involved?"

"Not really, well, yes and no. Although Major Nsenko was his initial contact, Nsenko with Tsygankov, dressed up the package to Hough as a Russian Mafia-funded exercise; so we are pretty sure the link to the KGB, except for a rogue officer in the shape of Tsygankov, is fairly tenuous and well hidden. Hough for his own reasons is fanatical and was desperate for money for his cause and his people. The people that we sponsored in the venture did it for the noblest of reasons, their 'cause', and they always declared that if they were successful they wanted payment for their efforts to boost their party funds. Tsygankov recognized that, as an idealist, Hough was a problem and he isolated him from the operation as best he could, even to the point where Tsygankov had Hough hire Saied through intermediaries so that neither of them would meet formally, although Tsygankov did attend a meeting with the two of them present but he sat silently in the background in order to decide if Saied was the right man for the job; from his achievements the other night, clearly he was. Well, we now have their costs and price and it's outrageous. However, I've discussed it with the Secretary and he feels we must pay up as we want it for ourselves. Quite a coup for the department, I think."

"Forgive me, Director, we want what?"

The director peered at his deputy through the thick lenses of his glasses; his round red face frequently had a startled expression that made him appear to others like a slightly retarded schoolboy. Despite this engineered comic look, he was respected, not just because he headed the largest and most important directive of the KGB, but because he was a shrewd operator with an exceptionally quick, clever brain backed by a political awareness that his fellow directors recognized and were wary of.

"Always straight to the point, eh, my dear Sergei? So be it. We're talking about an electronic counter-intelligence device that can unlock our competitor's communication computers, which have hitherto been denied to us."

"First take, that sounds like a bit of science fiction to me, sir. We have been working on such an idea for years to my knowledge and, with all our resources, still have not cracked it. So how did they, a second-rate state, succeed where we have failed? How could such a device work?"

"I haven't the slightest idea, my dear Sergei," the director laughed out loud, a roar ending in a chuckle, "But I'm assured it is feasible. So now let me give you the details. Seconded to you for the duration are the following: Lt Col Yuri Ivanovich, Technical Directive 'T', who will brief you on the device and explain it to you, I hope, and Major Valeria Gershuni of Department Five. She is good at her job, well connected and may be useful; she is already briefed and having worked on this mission with the Spymaster, she is as deeply involved in this mission as anyone. And of course you can have anybody from our department you think fit, but I would prefer you keep the team as small as possible, for security reasons, you understand. Now, is there anything else?"

Keep it small, thought Polyakov, in case it all goes belly up, but he didn't say so, instead he asked, "A supplementary question only. Is it not possible to get Major Nsenko simply to send the device through a diplomatic courier bag or box as normal?"

"Good question Sergei, but for a number of reasons it is not possible. To begin with the device, as I understand it, has to be reconfigured for our use or perhaps the more correct terminology would be recalibrated. The only man who currently knows how to do this is in Guatemala. Before you ask, the man is one of Hough's team, some engineer who worked on the device in its early days but left the design team over some issue. Hough targeted him and he has had his knowledge refreshed recently by one of Hough's men. Hough chose the engineer, contacted him in Guatemala and set him up for this job. The whole of this phase was under the watch of Major Nsenko. This man has now built a test bed out there to reconfigure and prove the device to us before we buy. There is a need for peripheral kit to make use of this machine, I am told. Even so, as I understand it, there will be some fine tuning and adjustment to do once it's back here in Moscow. Last but not least, the engineer refuses point-blank to leave the country. I think my other reason is that I don't like loose ends and I want you to brief Major Nsenko and Colonel Tsygankov personally that once the machine is proved and you are convinced our technical directive can handle and replicate the device as necessary, all links to us are to disappear."

The director's inference was unmistakable so Sergei simply added, "OK, understood, Director. Timings?"

"Colonel Ivanovich's Department T has the technical details, but you have about four days." Great, thought Polyakov, four days to mount an exercise on the other side of the world.

"Sir, I think it is imperative that we have someone from the Illegal's Department," Sergei was thoughtful.

"Really, why do you say that? They will have some on station there."

"That's as maybe, sir, but you know the way it works. If I use their man out there, his controller back here will want to be in on more of the show. Further, I would not be totally confident that they would not feel the need to report back to their directorate. If he or she is not under direct command, loyalties can be divided. Lastly, we could do with a Latin American expert and speaker with us to ensure that we don't do something stupid and attract attention out of ignorance of the country's culture and customs etc."

The director closed his bird-like eyes behind the pebble glasses. He knew what his deputy meant. The KGB had two weaknesses, if you discounted its enormous size which made it so unwieldy. One was interdepartmental jealousies, the other was that each department seemed to work in a watertight compartment and duplicated much of the work that may be being done by another department without either of the parties being aware they were working on the same thing.

It really was a terrible waste of resources, thought the director, but until things changed and a more open attitude was taken by his fellow directors, nothing would alter. He also knew that he and his counterparts perpetuated the system and until they changed the culture of mistrust, it was business as usual. He agreed that he had little choice but to accede to his deputy's request; Sergei was of course correct in his appreciation of the situation, but it would mean approaching the head of the Illegal's Department, a man he could barely tolerate. He shrugged his large shoulders in a very Russian way, picked up his phone and dialled his fellow director.

After a brief conversation he turned back to his deputy, a smile playing on his lips. "You have been given Major Sergei Alcksandrovich. They assure me he is competent. He is a Latin American specialist on Guatemala and has spent time there on several occasions."

"Very satisfactory, I am sure he will be invaluable to me. We will be operating far from base and may need his contacts in short order," Polyakov carefully added the man's name to the list. Now we are four, he thought, six if included Major Nsenko and Colonel Tsygankov.

"Nothing else I can think of for today," said Polyakov collecting his papers and rising.

"No? Good. I too have nothing more. I will be out for the rest of the day." The director rose from his desk. "If you do need me, which I'm confident you will not, I will be in Red Square with the other party leaders taking a salute. Then for the remainder of the day, I'll be with the inner circle; we must sort out the American grain embargo, the Siberian pipeline problems and that damned adventure we took into Afghanistan." He looked heavenward, "Will we never learn?"

"Every country must have its Vietnam to really appreciate how much a neighbour wants your help," commented Sergei with a wry smile.

"Our Vietnam, you say, eh?" mused the director.

"Could be," Polyakov said, suddenly serious.

The director noticed the change. "You're too soft, that's your problem, Sergei. It will all turn out all right in the end, never fear. Who thought up the Afghanistan mission anyway?"

"You did sir."

"Well, there you are. Have confidence in your Director. Now, I'll see you tomorrow. Tell me what's what then. Another thing, I noted your comment about the South Africans cracking a problem we hadn't. Never forget, my dear Sergei, that it's all about people and the right man in the right place at the right time, it was ever thus in every endeavour and walk of life. Here ends the lesson to you for today." It was a dismissal. The deputy, smiling, excused himself and left the director dressing for the cold outside. God forbid he should succeed the director, thought Polyakov. The appointment was political; he preferred his executive role far more.

When he arrived back in his own suite of offices he gave his secretary the list of three names and told her to call them for a meeting in an hour in his office and for her to attend to take notes.

She began to tell him that he had appointments all day, but he just smiled and told her to cancel them and reschedule them for tomorrow. When she started to tell him that tomorrow was a full day, he put his arm round her and said gently, "Cut all the appointment times in half and we will get through."

The secretary was an attractive middle-aged woman, intelligent and reliable. She looked up at the deputy towering above her and eyes shining said with feigned annoyance, "You're the boss. Not sure everyone on the list is going to be best pleased."

"The boss I am, and if people are unhappy, just sooth them the best you can. You're really good at that." He gave her a squeeze. "Do me a favour, pull the profiles on those three; I would like to know a little about each of them before I have the meeting."

He went into his office, not quite as big as the director's but decidedly more comfortable, and sorted through his urgent mail for half an hour before his secretary appeared with the files of his new team.

He sorted them into priority. The technocrat was the first folder he looked at. He read – Ivanovich, 38 years of age, good technical background in electronics and computers. He had been with the KGB for 16 years, working on computer developments. He was a specialist in communications and electronic counter-espionage. Two forays into the field. He had done one successful tour in America and another tour with the Soviet Exchange Mission in West Germany, SOXMIS. A solid dependable engineer was the deputy's conclusion.

The next file belonged to Alcksandrovich, the Illegal's man. He was 45, had been with the Latin section of that directorate for 20 years and had been promoted from the ranks. His file showed he had spent half the time in the field. The profile impressed Polyakov. The man had spent time in Cuba and Mexico as well as Guatemala, undercover recruiting and seeding moles. He was glad to have the man with him, especially as one entry showed that he had worked with the good Major Novisti Yuri Nsenko on more than one occasion.

With a sigh he picked up the file of the agent from Department Five. He understood the need for such people and had used them himself on occasions. It just seemed, and he knew that many of his colleagues felt the same way, that whenever one of these people was involved it led to a sometimes unnecessary killing. Feeling growing annoyance for some inexplicable reason he snapped open the folder. The photograph pinned to the flysheet was that of a very attractive woman. The frown that had begun to form gave way and with some pleasure he unclipped the photo from the file and studied it for a few moments. He chuckled to himself. He was thinking that this could be a little reminder to him from the director that he knew of his deputy's weakness for a beautiful woman. Major Valeria Gershuni was certainly that.

Dragging his eyes from the photograph he began to read the file, suddenly interested to know more of this woman. It read: Name – Gershuni, 31, ex-Swallow, one of that band of exceptionally beautiful Russian women that many an important visitor, diplomat or military attaché has regretted meeting. She had left the Swallows and had been commissioned into her present department after she had demonstrated a willingness to kill. Her list of covert operations was prodigious for one so young and she appeared to have operated in most parts of the globe. Slightly shocked by her bloody record he looked back at the photograph that showed a woman with a slightly round face and flawless complexion. Cat's eyes, he thought, with a ski-jump nose, short fair hair framed the face and the eyes were complemented by a full smiling mouth. He had seen those features before somewhere, another family member perhaps.

He had barely finished shuffling the files back into order when his secretary appeared again to tell him that the team was assembled in the small conference room adjoining the office. He gave her the files with a wink; after reading about the major he was comforted to have his uncomplicated, warm and loyal secretary at his side, "Come and take notes then, let's see what we've got." As he and his secretary entered, the team that had been talking freely to each other stopped; all came stiffly to attention and waited.

Polyakov broke the ice quickly, welcoming them with a warm smile, whilst introducing himself and his secretary and drew the team to the table. When they had settled themselves, Polyakov addressed them in his easy manner. "Now, introductions; you know who I am, tell me about yourselves and the reason you are here."

Once the three officers had finished their brief introductions, Polyakov summarized the preliminaries, including what he knew which, he conceded openly, was not a great deal and something that worried him slightly.

"As you will now have appreciated, I only have the barest of detail and I'm hoping that Colonel Ivanovich will be able to tell us more. Colonel, please..."

The colonel was what the deputy had expected, more a scientist than a soldier. Although the colonel would have been tall if he had straightened up to his full height, he stooped and deceptively, looked of only average height. He was thin to the point of fragility and looked more like 60 than closing on 40. The deputy summed him up as a beaten schoolmaster.

The colonel rose, shuffled a pile of papers while adjusting his glasses over his bony nose with his right index finger and peered almost timidly at the audience. If he was nervous it didn't show once he began. He had their full attention and he knew it.

"Ladies and gentlemen," his voice was steady. "I think that I should give you some insight into what this device is that we are about to recover or, should I say, collect. I should also add that the recovery of the device is not the end of the game. The device is part of a package which will enable us to carry out a much larger operation. Without the device, however, the operation cannot go ahead," he paused and looked at each of the other members of the group, smiling he said, "Hence the high-powered team dedicated to its collection and the price we are prepared to pay."

He was enthusiastic in his manner and even Polyakov could not help but be impressed and be swept along by him. He waited for the colonel to expand on the operation, but he did not. Instead he told them about the device.

"And now the device and what it does..."

"A moment, what is the full operation that you talk of?" Polyakov interrupted. The colonel looked at him, not quite understanding the question.

"Sir?"

"You mentioned that the device was a means to an end," Polyakov prompted him.

"I'm sorry sir, I assumed that you knew," he was clearly embarrassed.

Polyakov cursed himself but let the colonel off the hook by saying lightly, "We will talk of it later, after this briefing. Just so you all know this whole matter was raised to me only a little before you were called and, as I said, my knowledge of it is only by its most sketchy outline. Perhaps for good order and to help us stay focused, we will continue to confine this meeting to the device and its collection. The machine you are now about to tell us about," he raised his eyebrows and indicated with his hand that the colonel should continue.

"Yes, thank you sir," Ivanovich rubbed his brow collecting his thoughts. He was concerned now that he had compromised something. How was he to know that the deputy and this team did not know the whole story? He dismissed his thoughts and got back to the matter in hand. "The device – its origin is South African. It was developed by their people and is..." he paused, "...a communication encryption spying device."

He could sense the mood had changed to one of curiosity and, to a degree, distrust around the table. They were all wondering what the other part of the task was. He glanced above the deputy's head to the picture of the Russian soldier carrying the Red Flag in a victorious stance; he drew comfort from the image it imparted and briefly drew himself up to his full height.

Alcksandrovich stirred in his seat, "What does this machine do?" he looked at the engineer. "You say or imply that it's a bugging device of some sort." He looked round the table quickly to see if he had spoken out of turn. Polyakov simply nodded his approval and the team looked at the colonel expectantly.

He felt the warmth of the meeting return and went on quickly, "It's really quite simple, or the principle is," he grinned. "When you clamp it on a line, let's say, a computer lead, it listens; actually it monitors the pulse radiation, on, off etc. It works out the current passwords and handshakes flowing between the central processor and any remote terminal, hence my reference to a communication spying device. It observes the handshakes between the two locations as they synchronize themselves and determines the level of access. It processes the intelligence and then is able to sign on."

"How can it do that without detection? The supervisor's terminal is sure to detect if a strange terminal signs on, even if it does have the right password, handshake as you put it. And what about the encryption box?" It was the Illegal's man again.

"Ah, now that really is the clever bit."

"I thought the first bit was pretty clever," the deputy put in with a chuckle, "Eh, Valeria?" he gave her a wink. The men laughed; only his secretary uncrossed and recrossed her legs in slight annoyance. Polyakov knew the gesture so he winked at her too and she beamed at her boss's familiarity, the beautiful lady major quickly forgotten.

"I take your point, sir," the colonel ran his hands through his thinning hair, not quite sure how to explain the next part to the non-technical gathering he had before him. "I will try to keep it simple. When the device is ready to perform its duty, it chooses a time when the remote station is transmitting and cuts in. It sends a holding pulse or polling pulse if you like, to the remote station. And at the same time starts working to the main computer. Hence the main computer thinks it's working to its station and the remote terminal simply thinks it's time barred from the main machine for a time. We are talking thousandths of a second. Lastly, when the whole thing's working, the device lets the remote through but works, that is, schedules its requirements between the real stations. Therefore we can now work undetected, while the machine appears to be working quite normally."

Polyakov frowned, "I have a question. This machine sounds fantastic but surely we are in this game too, and I take it this machine, even if it gets through the computer locks, surely it cannot work on a scrambled line?"

"We are in this game but these machines have to be dedicated to compatible computers. This one will be compatible with one of our competitors where we very much want to know what's going on. You are also right, sir, when you say that this will only work on an unscrambled line. I mentioned before that there was another part to this task." The colonel looked at Polyakov.

"OK, enough. Thank you, Colonel. Any other questions so far?" He looked round the table.

Alcksandrovich indicated he had another question, "How will we know the machine when we see it and how can you be sure we are being offered the real article and not a fake?"

"Good question, sir." The colonel unrolled a set of blueprints, "They sent us some of the plans and we believe from the evidence that what they are offering is technically feasible. As I will be at the handover I can verify it there and then and check if the machine actually works."

Polyakov raised his eyebrows and made a note on his pad. He hadn't really expected the technocrat to be going into the field but he didn't seem to have much choice.

"Are there any further questions?" The people at the table shrugged. "OK, then who is going to brief me on the timings and the exchange arrangements?" Polyakov leaned forward gazing round at the team.

Major Valeria Gershuni rose to her feet, "With your permission, I will, sir. These updated briefing notes were handed to me by your director on his way out to pass on to you and the team, and there are copies for all here." Her voice was husky and she read from the director's notes, summarizing as she went. "First, a little background; around three months ago Major Nsenko, the department's man in Guatemala, was approached by a half-caste man who gave his name as Thomas Hough. He works in South Africa as the security manager for a government classified computer research centre. He offered to us for a price the device that the Colonel has taken great pains to describe. The price was so high that our man felt that there had to be something in the man's claim of its importance. The Major put the man's offer to us here. It was felt that it was important enough to brief the Director." She dropped her eyes, conscious that the director had not told his deputy. "What the Director did with it I don't know except that the offer was accepted and outline plans for its reception have been made," she eyed the colonel, for he obviously did know, "But I have just received these updated orders that lays out the method by which we are to make the exchange."

She pulled a paper from her tunic and read out the director's orders. "Phase one, Colonel Ivanovich and Major Alcksandrovich..." she looked at the two men and Polyakov for permission to continue, again he nodded, "...are to leave for Melchor de Mencos tonight, laying over in Mexico; they have four days from now to prove the device. You will be met by Major Nsenko who will take you to the man running the test and Nsenko will leave you with him and have no part to play thereafter. Your papers and travel documents you can collect from me after the meeting." Gershuni paused for questions; there were none so she continued.

"Phase two: within four days' time from now, the man who is proving the device to us and reconfiguring it for our use will meet you, sir," she indicated the deputy director, "and myself, with the device, at Melchor de Mencos airport, subject of course to Colonel Ivanovich signing off on the device's capability. We are to be at the airport where we will make the exchange, with the pay-off of ten million US dollars. The funds are being sent through to the local bank in Melchor for us to collect well in time for the exchange. The Deputy and I are booked to travel tomorrow evening. I will, of course, sir, bring your documentation to you later today."

Valeria Gershuni looked at her notes once more and added, "Before taking any questions there is supplementary information that may be helpful or useful for you to know. Firstly, coordination so far with the third parties has been led by Comrade Colonel Tsygankov. He also arranged for Jean Saied, the mercenary leader who stole the device, to take it to Melchor. Secondly, Colonel Tsygankov is not stood down for the moment until the device is to be used. I don't have any details on that matter. Thirdly, Saied is an extremely resourceful and dangerous man who is working both for them and us. We are asked by Colonel Tsygankov to nurture him. He will be at the test and the exchange. It is apparently part of the deal that he is to be paid in full by them, but Colonel Tsygankov has further plans for his talents. I have completed my briefing. Are there any questions?"

"How will we recognize Major Nsenko at the airport?" It was Polyakov.

"It will not be a problem," she smiled and her face lit up. "Nsenko is a little old-fashioned and apparently dresses always in a dark brown, double-breasted pinstripe suit with brown shoes." The people in the room roared with laughter, the tension of the moment lifting. Polyakov thought the team appeared to get on with each other and the mission, if nothing went wrong, could be amusing.

"Thank you, that seems straightforward enough," Polyakov was still rocking in his chair with mirth, "Will the man be alone?"

"No, he is the guest of the local terrorist organization there, as far as we can make out. It's a reciprocal arrangement between the banned African National Congress and the left-wing guerrillas there. Saied will also be there to ensure all goes well."

Polyakov waved the major back to her seat, "Good, thank you; I believe we are now in a position to execute the plan. One thing that does worry me slightly is the local involvement. What's their strength? Do we have any influence?" the general looked at Alcksandrovich from Illegal's expectantly.

The man cleared his throat. Polyakov studied him for the first time. He was dark-haired and thickset and his facial features could easily have marked him out for possibly a Spaniard or Italian. Even his mannerisms were Latin. When he began to talk it was with exaggerated movements of his body and hands. He didn't seem to be able to keep his hands still; it amused the general and he warmed to the man he had thought might have been a dull companion; he wanted to smile but didn't. What Alcksandrovich had to say was not encouraging.

"Hard core there are about five thousand or maybe a few more. They are hunted aggressively by the Guatemalan army but it's such an underdeveloped country in terms of logistical infrastructure, with great areas of wilderness, that they are rarely caught in any great numbers. Our involvement is fairly low key as is the Cuban link in El Salvador. Guatemala is close to the American's sphere of influence re Mexico and Panama. The British are in Belize protecting the Belizeans from Guatemala's stated aim of getting access to the sea on the other side of the isthmus through Belize. To me it is all too obvious that they are there at the American's, if not behest, for their benefit, as it secures local borders. I'll check out our people there before we go and make sure they are available if we need them. I'll try to get one involved, attached to the party that is hosting the South Africans and our party. But no promises, just in case what's there is not acceptable."

"Good. Now, what about this airport for the exchange? Where is it?"

"The airport is right up against the border between Belize and Guatemala," Valeria Gershuni answered.

"Is it an international airport?" Polyakov wanted to know. "Can we fly in direct and out on the same day?"

Gershuni responded, "No, sir, not by any imagination. We believe that the four days requested are to enable the courier to move up with the device from Guatemala City, through the safe terrorist-controlled jungle highways and, with the engineer, prepare the device for our scrutiny."

"Major, I must admit, I am a bit lost. Why the Belize and Guatemala border for the exchange? Surely it would make more sense to have the exchange at the Guatemala City international airport? Why all this cloak-and-dagger stuff in the jungle?" Polyakov queried.

"The issue is that the engineer who is to reconfigure the device and prove it to us has set himself up on the border between the two countries, a short distance from the dirt airfield runway. It seems he is playing safe so that he and our hosts can border hop if they need to. My plans were that we either charter a small aircraft from the city airport or we drive up. Both options have some risk. But, as it turns out, Colonel Tsygankov has a charter standing by in Mexico City."

"Do we have any more on the hosts? I mean the particular group of guerrillas who are involved with the engineer and with whom presumably we will meet at some stage; and what of this courier?" Polyakov looked at Gershuni and Alcksandrovich for an answer.

Gershuni said defensively, "The courier is Colonel Tsygankov's man, the mercenary, Jean Saied, the man who led the team that acquired the device. As for the local guerrilla group, I simply don't know anything about them." She hesitated and riffled through her briefing notes.

Alcksandrovich came to her rescue, "Well, General, I for one do not trust them. They are not normally as well organized as other guerrilla groups in South America, just a disenfranchised group from what I can make out. If the government forces would stop to do a bit more with the hearts and minds of the people there instead of having a civil rights record that is worse than any I can think of, they would easily defeat the rebels and bring these add-on peripheral freelance groups back into normal society. Be that as it may, this group is likely to be undisciplined, clannish and probably normally drug trade driven. All this means is that they will be unpredictable, a dangerous cocktail for us to be involved with. How they got mixed up with the ANC is a mystery to me."

"Your thoughts are noted. Now..." Polyakov lent back in his chair; he was thinking of what his director had got him into. Did his director know what a mess this was and could become? Polyakov thought generously that his director knew precisely what he was doing and that he wanted Polyakov to win through for him and that was a compliment, so he had better do the best he could. The small group around the table was waiting for him to speak or comment; even his secretary leaned forward as the minutes passed.

"General," she prompted him.

His secretary's prod bought him out of his trance. "Thank you, I just needed a moment to digest the information that the team has passed over in such a short time. OK. Gershuni, you are in overall command in the field. Your primary task is to get us all into Guatemala, up to the border then get us out and back here. As Tsygankov has a charter, I think we will all go together. Let's keep it simple. Major Alcksandrovich, your role is adviser to the good Major Valeria and to ensure that there is assistance available to you should it be required; I also want, through your contacts, to acquire such weaponry as is appropriate for self-defence and ready for us to have when we land in Mexico City. I do not want our people permanently stationed in that country to be involved. It is getting embarrassing, the number of our people various governments round the world are returning to us for activities that are, shall we say, incompatible with their duties. It would be very embarrassing to us as a group to have anyone returned from a country so close to the American borders."

He paused, "Any questions? No? Right, Colonel I would like to see you in my office." Turning to his secretary, "Take the two Majors with you; see that arrangements for our journey are made without delay and draw up the papers for the money. Get the director to sign the requisition. Valeria, tie up all the details before you finish tonight and then come and brief me when you are ready to do so. The team is to be ready by tomorrow night. Sergei, sort out your contacts. Come and see me later, latest early morning, and let me know what you have arranged." As he rose, the team rose and stood at attention until he and the colonel had left the room.

Chapter 5

SOUTH AFRICA – LATE IN THE DAY

Leaving Wolff and his men to squeeze more information out of Hough, Paul Vintner made his way reflectively down the stairs to the control centre and as he pushed open the door was surprised to see Bob Coveney with his sleeves rolled up; he had, with six of his men, already sorted all the evidence into neat piles; they looked about finished. He looked at his watch and was equally surprised to see the time, which showed just after one in the morning. Where had the last four hours gone, Paul puzzled to himself.

The young inspector looked up as Vintner made his presence known. Vintner had been upstairs for four hours and felt dry and drained. He collapsed into an easy chair, undid his tie and closed his eyes for a moment. Where had Hough said just before he clammed up – Guatemala? He dismissed it; maybe Wolff would get something more from their detainee.

The men continued their task so he squeezed his eyes and opened up the dialogue, "You look as though you've all been very busy, so busy in fact that you've forgotten to make this very senior officer a cup of tea." The men stopped and looked at the chief inspector.

"Right you are, sir. OK, ten minutes break. Morris, your turn for the tea." Sergeant Morris got up from his work mouthing, "Why me?" He knew he wasn't the youngest by a long way but he was the most junior.

While they waited for the tea Vintner questioned the inspector. He didn't believe that Hough had simply left all the evidence for anyone to find; it didn't fit the man's methods or his background.

Coveney laughed, "Damn right it wasn't just lying around. And if it hadn't been for a neighbour who had taken a dislike to Hough for some reason or other we would never have got him. The evidence was not in his house but in one up the street two-doors away. She had seen him going in and out at night. She didn't think anything of it because she knew he was caretaking for a few months for a neighbour. But she was suspicious, as he had been going in there regularly these past few weeks. Hough must have thought he had it made. When we broke in, there was all the stuff on the dining room table. If it hadn't been for that woman or we had gone to his house when she wasn't there, we would have found nothing. We checked his place of course. It was totally clean."

Vintner let out a whistle. God, they had been lucky. He thought to himself; let's hope that our luck, now begun, holds until we get the device back. Of those involved in the investigation, only he and Wolff knew what the device did and how important it was. The minister in charge of state security had given them one order, "Find that machine irrespective of cost, irrespective of resources." If the machine were to turn up on the world market or if its capabilities were to become known, the fact that it was from the government Research Station was felt to be an embarrassment that the South African government did not want to have to face. They were, some would argue unfairly, seen as a rogue state by some of the international community as it was, without being accused of building a computer spy machine.

"Bob, would you like to tell me what all this represents?" Vintner asked, waving his hand at the pile of evidence.

"Yes, I will certainly try."

"Does it implicate any locals?" Paul needed to know if there were more dissidents they needed to pick up.

"A couple of local people are named, but they are, or appear to be, minor parties and we will pick them up later." The inspector paused to pick up his notes. "He is a very exceptional man, our Hough. He definitely had an out-of-country sponsor and funding."

"Interesting you say that. How did you come to that conclusion, Bob?"

"One of the books is an account of monies placed into a Swiss account by parties as yet unknown. It shows various sums of money, some paid to the mercenaries. Their names are in code but from the general structure of the account you can tell it's payments of that kind. All the donations, or rather payments, are the same. It looks as though the men were paid in two instalments, one before and one to be paid after the raid. There are other payments too. And the headings clearly show what they are for. For example: Weapons, Transport, Clothing etc."

"Let me see the book please," Vintner stretched out his hand to take the ledger from the inspector.

The inspector flicked his fingers at one of the men who dug it out of a pile and handed it to the inspector. "Here you are Paul," he was feeling pleased with himself and it showed. Vintner noticed the look of success on the inspector's face and inwardly smiled; in the inspector's place he would be feeling pretty pleased with himself too.

Vintner studied the book for a few minutes. "It looks as though he was keeping this for presentation to someone. Did you find the airline ticket close by this?" Vintner's mind was working furiously.

"Yes, sir," one of the policemen answered, "The airline ticket was tucked in it."

"Hmm," Paul looked at the entries carefully. "What's this?" In the list of supposed code names he had picked out three that had only one payment due against their names, "How many dead did we find at the centre after the raid?"

"As you know, none of the raiders, but all of the Defence Force soldiers plus the two policemen that went out to investigate the shooting that had been heard."

"What about other evidence on the raiders?"

"There was nothing to identify them at the site. The shells they used were picked up and taken with them and no fingerprints were found, nothing. But they did make a mistake," Bob said seriously.

"Oh what was that?" Vintner looked up from the account book.

"Forensics found two sets of prints on the boot of the police car; they got careless after the raid or they were in a hurry."

"Did we identify them?" Vintner was alert.

"The results have just arrived at headquarters and we were just about to call them back for the names and then come upstairs to let you know of the development when you came down. Both men were on the Interpol files as known terrorists, freelance. Headquarters went back and asked for known associates."

"Good, now let's see if there is anything in the papers relating to them." The inspector went to the phone and called the duty desk. It was several minutes before the central police duty records officer came back on the phone with the answer. The inspector took the call.

"The names of the two men were Joseph Mataluzee and James Kholo."

Paul Vintner grinned. He studied the account book for a while and counted on his fingers, "Here are their initials in the pay book, albeit the names are encrypted into numbers with the use of a simple code, A equals 1 etc. It has to be them, I've only decrypted the first initials but clearly the names are in full from the length of the numbers. One entry in here deals with a large payment to an insurance company." Vintner was excited, "Right Bob, this insurance company is based here. Get one of your men to dig one of the directors out of his bed and find out who and what was insured. Priority on this, it may lead us to something significant."

Paul continued to study the account book and at last he looked up, "Bob, below the list of what we suspect are payments there is another coded name. But he gets three payments and the sum is many times larger than the others." Paul showed the entry to Bob, "Any ideas? It shows two payments still outstanding."

"May I see, sir?" Vintner handed the book to the inspector. "Yes, I thought so. See here," Bob indicated the line of the record, "there are three spaces left after his name. One is taken up by the first payment and the other two are blank. Curious don't you think? As you say, all the other men paid off had only two spaces with one filled in. The first payment is under the others." He screwed up his face. "Could it suggest he was to be paid in three instalments? If so it might suggest he was the leader."

Vintner looked at the young policeman; bright, he was, "Could be, could be. Let's just put that proposition on ice whilst one of your clever lads decodes this potential leader for us first and then we can check him out immediately."

Bob gave the book to one of his team who had made the mistake of looking interested in the exchange between the two senior officers and Bob demanded that he get the leader's name decoded in five minutes time or else the man would be back on the beat directing traffic.

Vintner moved on, totally focused now, "What else did you find?"

"There was a list of local phone numbers."

"Really, who did they belong to?" Vintner was interested.

"We are still checking them out; George over there is on to that," he thumbed over his shoulder to one of his men hunched over a phone book and on the telephone to the state phone company.

Vintner didn't show his impatience, the team had a lot to digest; he understood that investigation was not instantaneous but he added, "I'd like to know as soon as *you* do, George. Right, Bob, next please."

"There are photocopies of the security installations at the station and we found wax impressions of keys, the security type. We will have them checked out with the ones at the station. They could have opened up everything by key but they elected to blow locks and doors. Easy to do. Nice touch. It put us off the inside man's scent, for a while anyway."

"Next?" Vintner stated without let-up.

"Not really much else; there is a lot of material about illegal organizations that we may find useful in the future but, pertaining to the raid, very little."

"OK, where's that tea? Are you sure now that there is nothing to say for whom he was working? You would have thought he would have wanted some ace up his sleeve in case things went wrong."

"That's difficult to say. From what we have seen so far it does look as though he was working alone. That is except for our assumption that he had a banker backing him."

"That does tend to confirm what he himself claims. The only other possibility is that he is working with someone. But I don't think so. Until we prove it differently then we will assume that he was working alone except for a backer. There must be something about getting the force together though, surely?"

"Sort of, it's not much," the inspector retrieved a document from the table.

Vintner read it carefully; it was more of a checklist with notes. The fourth line read; *Raiding force agreed. Saied will organize everything for the price. Ship Boats Guns, men, explosives etc.* And the fifth line went; *Plan accepted Saied can do it.* Vintner scanned the rest of the list. It didn't mean much to him, but his eyes kept returning to the fourth and fifth lines. The more he looked at them the more he was sure there was something more there. In exasperation he passed it back to the inspector, "I'm missing something; look at lines four and five."

The men in the room crowded round the inspector. Just then Morris brought the tea round. He glanced at the list as he handed the tea round, "That's a funny way to spell 'said' with a capital letter."

Vintner looked at the inspector and they said together, "Where is that decoded list of names?"

"Just finished," called the policeman decoding the first name, "Jean Saied."

"Let's not get too excited boys. This name is obviously Aramaic. Unless it is 'Said' but I don't think so. Bob, get on to the Israelis and get them to send over the wire the profile of anyone with that name who is known to them. The Israelis are very good at keeping tabs on their errant children, especially important ones, and he must be one," he laughed. "Then Interpol, they may have something. Don't forget, if this cove is leading hit parties of this size and looking after operations of this sort, he has to be known. And he would have to have been trained by someone." He thought for a moment, "Try the Americans and the British too. Yes, that should do." He sipped his tea while the room bustled to do his bidding.

The room was well appointed for this operation and the numbers involved. It was spacious; as well as the easy chairs it had half a dozen desks all with telephones and another table with a short-wave radio which sat humming in a corner of the room. The room was well lit and samples of native art hung from the walls. One wall was taken up by a huge map of the city and its surrounding countryside. Vintner thought silently to himself that the intelligence service certainly lived well, the best of everything.

As to the device, he was no further forward. Suppose, Paul thought, Hough with his through ticket to Guatemala was going there to meet up with the machine? Who would he be meeting? Who would a man like that trust? Could it be this Saied? And Bob had suggested that the second and final payments to the man could be tied into that. It was possible. But if it was, how were they going to find the man now in a country that had no ties with South Africa. He shook his head to clear it. He was tired and his head felt crowded with thoughts of this possibility. He wondered how Wolff was getting on.

"Bob, are you absolutely sure there is nothing about the machine in all that stuff?"

"Not a damn thing, it's as though he were happy to broadcast the raid and a few titbits on the machine, but regarding future meetings, link-ups etc., he must have everything in his head." The inspector looked helplessly at his senior officer, "All we have is his ticket tonight to Guatemala."

Vintner was suddenly alert, "Jesus, what time does the plane leave?"

Bob picked up the ticket from the evidence table and studied it before responding, "It left an hour ago, why?"

"Damn, we should have put someone on that plane! We may have been able to bluff our way in with whoever was meeting him at the other end. Do you see, by sending a substitute?"

"We may not be too late; we might be able to catch it up. The journey route is unnecessarily convoluted, London, Miami, Guatemala, with an enforced stopover in London. We may be able to catch up, there or en route. You cannot fly to Guatemala direct from here, so there may be other options."

"Get on to it now, priority one. Now, please Bob."

Vintner left the room and dashed for the interrogation room. He burst in. Wolff sat in a chair, arms by his side, he was covered in perspiration; the other secret service man was slumped against the wall. In the chair, eyes bulging, was Hough; his head was back and his tongue protruded from his mouth. The man had a series of black and blue marks on the exposed skin of his arms and chest. It was clear that he had taken a terrible beating. An arm looked broken and dangled uselessly. There were burns on the man's face. All this Paul Vintner registered in one glance before turning his head away. It sickened him and the stench of the room from where Hough had fouled himself made him nauseous. In his last agony Hough had messed himself.

Wolff looked up dully at Paul, "He's dead."

Vintner growled and Wolff told his man to get out and wait downstairs. When he had gone, Vintner took Wolff by the arm and led him out. Once outside he let go of Wolff's arm and motioned him to follow him. Vintner led Wolff into the garden. He was slightly shocked at his colleague's state. He had supposed that a torture death would have little effect on him.

He was obviously wrong and in a minute or two, once Wolff had breathed in the cool night air and walked round the garden of the house, his colleague confessed, "I know what you're thinking and you're wrong. I don't kill defenceless people whoever they may be. I leave that to our specialists." He spat into the coarse parched grass that formed an excuse for a lawn. "The whole thing sickened me, if you want to know." He retched but nothing came up.

"Did you get anything out of him?"

"No, apart from a few involuntary grunts he never said another thing. He was a very brave man no matter what his fanatical beliefs were. He may not have looked very pretty but he died with dignity. He just seemed to switch off to pain and slip away from us. It was as though he made up his mind to die and just did."

"OK, are you feeling better now? I need you to be calm and ready to take in a series of developments and how we are going to move forward on them. Time is short and I need your input, OK?" Vintner needed to focus on the case and the next steps.

Wolff took a deep breath and exhaled slowly, "Yeah, go ahead, I will be fine, just give me a chance to have a cigarette in peace and then I will give you my full attention." Wolff wiped his mouth. He took out his packet of cigarettes, flipped one into his mouth and lit it. A few deep draws and he turned to the ever-patient Vintner who was gazing up at a half-moon trying to get his thoughts in order. "OK Paul, ready; hit me with the developments."

"Well, we have made some progress. We don't know for sure where the damn thing is but I've got a few ideas. Come into the house, have a cup of tea and I'll tell you about it."

When they entered the workroom the men were silent. Vintner took the lead, "OK, we have lost our star witness. You," he pointed to the man that had been working with Wolff, "take someone with you. Clean up and then make it look like a hit-and-run." He jerked his thumb. The man collected a colleague and left. The man could see danger in Vintner's eyes and that Vintner blamed him for the mess upstairs. He couldn't get out fast enough.

"Inspector, what's the news on catching that plane?" Vintner had switched seamlessly into his normal calm manner.

"We can get a plane at five in the morning to London and catch the same Miami flight."

"Good, book four, no, five seats then all of you take a one hour break. Then I want you all back here with food and drink for all of us. Morris, two teas please."

"What plane?" Wolff was back; Vintner could see the unpleasant experience of the interrogation was receding from Wolff's consciousness and he was back in play.

"I'll start at the beginning." Vintner sat beside Wolff and told him his plan.

Chapter 6

MOSCOW – LATE

After Polyakov had grilled the colonel and extracted the whole plan from him, not just the retrieval of the machine, he was furious. How could the director, he thought to himself, go on such a high-risk venture without his deputy's knowledge and help? He kept returning to the colonel's words; at first he had not trusted his ears.

"You are going to do what?" Polyakov said softly but with a threat in his voice.

"We are going to link the device into the NATO battle computer." The colonel, sitting in his chair in front of the general's desk, felt very uncomfortable to the extent that perspiration was forming on his brow.

"And how do you propose to do that? This thing only works in clear language." Polyakov was on his feet.

"Yes sir, but you must appreciate that we have been working on this conceptually for the last five years, waiting for such a device, as is now within our sights, to become a reality. It's been my project from the very start but we were only able to move on since the man, Hough, quite out of the blue just over six months ago, came to us."

Polyakov stood in front of the colonel, arms folded. "You had better tell me the whole of the story from beginning to end and don't leave anything out. Do you understand?" Polyakov bent over the sitting colonel and whispered, "This is not your problem, it's above your pay grade, so have no fear that it is you I am concerned or annoyed with. Now let's have the story." Polyakov patted the colonel's shoulder and returned to his desk. He settled himself in, leaning back with his eyes closed, "Begin, please."

"Yes, General." The colonel lowered his head slowly looking at his hands folded on his lap. He was not a coward but knew that he was in the presence of the second most important man in the directorate who wielded near total power and to refuse to tell all could mean death sooner or later.

"Who is involved in this with you, Yuri?"

"Those who know about this apart from you now, are the Director, Colonel Tsygankov, one of my people and one other."

"Who is the other?" The deputy's voice was insistent.

"He is an electronic installation engineer working for the contractor building the new NATO computer hard and software. He is a member of my team and has been in deep cover since we thought this mission up almost five years ago."

"OK, OK, you have someone on the inside. I am nevertheless amazed that his cover has not been blown if he is working on such a contract, what about security clearance? He surely must have been checked out thoroughly?"

"Indeed General, that is so. We took great pains to build a legend for him. Whilst nothing is perfect, they would have to dig deeper than they do to find out he is not who he purports to be. We rebuilt his history from birth."

"Well," said Polyakov, "as everything rests on him being able to carry out his task, let us hope so. No doubt the Director was involved in this and therefore I take comfort from the fact that he is an old master in that regard." the colonel confirmed with a nod so Polyakov instructed, "Now, please continue with your story."

"It all started, as I said, five years ago when we knew that they were going to design a new machine to replace the current battle computer. You know how it is, sir, technology moves on so fast and you need to increase the speed and file sizes etc. as time goes on. We dreamed up a scenario that was feasible, if not technically possible at that time."

Polyakov rose slowly to his feet and paced around the back of the colonel's chair. Polyakov had an awful premonition of what he was about to hear. The colonel rubbed his hands through his hair. Polyakov had noticed the colonel's habit of playing with his thinning hair before and it both amused and mildly irritated him at the same time.

"Get on, Colonel." So much for profiles, Polyakov thought, returning to his desk and throwing himself back in the high-backed leather chair.

"When the Director did one of his periodic tours of the other departments, as he does..." Polyakov smiled to himself; the old man was incredible, "...I put it to him..." said Ivanovich.

"Put what to him?" the general was now leaning forward, resting his head in his hands, elbows on the desk.

"...that we build a device like the one we are after and that, at the time of the construction of the new computer for NATO, we build a tap into the master supervisor's server/terminal. You will understand that all intelligence to and from the computer has to go through his terminal one way or the other."

"Bloody hell," Polyakov had left his desk again and began to pace around the room, "Why now?"

The colonel moved uncomfortably in his chair, "There are two reasons. One is that their computer is nearing operational readiness and two, we here met unexpected difficulties in producing our spy machine. Timing is not necessarily critical in that we could put the spy device in later, as I understand our man will be snagging and developing the machine for years on his contract. It appears from what the Director indicated to me that he is in a rush. He mentioned that we had that unfortunate defection to the British and, with leaks from someone and the spy network in Europe, including our KGB operative at NATO HQ, he doesn't feel he can wait. With the device from South Africa we can be operational in a few months."

"Forgive my layman enquiry, but I always thought that their computer suites, like ours, would be screened and that any foreign devices would show on their detectors, plus, even if we can read the intelligence with this device, what about encryption? What about getting the information out to us? Real time was mentioned."

"Ordinarily, yes to all your points; but we would be able, with the device capabilities, to overcome the issues." The colonel warmed to his task, "Our bug in the supervisor's terminal, a very sophisticated one which I will tell you more about in a moment, does not transmit in the normal way. It is linked undetectably to the power supply. It pushes harmonics down the power supply line."

"What do you mean, pushes harmonics down the line?"

"The bug in the supervisor's terminal converts the intelligence it receives into harmonics, encodes the received intelligence and these encrypted waves pass down the line undetected to a receiver outside the security area. Here we pick them up by plugging in our spy machine to decode and amplify the signals and transmit them direct to Moscow centre," the colonel paused. "Do you see, sir?"

"I see the concept, but why do you really think that they will not suspect? Surely they will pick up your signal and will clean up the line."

"Not a chance, General. The harmonics are not regular and, remember, they have been scrambled. The signal is so weak that it will look to any tests like normal radiation on the cable, just unintelligible noise."

"You'd stake your life on that, would you, Comrade Colonel Ivanovich?"

For the first time since he had met Ivanovich, Polyakov affirmed his respect for the man when he answered, "I already have, sir." The colonel's face was bland. He meant it.

"So be it. I will do everything in my power to make your, in my opinion, foolish venture, work. Do I fully understand that the only thing standing in your way to getting your project operational is the device we now propose to buy from a dubious unknown source?" Polyakov's brilliant grey eyes smiled at the colonel who let out his breath, clearly the telling had been stressful. "Humour me a little longer, Colonel, I am still curious about the hardware in the supervisor's terminal. Will it pick up all data to and from the mainframe i.e. all intelligence?" queried Polyakov.

"Oh yes, General, it most assuredly will."

"Secondly, when their engineers service or troubleshoot the console, will they not see our extra, unnecessary hardware and wiring?"

"We don't believe so; we have taken great pains to disguise our kit. For example, for your ears only, we redesigned one of their components so that it not only appears to and does its job for them; it also performs our tasks too. This component, or rather chip, is the one that gathers intelligence with our transmitter included in the chip. It has a lithium battery embedded which has a five-year-life; this is quite normal and will be changed out in its turn. The spares back-up package is quite extensive, as you would expect. The nature of the beast is that its components cannot be bought off the shelf and our engineer cleverly coded the part number so one of our own components would replace the part. You might say that when their engineers change out the component, they will not only be perpetuating our capability but doing the work for us!" the colonel laughed for the first time, "Would you like me to go on?"

"Please, this is as fascinating as it is unbelievable."

"The last bit then. We, or rather our engineer, will modify the console to embed in its metal structure the chip receiver-transmitter I have described. The transmitter we use also scrambles the signal. Rather, I should say many chips. We have put in resilience so that the encapsulated chips in the console's metalwork trigger the lithium batteries of the next set of chips once the battery in the previous chip is running out, and so on. We have built in twenty years of life, as we expect in that time frame the whole machine will be replaced." He paused, "Remember the machines are not your average PC and their life and life-enhancement program is planned for extended use."

"Hah! If this works they will not have many secrets after twenty years." Polyakov laughed out loud, "This is crazy, absolutely insane. A thought occurred to me, is this set-up of chips a two-way process? Can we input into them?"

The colonel dropped his head into his hands, "Yes and that is precisely what got the Director so excited."

"Wow! This is past insane." Polyakov was appalled when he considered the danger of such a capability in the wrong hands. Polyakov could see from the colonel's body language that he was also worried, "OK, what else don't I know?"

The colonel blew out a breath. "Clearly the Director wants us to replicate the device and its supporting chips so we have the option of infiltrating other computer systems, NSA, CIA, M16, the Israelis, some Arab states, Asian etc. over time."

"Yuri, for clarity, do I understand that if we fail to get this device, you can still produce the desired result but the time frame is simply unacceptable to the Director?"

"Exactly so, Comrade General; I cannot see our technicians producing a device like the one we have been offered for a few more years at least. Even though the technology is proven, it's the micro level that is defeating us currently." The colonel fell silent.

"What you really mean, surely, my dear Yuri, is that you have hit snags that a little country like South Africa has solved and you don't know how to solve them without pinching somebody else's breakthrough?"

The colonel's head shot up, "We would solve the difficulties eventually." His voice was firm. Polyakov at last could see the man had courage, which was to the good considering where they were going. He had pricked the colonel's skin by attacking his professional pride.

Polyakov smiled, walked over to the man and patted the colonel on the shoulder again, "Of course you would; but, as you say, not in time for the Director. A drink for you?" Polyakov stood by his cocktail cabinet now, holding up a brandy. The colonel shook his head. "As you wish, Colonel, however I need one, I think." The general moved to signal the end of the interview, "Right, that's all for now. I'll see you tomorrow. I need some time to think about what you have told me. What has passed between us remains in this room," Polyakov shook the colonel's hand.

The colonel rose, hesitated as though to say something, changed his mind and walked to the door; Polyakov called after him, "I shall tell the Director that I ordered you to tell me about the whole matter."

Relief flooded the colonel's face, "Thank you, sir." He saluted with the air of the reprieved and left.

Polyakov rang for his secretary. When she entered the office, she found him angrier than she had ever seen him. He stood at his desk with his hands clasped firmly behind him, "Get me the Director on my private line." He swivelled on his feet to look out of the window at the gathering dusk. His secretary moved to comply with his order. "But first, my angel, pour me a scotch, a large one, and give me a hug, this brandy is like petrol," he put down his glass hard in disgust.

Chapter 7

MISS OJUKO

As one of the five people picked up the night before, Miss Christiana Ojuko was a very frightened woman. She sat at her desk in the research station close to tears. The events of the previous day were still vivid in her mind.

Miss Ojuko was in her middle thirties, tall and pleasant to look at, with a good figure and fine, lightly coloured features. Perhaps that was what had attracted Hough to her in the first place and, because of his position, she to him. He had been older but quite a catch in her eyes. It was rumoured that he had also been picked up last night and that worried her further. Hough had represented a step up the social scale, or so her intimate friends had said. Their affair had been secretive, which she found an excitement in itself. She suspected he was more than he appeared, as a security manager at the station, but she didn't really know. She was to find out quickly that day.

She was acutely aware that the South African police would soon find out that they had been secret lovers, her only worry was when and would it make any difference. She shuddered as she contemplated being interviewed again by the men she had met last night. They had been brash, confident and cruel. She had no illusions that they could make her confess to anything. She had only been at work for an hour and already the absence of Hough and combined with her own fears made her suddenly tremble.

She got up from her desk and went to the window of her office again and looked at the remains of the security lodge. Hough was not in sight.

Normally he sat at the desk in the lodge but there was a new man there. As she returned to her desk she heard another secretary in the room gasp. The girl snapped her newspaper shut. Christiana's sixth sense told her something was wrong and she went over to the woman.

"What's up, girl?"

"Nothing, girl, go and sit down. Get on with your work."

"Come on, let's see, la."

Christiana opened up the paper slowly. It was the *South African Times*. As she let the paper fall open the picture of her lover stared up at her. The picture was not good and the body had been photographed where it had been found. The body was crumpled in the pose of a broken doll. The caption was what drew Christiana's attention. *"Mr Hough of Cape Town killed by hit-and-run driver on the way home after work last night. The city police were..."* Tears blurred the print. She closed the paper and let out a cry. The other girls crowded round her. There was little they could do to comfort her.

After a while she went back to her desk. If she had been frightened before, she was terrified now. What had Hough said to her? As their life together tumbled through her mind, a kaleidoscope of images and sound bites, she kept returning to the fact that she had to do something.

She remembered Hough had given her a key to a safety-deposit box the day after the raid. She fingered it in her handbag and brought it out on to her desk. For a moment or two she stared at it. What had he said? He had told her that if anything happened to him she was to take it to the bank, withdraw the envelope she would find in the deposit box and take it to the British Embassy where she would be looked after. Anything else in the box was hers to keep.

She collected her things and left the office. The other girls understood and let her go saying they would cover for her. She booked out at reception and ran to the bus stop at the top of the road out of the research station. While she waited for the bus she bit her lip. Mustn't cry; he was dead and now she must do what he had asked. A bus passed the spot every ten minutes and half an hour later she was standing outside the bank.

Normally a confident person, today she felt exposed entering the bank and felt that all eyes were on her. Her modest earnings meant that she didn't have an account and the cool, high-vaulted marbled reception area of the bank overawed her. Taking a big breath she advanced to the enquiries desk. Another customer walked in front of her and she almost lost her courage, but she waited quietly for him to finish his business and then it was her turn. The teller didn't even look up.

"Please sir, I am to open a box here."

The teller eyed her suspiciously. "You want to what, madam?"

"See here," she fished out the key and held it up for his inspection.

"Wait there, please," the man left his desk and for a moment she almost panicked and fled. A door to the left of the booth opened and the man stuck his head out and beckoned her into the inner bank complex.

She followed him, clipping along behind him in her high-heeled sandals. He led her into the depths of the bank. They stopped outside a huge strongroom in which an armed guard sat. The teller smiled for the first time.

"Now madam, may I see your key?" he studied it and then left her. He went into the strongroom and removed a box from the bank of seemingly endless others. When he returned with it he took her by the arm and steered her into a side room. "Now I will leave you to yourself. When you finish, simply relock your box and then give it to the guard. He will see you out." With an acknowledgment he left her alone. When she was sure she was not observed she took out her key again and inserted it into the lock. She hesitated for a moment, tears beginning to cloud her vision. She wiped them away and with a determination borne of panic, turned the key in the lock and swung the lid open.

* * * * *

The investigation team had reassembled again an hour or so after Hough's death and they were a pretty tired and subdued group. Even Wolff seemed to have withdrawn into himself again. It was left to Vintner's coldly analytical mind to cajole and bully the men back into action.

The first phase of the operation was to get them both on to the plane and make the rendezvous in Guatemala. It had not been without the greatest difficulty that they had persuaded the minister that they should both go. Eventually he was persuaded that the team left behind, led by Bob Coveney, was more than capable of following through on the investigation at this end. They had had to promise to keep in touch with the inspector and the minister every eight hours and also when they changed locations. He had argued with the minister that they had two choices; one was to try to bluff Hough's contact from the South African end. The other was to get there, identify the contact or, possibly, Saied, follow him or them and retrieve the device. Whatever they both felt and believed, they had to follow the device. They had had to acknowledge to the minister they were going into the unknown but they didn't see any other choice.

They now had the information and descriptions from the various agencies they had contacted with urgent requests on the man, Jean Saied. The Israeli information seemed the most reliable and was backed up by a report from the Americans who had also identified Saied. They had his picture, albeit a couple of years old, but it was clear and they would have no difficulty identifying him. He was undoubtedly a dangerous and intelligent terrorist, experienced and no pushover.

It was barely two hours before the plane and Vintner began to release men on to other parts of the investigation and handover the 'in-country' investigation to his inspector, with two of Wolff's senior men assigned to support as necessary. A small team had been put to analysing the Hough documents.

Around mid morning the team made the connection between Miss Ojuko and Hough but it was long after Vintner and Wolff and their support had flown out. There had been several references to a 'Chris'. The men had assumed this referred to a man; it was only when a tired aide put together a reference to the note *flowers to Chris* and later a scrawled address in the back of his pocketbook that the policeman checked out the address and, found it to be that of Miss Ojuko; putting the picture together didn't take many more minutes. Once he was certain of his facts he went to find his boss. When he told the inspector, Coveney's head shot up. They had had her and had let her go.

"Bollocks! Pick her up and quick. If she's seen the picture in today's paper she may go into hiding or on the run. Get it broadcast, get the local men to pick her up from the research station."

"Could we use the guards there to hold her?"

"Do it." Bob was furious with himself for letting her go last night but he didn't show it to his men. It had not been his decision anyway and they knew it.

The policeman rang the guards. He stayed on the line waiting while they checked that she was there. Bob watched his man's shoulders slope as the voice at the other end informed him that she had booked out almost two hours ago. And they had noticed her boarding a bus for town. Bob nodded his approval as his man got the centre to tell him what she had been wearing. Bob straight away dialled police headquarters to put out an immediate request for assistance and told them he would fax over a picture and description. He collected the notes and picture they had on her and got his colleague to relay them together with details of her description.

He added, "Make sure they get that picture of her out to the officers on the beat and traffic cops right away."

* * * * *

Miss Ojuko stared into the box; it was so crammed full of items the lid sprang up as she undid the lock. On the top was a thick envelope addressed to the British Embassy. She lifted the envelope out and beneath it were wads of banknotes. More money than she had ever seen in her life. It was in US dollars and sterling. Beneath the bundles were a score of old gold coins and small platinum ingots; a small velvet bag held a dozen or more heavy diamonds. She looked round and then hastily crammed the contents into her large handbag. To get it all in she had to empty her bag's contents out and these she crammed into the empty deposit box. She didn't need them now; she felt no guilt but her heart pounded; it was obviously meant for her. Hough didn't need it and he had never spoken about any relatives. Her heart pounded with excitement more than anything. She forced herself to calmly relock the box, hand it back to the guard and unhurriedly let herself out.

Once on the street, the fear she had felt earlier that day returned; there were too many people about. She crossed the street to a local café and went in. Once inside she headed straight for the ladies room where she locked herself into a toilet closet.

Opening her bag carefully she selected the letter. She had almost decided to flush it down the toilet and take her chances with her new found wealth to make a run for it; she hesitated for a moment but after pausing she slit open the envelope.

She wondered if there may have been more money or something that could be turned into money. She found neither but what she read was more valuable than either to her right now. Hough in his neat writing had in a few short paragraphs laid out the reasons for the raid and the plan for the disposal of the device afterwards.

The concluding paragraph read, *"This letter should be delivered in the case of my death or demise by Miss Christiana Ojuko. My cause is lost so I do this for her. My price is that you get her out of South Africa to England and give her a British passport. She will be in great danger if you do not do this for her."*

He had signed it. She looked at his signature and burst into tears. The tears cascaded down her round cheeks and dripped on to the letter to which a selection of the device's blueprints was attached. She wiped them off and got herself under control. She folded the contents of the envelope carefully and put them back. Leaving the cubicle, she washed her face and straightened herself up.

Her mind was in turmoil; should she go to the police and hope they would look on her as an innocent party in the affair or should she go to the British? In her heart she didn't believe that the police would treat her well and were bound to steal the money. She decided to try the British.

The British Embassy was not in Cape Town, she knew, but in Pretoria, although there was a British consulate in Riebeek Street not far away and she decided to get there first as quickly as possible. Back in the brilliant sunshine outside the café she screwed up her eyes and looked up and down the street.

There was a black policeman, a young constable, about 20 yards from her, who eyed her. She smiled at him and crossed the road at as natural a pace as she could manage. The policeman followed her with his eyes; it was lucky for her that he was young and inexperienced. He had taken the urgent call about a black woman and the girl who had smiled at him did fit the description. He was undecided. Christiana could see him still looking at her and she mixed with the crowd moving to the corner of the street in rising panic.

Her mistake was to look back. They were now separated by a 100 yards but their eyes met and they both knew in that moment that a chase was on.

The policeman let out a yell and started across the road. His passage was halted by a few fast moving cars but only momentarily.

Christiana rounded the corner and kicking off her shoes she hitched up her skirt and fled down the road, her precious bag clutched tightly under one arm. 30 yards up the road was a turning to the left, she took it and then the next right and into a shop. She sensed, rather than heard, the police whistle go by in the street she had turned off. She was out of the shop and backtracking. A taxi stopped a few yards up the road and she was in it before the passengers had really finished getting out. The taxi driver scowled at her, but once he had taken the fare, mellowed. She was after all another customer.

"Where to, Miss?" the taxi driver leaned over to look at his new client and was struck by the leggy woman in the rear seat trying to make herself as small as she could. She's in trouble, he thought, but, with a taxi driver's intuition, decided she was of no danger to him.

"British Embassy, la," Christiana made her mind up instantly that Cape Town was not safe for her and as she had the money she could afford the trip to Pretoria.

"Come on, it's only round the corner," the driver retorted crossly.

"No la, not the consulate, the embassy in Pretoria," Christiana clarified breathlessly, "Please, quickly."

"Wait a minute, it's a day there and a day back for me; never been that far out in my life," the driver protested.

"I've got my reasons," she fished in her bag and brought out two US hundred dollar bills, "Here, on account."

The driver shrugged, grinning. Christiana looked back and just had time to see the young policeman reappear looking breathless and confused. She slid further down in the seat; the driver noticed but just shrugged again. It wasn't his business what trouble the young girls of today got into and he wasn't about to get involved with the police. By the time he had given a statement his shift would be over and the boss would not take it kindly if he hadn't earned the price of a beer that day. Anyway this fare was something every taxi driver dreamed of. As they drove out of the city, a price was agreed on. It would be midnight before they arrived at the embassy gates.

It was nearly four o'clock in the morning before the documents Christiana had brought with her were fully appreciated by the duty resident Foreign Office official.

He arranged for refreshments and a bed in the embassy for Christiana. Her fate could be sorted out in the morning when the day shift came in. His duty was to get the documents and intelligence to London without delay.

The communication centre deep in the embassy was always manned and he made his way there as soon as he had handed over his charge to the duty housekeeper.

Chapter 8

LONDON
THE NEXT DAY, LATE AFTEROON

In the intelligence service building in Central London, Major Rodney Brown, retired, was just clearing his desk for the day. He glanced at the electric clock on the wall of his tiny office which he shared with two others. It was only 5pm. He felt a little guilty leaving early but tonight he had a date with the tall, leggy redhead, Miss Caroline Webster from the South American section.

Rodney was Brigadier Robinson's section head with particular responsibilities, together with his counterpart in the Foreign Office, for keeping 10 Downing Street up to speed with developments on a day-to-day basis. His morning meetings were a chore he put up with whenever the brigadier was away but his real interest was the Eastern bloc and especially Mother Bear.

A leg wound from his early service days in Borneo kept him desk-bound for the most part but he did escape now and again for a foray into the 'field'.

He checked his unruly fair hair, which was always in disarray; he wore it far too long for his boss's approval. Rodney didn't care and neither did his boss really. Rodney was good at his job and had the distinction of having his own mole in the KGB. The contact was called Chekhov the Second. Whether the person was male or female, the boss didn't know – only Rodney did. All the boss cared about was that Rodney got fairly regular tips from Chekhov that were invariably important. The boss hadn't even been able to work out which department his mole worked for; the intelligence he received via Rodney didn't point to a particular directorate as it was so diverse and covered a wide variety of subjects.

"Sir," Rodney's intercom squawked. It was from the duty room. Rodney looked at the machine. He was tempted to ignore it – he didn't want to be late tonight but discipline ruled and he flicked the speak switch.

"Yes," he said shortly, "Trying to get out of here; can it wait?"

"Brigadier wants you."

"Bugger, he's supposed to be on leave."

"What's that, sir?"

"Never mind; what does he want?"

"You, at number ten by six tonight."

Rodney was not pleased. He had been standing in for the brigadier for the last two weeks while his boss was doing something special with the director general of Box 5. Standing in for the boss had meant many nights working into the small hours and early mornings getting ready for prayers, the director's briefing to all sections. Still, he had enjoyed it, he just wanted this night off.

"Tell him I'll be there," confirmed Rodney wearily.

"I don't think he wanted a reply, sir," the duty officer chuckled over the intercom.

"Cheeky sod," said Rodney throwing the speak key forcibly, not knowing whether he was commenting on his boss or the duty officer.

Rodney sat back in his desk and decided he might just as well work until the appointed hour then decided he would go to the canteen to fill up on food as the brigadier's evening meetings often went on into the early hours.

He tried unsuccessfully to contact Caroline Webster. He imagined her getting ready to go out and being disappointed when he didn't turn up. It had taken him two months to get her to the stage where she would accept a date and now he had blown it. He didn't fancy his chances for a rematch. Rodney then called up the duty officer and told him to get him a staff car for a quarter to six to go to Downing Street.

Rodney was dropped at Number Ten at five fifty-five and told the driver to go back to the pool; he would call if he wanted him again. The Number Ten staff and police knew him well from his daily visits to complete his bit of the red book and cheerfully waved him in.

He reported to a woman receptionist and after he had signed in she directed him to a side reception room on the ground floor. He had not been in this room before. It was very comfortable with a desk, some fine paintings on the walls of past British heroes and politicians, an open marble fireplace in which a large basket of flowers resided, and two easy chairs separated by an oak coffee table. The room oozed class and calm and he relaxed into one of the two chairs. The time ticked by and he began to doze. It must have been well past seven o'clock when the brigadier gently shook him into consciousness.

"Job too much for you?" the boss towered over his aide and a smile played on his lips. He was nearing 70 but his ramrod back, silvery black slicked-down hair and severely clipped moustache made him look much younger.

Rodney stretched and shook himself, rubbing an arm that had gone to sleep, "Got to admit it's been a full week or so, sir, and I did have a date for tonight with a young lady I have been working on for a while."

"Sorry to have messed up your evening; I am sure the lady will understand. Anyone I know?"

"Caroline Webster."

"Shame; but she is far too young and far too good for you. Nothing more pathetic than an ageing playboy," the brigadier was teasing him but Rodney knew it was out of affection not malice. He sometimes thought the brigadier saw him still as one of his 20-something subalterns who were game for anything. Now in his mid forties, Rodney had long accepted that the old man's humour would never improve. On the other hand, at least the old man had a sense of humour.

"Thank you sir, you're all heart," Rodney chuckled.

"Well, there you are, what more can I say? Glad you've acquired the habit of being able to work long hours because I've got a little job for you and your team."

"What team?" thought Rodney out loud. "More like team of one; me!"

"The job will take up a few more hours of your dour life in the next few days," said the brigadier seriously, ignoring Rodney's quip.

"I hope that this is important, sir. My date tonight was a very significant one, despite your unkind words about my ageing playboy image." Rodney stood up to ease his leg and paced the floor. An old wound troubled Rodney from time to time and he needed to walk the leg to ease the muscles.

The brigadier threw himself into one of the vacant chairs, "Yes I know, she told me."

Rodney glanced at the old man; he had known all the time.

"Yes, Miss Webster was most put out, but when I told her you would be working with her she became really quite mellow, can't think why," this time the brigadier chuckled. "And now, let's get on." He pulled a long signal from his hip pocket, "Read this." Rodney took it and settled himself in the other chair. "Read while I organize a drink for us." The brigadier pressed the service bell and a valet arrived with a tray containing a bottle of whisky and jug of water.

"Just put it on the desk, please," the brigadier ordered. The man put down the drinks and left. "Rodney, whisky and water?"

Rodney looked up from the papers, "Fine," and returned to his reading. Finally, Rodney put the signal aside on the desk and picked up his drink. "That's a Central American, Latin Desk affair surely?" he waved his drink at the signal.

"Under normal circumstances you are, of course, right. There are one or two aspects of the case that led me to the decision I should use you and some of our people." The brigadier got up from his chair and began to pace the floor; it was his habit and helped him to think. "You see, the Russians are involved, that is made clear in the signal, albeit through an intermediary."

Rodney interrupted, "How can we be sure this is not a gambit of some sort put together to embarrass us? The whole plot seems a bit far-fetched."

"I disagree with you. And our man in South Africa does too. I admit to the possibility but discount it. Anyway we have to proceed on the assumption that it's not. Where's your spirit of adventure, boy?"

Rodney thought but didn't say, "Gone with the responsibility and lack of sleep of my new job." Sleep deprivation was something he thought he had left behind when he retired from the army; they were the past masters at creating it.

The brigadier continued, "I suspect that the Russians will be coming for this trinket themselves, if it's true and all as they say in the signal. As you are only too well aware, they would generally act through third parties abroad but in this case I suspect that the prize is too valuable to leave to others," he finished. Then as an afterthought he added, "It occurs to me that your 'mole' may have something to add if you can make contact although, as you see, we barely have three days to catch up with the exchange and time is at a premium."

"Where do I come in?"

The brigadier looked at his subordinate. It was not like Rodney to rush him; but since the Cyprus affair, Rodney had at times grown distant. No, that was the wrong word, their relationship was as good as it had ever been, but there was, he reflected, an unwillingness to take everything at face value. Robinson could understand that their relationship would never be the same since he had ordered Rodney to kill in cold blood but that was nearly four years ago or was it three? Rodney had to get over that, perhaps this break from routine would help. For various reasons, the brigadier had decided to rope in his second in command in an attempt to get back that very special, open working relationship that they once had. Now he had analysed it once again, on the spur of the moment, he had another thought and that was that Rodney was simply maturing into an exceptional 'aide-de-camp'.

Getting back to the matter now in hand, "Where, indeed? As always we seem to be up against a time constraint, which means very little time to plan. We have three days, possibly four from now to foil their plans. Since we received the message from South Africa, I have had a few hours to evaluate our resources, strengths and weaknesses in that part of the world. The exchange point is close to Belize where we have a force deployed in support of the Belizean government, as you know, and by the way, your brief for Sir Peter last week was very informative, well done on that. But our responsibility there is mainly confined to intelligence collecting; we do not have any operatives in the theatre that I could use and feel confident of success, so I'm going to have to put a team in. There are two men out there that we could make use of. One is the intelligence officer on the Governor's staff but for diplomatic reasons I only want to use him on our side of the border. James Collins, who you know well, is also out there. You will need someone with some idea of the terrain, it's quite evil in the jungle there, I believe."

Rodney allowed himself a smile, not just because the brigadier mentioned his protégé, Major James Collins, but because the old man had just said, "*We* could use". In other words he had just handed the mission to him, the '*we*' being Major Rodney Brown. The brigadier did not notice Rodney's cynical smile and went on, "I'd like to put Mould and Sharky in the field also, plus anyone else you feel would be of use."

"I'd like to go myself. I think I should be on the ground there; it's a bloody long way from London," said Rodney, "but I assume the department will need me here?"

"I suppose I could cover for a few days. To tell the truth there's not much left to do here on the project that has taken me away these last few weeks. It's a red stamp job from now on, for our political masters to sign off. If you really think you need to go I'll cover your desk but I will get Graham Swain to keep the routine going; fair enough?"

"Yes, sir," Rodney began to brighten a little; any chance to get away from his desk, even for a few days, would be welcome.

"Right then, you've got the details in the signal. The mission is known to the PM and the Foreign Minister. Sir Peter Gray insisted on telling them when I briefed him, goodness knows why. And, not least, I've got Miss Webster from the Latin Section for you. What more could you ask? I'll be over to your office at eight tomorrow and I expect to be briefed on the way you intend to handle the affair. I've taken the precaution of block booking six seats on the Washington shuttle midday tomorrow and onward reservations from there to Miami and then on to Belize. You will be met at the Belize airport by the Governor's man and later Major Collins. Roughly speaking, you should have a forty-eight hour window to get the team etc. in place out there; any questions?"

"None at this moment, but I will have my thoughts and questions ready for you in the morning although there is something that we haven't discussed," Rodney stood.

"What is that then, Rodney?" the brigadier sat up in his chair.

Rodney scanned the long signal again before folding it up and pocketing it, "If this device does what is claimed and, assuming it is the KGB who are involved, what do the Russians want to do with it? Or rather where do they intend to use it? By definition, if it is as claimed and capable of handling mega data and graphics streaming at high volumes, it has to be based on some new technology."

"Good points," commented the brigadier "and ones that have been on my mind these last few hours." He rubbed his long nose, "I will handle both your questions, where might they use it and what is it? I will get Graham on to it tonight; he will need to wind up the analysts and R&D."

"Sounds good to me." Rodney had been frowning, "Do you want me to contact Chekhov now or wait till we get back?"

"Been thinking about that and on balance I think we should wait, just in case. We don't want to take the chance of tipping their hands at this stage, in case Chekhov is playing both sides of the fence. Enough for now?" Robinson swirled his glass of whisky. "Good, now here's mud in your eye and to success," the brigadier offered his glass to Rodney who chinked his against it and they drained them together.

"Miss Webster is waiting outside; I've told her very little so you can start the exercise from scratch with your entire team."

Rodney was about to take his leave, when he turned back. "Could I ask you kindly to check out this man Hough that the signal refers to? Seems he was one of ours at one time," the brigadier grunted an affirmation and Rodney left him in the room waiting for another call from the PM's office.

Rodney found the delectable Miss Webster waiting for him in the foyer of Number Ten talking to the policeman on duty there and he admired her as he approached. She was a good five feet eight, tall for a woman but she was well proportioned with medium length, wavy red hair that curled round her full face. Rodney suspected she was a year or three, possibly more, younger than him but he didn't care. She had a set of green eyes that set him going every time she cast them on him. The policeman stiffened as he saw Rodney approaching and Miss Webster, aware of another presence, turned to see Rodney as he came up to her.

He nodded, acknowledging the policeman and then to her, "OK, Miss, just a quick call to my people and then dinner for you and me. They will take a few hours to assemble so why don't we keep that dinner date?"

"That's a lovely idea. There's the Sherlock Holmes pub within walking distance and I could do with a little fresh air. This place always seems so stuffy to me."

She smiled at Rodney and he winked at her, "That's my girl!"

Chapter 9

MOSCOW – LATE EVENING

As the British embassy was arranging to spirit Miss Ojuko out of South Africa, the director and his deputy, General Polyakov, sat locked in conversation in the director's office. They had spent the evening going over the team's plan to deploy to the target area. A bottle of vodka stood half empty between them. As the night drew on and they exhausted all the possible avenues that would either spell success or disaster, Polyakov looked for the opportunity to bring up the second phase of the task. He listened to his director ramble on until he touched on the NATO Alliance; he saw his chance and questioned his director's phase two.

The director's response was open and enthusiastic, "But why not?" the director beamed.

"I believe that to foist the spy device on the West is an unacceptable risk; they are bound to find out. I know our technocrat assures us that his spying will be undetectable, but do you really believe that the opposition is so far behind us technically that they will not realize eventually?" Polyakov poured another drink for them and waited for his master's reply.

"You are right, of course; I do not expect our prying to go undetected forever. Possibly long enough, despite, as you say, the assurances the Colonel has given, but the very idea that, even if it merely works, fills me with excitement. Think of the consternation in the Western camp when they realize that their precious computer has been interfered with." The director made a sign more reminiscence of Churchill than a Russian and he laughed.

Polyakov allowed himself a smile but underneath he was as cold as ice. His mind was racing. "Director, I must say that I think we are playing with fire. I don't think the West will take the rape of their computer lying down; I think they will react strongly."

The director was suddenly serious. "What do you think they will do?"

"I think that at the very least they will turn the Cold War into a frozen one. Good God, sir, you are tampering with their very existence. At worst they may do something that we could all have cause to regret."

"What do you mean, they may do something we could all regret?" the director was looking at his deputy wanting him to expand on his statement.

"You forget, General, that I have worked for you for many a long year and I know that you will not simply use the machine to spy; you will want to use it as a facility to feed their machine as well."

The director was silent; he sat for a long time staring past his deputy. When he spoke it was with an energy and fervour that Polyakov had not known before, "Of course you are right Sergei. We will not simply be going to listen; we are going to feed their machine too."

"They will realize, surely?" Polyakov thought the whole thing incredible and began to wonder if his master was going mad.

"Consider the following premise," the director chuckled, he was enjoying the session with his deputy. It was not often he could tell this intelligent man anything he didn't know. This was one operation he had wanted to keep from him until it was well under way. Only the director and the secretary of the central committee knew the whole story. He continued, "If we have men in positions of power in the civil service, the trade unions etc. of our competitors, what makes you think that we don't have men in their military organizations as well, at the very highest levels? Why not also at the NATO Headquarters?" He opened his hands out to Polyakov, "Plus I am not so sure the device will be found. I don't think their sweep equipment will find it simply because there is nothing to find in the conventional sense, I am not as pessimistic as you."

"Yes, I know, but at the highest levels. You cannot have enough to influence; what about the conscientious operator that knows something is not quite right and cannot be got at?"

"Depends what you mean by 'got at' doesn't it?"

"I mean manipulated, carried along with the rest of the sheep."

"He is the man we do get at, you know this!" The director's eyebrows went up "These men are so vulnerable, it's pathetic," he said dismissively. "When there are such men, we must decide that where there is a hint of something untoward, we send the wolves out to cut the man down, such as an unsolicited telephone call to the customs post that a military man is cheating the customs by carrying something through, such as wine in excess of what might be reasonably expected. It is just too easy to get someone put out of the way, with no collateral damage."

"You don't mean...?" Polyakov sat forward.

"No, no that was but an example to show their vulnerability. What do you take me for?"

"He was a good soldier even if he was on the other side."

"Yes he was; yes, too good." The general thought back to the NATO general he had caused to be dismissed from the service when the KGB found out he was going to take significantly more than his port allowance out of the country. It had been a bloodless assassination and one the director had some conscience over.

Polyakov was disturbed; he knew that there was more to the task than the director was telling him; he must find out. "Sir, I have this feeling that you are going to tell me more. I don't see you being involved in this episode to the extent that you are if there is not something more. I do not believe that simply listening to them and feeding spurious data into them is the main object of this exercise," he sat back waiting for the director to challenge him.

"My dear friend, the final objective will be..." he leant forward, picked a sheaf of paper from his desk, turned it over and handed it to Polyakov.

Polyakov took it. The paper was headed 'Operation Back Door', he read and then reread it. "Sir, please reconsider, this really is fraught with danger; it's too dangerous. If you fail, it is the end of everything we know and hold precious."

The director snatched the paper from Polyakov, "It will work, it must work – and you will implement it. Until our objective is achieved, you are relieved of all other duties. I will carry out your tasks. This has the approval of the Secretary; there is no room for manoeuvre, you are to do it. The teams you need have already been set up. It now behoves us to wait patiently to hear that you and your team has gone to the Americas and have been successful."

"I see," Polyakov felt drained. How could they play such a dangerous game? This was more dangerous than any Cuba affair.

The director pressed a button, the doors opened and his secretary entered carrying a pile of sealed envelopes. "General Polyakov," the director indicated to his secretary that she should give them to his second in command. Polyakov smiled and took them from her. She was no oil painting but she was good at her job and was feared as much as the director was. After all, she had his ear day in and day out. She could make or break any ambitious official who was a threat to her boss.

"Everything you need to know is in those envelopes, read them tonight and come and see me tomorrow. You know I am really looking forward to my part in this."

"What part, sir?"

"Why, looking after your job. I'll really be able to get to know my people again."

Polyakov didn't say anything; he reckoned that he had got the worse deal. His department could ride the director for a few weeks or even months and recover if anything went wrong. He had a task that, if he failed, would be the end of him and many others as well.

When he returned to his own office much later his secretary was still there. She was waiting for him. He felt in need of support, somewhat sad and alone. She sensed his mood that he was in some sort of trouble or under pressure. As he sat at his desk working on his papers she fed him coffee when he called for it. When he had finished he folded his papers and sat back in his chair, eyes closed, thinking. She came up behind him and gently massaged his neck. It soothed and relaxed him. That night he would take her home; in the morning their normal boss – secretary relationship would return, until the next time.

* * * * *

At home, the director of the most powerful organ of the KGB lay in bed awake, listening to his wife breathing easily beside him. He stared at the ceiling for a long time. He had embarked on a dangerous course. The task he had set himself was beyond him. He knew that only his aide, Polyakov, had the ability to carry the task through to a successful conclusion. Or did he? Did any man? The director turned the problems over and over in his mind and the possible consequences of failure.

He didn't sleep and watched the hours pass on the bedside clock until dawn showed its face. What he hadn't told his deputy earlier was the real reason for the theft of the device and the elaborate plan to rape and seed disinformation direct into the NATO computer. Why he had not done that earlier was, he now realized, a mistake. It was an ambitious plan that probably wouldn't come off but it was important enough to flush the mole he knew existed; a man close to the Soviet leadership, or at the very least, high enough in the KGB to be party to all that was going on or to have access to the secrets of state. He dismissed his thoughts, comforting himself with the thought that after all he had given his word to the General Secretary of the Party to keep the plan to themselves alone.

He swung his large frame upright on to the edge of his bed smoothly, without wakening his wife. Quietly he went to his dressing room and began to prepare himself for the day ahead. He was not overly concerned that Polyakov had pushed back over the use of the device. All Polyakov had to do was what he had been asked, surprising as he knew Polyakov was an ardent believer in the Portuguese mantra, "The only problem that can't be resolved is death."

Chapter 10

GUATEMALA – DAY 12

The Arab was concerned; he had met the hosts when he arrived. There was an instant distrust of them and wariness of him on their part. He didn't know how they would react when he informed them that Hough had not arrived. For the most part, in spite of his earlier reckless youth, Saied had seen it all and worked with every variation of miscreant and would-be hero. He was now a well trained, experienced and mature soldier of fortune. This band he had to deal with were not part of the main insurgence forces and most were simply peasants mixed with a liberal sprinkling of malcontents and criminals with a grievance – ignorant, uneducated and, for the most part, high on coca leaves and other drugs. They were unpredictable and this made them dangerous. Admittedly, there were one or two idealists who wanted change but they were, for the most part, marginalized. Saied could not understand why Hough had chosen these people over the regular insurgents.

He had been at the airport in good time to meet the plane that should have flown in with Hough. He had waited expectantly for him to appear; Saied couldn't know and there was nobody to tell him that Hough was dead. Whilst there were contacts back in South Africa who Saied could contact and who could have told him of Hough's demise, Hough had not let them know how to contact Saied. He didn't do this because it was his insurance policy.

Eventually he went to the enquiry desk and asked if a Mr Hough had arrived or if he was on the plane's manifest. The clerk took his time but eventually confirmed that he wasn't. Puzzled, the Arab decided to wait the four hours for the next incoming connecting flight. If Hough didn't arrive after that he would phone one of the contact numbers he had been given by Hough. Saied had never met Hough in person; the arrangements had been via third parties and the Russians but he had Hough's description from Tsygankov.

* * * * *

Wolff's party were on the next flight and, he hoped, in time. The team consisting of himself and Vintner and two secret service men, plus an undercover agent whose resemblance to Hough was remarkable and would pass scrutiny to the casual observer. His task was to pass himself off as a substitute for Hough from the brothers of the ANC. These undercover men were well used to operations overseas and they were very good at it.

Because of the South African standing in the eyes of host countries they were particularly good at survival in hostile environments and that definition would certainly apply to Guatemala.

Guatemala is a land of contrasts. A rough coast road leads to the cattle lands which in turn leads to mountains and hinterland, lands of dense jungle that few men have set foot in. It was a land of the very rich and the very poor. This time of year before the rainy season it was hot and humid. The country's regime was right wing, ultra right; its forces, around 18 to 20 thousand or three divisions, were considered good and well practiced. They had to be with a core of left wing, Cuban-trained, guerrilla force of several thousand to keep under control. They could probably have got rid of the guerrillas but the way the ruling regime treated the poor and natives made terrorism an attractive option, or at least the lesser evil. In the powerhouse of Guatemalan government and the guerrillas' domain, murder and political assassinations were frequent occurrences on both sides.

Wolff was frustrated and angry; they had missed Hough's planned flight so they were on the next plane that Saied now waited for. There had been the normal interminable wait through American customs. They really were the worst in the world for keeping travellers waiting. Nothing Wolff could do would hurry the immigration up and they missed the planned flight by minutes. As the plane turned to take its final run into the Guatemala City airport he had a last word with his man.

"Joseph," he spoke to the black agent beside him, "as soon as we get down we split up. Get to the enquiry desk and get them to put a call out for the party meeting Thomas Hough. From there you have to take it as it comes." Wolff quizzed Joseph Kimba with his eyes.

"No problem. You just keep my back covered. OK?" Kimba was not overly worried.

"OK." He beckoned the other two from across the aisle, "You two know what to do?"

"Get a hire car, wait for Joseph to appear and follow him; you will be in the Recent Hotel after you have fixed cars, shooters etc.," the agents John Van der Veldt and his partner Den Jordan chorused.

"Good, let's hope we haven't missed the contact or we will all be on the next flight back," Paul Vintner commented dryly.

The jet engines gave a final roar as the plane touched down, bounced slightly and slowed, then cruised up to the terminal building. In the airport Saied moved to an observation vantage point. He watched the passengers disgorge from the plane. They were a little way off but he didn't immediately see anyone who matched Hough's description. Was Hough there or wasn't he? One or two coloured men did get off the plane; one was close in build and colouring. Slightly unsure he returned to the terminal concourse. The passengers would be another half hour before they appeared in arrivals; he went to the international phone booth and booked a line to South Africa. He paid the man at the cable desk a fee and waited for the call to come through.

As he waited, he watched the passengers being processed by immigration; he was disgruntled and felt let down. When the call came over the tannoy he didn't catch it at first. He thought he heard it and stood up straining. It came again.

At the enquiries desk was a black man, younger than he had thought Hough might be, small, wiry but well dressed and well built. The man was casting around as though waiting for someone. Saied sensed that this man was waiting for him but was he Hough? The man asked the girl to call once more.

She did but when she turned round the man was gone. Saied had taken him by the arm and told him to follow. Once outside in the brilliant sunshine that made both men squint Saied wanted to know if he was Hough.

Joseph Kimba looked at Saied and knew immediately that the

subterfuge would not last the course. He was experienced enough to understand that even if he fooled Saied there would be someone further up the line that would know he was an impostor. He had one chance and he took it. When in trouble tell the truth. He smiled to himself. No plan survives the first contact with the enemy.

"Hough is dead, killed by the secret service." Joseph saw frustration cross the other man's face.

"What happens from here?" Saied was nonplussed, all he saw was his money receding; but he did have the device he reasoned. "How did the police get on to him?" He seemed to pull himself quickly back to the situation facing him, Joseph thought, this Saied was a dangerous man indeed. "What happened? He seemed to have himself well organized and all angles covered from what I knew of him. Did he talk?"

"They raided his house and found something, I understand; anyway that's all past, what we want is the device." Kimba's voice was casual. He loosened his tie, lit a cigarette and blew smoke into the humid air. "Is there somewhere we can go and talk?"

"Did he talk?" Saied repeated.

Kimba looked at the man. "We don't think so. He was a strange man, we didn't like him." Kimba tried to get some authenticity into his voice. He succeeded.

"Yes he was. I didn't entirely trust him either although I didn't meet him. If it hadn't been for the sponsor I would have walked away. His demands and irrational attention to detail in his instructions to me were paranoid. Now, before we go I want the answers to a few questions because when we join our hosts we will not be able to talk freely. They are a suspicious lot at the best of times."

"Sure."

"Come walk with me, there is a local refreshment stall near the car park just over there and we can get a cold drink and find a place to sit under the trees."

They strolled without talking through the dusty edge of the car park to the stall on the side of which a few locals leant, eyeing the strangers. There was suspicion and hostility there, both men knew it. They collected their drinks and moved away from the stall to a grove of shading trees.

When they were settled Saied opened the conversation. "Is there any change in the plan to exchange the machine with his buyers?"

"No," Kimba knew that nothing had upset the present arrangements;

they wanted the device back but they also wanted to know who was responsible for the incident.

"Hmm, so we have three days to get to the airstrip up country. The people here see no problem there, but I have my reservations. They want us to travel along safe routes and that will mean travelling at night and mostly across country."

"Why can't we simply fly up ourselves and meet them there? We could save time and effort."

"More than one reason, as I see it. First and foremost they insist on it; they are worried that if we go through what to you and I would be a sensible route, some official will see the device and confiscate it." He looked at Kimba, "These men Hough enlisted are unpredictable but, for all that, they are cautious and have survived this long so I am not going to piss them off."

Kimba raised his eyebrows. He only hoped that the backup team could follow him.

"And now," Saied continued, "you owe me some money, my second instalment; my third, I am led to believe, will be paid by the sponsor."

They had taken a chance and equipped Kimba with the amount of money due to Saied according to Hough's cash book.

"I would like my second payment now before we go any further."

Kimba opened his day bag and handed Saied a sealed envelope. "I think you will find that correct."

Saied hefted the weight in his hand and smiled, "I'm sure I will. Now come on, let's get out of here." He remembered his call to South Africa and he turned to lead Kimba away. "Wait here, I've just got to bank the money in one of the terminal banks." He left Kimba alone, somewhat bewildered and for a minute he was worried that Saied had done a bunk until he realized that he could stand at the only exit doors to the airport. Quickly he opened his briefcase, took out his notebook and wrote what Saied had told him about the exchange and then put the note in his pocket; ripping the page from his notebook, he was sure that he could slip it or drop it to the team. He looked round; there were a lot of people about but he could see his men looking at him so he made a play of screwing up the page and throwing it to the ground. He then walked back to the terminal entrance.

Saied went up to the overseas cable desk and asked the man to cancel his call. "But sir, it's here now, you might as well take it, you've paid for it," the man indicated a booth to the side of his desk; Saied shrugged.

"Hello, anyone there?" the voice on the other end was calling.

"Yes this is Hough's man in..." the voice cut him short.

"Hough's dead man; can you carry on?"

"Yes, I know. Listen, I booked this call before your man arrived. When Hough didn't arrive I was concerned for a moment. But all's well now."

"What man? We didn't send anybody. Hough never told us where the drop was to be. So who is the man you've got there then?"

Saied's eyes closed to a slit. "I don't know, but he seems to know enough about the operation to be convincing. Who do you think he can be?"

The man on the other end of the phone was silent for a while. "Listen, Saied, they had Hough for a night and we know they searched his house and another he was looking after. I think your man must be BOSS."

"BOSS?"

"Yeah man, you know, the old Selous Scouts-type secret service."

"As if this was not difficult enough," Saied was pissed off and the feeling was transmitted to the other party.

"Yes it is. That's why they pay us well. Be careful – they rarely operate alone," the man warned him.

"Leave this to me. You can't do much else can you?" Saied spat down the phone. Working with amateurs was always a mistake.

"No; do you need more help?" the man was at least trying to be positive.

"No, I do this alone; I'll call you when all is well. Thank you for the warning." Saied cut the line.

Saied replaced the receiver thoughtfully. He rubbed his chin. He now had two choices; one, he could fulfil his contract, or he could sell the device straight back to the South Africans, for a fee. He suddenly had another thought – I could sell it to the buyer and keep the money for myself. Undecided, he would let things ride. For the moment he was in no danger until he revealed the whereabouts of the device. He'd have some fun with the coloured man until then.

"Where you been man?" Kimba was a bit miffed at being left for so long.

"Banking my money and I had to relieve myself; we have a long way to go," Saied dismissed Kimba's remark casually and took Kimba's briefcase, leaving the black to carry his own suitcase. "Got a car over there at the back of the airport; come on, we will get it and go see our hosts."

Wolff's men watched them go, the note they had read from Kimba meant they had just time to change the saloon they had booked for a Toyota 4x4. They moved off in their hire car at a respectable distance. Fortunately for them the country around the airport would be flat enough for them to follow the two men from a distance. They watched the targets get into Saied's car and drive off to the city centre.

Following Saied into the centre of the city and then out into the suburbs through the squalor of the shanty town on the city outskirts the 4x4 with its tinted windows was a good cover as there seemed to be two sorts of domestic vehicles, mainly old rusting wrecks and 4x4s, so they blended well into the background.

Saied suddenly pulled up at one of the wooden clapboard shacks. Wolff's men had to drive past and by the time they had turned round and retraced their steps, Saied and Kimba had got out of their car and gone inside the shack. Kimba had looked round for his men before entering the building but failed to see them. He just hoped the team had picked up his note and had him covered.

In the city, Wolff and Vintner had arrived at the hotel to be greeted by the manager before being handed over to the reception desk. "Mr Wolff and Mr Vintner, welcome. Your rooms are ready and I hope that your stay with us will be a pleasant one." The desk clerk at the hotel scanned the register as Dieter and Paul signed in, reading it upside down with practiced ease.

"Thank you, we expect to be here for a few days," Paul confirmed as they handed over their passports for the clerk to book in to his police register.

"Thank you. I'll bring your passports to you within a few minutes. You can stay as long as you like." The clerk retrieved the hotel register, "There is a man waiting for you in the bar, gentlemen," the clerk's English was good with little accent.

Wolff was surprised, "Really, who?"

"I don't know him. I've seen him around, he is a local hunter of sorts, has a sports shop in the city, I believe; your keys."

"Thank you. We will join him. Could someone take up the bags?"

"Of course, sir."

The bar was dingy but thankfully cooler than outside, as was the hotel.

The bar was gloomy even at this time of day. It was well appointed, that was for sure; Wolff had rarely seen so many bottles on display. The bar was constructed out of rich local mahogany darkened with age and smoke and it took up two sides of the room. At the far end sat a solitary figure sipping beer.

The man saw the South Africans enter the bar and waved them over, "You must be Wolff and Vintner," Wolff nodded for both of them. "Had a cable from Bob," the man had a lazy Midwest drawl but didn't look like an American, "he said you and a few friends were here and wanted to do a bit of hunting in the jungle. He asked me if I could fix you all up," the man pulled one eyelid down; it was more than a wink. He held out his hand, "Jim Bonner at your service."

Wolff took his hand, studying him. Bonner's handshake was firm but not dominating. As tall as Wolff but rangy and the easy smile and grey eyes went with his demeanour. "Well Jim, what can you do for us?" Wolff smiled charmingly but his eyes, if Jim Bonner could have read them, would have seen the slight distrust in them.

Bonner flicked his fingers and the barman came over. "Beer for a start eh?" and then to the barman "Freshen mine too, will you."

When the beers were served Bonner took them to an alcove table. The room was cooler in this corner; a few ineffectual fans moved the still air round but even so Wolff found himself sweating. Bonner noticed, "You'll find this place as hot as South Africa but considerably more humid. I take it you want a complete outfit for a hunting trip; sidearms?" The question was not an idle one.

Wolff was wary, "Why not?" Bonner shrugged.

"How soon do you want the outfit?" Bonner probed.

"Now," Wolff said casually.

"You must be bloody joking, mate," Bonner spilt beer down his front, "Take a few days to get the stuff together," he brushed the beer from his front.

"You're a businessman, I presume; what does it take to get the stuff now?" Paul put in quietly and sipped his beer watching the man.

"Well, the basic gear I've got in the shop and I've got a Land Cruiser you can use which can be fully kitted out tonight with provisions etc., but the government license to carry guns for the trip and the hunting license could take time. You know what these places are like, takes backhanders to get your dustbin emptied." Bonner didn't meet Wolff's gaze. "We don't get many South Africans hunting here; that alone will raise interest."

Neither responded to Bonner who shrugged, "Your business; let's go to my shop, draw the stuff and think about the paperwork later. What do you say?" Bonner seemed to have accepted the situation.

Wolff showed feigned delight, "Thanks, Jim, sounds great, my friends and I really want to get away to make the most of our time and opportunities."

"It'll cost," warned Bonner.

Wolff shrugged, "Money is not the problem, time is. Don't get a holiday very often in my business."

"What business would that be?" the man was probing.

"Oh, insurance," said Wolff, draining his glass, "Let's go," he tapped his wallet pocket, "Time is money, Mr Bonner."

"True, come on then. Take you over to the shop right now."

* * * * *

Back in the shanty town, Kimba's eyes adjusted to the gloom. He stood in what was the front room of a shack that also housed the bottled-gas cooker on which two battered and blackened saucepans rested, one with steaming rice and another that had a fish mixture in it. One was being stirred vigorously by a surly mature black who glared at Saied and Kimba as they entered and then went back to his cooking; he neither acknowledged nor welcomed them.

A few rickety doors led off from the main room, and from one they could hear the grunts of a man and woman in play. Saied looked at Kimba and raised his eyes to heaven but said nothing. He put Kimba's case in one corner and indicated that he should take a seat at the crude wooden table in the centre of the room. Apart from the chairs round the table and the cooker there was no furniture of any other kind. A picture of the Virgin Mary swung drunkenly in a fading, chipped gold-leaf and mildewed frame on the far wall and around the cooker hung an array of cooking utensils. The place was dirty and smelled strongly of sweat, damp and food. The compacted earth floor was uneven and covered in rubbish. Kimba looked round in disgust.

"Thought your brothers were badly off in South Africa?" Saied sneered. He had spent most of his life in squalor one way or another but he would bet his last dollar that this black hadn't.

"Everything is relative. Could say this place would make a good hotel in time," Kimba grinned.

"Most of South America's poor quarter is like this no-hope place. Is it any wonder that the people here will follow anyone who promises them something better?" Saied commented without emotion.

The sound in the bedroom had stopped. Shortly a man appeared framed in the doorway. Kimba could see past him to a dishevelled bed on which a woman sprawled naked in a satisfied pose. The man closed the door and Kimba transferred his gaze to him. The man was classic Latin, quite young and in good shape. His clean-shaven and neat appearance contrasted as starkly with the surroundings as did Kimba in his lightweight suit.

The man broke into a grin, "Welcome to my country; it's Mr Hough is it? Saied has told me a lot about you," his English was broken and Kimba had to concentrate to catch what he said.

"No, Roberto," it was Saied who spoke, "Mr Hough is dead; this man is taking his place."

"No matter, if you are my friend I kill you for nothing," the man put his head back and laughed. It was obviously his favourite English expression and Kimba was to hear it repeated.

He banged the door, "Heah! Bring the beer." He winked at Kimba, "Let's drink and eat and discuss this plan of yours."

"That sounds like a good idea. I want to get this over as quickly as I can." Kimba turned to Saied, "Where is the device now?" He held his breath.

"Safe," was all he got as a response.

Roberto looked from Saied to Kimba. He sensed the sudden tension; Kimba noted the change too and decided to play it as offhand as he could.

"Good," he said casually, "How about that beer; it was a long dusty trip." He smiled good-humouredly then turning to Saied, "What are the plans? I was brought in very late as you can imagine. They told me to get on the plane, meet you here to give you a hand and see that it all goes well. It was all a bit of a rush. Sorry. They gave me the authority to take any decisions on their behalf and to see the transactions proceed smoothly and without fuss. Now, where do we go from here?" He looked at Saied and the Latino for information.

Roberto shrugged and pointed to Saied. Saied gazed at the table as if in a trance. "Well, we will leave here tonight, possibly tomorrow

night, it's up to Roberto," Kimba's heart jumped, could his people move
that fast? "Then we will travel through the back roads for two days,
travelling at night only. Spend a day or so in the jungle and then move
to the rendezvous. Meet the sponsor's party and the engineer who will
prove the machine to them. If all is well, we make the exchange. They
pay me off and return you to your people and they collect the reward
from the sponsor, I suppose," he sat back looking at Kimba, daring him
to ask a question.

Kimba took out his handkerchief and wiped his forehead and then
the back of his neck before finally blowing his nose and replacing the
handkerchief into his pocket. He exaggerated the performance to give
himself time to think and avoid Saied's eyes which he found disquieting.
It was almost as though the man was playing with him.

It was Roberto who, in his innocence, let the cat out of the bag. "You
can fly from the airport there. No need to come back here. Better, really,
if you will be carrying money?" the reference to money was a question.

Kimba shrugged, indicating he didn't really know what he would be
carrying.

"Anyway," the Latino continued, "flying from Melchor de Mencos
Airfield you can fly to anywhere in a light plane. No customs going out
to stop you," he winked at Kimba.

Kimba decided he didn't like this man; he was loose mouthed and
unprofessional, not what he had expected. He noticed the contempt on
Saied's face as he looked at Roberto. Surely the man should have caught
on from the earlier conversation that he didn't want to tell this black man
the whole story.

Saied was angry but he gave an outward appearance of calm, "Roberto,
where is this beer you promised?"

"Just so I understand, could you explain why can't we fly up and save
time?" Kimba queried looking at Saied for a response.

"Couple of reasons really; principally, our host insists his men don't
fly as they are known and we would all be picked up and we may not
survive that. Almost as important, if we were picked up, they would
almost certainly confiscate the machine." Roberto nodded his head at
Kimba to give support to Saied's explanation.

Roberto got up and went into the bedroom; he reappeared quickly,
"We are out, man," he pointed to Saied, "you come with me to the shop;
we will get a couple of packs to keep us going until we leave." Kimba

began to rise, "No man, you are our guest; you stay and keep this cook and his daughter company, we will not be long."

Kimba was left alone with the Carib; he tried conversation but the man ignored him. The girl appeared in a loose shift dress and bare feet; she was no oil painting but she was fulsome. She gave Kimba a smile and sat down opposite him.

"What you doing with this lot of hotheads, man? They are no good. Nice boy like you should keep away," she was friendly but her words were not without warning.

Kimba decided to get what he could from her, "Just business; anyway, what are you doing, you and your dad with this lot?"

"Got no choice man, help them or die," she drew her hand across her throat and bulged her mouth but her eyes were lit up in amusement. "Anyway, they are always good to me; they give us money and protect me and my father," she indicated the old man. "They help us to live a little longer;" she leant over the table confidentially, "saving enough to go to America one day."

Kimba took his cue, "How much more you need, girl?"

She was suspicious but conceded, "Maybe another couple of thousand."

"US dollars?" Kimba wasn't sure if he could use the girl's need for money to his advantage later. Could he trust her? Probably not, was his final thought as he died with Saied's knife driven through his ribs. He had not heard Saied re-enter the shack. Kimba stiffened in surprise, then the pain and then his heart burst; he collapsed on to the table and, as he did so, Saied withdrew his knife quickly, snatched up Kimba's briefcase and threw the other case at Roberto, then both fled from the shack, through the bedroom and out of a back window.

When Saied and Roberto had left for the beer, Saied had noticed the 4x4 in which two men sat parked up in the street in the shade of one of the houses. Kimba's backup; had to be. Saied sent Roberto to have a look while he found a place where he could not be observed. The men in the car tried not to be obvious but Saied could see they were interested in Roberto. Proof enough for him. They had been followed and were compromised. The other giveaway was that the car was hired and white men do not wait around in this part of the city without a very good reason; instinct told Saied who they were.

Roberto rejoined him and they walked to the beer shop almost opposite the car. He told the Latino of the complication and it was all he could do to keep the man from panicking and running there and then.

They bought the beer and innocently walked back to the shack. Saied came to his decision as he entered. Stealing up to Kimba while he was engrossed with the black girl with his back to him, he killed him.

As the men fled, the girl let out a scream that carried to every corner of the street. Kimba's backup team heard it and were out of the car in seconds, pounding towards the shack.

The neighbours followed them, crowding them initially, but the two men were there first, blocking the shanty doorway and, as they burst in, the girl's scream stopped suddenly, replaced with a silence borne of fear.

One BOSS man barred the door so that the neighbours had to peer between his arms and legs to see what was going on. The other man checked out Kimba; he was very dead, the lower part of his body was covered in an ever darkening pool of blood that flowed on to the dirt floor.

He lifted Kimba so that he could remove his wallet and other identification from him; to the police, he would be just another unknown black.

When he finished, he turned his attention to the girl and her father, both now cowered together in the far corner of the room. He made a motion to his sidekick to close the street door.

When this was done he approached the father and daughter. "Where are the two who did this?" The man's accent told them that he wasn't local. The girl started to wail and the old man looked scared. "Come on now," he advanced close to them, "Who did this? Where did they go?"

The girl looked from her father to the two men, "You friend of the black man?"

"Yes, very good friend; damn, now the police will come for us," but his gesture paid off.

"OK," said the girl wiping her tears. "You pay me, I tell."

His companion was hurrying him. They didn't want to be caught there and the police might arrive soon. He'd pay for quickness but it was against his principles; he would rather have forced it out of them.

"OK," he took out Kimba's wallet and drew the bill roll from it. He waved it, "Talk, damn quick."

The girl snatched the money, "You tell, father."

The old man's watery eyes surprisingly showed no fear, "You..." he started in a quivering voice, "find dem at Melchor de Mencos airstrip, three, four days. They got a place two miles north from the airstrip, half mile in from the border, dem going to drive and work there before airport business, don't know what that is but they mentioned sponsors, that's all we know."

John Van der Veldt placed his face close to the old man's, "If you lie to me I will come back."

"I tell you good. For what they do to me and my girl, I hope you kill them. I know they will be there because they have some business; I don't understand it, but they go for much money..." before he had finished the two men were gone.

* * * * *

Vintner, Wolff and Bonner were in the shop; they were quite alone. Bonner's other staff had been sent away; the arrangement suited Wolff, the less people in the know the better. Bonner's shop was a gold mine, he had everything Wolff needed. In the keep at the back of the shop was a store for more weapons, these were not the sort dedicated to pure hunting. When Wolff asked Bonner how he was allowed to hold such armaments the man just evaded the question.

The Land Cruiser was brought to the back of the shop and loaded. Wolff took enough equipment to camp for a week if necessary; Bonner got more and more interested as they worked on. Wolff was convinced that the man must be in the pocket of the local authorities and this disturbed him; but how else could the man function with impunity in this country?

Two hours later they were happy that they had forgotten nothing they would need; they could get food and water later; "OK, that's it, let's settle up." Wolff was sweating and Bonner was no better, "Travellers' cheques, US dollars all right with you?"

"Fine with me; you really were in a hurry, where do you intend to hunt?" Bonner went to his fridge in the rear of the shop and drew three beers from it. He pulled off the metal pull tops and handed a beer to Paul who was concentrating on the cheques.

Wolff accepted his before asking a question of Bonner, "Jim, tell me, have you got some maps we could have?"

"Yah, I have got a complete pack somewhere, of the parts that have been mapped properly. Do you know there are some parts of this place and Belize over the border that no white man has ever seen, never mind mapped?"

"Is that right?" Wolff was genuinely interested.

Bonner upended his can and squinted at Wolff, "Yah, and man, some of this jungle is the worst you will ever see. Let me get those maps."

As Bonner returned with a wad of maps in a roll, he shuddered, Wolff looked at the man in surprise, "You all right Jim?"

"Yah, ghosts of the past. I've had a few bad trips in there that I never thought I'd get back from," he smiled. "Want a guide?"

"Thank you, no, my friend and I are pretty good in the jungle."

Bonner laughed, relieved, "Trust me, you'd better be. I'll throw in a first aid kit; I hope you'll not need it."

Their business completed, Bonner tucked the cheques into his coat pocket. Wolff suggested that they drop Paul off at the hotel in case the other members of the hunting team had arrived and he and Bonner would go for a drink in a local bar and have a meal. Bonner could tell him about the country, its terrain and its dangers.

Bonner was only too agreeable to find out more so having locked up the shop and set the alarms, they went to the hotel, dropped Paul off, then he and Wolff drove to a bar on the coastal road just outside the town. From there, Wolff could see the civilian airport in the distance, and was surprised at the number of military jets operating from it. But, as Bonner commented, "In a state like this, where does the military and civil authority part?"

The bar Bonner had chosen was used by a few locals and there was no evidence here of any authorities. The food was local, spicy and there was a lot of it. As the evening wore on, Wolff plied Bonner with drink, first beer and then the local rum. The drink loosened Bonner's tongue and it was clear to Wolff that the reason Bonner was able to operate in the country at all and to ply his trade was that he was in hock to the local police chief who gathered intelligence on Bonner's customers; Wolff decided that they would either have to take Bonner with them or he would have to disappear for a time, if not permanently.

It was late evening when Wolff poured his merchant hunter friend into the Land Cruiser. He headed away from town and up the coast. About five miles out, he turned off the road and drove up to the cliffs. The surf pounded on the rocks far below. Bonner raised his drunken head from his chest; Wolff hit him on the chin and Bonner's senseless head bounced off the windscreen on to Wolff's lap. Wolff shoved him right down, and opening the door, pushed him out on to the ground. Wolff got out of the wagon and dragged Bonner to the cliff edge. Then he smiled. Not the old boy's fault that he was a snitch; he had to be to keep his business going. Also, he could see Paul's outraged face if he told him what he had done; so he dragged the unconscious Bonner back to the wagon and threw him in the back. He trussed the recumbent form and gagged him, then hid him under a pile of sleeping bags and the tent they had hired earlier. "Well, Jim, you did offer to be our guide but I don't fancy your hangover in the morning."

When Wolff arrived wearily back at the hotel, Paul and his two men were waiting for him. When he heard about Kimba, he was angry and swore to get even. The news that they knew where to go did little to pacify him.

Paul had been planning ever since he had heard the developments. His plan was simple, two would fly up and two would drive up. Wolff, weary as he was, saw the sense in the plan but wanted to input. He told them about Jim resting in the back of wagon. He would drive up with Den Jordan tonight. Typical of this part of the world, some shops were still open and they could provision for the trip. He felt he could convince Jim, when he woke, that he had agreed to go with them and had fallen over and knocked himself out; he had been so drunk he would not remember. Paul and Jon Van der Veldt would fly. It was agreed. Wolff told Den to grab his things from the 4x4 and threw the wagon keys to him, asking him to wait in the vehicle. He would join him in ten minutes.

Chapter 11

LONDON – DAY 12

In Rodney Brown's office, his team, along with Graham Swain, sat ready for their final briefing. They were all subdued, heads drooping. They had worked into the early hours on the plan they intended to follow when they got to South America. Rodney was the worst off for when they had finished he had carried on rearranging and confirming the travel arrangements and their reception in Belize. From Belize they would launch their efforts to acquire the device.

Whilst Rodney sat at his desk putting the final touches to his orders, the remainder of the team, Mould, Sharky and Caroline Webster, drank coffee and waited. The brigadier would arrive shortly and sit in with them.

When Rodney had finished, he relaxed in his chair and threw his pen on to the desk. He put his hands behind his head, and leant back in his chair with half-closed eyes. He watched them, half listening to their conversation.

Mould and Sharky had with him for years, and he knew that the two were dependable and could be relied on to carry out the most difficult of assignments with very little fuss or bother. He knew them to be solid and resourceful. Miss Webster was another kettle of fish altogether. Apart from their budding relationship, he knew nothing about her except that she didn't appear to have any close family and had entered the service from Cambridge. She had probably been recruited there for all he knew. It would be a familiar pattern. He turned his thoughts to other things.

It had only been a few years since his team had been involved in the

Chekhov case that had led to a massive round-up of the Russian agents in Western Europe and leading from there into the States. He wondered what the other side was doing to retaliate. He had seen little evidence that they had done anything but slink off with their tails between their legs. In his heart he knew that they must be up to something; it was their way.

He felt suddenly excited at the thought of this foray into the field again, and a possible coup for the department.

The UK, like most countries, has a department for looking after external security threats and such external activities as the game dictates. Its sister department looks after the internal security of the nation. The rivalry between the two departments was legendary and was sometimes taken to dangerous lengths. Since the Chekhov affair, the external department had had little success and needed a win to gently remind the more conservative internal sister that they still had teeth. Rodney's small section was an offshoot of the main body of the secret service that had been set up as one of the special project teams; these teams were led by Brigadier Robinson; Rodney's team, covering discrete projects in the Eastern bloc, was well placed to support the main Russian desks especially during the Chekhov affair.

Rodney knew the sister agency was having unprecedented success at the moment and that just increased pressure on the teams. They were accelerating the need to infiltrate the more militant organizations in the UK that were threatening the 'very fabric of our British society' as Rodney had heard a pompous colleague in the Home Office tell him grandly at a recent meeting.

The rivalry between the two was the best weapon of accountability the state had. For when was an issue, domestic or foreign venture, ever truly separate from each other? Hence Robinson's section. They kept an eye on each of the agencies who guarded their territory jealously. Even so it was not unusual, rather like the KGB, for one department to be working on the fringe of the sister organization, from opposite ends of the same case, only to meet the other in the middle. Unlike the KGB, the directors did speak and there was a modicum of trust and respect between them. It was therefore for the directors to get together to decide who completed the job. That didn't mean that there was not any infighting to win the prize. The departments were not too keen on working together. It didn't quite equate to their idea of cricket and they didn't do it with a good grace but the Joint Intelligence Service chairman normally prevented blood being spilt, literally or metaphorically speaking.

Rodney chuckled as he thought on; the rivalry between the people of different agencies was interesting to watch. The system worked and rarely were there gaps but when there were, they were big ones of the Burgess and Blunt type. Rodney frowned, God, that he should ever overlook someone like that in his department.

The brigadier entered and his musings were cut short. "Morning, sir," Rodney got up from his desk and went to welcome his chief. "Sharky, get the Director a coffee, please." Sharky was already on his feet; as the junior member of the team he knew his place.

"Thank you, usual, please, Sharky, and bring another cup, we will have a guest in a few minutes." The brigadier took off his coat, threw it on the other desk and then sat on it, "Bloody awful office you've got here Rodney. This the best I can give you?" Robinson looked round at the magnolia walls and twenty-year-old furniture.

Rodney laughed; it was a standing joke that their department's accommodation was the worst in the ministry, "Did think of moving into yours in your absence, sir, but your secretary wouldn't let me."

"Ah, what it is to have a good secretary. Old Miss MP is worth her weight in gold." This time they all laughed; since Ian Fleming had immortalized Miss Moneypenny, the brigadier's secretary and the others who worked for the bosses were invariably renamed. It made them feel good and it was good for morale. "To business, Rodney, the PM is particularly interested in this one. Her political and scientific analysts have both been tasked to keep an eye on the project. In fact the political man is coming to listen to your briefing and then he would like to have a few words with you," the emphasis indicated that Rodney's team was not included.

"When will he be here, sir? The team and I have a lot to do and not a lot of time to do it in," Rodney said firmly.

The brigadier raised his eyebrows but said nothing and instead looked at the large round government-issue electric clock on the wall and checked his watch, "He will be here in five minutes, no later. What's the rush? Anyway, your clock's five minutes fast, Rodney."

"That's so that I am never late for a meeting." Robinson smiled at the heavy irony leaving Rodney to continue, "We leave on the Washington shuttle mid afternoon to pick up the connection to Miami then to Belize, which gets us there in the morning."

"Soon as that? I see."

"Got to sir, or we won't make the rendezvous. Remember they have the advantage of knowing the ground. We will need a day to get the feel of the place even though I have the area being inched over by Collins as we speak. I spoke to him last night and he volunteered to go in and try to pinpoint the target hideout."

They were interrupted by the political adviser's arrival. He was a small round man in a sports jacket and flannels, dark hair and very Essex. He was around 50 and didn't look anything out of the ordinary, but was reputed to be the best brain on the PM's staff; a college professor on loan, his advice was listened to and rarely questioned. They were a little surprised by his nondescript appearance as he didn't seem to fit the picture but he was about to enlighten them. The professor, as he was referred to, made himself known to them all and then asked if he might address them before Rodney gave them their orders.

Rodney made way for him at his desk and joined his team. "Lady," he acknowledged Miss Webster, "and gentlemen, what I have to say should have more properly come from your director, but..." he smiled apologetically and pushed his glasses back against his face with his index finger as they began to slip down his nose – it was a well rehearsed gesture done to focus their attention, "...this task of yours is most secret, it goes without saying; it is to be covert. If you fail or get into difficulty, we will disclaim all responsibility for you. In other words you will languish in a Guatemalan jail for the duration," then added sorrowfully, "or worse. Our relations with the Belize and Guatemala governments are, and always will be, difficult; you are small fish and so are totally expendable. You will arrive in Belize as tourists and as far as we are concerned that is all you are. You can expect no official help although the intelligence officer there knows you are coming and will have some equipment for you. After that you are on your own." He paused to let his words sink in.

Not quite true, thought Rodney, but didn't think he would enlighten him about his arrangements with James Collins.

The team was silent, they were used to getting this sort of statement from their boss but, coming from this man, it reinforced the inevitability of it. It was a death sentence if anything went wrong. The same briefing from their own people was routine but all believed in the back of their minds that something would be done in the event. In this case they were left in no doubt that they were definitely on their own and could not expect a reprieve.

"OK, here is the good news," the professor beamed at them, "You would not be going if we didn't think you would return with the device which, if we have got our mind round this correctly, will leap us ten years ahead of the competition, if the machine comes back intact. Intact! If you get your hands on it please do not drop it, run over it, shoot it up or whatever. Thank you." The team laughed. Rodney looked at his people and sensed their lightening mood; it would be up to him to keep morale high and motivate them. The brigadier caught his eye and nodded to Rodney that he should now take over.

"Thank you for being so frank with us, Professor. Your words are well taken but I don't think we will let you or the Brigadier down and we will try not to scratch the paint on the machine, if it exists and if we get our hands on it, as they say," Rodney said confidently. Rodney invited the professor to take his vacant chair so that he could continue with the briefing. Behind Rodney's desk, pinned on the wall, were two maps, a large-scale one of the border area that they were to operate in and another superimposed on an aerial photograph with colour chinagraph of the airport at Melchor de Mencos.

"Right, orders," Rodney paused, "Our aim is to liberate a computer spy device before its intended recipients who, as far as we know, are the Russians, get hold of it. They should make the exchange at the airport, that is, the machine for the money at this airport." He described the layout and then went on to his large-scale map and briefed the room on the general area and possible approaches to the objective. "A few facts about the place we are going to; Belize is long and narrow and about the size of Wales; the long border between Belize and Guatemala is jungle and swamp; there is some relief in this area where we are going to, the south of the country," Rodney showed them on the map, "but not much. See the town of San Jose on the Belize side and the site of antiquity, Xunantunich, about a mile to the east; a mile further and that's the border; less than two miles further is the airstrip at Melchor. Hook north-east and you see the hamlet of Montufar. Target one is the house and compound half a mile west of that. This is where Hough wrote that the engineer lives and works." Rodney paused for his team to take all this in and to give them a chance to look at the map. The team took notes then settled back in their seats and Rodney continued, "Factors we must consider: one – our accumulated knowledge of the opposition indicates to me that they will not be in any great strength, a few heavies and a technical man, maybe someone senior with authority. But we must be aware that unlike ourselves they will not hesitate to use the people they already have in the country to back them up, so we face a difficult task with the balance in their favour, of that I am sure. Our side consists of this team and the intelligence officer out in Belize, plus Collins. They will supply our sidearms, transport and supplies but the rest is up to us. Graham will stay here and be our longstop."

Sharky held up his hand, "What about Collins? He is pretty resourceful and already out there. He must know the country and could be of some help."

"Resourceful he may be, but he is only involved insofar that we will draw our equipment from him etc. He is, after all, the force supply officer for the theatre. No, the last time we used him was a one-off. He is not to be involved this time. We all know him and it will, as we know, be difficult to keep the reins on him." He continued, returning to the maps, "The general area we have discussed, but what I want you all to bear in mind is that if for some reason we get pulled out of the immediate area of the objective, even if only by a few miles, we will be in some very inhospitable country; literally miles of swamp, heavy forest and bad jungle will frustrate us if we are not very careful. For this reason..., oh yes, also, the swamps and rivers contain predators. In fact the animal life of the area can be pretty off-putting; poisonous snakes, spiders, reptiles, enormous catfish, all the way to large cats," he paused to get his breath and Mould and Sharky exchanged glances with each other, grinning as they saw their lady member staring white-faced at Rodney, "For this reason, the kit we will pick up in Belize will be survival orientated," he had noticed the Mould, Sharky exchange, "and you two," Rodney brought their attention back to him, "may have to carry most of it." The pair groaned and Rodney chuckled.

Rodney returned to the map. "Safe Base is here, a quarter mile further on from the antiquity site at Xunantunich, from which we will also start out on the mission. The base will be set up by the time we get to Belize," he indicated a point only two miles from the border and gave them the coordinates, "Whilst Collins is not allowed to play, he will secure and man our base, and so if anything goes wrong or you get separated and need to run for it, this is where you will find safety. And if all goes well, this is where we will take the device and from there we will get picked up."

"How will we know what to carry and take?" it was the shaken Miss Webster.

"Don't worry about that; it has all been worked out and you will have a chance to see it all and understand why we take what we take and how to use it when we get out there. There will be enough to sustain us for a good few days and enough ammunition for a sustained firefight which hopefully will not be needed. Now, let us consider timings. Our arrangements should get us to the base camp at least 24 hours before the raid; surprise should be on our side. It is highly unlikely that anyone will recognize any of us. The only exception is likely to be Miss Webster as she is from the Latin Desk, but even then it's highly unlikely that any of the people out there, field men, will know her face. Now, any questions so far?" Rodney took off his jacket; these briefings in front of the two senior officers always made him sweat; there was no reason why they should but they did.

"Communications?" queried Mould. Mould was a northerner, he seemed slow to those who didn't know him but he was thorough and had a good sense of humour which spilled over into pranks that often led him into trouble with his peers. That was for fun. Next to Rodney he was probably the department's best all-rounder.

"We will each have a small individual radio, range about ten miles, with our own frequency and they are secure." Mould crossed the item off a list he had in front of him.

"Plan of attack?" Mould looked at his list again.

"Got to stop you there as you have strayed into an area I want to discuss first. If I don't answer your question in the next few minutes ask it again. Now we know that this device was taken from the South Africans and that they arrested one of the key players. There is nothing to say he didn't spill enough information for them to be on the device's repatriation trail too; so there may be a third player on the ground; we don't know, but in the plan of attack we will consider them too. The letter Hough wrote also talked of the device being proved to the Russian's by the engineer at the engineer's lab close to the airport. His location, according to Hough, is two miles to the north and a half mile from the Belize border right here, unfortunately on the Guatemalan side. But only three or four miles from our base as the crow flies." Rodney pointed again to the aerial photograph and a house set in the jungle surrounded by what appeared to be a concrete wall, to ensure the location was being burnt into their brains; he pointed out the track, tracing it with his finger, that left the engineer's isolated house and led towards Melchor and the adjacent airstrip and on to the nearby border post between Guatemala and Belize.

"What if they do not move out on foot?" Mould again.

"You mean between the house and the airstrip? They are bound to have some form of transport. Thought about that, the intelligence officer is having a car left for us; we will get the keys and location from him when we arrive. I suggest we stash the equipment in that until we need it." Rodney waited; nobody seemed inclined to interrupt, "Good; I also arranged for a fast light aircraft to be flown in from Mexico; it will be on the field for that day." He frowned, "It is of course difficult to know what is going to happen at the airport but I've tried to allow for all contingencies."

"Tell me Rodney, how do you intend to relieve them of the device and where?" it was the professor. He had leant so far forward in his chair that he was in danger of falling out of it.

"Timely, Professor, as I am now going to answer both yours and Mould's questions. Proposed action plan is that as we will have at least 24 hours before the exchange, we will use that time to recce both the engineer's house and the airport and see to the loading of the vehicle. If there is a chance to snatch the device at the house we will, but I believe it will be too heavily guarded for us to do that. Therefore the likely plan is that, when the exchange is done at the airport, in essence, we will simply snatch it from them, make for the charter plane I just mentioned and make a run for Belize. If the exchange is to take place somewhere else, and this is more unlikely, then we will have to do what we can, depending on the place and the circumstances."

The professor was not to be put off; even the brigadier gave him a sidelong glance when he asked his next question. "Accepting what you say, i.e. that you can only plan so far ahead, do you have the means at your disposal to allow you some flexibility apart from your flip over the border in the aircraft? What other escape routes do you have?"

Rodney swallowed, "A good question," he stood up and again went to his maps. "The border is not tightly controlled except on the main crossing point just up from the airport. I don't see therefore any great problem in getting across in the jungle a few miles to the north. Our planning will continue once we leave here. By the time we get to Belize, the team and I will have selected several crossing points and determined the routes we might take."

The professor nodded, sitting back in his chair, "That seems most satisfactory. By the way, I believe you are right in your assessment. I believe that the exchange will take place at the airport. It stands to reason that both parties, the South Africans, for that is what they are, and the Russians want to get out of the place as quickly as possible, each for their own reasons. But I'll give you another reason from the South African side if you like, or at least a thought. The people they have teamed up with, the local guerrillas, are not your actual boy scouts and I believe that the South African, or this man Saied, or whoever they have there now will have realized, if they didn't know before, that the international brotherhood of terrorism is only as good as the individual groups can afford to be. It is clear that a great deal of money is at stake, therefore I believe that if the exchange were to take place somewhere other than the airport then all the South African delegation would get would be a dead Brother or Brothers and an Arab."

The brigadier stubbed out his cigar, "You could be right at that." He glanced at his watch, "OK, team, I suggest you get on and sort out the fine details; you haven't got long. By the way Rodney, what about the BOSS, are they anywhere on the horizon?"

"That, sir, is an unknown. I have to assume they know as much as we do. They may have had a breakthrough in their investigations and could be a day or two in front of us. I would be happier if you could keep an eye on them for me and let me know any developments on that score," Rodney requested.

"Of course," agreed Robinson. "Graham, please come and get me in an hour from my office and we will together see what we can find out about BOSS. Must say I preferred it when they were the Selous Scouts. Now Professor, are you ready?" the brigadier was hurrying him. The professor took the hint; he made his goodbyes to the team, wished them good luck and reminded them again of the conditions that had been imposed on them.

Chapter 12

THE DAY AFTER

Saied and the guerrillas had moved into the Melchor de Mencos area early that day. The guerrilla faction that Saied had found himself with was relatively small in numbers; Roberto, their leader, had three section leaders, each with half a dozen men. Two of the sections were out in the jungle with other groups promoting the campaign. The remaining section leader, Ramos, and his men guarded the engineer, his house and the compound. The KGB major, Novisti Yuri Nsenko had also appeared that morning, alone; how he had got there was a mystery, he just appeared at the gate of the house mid morning.

The compound was larger than Saied had expected, covering around half a hectare with a four-bedroomed house in the middle. The white house was wooden clapboard typical of the area and well maintained for its age, at least early 20th century. A raised, broad, covered veranda ran round all four sides of the house. Saied was amazed to find the large downstairs was completely open plan with a substantial open fireplace in the middle of the room opened up to the top floor. There was a staircase to one wall and the room was split into a kitchen area and a dining area with a table that seated ten, the rest of the room being taken up with four double-seater settees clustered around a large television fed by a satellite system on the roof. To the rear of the house was a brick workshop the size of a triple garage which housed the engineer's tools and workbenches. A large generator was in a separate brick hut standing apart from both the house and the workshop.

When Saied arrived at the house with Roberto they met the engineer, a short white-haired Scotsman who introduced himself as William McKay. He was in his late sixties but still wiry and energetic. As soon as Saied arrived he hustled him up to the bathroom so that Saied could wash the jungle dampness off him. When he came back downstairs, much revived, a hot breakfast was on the table. Roberto had disappeared, so he was left alone with McKay. While Saied ate, McKay told him of his life in Guatemala where his father had been a shipping agent and how he had come to love the hinterland. He explained how he had become an electronics engineer working the oceans on ships and latterly at the research station in South Africa, and how he had become tangled up with the project and then Hough. Whatever, it gave McKay the opportunity to indulge a lifelong passion and so here he was.

After breakfast McKay took Saied to see his workshop and laboratory. The building was secure with a sophisticated alarm system. Inside, it was crammed with electronic gadgetry and Saied wondered how on earth the man had got all this equipment out here. They were interrupted by a knock on the workshop door and McKay admitted a stocky bear of a man. Despite his craggy appearance he had charm and when he smiled Saied put his age at around his own.

"Good morning, Mr McKay, and you must be Saied, Yuri Nsenko, pleased to meet you at last. Tsygankov speaks highly of you. Call me Yuri." Nsenko extended his hand to Saied. His voice was well modulated without any trace of an accent.

Despite his normal reserve at first meetings, Saied warmed to Nsenko immediately, "Happy to meet you."

"Good. Now, William, can we see this device that has caused such a storm?" Yuri opened his hands out and up.

"It's here," the device was on one of the tables with other electronic modules linked to it. "What I have set up is a simulation of exactly the way I was told you wanted it to work, with a replicated supervisor's console here," he pointed to an electronic array, "and the receiver transmitters here and the receiver decoder here." McKay looked pleased with himself, hesitated and then continued, "In these boxes are all the necessary paired chips etc. I have written the whole thing up in this quick start manual," McKay picked up and waved an inch-thick wad of papers. "Everything's calibrated, so my job is done."

Yuri pursed his lips and thoughtfully commented, "Almost, we still have to show and prove the model you have set up here to our engineer,

Colonel Ivanovich."

"Do we know when he will arrive? Can't be too long now, a day or two?" Saied turned to Yuri. Saied would be only too glad to get out and back to where he felt safe.

"I think it is unlikely to be tomorrow, more likely the day after but they will contact us nearer the time."

Saied grunted. What he wanted more than anything was to recce the route to the airport and the airport itself, as well as the border crossing. He would feel better when he had the lie of the land in his mind. He discussed this with Yuri who agreed with him. McKay said he would get hold of Roberto and arrange for transport to take them for their look round. But first McKay insisted they relax for an hour and while they waited for the transport they should take local coffee with him on the veranda. He would get his house servant to make it.

An hour later, Roberto turned up on the veranda looking refreshed and ready for anything; he had brought with him an open-backed and very battered Ford truck.

The three of them sat in the front seats and after a trip round the local tracks had made their way into Melchor. Roberto drove round the village to a vantage point near the airport and smoked while Saied took a few notes and searched the airfield. Yuri appeared disinterested but Saied knew he was not and he too would be doing his appreciation of the current situation and what might face them shortly.

There was not a great deal to see. The airfield was on the eastern side of the town, if that was what you could call it. Shacks, for the most part, clapboard construction with corrugated tin roofs and typical of many a shanty town. Here and there were signs of wealth. After all, this was one of the few border crossing points between Belize and Guatemala. Melchor had a sister village over the border; in effect both existed as transit and trading posts for each other and both would grow as the political situation between the two countries improved. The airfield itself stretched from north to south the entire length of the eastern side of the town.

The airfield plus the town could all have been crammed into a two kilometre square. As the afternoon drew on the sun began to slide lower. Roberto dozed in his driver's seat and Yuri began to fidget with boredom. Saied became uneasy as he studied the border crossing. What concerned him was the number of soldiers that seemed to be around.

He mentioned this to Roberto who opened one lazy eye to explain that it was normal with the Belize border only a mile away and being one of the few access points into the country meant there was always a presence. They were probably looking for people trying to get in or out illegally. Saied was unconvinced and asked them to drive on. He had seen what he wanted.

The guerrilla leader started up the ancient engine and the old car chugged into life. Roberto drove a short way to one of the native bars in Melchor and honked his horn. Two men came out of the bar and walked up to them. Roberto spoke to them rapidly in Spanish then looked at Yuri. Yuri grunted his agreement.

Roberto explained, "My friend, we go south now for about five miles and we will stay there tonight and tomorrow until the evening, in a little village where we will be welcome, then tomorrow evening we will return to the house of Señor McKay and await the other party for the demonstration."

The leader gave a further curt order to his men who left without a word, "I tell them to stay in the town and let us know if all is well for us to return tomorrow night. You would not be bothered, but the soldiers here, they know me and I must be a little careful. Also Señor McKay is well known and does have visitors so the time we spend at his house needs to be minimized." He let out the clutch and the truck lurched forward. "And," he added casually, "my men will tip off the local police, who work for us. Unfortunately the soldiers don't, so if your BOSS men end up here our friends in the police will take them in and hold them until we have concluded the business and you have all left the country."

Saied nodded his acknowledgement. His initial impression of Roberto and his friends in the city had been that they were a disaster but, as they had travelled through the country, the young man had become more and more professional and confident in what he was doing and his men had become more serious and vigilant. The backwoods were obviously their habitat and the men showed the cautiousness of jungle animals. They were in their natural element up here in Melchor. The town was set in low country and the jungle-covered rolling hills stretched to the east with the valleys in between carrying teeming streams that joined and built themselves into the mighty rivers of Belize that flowed to the ocean.

Chapter 13

THE RUSSIANS

It was late at night and Polyakov and his party were settling into a hotel in Mexico City. In the morning they would meet for a final conference together and then enjoy the city for the rest of the day. The plan was to fly direct into the Melchor airstrip late that night in a privately chartered twin-engine fan jet aircraft. Polyakov planned for the engineer to work through the night to satisfy Colonel Ivanovich that the device would perform the task it had to do. The eight hours overnight should give the technocrats plenty of time. Polyakov then planned to have the device and its peripherals shipped to the airport and the handover of the money for the device would take place in the early morning.

The major, Sergei Alcksandrovich, Polyakov's Illegal's Department man, had made his contacts in Guatemala and then with Yuri. The scene was set.

Chapter 14

THE SOUTH AFRICANS

A few hours earlier the two teams of South Africans rendezvoused at the airstrip. Jim Bonner, the hunter who had outfitted the South African crew, had been belligerent when he woke to find himself in the back of a bucking Land Cruiser in the middle of the night. Wolff had placated him early with the promise of a bonus if he got them to the airstrip in time to meet Vintner and reminded him of his offer to come with them anyway.

"I did, but not like this, you silly bastard," was Bonner's only retort. After that he brightened and warmed to his task as guide, despite a hangover that threatened to shake loose his brain as they bounced along. Wolff was fascinated by the environment as they travelled and compared the green jungle world they found themselves in to the South African veldt.

Bonner's knowledge of the country was extraordinary and his running commentary on everything from the vegetation to the animals and the country's history made the long tortuous journey bearable and interesting. He found the most unlikely places in which to refuel the Land Cruiser; Wolff recognized that without Bonner they would have run out of fuel along the way.

At Melchor, they all thanked Bonner for his help and support and sent him back on the small aircraft Paul Vintner had chartered to fly up. The pilot was only too pleased to get home for the night and promised to return in the morning. This charter was lucrative but sleeping in the plane for several nights held little attraction for him. They waved Bonner off and then the four men gathered in the Land Cruiser.

Wolff was unusually nervous and apprehensive and Paul noticed that the strain of the journey and the situation showed on his face. The town was small enough but how did they find the man Saied? There was a small building that was an excuse for a terminal which, they realized, they could not simply sit in or they would be too conspicuous. Wolff had a fear of them being questioned. From what Bonner had told them the border area seethed with informers and the authorities were nervous.

"Listen," Wolff began, "this is what I think we should do. Time may be short. Let's drive from here and recce the engineer's compound, just a drive by for now, and gather what detail we can, followed by a more detailed recce on foot in the morning. Then between here and there stash the larger weapons in the bush. Keep the handguns with you. After that, go into town and see if there is somewhere to stay overnight. Or would you rather stay in the bush, your choice?"

Jon Van der Veldt spoke first, "Personally, a good night's rest would be my choice if we are to be at our best tomorrow. There is a risk, but how much in this green hell I do not know."

Den Jordan shrugged, he was easy either way, so it was left to Paul to give the casting vote, "I tend to agree that we need a good meal and a good night's sleep."

"So be it." Wolff started the wagon and drove off the airport and on to the track that led towards and past the engineer's house. As they approached the compound, they slowed to drive carefully past. A guard rested on one of the large gateposts at the end of a short drive, looking at nothing in particular. He raised his head as the vehicle went by but showed no obvious interest in it. By his side was a machine gun propped against the closed gate.

"Interesting," commented Paul, "Wonder how many there are with him."

"We will find out tomorrow. Now let's get back to town," Wolff directed.

After half a mile, Den Jordan tapped Wolff on the shoulder, "Boss, stop the vehicle over there in the bush."

Wolff stopped the wagon and looked back at Den questioningly.

Den's voice was steady, "Listen, boss, I want to get into the bush opposite the gates; you will have noticed that on the other side of the road it's only a hundred yards to the edge of the jungle," he looked at the other three, "the intelligence I can gather in the next twelve hours or so could mean the difference between success and failure. I picked my spot as we went by, so if you don't mind, I'll grab the kit I need from the back of the wagon and trek back there on foot."

Wolff smiled, looked at Vintner and then back at Jordan. He put his head on the steering wheel as he considered the suggestion. Jordan had joined him from the infantry and he was at home in any green environment. "Thank you, Den, good idea. Don't get bumped. Don't get caught. Don't get eaten or anything like that. Do make sure you are at this location at dawn, whatever time that is here. OK, off you go."

Den grabbed the kit he felt he would need for most contingencies that might arise and then added extra water and rations. Finally, he picked up a hunting rifle and its powerful scope; he stuffed his bergen with supplies and shelter materials and slung the rifle over his shoulder. When he was ready he slapped the side of the vehicle and hoofed it. His plan was to take a wide circle approach which would give him time to look at the country he was working in. Like any experienced soldier, he believed that time spent in looking round was never wasted.

The others entered the town from the north, having done a circuit; they had missed Saied and his team by minutes. There were a few bars in the town but there didn't appear to be a hotel of any sort. They stopped by one bar and checked that they were not an item of interest before Wolff got out of the truck and entered through the double open doors. The bar owner wiped down a few tables from the late lunch crowd before looking up. He greeted Wolff in Spanish; Wolff asked him if he spoke any English. The man said slowly, "A little," so Wolff asked him if there was anywhere in town that could put them up for the night.

"You mean a hotel, señor?" the man hung his head to one side.

"Yes, a hotel near to the airport," and by way of explanation, Wolff added, "Some friends of ours will be flying in tomorrow."

"Sorry, señor, nothing; but maybe my friend can find you rooms in his house for the night and you can eat here. Is that ok?" The man stopped his work, "You English?"

"No, South African."

"Oh, long way from home, eh?"

"Yes, a long way," Wolff didn't feel like talking. "Could you direct us to your friend's house? We have been travelling for some time, and we would like to get some rest."

The man looked past Wolff and could see the other two men sitting silently in the jeep, "Three of you want to stay, yes?"

Wolff simply nodded.

"OK, you come with me, the others can follow in the car. The house is only round the other street. Clean up and come back for a meal here in an hour. Come early, have a drink." He waved Wolff out of the bar and then followed him. The sun had lost its glare in the sky, but it was still humid. The still suffocating hot air made the South Africans long for the dry, dusty climate of their homeland.

Chapter 15

THE BRITISH

The BAC III fan jet of the Transportes Aereos CentroAmericanos airlines made its final turn over the Caribbean Sea with its protecting barrier of scattered white coral reefs, some breaking the surface in a ribbon pattern, and, dipping its wing, headed in to land at Belize airport.

Rodney looked out of the aircraft window as the wing dipped to give him an amazing view of the coast, a ribbon of silt-laden fresh water washed on to the immediate coastline of Belize from the Belize River. In the mile or so of effluent, giant catfish scavenged the seabed and fought other nightmarish creatures. As well as the main river, the silt seemed to ooze out of the mangroves that fringed the coast; the contrast between the brown water hugging the coastline and the blue waters was stark. Rodney remembered, for no particular reason, that Belize had a barrier reef that only the Australian Great Barrier Reef could surpass. Then they were over dense jungle, Belize City and making their final approach eight miles further on, to land at the international airport, an airstrip hacked out of the dense forest and swamps.

Like the South Africans, as they got off the plane the temperature and humidity hit them like a solid wall. It made them gasp and even Rodney, remembering his days in Borneo, had forgotten the experience of humidity like this. By the time they were in the airport reception area they were running with sweat.

The intelligence officer, Paul West, met them. He made it immediately clear that he didn't give much for their chances, but that he would do his best for them. They transferred immediately to a Beechcraft light aeroplane and were soon flying south-west across the jungle canopy which covered all but ten per cent of the country.

Rodney mentioned the terrain to West, who smiled, "Yes, it can be a nightmare down there and it is all too easy to get lost. It's not just the terrain you have to beware of."

Miss Webster shuddered, remembering the briefing in London. Across the aisle, Rodney reached out and squeezed her arm to reassure her. She smiled weakly back.

The Beechcraft flew in and out of wispy clouds. The team lost track of time and were completely disorientated. Just over the hour, the aircraft dipped below the sparse cloud and coasted down on to a grass strip in a jungle clearing. As the aircraft come to the end of the runway, the pilot expertly turned the craft around and headed back up the landing strip, turning at the end to place himself in a position to take off.

As soon as they alighted with their luggage and stores, the aircraft took off again and they were left with the feeling of being somewhat alone in an alien environment. Only the presence of the intelligence officer gave any comfort. After a few minutes they heard engines approaching through the jungle. Three Land Rovers appeared; in one of them Rodney recognized the cheerful smiling face of Major James Collins. But it was the white Range Rover that took their attention. It was the Force Commander of Belize and he was driving himself.

The commander's face as he alighted showed that he was not at all pleased to have spooks on his patch. He didn't like what was going on and he made it clear that Rodney and his people were not welcome.

"Whatever you do, you must not, repeat, must not, compromise the governor, who represents the British government." The commander eyed each of the team and his jaw was set. "Have you any idea how much crap will land on us if you are caught and they discover who you are and what you are doing? This theatre is not technically at war with its neighbour, at least not declared, but a spark could ignite the existing tension and matters could change in an instant. Gods! What is London thinking of?" He was not being unreasonable since what they were about to do could, if they were caught, fan the flames of an already difficult situation between the Belizean and Guatemalan authorities. "Now that's the official bollocking," he smiled at last, "Good luck, don't get caught and don't give me regret to have ever known you." He shook hands with each of them. Waving goodbye, he collected Captain West, the intelligence officer, indicating that he could drive the commander back from whence he came.

Only when the commander had disappeared back into the green world did Collins dismount from his vehicle.

"Welcome to the jewel of the Caribbean," James shook hands warmly with Rodney, Sharky and Mould, and gave Miss Webster a peck on the cheek. It was a throwaway gesture but it made her feel a little more secure.

James had come well prepared. Inside half an hour they had all changed into jungle greens and boots. They felt more comfortable and began to unwind from their journey.

Rodney wanted to know what the immediate plan was. The evening, only a few hours away, would soon draw in and he knew that within a quarter of an hour of dusk it would be tropical pitch black; already the insect life was increasing and they were forced to liberally douse themselves with insect repellent.

He desperately wanted to get a little closer to their objective. James reached into the driver's seat of the Land Rover and took out a well marked map, "The area we are in is called Central Farm," he stabbed the map. "We are going to follow the road for about twenty miles to the west and then turn off north to an old Mayan temple complex at Xunantunich, here."

Rodney and his party looked at the site on the map. Mould measured the distance to the border and then the distance to Melchor, "Hmm, that puts us only about a mile, less perhaps, from the border and maybe another one to the airfield at Melchor. Bit close, isn't it, mate?"

"No, I don't think so under the circumstances. Plus, I have got to think about your ageing bones. You see the border security effort is concentrated at the town crossing in Menchos itself. It is unlikely that there will be any patrols out at night, there never are, and you should be able to slip over without mishap. I can take you to the border but from there you are on your own. Whilst I am sure you have your plans, I would recommend you recce the airfield tonight ASAP, as it's lit and the going is not too bad. Then, get a good night's sleep and start out for the engineer's house before first light. The going there is not so good and you will need to see the ground underfoot as there are some areas of swamp pockets and you don't want to get your new clothes wet yet." James apologized once again that he could not come any further as it was more than his job was worth.

"That's OK James; you already appear to have done more than was asked."

"Yeah, that's a fact," Sharky added.

"Wish I could do more. You realize that you will have to change back into your kit to go over. You would certainly be stopped in that get up. Although I have to admit Miss Webster looks great in her outfit."

"Why, thank you James. But for goodness sake please call me Caroline," she smiled at James and he grinned.

"Right, Caroline it is." He got up and waved to his sergeant major, "Ian, I want you to take two of the party in your vehicle and take the lead to the base camp."

"Yes, sir. As it might be dark when we get to the ruins, no one's going to be there so we can take the good track to it before moving into the bush. The lads will have set up base camp by now so the dinner had better be ready for our guests."

"James," it was Rodney, "what about tourists at the monument, the base camp is not far according to the map?"

"I am sure it will become a tourist destination sometime in the future but in these uncertain times, apart from the odd trekker and our patrols, it's a pretty deserted area. There is no accommodation on this side of the border for several miles. I believe that the area around the ruin will be the best place to spend the night."

"You mean we are going to spend the night in the jungle, you are joking aren't you?" it was Caroline, and she wasn't impressed.

"No, I'm afraid not. But don't worry, we've brought plenty of insect repellent with us," Collins said sympathetically. "The ruin area was extensively dug some years ago and where we are going is a short ride from the main temple, a smaller one. It's off the beaten track, so safe; we can spend the night inside it with a smoke fire. Nothing will bother you," James said comfortingly.

"I just hope you are right. I don't like crawlies, and I have never spent a night in the jungle before."

"Then it's an experience you won't forget. The night sky here doesn't seem somehow quite as expansive as the Middle East but it has its own charm. The jungle night noises and rustlings, as well as thumps in the night will be sounds you will never forget." James suddenly smiled, "Tonight you are Jane." They all laughed and even the sergeant major smiled at his officer's attempts at quieting the fears of the young woman.

"If you and Rodney would like to go with Ian, I'll take the remainder. Let's go."

Sharky and Mould crammed themselves into the front seat with the major. "Interesting that you call the man by his first name," Mould remarked.

"God, you are a snob," was Sharky's retort, "Didn't your officer ever call you by your first name, then?"

"No he didn't, although he did call me other names, but I'm sure I can't repeat them in mixed company."

James said quietly, "I think there is a time and a place. Ian, apart from being a good sergeant major, knows the game. Anyway it works; give a little, and receive a little, don't you think?"

Chapter 16

POLYAKOV MEETS TSYGANKOV, THE SPYMASTER

It was about this time that the phone in General Polyakov's hotel suite rang. It was the receptionist, "Sir, we have a gentleman here who wishes to see you." Polyakov guessed it was Tsygankov, expecting him to surface around now.

"Please put him on the phone," Polyakov told the desk.

"Good evening, sir," Polyakov recognized the quiet tones.

"Good evening, come up to room 3016," Polyakov grimaced – the director's hatchet man was here; Colonel Carl Tsygankov, the Spymaster.

Polyakov poured two whiskies and set them on the low table between the two settees. He went to the door and left it ajar. He sat and waited. When Tsygankov entered the room, closing the door quietly, his tall, spare figure bowed slightly. Polyakov didn't get up but waved the colonel to the other settee opposite him.

"It must be important for you to break cover before we fly," Polyakov raised his glass to his guest.

"Possibly," Tsygankov leant forward and took the tumbler of whisky, raising it in a salute. Polyakov noticed he used his scarred hand to lift the glass. "It is a nuisance really but these things are sent to try us; the Director called to let me know that a party of four, possibly, British Secret Service took off on a flight from Miami to Belize after lunch today, and was I interested. Of course, I told him. They will be in Belize by now. Major Nsenko, also called me. The South Africans are in Guatemala at the border area.

"How many South Africans? What are they?"

"We know there were at least three. But now at least definitely two, as Saied killed one who was masquerading as a friend of Hough's."

Tsygankov got up and stood before him; his exceptional height and the vivid redness of the scar in the middle of his left hand, front and back where a knife had gone through it, stood out. The Russian surgeons had done what they could, but the hand had an open claw-like appearance. In the man's skull-like head, the cruel mouth curled into a smile. He reached into his inside jacket pocket and brought out a sheaf of signals which he placed in front of Polyakov. Polyakov stared at the signals in front of him and as he sat twirling the whisky glass he felt a surge of alarm. The man's quiet voice stilled him for a moment as he sat back down.

"My dear General, you tasked me to keep an eye on things. Well," the man settled himself and saw Polyakov's eyebrows rise imperceptibly; he didn't care, his career had been damned years ago, "as I said, the South African situation was phoned through by our people in South Africa. Their investigation confirmed that a Major Wolff and a party did go to Guatemala. One of them is dead and the others have moved up country. This has been confirmed as far as possible by our people out there. There is, by the way, a hunt on for the South Africans. The local Guatemalan police want to speak to them about the death of their colleague. They have been tipped off that they will be found in Melchor de Mencos very soon; the police are having help. One can assume that they will soon be neutralized."

"They must be." Polyakov went through his signals on the table, "What about the British?" he said in exasperation; so much for a smooth ride; this was turning into a fiasco.

The brigadier held up his scarred hand, "You will recall, sir, that I have spent a good part of my career in and out of London and the disaster we suffered."

"Yes, the Chekhov affair, what of it?" the general said impatiently.

"Simply this, the man who was responsible for the debacle was Major Rodney Brown. I have kept tabs on him ever since. He is a rising star in their service; I shouldn't be surprised if he takes over the section one day."

"Are you about to say this man is on his way to Belize?"

"He is there."

"Bloody hell!" Polyakov said, "I remember the incident. What's the man like now?"

"Who, Brown?" Tsygankov dismissed Brown with his hands. "Not impressive to look at but," he paused, considering, "he has a good brain and is resourceful. No superman, in fact he has a leg that was badly wounded in Borneo."

"What about the team he has with him?"

"Mould and Sharky. Both are loyal, intelligent and tough."

"Is that all he has with him? You said there were four of them."

"No, there is woman in her mid thirties; along as an expert, I should think. Probably not much more than a desk officer, I would say. Yes, she is the local expert and interpreter, nothing more. We don't know her. She is certainly not a Valeria Gershuni, of that you can be certain." Tsygankov was dismissive.

"There is no chance that their visit is for some other reason?" Polyakov was clutching at straws and he knew it. "No, of course not," he shook his head in disgust with himself. "Your suggestions, you have obviously thought about it?" he saw the colonel's face break into a grin.

"Yes I have; there are several options open to us, but we must keep the aim of the exercise in mind." The colonel looked at Polyakov. Polyakov was looking at him; he had thought the man's dead eyes were washed out but they were in fact light blue, they matched the colonel's code name, rather than his nickname of the Spymaster; he was known to both sides by the code name 'Blue'. However, the general's face told him nothing; "Very well, General," Tsygankov continued, momentarily annoyed that the general had not picked up his signal to input. "We must go ahead but ensure the British are kept away at the critical time. I am the only one you have who knows Brown. I will fly with you but stay on board the jet. Its windows will give me sight of proceedings on the airstrip."

"Are you sure that they will try to take the device at the aeroplane?"

"Yes, if they do their sweep of the area they will soon realize that the engineer's house is too well guarded."

"Agreed."

"I know our man and he will have to come across the border close to the town, say three or four miles north or south. A minor incident to tighten up the border there should be enough to stop him."

"You are assuming that he is not there already."

"He won't be yet, early morning is the best he can do, of that I'm sure."

"And if you are wrong?"

"There is nothing he can do, effectively, unless he has a platoon with him to take the engineer's house and that is not going to happen. The British are paranoid about keeping the lid on the situation there."

Polyakov was undecided but he had little choice other than to accept the solution he had been given. "Are you sure there is no other way of stopping this man? What about getting somebody to ferret him out?"

"The country, whilst sparsely populated, is mostly impenetrable jungle, we would never find him. And anyway, who do we use? We need the assets we have there to guard the device," Tsygankov replied.

"Do what you can then. You have my full authority to do what you must. Don't fail me."

Tsygankov bowed in his chair. "Please tell your people I am joining them. I'll forego another whisky, if you don't mind. But I'll drink a toast with you to success," he stood up and raised and drained his glass. "Until tomorrow, sir, I'll bid you goodnight."

Polyakov checked him before he could leave, using his first name for the first time, "Carl, this is not to turn into a vendetta."

Tsygankov stopped and turned to Polyakov. He held up his damaged hand, "If you mean is this for revenge, I don't think so. I would like to even the score that is true. Revenge is always best taken cold, don't you think? Besides I've never been vindictive in the context of an enemy and I don't intend to start now."

Once the man had left, Polyakov relaxed into his sofa and gazed round his hotel room until his gaze fell on to his ink blotter and the scattered papers on it. He went to the desk, selected a clean sheet of paper and began to write an account of what had happened and what he planned to do. His training as a young staff officer taught him to document anything of importance; he knew this was the time to get something on paper, just in case. Back in Moscow he had a rubber stamp with an umbrella on it in his desk drawer that he kept for just such moments as this, and he would have religiously stamped his copy with it if he had been there.

Chapter 17

BELIZE – THE JEWEL OF THE CARIBBEAN

The Land Rovers drove under camouflage nets suspended from the ruin and the trees that surrounded it and the nets adjusted, immediately, hiding them from the way they had come. They had arrived. Getting out of the vehicles, they were surprised to see the base camp was all set up; it was fully functioning and food had been prepared. The camp was in a small jungle clearing with a tight, little-used track leading into it. One end of the camp was now blocked with the Land Rovers and, at the other, the nets were strewn on to the small temple ruin.

A SAS sergeant came forward and introduced himself to them all, "Call me Staff and we will get along fine." Rodney raised his eyebrows to Collins.

"Think the reason for being here is safe with 'Staff'. We share half the hut with him and his training team. They owe us some favours." James smiled. "Right, please eat and let's gets down to business."

An hour later, at eight o'clock that night, they reassembled refreshed and dressed for the night operations. They sat on camp chairs in a circle inside the temple, leaving space for a battle board with a map and other data pinned to it.

Rodney took the floor by the board, "For our new team members, a general outline of the mission. The mission is to steal a device taken from the South Africans by others for the Russians. Who knows what? I have to assume that the Russians know we are in the field. The South Africans don't. The Russians have local help, we think, a small band of guerrillas.

The Russians are expected to fly in over the next twenty-four hours; they will go to the engineer's house here at this location," Rodney indicated a point on the map and then continued, "to have the device proved to them," Rodney again pointed out the engineer's house. "I propose that we will carry out two visits. One tonight to the airport here, note its relationship to the house, the border, base camp. The other recce at first light will be to the engineer's house. From the map and aerial picture you can see the jungle comes up to three sides of the compound. To the front is a short drive and then there is scrubland for about a hundred yards and then jungle again." He took a breath before continuing, "The purpose of the airfield visit is to see for ourselves what it has to offer in the way of cover buildings where we can hide, blend in, whatever, for a while; and what the security arrangements are. The purpose of the visit to the house is to check out what strength the opposition is and as a permanent observation post until this is over."

"Dispositions: All four of us will take a look at the airstrip tonight. We leave in an hour; Staff will be with us and lead us in. Blackout kit; we are not going there to mingle with the natives. First light, Mould and Sharky make their way to the jungle in front of the house and set up the observation post. Once it's established, Mould, I want you back here by midday latest. Any questions so far?" Silence was the response.

"Plan existing," this got everyone's attention, "although Sharky will observe the house, I don't think we can get the device off them with our small force but we need to check it out. There is a potential to ambush them on the road to the airport but that would rouse the country. So until we know differently the plan is to take the device on the plane. Now it's going to be a small charter and we will have the luxury of only having to deal with the Russian team and crew."

"Bloody hell!" Staff was impressed.

Rodney continued, "It's not all bad news, Staff," but the astonishment on the faces of all the team was a spectacle to behold; "James, do we have the uniforms?" When James nodded, Rodney returned to his briefing, "We have aircrew uniforms for the four of us, so we will bluff our way on to the plane when the Russians are at the house and take the aircraft over. There should only be on board the captain, engineer and a steward so that should not be too difficult. The trick is to get the Russians on to the plane before we take them and that is the task of Caroline, our Latin-speaking air hostess. OK so far? If not please leave your questions until the end.

Assuming all goes well, there are a couple of outcomes. We silence them, tie them up, gag them and walk off the aircraft with the device and back to here. If that's not possible then we will have to fly off to a destination, and that part of the plan is not shaped yet," nobody interrupted him so he continued but he called for comments and questions.

"Notwithstanding that it's an interesting plan, it seems to me you are a man short. It would be helpful if you and your party knew when the Russians were leaving the engineer's house so you can take the plane. That could be a problem area as the longer you hang around the airfield in view, the greater the danger of being compromised," James Collins commented and got up to look at the map. "On the map it looks like the track from the engineer's house to the airstrip comes within a quarter of a mile of the border, which is not well delineated anyway. An observer could give you about five minutes notice if he were hidden about here." James viewed everyone at once and got a nod from the sergeant major and Staff. "Whilst we are not allowed to get involved by my boss, as overstepping the mark, we can offer that service to you. I would really like to have an observer near the front gate to give you more notice of the movements but that would be a career limiting move."

"Not worried about that are you, sir?" Staff questioned.

"Not really but I would like to make the pension," James was sanguine.

Rodney expressed his gratitude as he sensed that unless he stopped them at this point they would exceed their remit, "That is really good of you, more than I expected, as that was a concern I had and didn't know how to sort it. Now, what else have you brought for us? The team need to know."

The sergeant major opened up, "Eight radios, two will be used back to back and form a base station at this location with a good ten-mile range so they will cover the area of this operation; spare batteries etc. two vehicle-borne radio sets that can reach both battle groups and HQ at airport camp near Belize City if push comes to shove;" he looked at Staff, "and, courtesy of Staff, don't ask me where he got them for you, four handguns, Russian issue, with shoulder holsters and three Israeli Uzi machine guns, small enough to put in your 'flasher mac' pocket." He smiled, "Borrowed, begged or stolen, a dozen pairs of handcuffs; also four flight bags and the uniforms for your disguises as aircrew." He glanced at his list, "Water, iron rations, also a Silva compass for each of you and small set of civilian binoculars, but good quality, and one infrared and green light sniper scope. Don't lose that, we want it back, don't we Staff?"

"Very much so," Staff nodded. "Now let's get you lot kitted up; Major James and I are going to take you to the border and point you at the airfield. We will wait in the bush for you to return and bring you back here. One last thing, we will set the Silva compasses with a back bearing at the border so, if you get bumped, run like hell and trust the compass for base. Worst case, make for the big ruin down the road and then make your way back to here. Got it?"

It was clear to Rodney, Mould and Sharky that James and his team had already been on the ground and had worked out the route, which was a big help.

Staff got them up and put them in a line before he made them jump up and down to check they had nothing loose in their pockets. "Make ready your sidearm," he waited until they hand cocked their pistols and made safe with the safety catch on then checked them all. "Radios switched off, right. No sounds from now on, stay in touch with the man in front. I will stop about every hundred yards so count your steps. The last man slaps the back of the next man and so on up the line. I will only move off when the man behind me slaps my back. Got it? Now it's dark as lamp black until we get to the border. At the border opposite the airfield is scrubland and a few shanty houses so you will be able to see the object better. Don't worry about animals or anything else. Everybody got their night vision? Ready to go?"

Staff moved slowly and silently into the blackness that was the jungle. Mould was on his shoulder followed by Caroline, then Sharky followed by Rodney and finally James. Staff was as good as his word, stopping every hundred yards to ensure nobody had wandered off, so instilling confidence in the group. The jungle hemmed them in, vines and undergrowth tugged at them as they pushed through; the smell of damp mildew in humidity was like swimming in a stifling soup of stagnant air. Animals scuttled about and real or imaginary things dropped out of the canopy near them. Nightmare is what Caroline thought stumbling along trying desperately to gather all available light into her eyes to help focus on the broad back of Mould in front of her. Ten stops later the jungle thinned suddenly and shortly Staff waved them down and to his left. There was a natural rise and they lay along it looking south-east. The airfield was clearly visible. Staff took out the night sight from his bergen and adjusted it before passing it to the others who in turn spent some time scanning the target.

Between them and the runway some five hundred metres away was the odd low shack. None showed lights, and they didn't obscure the target. On the far side of the runway there were a couple of small hangars and three buildings. One was obviously a workshop with Third World junk lying around it. One was a reception building of some sort made out of clapboard, which even in the night looked derelict. It had a long lean-to on one side with a dozen tables and chairs. On one of the tables, a sleeping figure turned over in his sleep, possibly the nightwatchman. The last building could be the service building as it was fenced, enclosing a battered fuelling truck and two horizontal oil tanks. On the far side of the airfield, buildings could be seen increasing in darkness as they distanced themselves.

Staff's six senses felt a change in the night and then his keen hearing picked up the low sound of movement; he motioned them all back from the bank into the undergrowth. Soon the murmur of people could be caught on the night air; the sound of men approaching grew in intensity but their voices betrayed no urgency. The slap of equipment on equipment grew louder. The hollow ring of the patrol magazines told the soldiers in Rodney's group that they had their weapons slung or shouldered and the magazines were probably empty. Peering out through the undergrowth, Rodney could now see the upper parts of the men moving along the other side of the bank, just silhouetted against the sky. One of the men in the patrol glanced over into the jungle and seemed to look straight at Rodney but then looked away disinterested. The patrol continued on its way oblivious of the team who were as still as tombstones and with their breath held in. When the patrol was out of sight and the sounds of the jungle returned, Staff crept round each member telling them that the discipline of the outward journey would be repeated on the way back.

Staff's careful marshalling had them back in the base camp within the half hour. A brew of tea awaited them for which they were grateful. Free to talk at last Caroline turned to Staff, "Good job you picked up the patrol heading our way."

"Takes years of practice, ma'am, plus there is a trick you might like to remember. Apart from your ears at night you need to use your peripheral vision, watching for movement out of the corner of the eyes. I saw them almost as soon as I heard them."

"Staff, can you tell me what those thuds and crashes were that we heard in the jungle?"

"Yeah, damned deadfall, branches falling off the trees; very dangerous too, kills more men in the jungle and forests than any other hazard," Staff shook his head, "had a few close calls myself."

Rodney shook the last dregs of his tea on to the ground and called for attention. "Listen in, everybody; I need you to sort yourselves out. James, I want a debrief for all in ten minutes and then let's get some sleep," Rodney called, looking back at his scribbling in a notebook.

Everybody grunted acknowledgment.

When they had all reassembled back in the centre of the ruin and were seated in the camp chairs, Rodney was already waiting for them. "Let's get this over with; I'm going to take observations from everyone, Mould, you first."

Mould stood scratching bites and brushing himself off, "The area is patrolled but not aggressively, however the patrol size of eight men is too strong for us so simply walking across the scrub to the airfield in aircrew uniforms may not be an option." Mould returned to his chair.

Starkey didn't move but spoke next, "Agree, plus there are some old shacks, only a few, I know, but in daylight there may be more activity than tonight. The airfield is pretty bare, except for a few field buildings."

"Staff, would you like to add?" Rodney asked.

"Agree with what's been said so far. Don't think just walking in is an option."

"James, your input please."

"Agree, but I've got an idea."

"OK, let's have it."

"We will get you a hire car and have it delivered from Benque Viejo del Carmen, the sister village of Menchos, but on the Belize side of the border to this location. You simply drive through the border in your aircrew outfits and sit in the car until you are ready to drive up to the aircraft and take it;" James looked pleased with himself, "we can spot the aircraft arriving for you."

"Like it, but a few points," Rodney looked at the team, "First, Caroline, anything you would like to add?"

"I was thinking it would be a good idea to see who comes off the aircraft and who meets them." Caroline looked at Rodney, "And you and I should witness it because between us we know most of the faces."

Staff looked up, "Could work, if we bring the hire car to the main ruin down the track. You two see them off the plane and I whistle you back here, you get changed then off you all go. After all they aren't going anywhere quickly if they have to go to the engineer's house to see a test of the kit before they buy, are they?"

"OK, that's the plan. You two," Rodney indicated Mould and Sharky, "heads down; you are away at first light. Slight change, I want you both back here midday, 1300 hours latest," he turned to the Belize contingent and Caroline, "I'd like a few minutes of your time before we hit the sack."

Chapter 18

THE SOUTH AFRICAN

Den Jordan, now in his hide fashioned with two groundsheets he had brought with him and local arranged foliage was opposite the engineer's house, focusing all his attention on the gate as dusk fell. Den's hide was ten feet back in the scrub on a slightly raised mound. He had carefully eased the foliage away to give him an uninterrupted view of the front gate and walls. By turning left or right slightly he could monitor any approaches along the track road to the front of the property. Den had noted the change of guard several times and counted four different men in all. Once a white-haired, stocky, character had come out and spoken to the guard. He noted him in his book as the engineer. Den had made himself comfortable with a brush and foliage base over which he had laid a groundsheet to protect himself from the damp and insects. Over the top of his hide, he had stretched another sheet half a metre above the groundsheet. His rifle and machete to his side and his rations stacked, he smiled, as an ex-sniper he was in his element. Just like old times, he thought, the others don't know what they are missing. He was suddenly alert. He heard the approach of a diesel truck but it drove past the house without slowing. He had reached into his bergen for the insect repellent. The bug activity had picked up in the last half hour and he had rolled his sleeves down. He covered his head liberally with the repellent first and then his clothes before his ankles and boots. He had a camouflage face veil which he doused in the repellent and draped it over his jungle hat. His final act was to open the litre can of kerosene he had taken from the truck and he carefully poured it around the outer base of his groundsheet to keep off ants and any other crawling insect that may decide to join his bed. He was not bored; this situation had been his lifeblood as a sniper with the Selous Scouts for more than ten years and he revelled in the solitude of his situation. He listened to the sounds around him. He had heard the slither of the odd snake and the rustle of small rodents. In the distance he had heard the crashing of larger animals through the jungle but nothing came near him. This part of the world had more than a thousand species of birds and in the early evening they roosted noisily; to the left and front were bushes of brilliant red hibiscus and he watched out of the corner of his eye as hummingbirds jerked from flower to flower. He wondered what his three colleagues were up to but dismissed the thought and watched the guard on the gate relieve himself against the stone gatepost. He settled down for a long night.

Chapter 19

THE EXCHANGE

Before first light Staff had a brew and breakfast going and Mould and Sharky were up and dressed.

"Get this lot down you; leave the others to sleep a little longer, James will get them up when we have gone."

Mould was bleary-eyed and Sharky not much better but they perked up after sausage sandwiches and a couple of strong, sweet cups of steaming tea.

Staff sat with them drinking his tea, "I'd really like to come with you but the Major says it would be more than our jobs are worth; but what I will do is get you to the jump-off point so you only have less than a mile to go. We will retrace our steps of last night to the airfield and then I am going to run you along the edge of the border to the north for about a mile and a half; I will point out the track which leads to the target, say, a mile to the east. You can't miss it. I'll mark the trail as we go so you two office boys won't get lost."

"Thanks, Staff," Sharky grinned, "If it's not too much trouble, I would like to go a couple of hundred yards further, so I strike out and come into the ground say a half mile from the front of the target and then work my way forward."

"Reasonable," agreed Staff. "Get your bergens while I get you some rations and extra water to take with you. Dawn's breaking and it's time to move."

* * * * *

Den Jordan left his kit in the hide and moved out to await Wolff as they had arranged the day before. By nine thirty with still no sign of Wolff, which was perplexing but not worrying, Den felt exposed at the meeting place and made the decision to go back to his hide. Besides, he was hungry. He would see Wolff drive by in any case when he drove past the house.

* * * * *

Staff's small party moved from the vaulted ruins of the Xunantunich complex moving as fast as possible, but with caution, as the newly-risen sun began to make the jungle steam. The early morning jungle sounds surrounded them, with screeching monkeys in the canopy and every manner of parakeet; brightly coloured butterflies and other insects flitted on the foliage and scattered as the three men pushed up the trail.

When they reached the bank they had hidden behind the previous night, they could see clearly the packed earth airstrip of Melchor de Mencos. Further out, there seemed to be a lot of activity in the town itself. Staff halted them, got out his binoculars and focused them on the soldiers that seemed to be moving purposefully around the airstrip. He passed the binoculars to Sharky. Even as Sharky watched, a troop-carrying aeroplane banked away in the sky to the north and made its run into the town airstrip. He held the instrument on the runway until the plane had landed and the first of the troops began to disgorge from its innards.

"Staff, what's going on, is this normal?" Mould quizzed.

"I don't think so. I know that the Kaibil was here in some strength but the lot that has just arrived is ordinary infantry so they must be reinforcements not replacements. What's going on?" Staff had a horrible feeling that something over there was seriously wrong.

Mould asked what the Kaibil was and Staff explained they were special forces; when Mould asked what it all meant, Staff suddenly came alive, "Bollocks, it means one of two things," and even as he spoke two other troop carriers circled before landing, "Either there is trouble inside Guatemala and the infantry has come to hold the fort while the special forces go back and sort it out; and that's bad enough for us, the last thing we want is an unstable country over there or even worse. Or, and less likely, they are forming a mounting base and they are coming this way!"

"Yeah," Sharky had the scope now, "It doesn't look as though this is going to be such an easy walk in the park." Sharky suddenly stiffened and fiddled with the focus to get the best definition possible, "I know that face," he said almost to himself screwing up his eye on the lens piece, "Here, Mould, you confirm it. There, see, there are three men being led out to one of the military planes. Got them?"

"Seen, but I can't make out features."

"Take the scope," Sharky passed the instrument to Mould and waited impatiently.

"Yes, I know him, but I know his sidekicks better. What are the South Africans doing hobnobbing with this lot?" He continued to study them, "They are not hobnobbing, they are under guard," Mould took the scope from his eye and handed it back.

"Exactly, it seems that they were in the game too. Why didn't we know they had got this far? They are well out of the game now so, unless anything else has changed, it's us, the Russians, this man, Saied, and that lot," he swept the scope out towards the airstrip now swarming with military trying to get themselves sorted out.

It transpired later that Wolff and the other two had been taken easily when the bar owner had led them into a carefully prepared trap; it had been too easy and Wolff and Vintner were furious with themselves. They had been handcuffed and blindfolded and locked up until the police were able to put them on a plane for Guatemala City. Whatever their fate, Staff knew that they now posed no threat to them. He watched them disappear into the bowels of the transport plane and it swiftly took off, roaring into the blue.

He made a quick decision, "Got to go boys, you are on your own. Just do what I planned and you will be fine."

"A moment, Staff," Sharky looked at Mould, "My watch, my job. You need to go back with Staff and brief the boss. No argument, I will be fine. Now go."

Mould nodded; passed his rations and water to Sharky and then he and Staff left, both of them moving in leaps and bounds back down the track, disappearing immediately into the green jungle.

Sharky just shrugged and looked at the brilliant blue sky, feeling the heat warm his body, "God, but life's good," he mumbled. Sharky turned right and with one eye on the airfield moved silently inside the canopy. He found a well-defined game trail a few metres in from the edge of the jungle which gave him a swift route to his jumping-off point. He counted his steps, stopping every 250 paces and picked up a twig which he stuffed in his pocket. As he went on the sounds and sights of the airfield fell behind him. When he picked up his tenth twig, he moved to the edge of the jungle and referred to his aerial picture. He decided he was still 500 or so metres short of the point when he would turn inland. Two more twigs and he adjusted his kit so that he was comfortable with the weight on his back, checked his watch at eight thirty, drank a small bottle of water and wedged it in the fork of a tree as a marker, noted his surroundings, scanning and picking a few key features and then made his way unhurriedly into Guatemala.

The camp was up and bustling when Staff and Mould appeared in their midst. "What's up?" Major Collins was the first to realize something was amiss. Mould should not be there and Staff was sweating. The others crowded round, eager to hear what was going on.

"There is a lot of military activity, regular army is flying in, probably battalion-strength plus at the moment, and more were arriving. They have captured three men who were frogmarched on to one of the planes. Mould knows them, South Africans. I think, sir, we need to get on top of the main temple where we will be able to overlook the airfield and with the use of the scopes should see something." James nodded to the sergeant major to get the scopes and a radio.

"We will all go," James looked at Rodney who nodded his agreement.

Ten minutes later they scrambled up to the top of the Xunantunich temple and were scanning south-east to the Menchos airfield three miles away. The scopes they had were good and although they couldn't make out individual facial features, the numbers he could see were enough to alert Major Collins to the fact that there was an issue.

"Staff, I need you to observe for me and relay to Ian." James eyeballed his sergeant major, "Need you to man the Land Rover radio and relay what I send you to HQ." James got the basics done and then faced Rodney, "You are on your own now. Once we get preliminary reports away, we need to go back to base and it's 80 miles of shit roads, so we will need to break camp and disappear in the next half hour. Your car will be here in a few minutes. That's the best I can do. Sorry, got to go."

Rodney was sanguine in a crisis; he had a way of slowing his functions whilst his brain ramped up, "Thank you; you have done more than we asked already." He turned to Mould and Caroline, "Nothing has changed; our plan goes ahead."

* * * * *

Sharky was moving silently through the jungle towards the target, his machine pistol ready and held out to his front. His feet tested the ground each step before he put his weight on the forward foot. He loved this game, hunting was his speciality. At 300 yards out he caught a slight movement in the scrub ahead of him. Sharky went to ground and listened. It had been just a flicker of a man going down. He waited and saw nothing more. Sharky eased his bergen from his back and moved cautiously forward for another 100 yards. The thorns on the bushes in this area of pre-jungle hampered him and he had to move with care as they tugged at his clothing and he constantly had to stop and carefully extract them without making the foliage move. Moving his head from side to side, scanning ahead and using his side vision, he saw a man prone in a hide facing away from him. He was puzzled; his man was clearly watching the target. The build of the man was familiar, his bald patch was distinctive; Sharky worried that he had seen this man before, but was he friend or foe? He sneaked forward another 20 yards and found himself only 30 yards from the hide. The man turned his head and reached for something in his bag and brought out a water bottle. He took a swig and replaced the bottle in the bag. As he had turned, Sharky saw the side of his face, recognizing with relief an old associate; "Den," he whispered, Den shot his head round. It took him a moment to recognize Sharky and the surprise on his face was total; recovering, he motioned Sharky up to him.

When Sharky had crawled in and the men had grasped hands, Den whispered, "What in hell's name are you doing here?"

"It's a small world; I think I am saving your arse right now!" Sharky told Den; he went on to tell him what he had seen at the airfield and that the place was now hot. He told how he had seen Wolff, Vintner and another handcuffed and led into the plane which took off for the east.

Sharky, like Den Jordan, had been a sniper and Den had attended a course Sharky had run when he was on exchange. They had met professionally and in competition many times since. That they should meet here when both their nations were active in the same country was not surprising, they belonged to a small pool of men that excelled in what they were now doing in the bush of Guatemala.

"You still haven't told me what you are doing here?" Den was persistent.

"No way of softening this Den, we heard the Russians were coming to do an exchange for the device they took off you and we couldn't allow that."

"What do we do now? My team's neutralized and yours is still whole; at least it means all's not lost. If you guys do snatch it from the Russians, we can at least talk to you about it."

"Yeah, now what are you going to do?"

Den was silent for a while, his hands resting on his knees, "Only one thing I can do, help you bunch of misfits do the business. What is the plan?"

"That's my boy. The plan is for us, dressed as aircrew, to drive up to the Russian plane, take it over and, when the Russian party has finished its business in the engineer's house and returns to their plane, we grab them and the device."

"Neat," Den looked at Sharky, "Timing an issue?"

"Yeah, and that is where you could help us. Can you continue to do what you're doing? I've got a radio in my bergen back there in the bush. You can tell us when the Russians arrive and how many there are, plus any 'hangers-on', then radio to tell us when they leave for the airfield and how many there are, so that we know what we are facing."

"I can do that," Den smiled for the first time. "If and when you get hold of the device, what do you do then?"

"Now, that's a million dollar question and one we can't answer. Ideally we would like to get back in the car and drive it over the border. Don't know how that part of the mission will work out."

"Bloody hell, you're mad."

"Got to try," Sharky mouthed. "Listen, as soon as you give us the intel that the Russians are on their way to the airfield, make your way to our base camp. No way can you stay in this country now." Sharky got out his map and showed the location to Den. Don't think our support team will be there long with everything going on, they will bug out as soon as Rodney makes his move, if they have not already. I'll make sure that we leave you some kit and supplies in the ruin and ask them to wait if I see them. And here, take this Belize money," he reached into his pocket and shoved a bundle of notes to Den. "It should enable you to get a lift to Belize City airport if you need to. There you can get a flight to Miami and home. Find a Major James Collins at Airport Camp, nobody else. He will be back there by the time you get out of this and down to the camp which is, by the way, around 80 miles from our base camp. OK so far?"

"Yeah, thanks Sharky," Den was grinning now. He had a way out now which was an issue he had been wondering how to solve since Sharky had arrived and told him he was isolated. "Now, let's have that radio and map, you get back to your team. Any supplies you don't want, I could use and then I can get back to my task. While you sort that, I will tell you what I have seen so far."

"One last thing, Den, don't turn the radio on for an hour; I will need that time to get back. If they were to call and you replied before I get back, you may have difficulty explaining who you are. The radios have a scrambler so you can talk in plain speech. Come on let's get sorted."

It took Sharky a good hour to get back to the base camp; he had had to wait for a patrol to pass close to him. He was shocked as at first sight the camp appeared deserted. The Land Rovers and the paraphernalia were missing and it looked deserted. Then Caroline came out of the ruin dressed as an air stewardess.

"Ah, Sharky, you're back. How did it go?"

"OK, where is everybody?"

"Well, after Staff and Mould came back, all hell broke loose. We all went up to the main ruin and watched the goings-on from there; Rodney is still up there and Mould is checking out the hire car. Think you better go and see Rodney; he was hoping you would get back earlier than planned." She looked at her watch, 11.10. "I am sorting out our kit for the journey across the border. Just go back down the track to the ruin and then to its front and climb the steps. You will find Rodney there, you can't miss him."

"Sure, but first got any of the bottles of water? I am parched; it's hot and humid as anything here. Don't know how they stand it when it gets like this."

Sharky legged it up the track, swigging water and then dousing his head and shoulders with what remained. It cooled him but by the time he had climbed to the top of the mound he was hot again. He found Rodney with the scope in his hand squinting at the airfield, deep in thought.

Sharky approached him and made him start, "Sharky, you're back, thank goodness for that. The Russians have arrived; see the small passenger jet on the runway," he passed the scope over. "Four people got off and an aircrew of three got out just now and stretched their legs, seemed to book in to the airport control building and now the crew have returned to the aircraft."

Sharky swept the airfield and then focused on the aircraft. The blinds were down, he didn't think it was simply to keep out the bright sun. "Did we manage to identify any of the Russians?" Sharky handed back the scope.

"Only two of them; I recognized the head man, General Polyakov," Sharky whistled, "and Caroline recognized a Major Nsenko. Our problem is that we don't know when they will come back to the aircraft and take off, so it's good you're back early. We are going to bring everything forward and go for the aircraft ASAP."

"Boss, got something to tell you; got that covered."

Rodney tilted his head, was he going to like this? Sharky had the habit of generating surprises.

"I was getting close to the house and bumped into, well, sort of fell over the fourth SA man, Den Jordan, who I just happen to know, watching the target."

Rodney groaned, "Just what I needed, and what was the fallout from this reunion of old soldiers?"

"All good boss; Den is going to keep watch and keep us abreast of movements etc. He has one of our radios so we have comms with him. I asked him to let us know who went by and when the Russians left and how many were in the party."

Rodney grunted, "Robinson is going to have my guts for garters. On the other hand, I expect our people would have given the device back anyway, eventually; so, no harm done there, in fact, a plus; well done."

Sharky grinned. "Gave him some Belizean money and told him to get to the village on this side and to get himself to Airport Camp and find Major Collins to help him get to Miami. Come to think of it, where is the Major and the rest of them?"

"When Staff and Mould got back and James reported into HQ on the radio all hell broke loose apparently, it is not completely clear. Unsurprisingly, it's pretty chaotic at this moment, but according to James, as far as the intelligence cell can work out, the Guatemalans have declared martial law. Why? Because some of the generals have apparently asked for the resignation of the president."

"Who's that again?" Sharky asked.

"A tough right-winger, President General Rios Montt; he preached

Christian brotherly love and waged ferocious military campaigns against the terrorists and his own, thank goodness, not us."

"Formidable, eh?" Sharky whistled through his teeth and shook his hand as though cooling it.

Rodney couldn't help chuckling, "I wouldn't say he was a tyrant but his record on human rights wouldn't stand up to scrutiny, but tough, yes. I wouldn't be in the shoes of these generals who indicated he should retire, for all the tea in China."

Sharky wasn't impressed. "Look, boss, are you sure the whole thing isn't simply a ruse to move troops up to the border for something else?" He let the implication hang in the air.

Rodney viewed Sharky with interest then put a finger to his nose and tapped it. "Shrewd, Sharky, very shrewd. We simply don't know yet but preparations are going on in case." Sharky could see Rodney had more to tell.

"And?" Sharky said simply.

"And I'm afraid they indicated our mission is terminated." Rodney didn't say anything for a while.

"Who said so, this lot, or did it come from London?"

"London."

Sharky's comment was dry, "Well, that's all right then, because they said we were on our own anyway, so what has changed?"

"As you've brought Den into this, let's see if he has anything for us." Rodney took out his radio and called him up, "Den, this is Sharky's boss, what have you got for us?"

"Rodney Brown, I assume. The story so far: the Russians arrived, numbers four. Shortly afterwards a truck appeared with Saied and a couple of locals. Nobody has left. We considered when we were planning that they would need at least eight hours to get the tests done and satisfy a third party, so I am expecting them to reappear and leave for the airfield earliest 1700 hrs, latest, say, 2100 hrs if there is a snag. Whatever, this time of year you have the cover of darkness, dusk at 1630 hrs and dark, as you will know, ten minutes later, over to you."

"Thanks. We will listen out and be back to you later in any case, over."

"Roger, out." Den closed down.

"Well, he seems cheerful and he should know re. the time we have," Rodney relaxed a little. He was thinking if they could go in in the dark it would enhance their chances of success.

They heard voices approaching and looked down the mound to see Staff and three Gurkhas climbing towards them.

"What now I wonder," Rodney waved to Staff. "What's up?"

"Couldn't let you have all the fun. We're setting up an observation point here with radio comms back to base. I'm spare at the moment as I don't have a jungle course in training just now so the Major arranged for me to hang back, so to speak. Thought you lot were stood down?"

"Yes and no," Sharky countered.

"The Major said you lot were mad. Let me introduce you to my team." Staff introduced the Gurkha captain and while his two radio men started to unpack their equipment, Sharky spoke to the captain.

Rodney pulled Staff to one side, "Staff, we think we will be leaving here around 1600 hrs for the border and aim to do whatever we need to do on the airfield from 1800 hrs onwards, it would give me some comfort if you could keep an eye on us and relay to James anything if we screw up. I'll take one radio with me but leave the rest here with you so we have communication, if that's OK with you? Plus, need to tell you we have another man over there now, called Den, who you may hear on the waves."

"Who's he then? He wasn't with you when you arrived."

"Sort of refugee, South African BOSS, left behind in the bush observing the target when his mates were lifted; he's an acquaintance of Sharky's so that's good enough for me."

"And what is this Den supposed to do when you lot fly off?"

"Ah yes, Sharky told him to make for here as a landmark and then make his way to the local town and get a taxi from there to HQ and ask for James to help him get a flight to Miami."

"That's going to please the Major, I don't think. Don't worry if he gets here, I will look after him and get him home. OK with that?"

"Thanks Staff. I'll make sure he knows that. I guess we had better let you get sorted."

"No problem. If you two make your way back to base camp now, there should be a brew on by now and lunch; if you like Gurkha curry, you're quids in." Staff held his hand out to shake Sharky's and Rodney's in turn, "Just like to say goodbye to you and tell you that I think this is a suicide mission and you're too old and foolish to go against the odds. Not as if you were young and foolish; in fact you're a little long in the tooth for this game if the truth be told. Good luck anyway and don't screw it up for us here." There was a warning in Staff's voice and Rodney could understand where he was coming from.

"Staff, you're right on all counts, but 'dienst is dienst' or duty is duty as the Germans say and that's why we pick up our pay and we believe you do have to stay alive to get paid," Rodney smiled and Staff chuckled.

"Sod off then, sir, and you, Sharky, watch his back."

At the base camp, the Gurkhas had set themselves up and the cook was already feeding Caroline and Mould when Rodney and Sharky joined them. The team ate and rested the afternoon away. Then they started to get ready. Around four o'clock, Rodney called them all together and inspected them and their flight bags.

"We may have an hour of good light, left, and then it gets dark quickly. Caroline, I'm sorry. Good as you look in the uniform I have decided that it is simply too much of a risk to take you with us," Rodney dropped his head waiting for the outburst which was not long in coming and Sharky and Mould exchanged looks.

"If I said you were a sexist pig, sir," Caroline emphasized the sir but she was calm, "would you feel I was overstepping the mark? I would have thought that my presence would be a distracting and positive contribution allaying suspicion that you were up to no good."

"Yes but..." Rodney started but Caroline interrupted him.

"But me no buts, I am coming." She stood hands on hips daring him to contradict. Rodney and the others, taken aback, could only laugh.

"OK, let's go. We are going to drive from here to the village just this side of the border and check in with Den and then we will make a decision when to go. Sharky, get on the radio and let Staff and Den know we are moving now.

They found their way to the village easily and stopped at the border café just short of the barrier. The barrier was manned and there was a sangar of sandbags on the other side, a dozen yards or so away, where a machine gun team sat lazily talking to each other.

Den had confirmed as they entered the village that the Russians were still inside the target house; evening was fast approaching. The team got out of the car and nodded to the border guards who were much taken with the aircrew uniforms and Miss Webster in particular. Rodney and Mould walked over to the café and bought four iced cokes from the owner, a dark native. The café was little more than a kiosk with a few dirty rusting tables and chairs outside under an awning. At the risk of getting their new uniforms grubby they all settled down to drink.

"Last chance, team; once we leave here there is no turning back."

"We go," said Sharky, the others nodded in agreement.

"So be it. Good luck."

They made their way to the car, Caroline giving a brilliant, disarming smile to the guards at the barrier who grinned back. When they were settled, Rodney started the car and turned it towards the border crossing.

Pulling up he wound down the window. One guard walked round the car while the senior man leant into Rodney's window eyeing Caroline. He spoke rapidly in Spanish; Caroline responded calmly telling him that they were a relief crew. He accepted the explanation and indicated to a scruffy guard leaning on the barrier to lift it.

"Welcome to Guatemala," he said without conviction and waved them through.

* * * * *

At the target house, Saied sat with his local hosts drinking while the Russians were in the workshop with the engineer. The hosts were worried. At the moment they were safe and could keep themselves hidden indefinitely in the house. But the problem was now getting on to the airstrip since the army had arrived in force. They thought that Saied as an outsider and an accredited tourist could get away with it but the others couldn't and as Ramos observed they were, after all, looking for payment for their services. It took all of Saied's persuasive powers to assure them that if he did have to go alone with the Russians, he would make sure they got their share. They settled uneasily for his assurance. There was little they could do. Before the reinforcement they could have seen the exchange and seen that they were paid off, now they may get nothing.

In the workshop, the Russian party wanted to get away. Although the testing was nearly complete and had gone well and although they had reconfirmed that their flight was still cleared to go out, there was obviously a niggling doubt that they may be refused at the last moment. They knew that Colonel Tsygankov, secreted on board the aircraft, would not let it leave without them. Still, it was getting dark now and the one matter they had not checked on was the situation regarding night flights.

They were a team, albeit newly formed, and they all knew their place. The colonel and his unsmiling quiet stillness made them wary.

Of all the groups involved, Rodney's situation was the most precarious. He pulled the car into the dirt car park at the rear of the control building. As dusk settled in, they watched the soldiers that had been sitting around the airstrip move into the hangars with their kit for the night. The team was now flanked on either side by a dangerous enemy. They could go forward but not back. The British troops would be behind them now and in the jungle-covered land to their rear, the soldiers this night might shoot first and ask questions later.

As the sounds of night took over, Rodney turned his head to his people, "Now," Rodney whispered, "this is what we are going to do."

A foot patrol appeared, circled the car park and went out the way it had arrived. The darkness thickened as the night established itself.

Rodney held out three straws for them to see. "OK, no arguments. With all the artillery out there and the Russians due, it's time to commit and time to move. There's no way we will get away with a covert approach to this. The aircraft steps are down and the door is open. We will openly drive up to the aircraft, walk calmly up the steps, crew bags swinging, chatting. We duck into the cabin, take out our handguns conveniently tucked into our waistbands and do the business. We then wait for the Russians to arrive on board, close the door and take the device. Call the car back. Get in, drive back over the border." He held out the straws, "Shortest gets the driver's job." Rodney was still a little rattled that the charter he had organized had not arrived, leaving his options limited.

The building that they were parked behind was little more than a shack. It served as the airport terminal and along with the hangars was filled with soldiers smoking or sleeping.

So far it had been easy. Rodney had spotted the areas used for different functions, stores etc.; he was looking for as much cover for the approach to the aircraft as possible.

At six, the soldiers stirred and moved to the feeding area at one side of the airport. By the look of them they were a mass of infantrymen and other corps. Nobody noticed them in the car but that would not last. Rodney wanted to move even though he had the impression that the force was made up of several different units and they would be able to stay under cover as long as they needed to. An officer joined the soldiers with a senior non-commissioned warrant officer. The man had a millboard with him and started calling out names. He was obviously reading out the next 'stag' to man the perimeter foxholes and observation posts. Rodney watched the men peel out of the dining area, led by the officer and the warrant officer. They would be taking the men to post them and to brief them on their responsibilities and their fields of fire. Rodney watched the soldiers straggle off after the officer with their equipment. They moved well and Rodney could see that if they ever pushed into Belize these soldiers would not be a pushover. He was impressed and made a mental note to report his thoughts when he got back, if he got back. He shook the thought from his mind; of course they would get back. Left behind were about half the men who moved from the eating area back to their resting places. Now, Rodney thought, while all this movement is going on.

"I got the straw," Mould said with disgust. Resigned, he got out of the car and opened Rodney's door. Rodney got out and changed places with him.

"Let's do it," Rodney said quietly.

Mould started the car and drove carefully along the route to the aircraft that Rodney indicated. With the few lights that were now on around the airfield there was just enough illumination to see, so Mould showed no lights. He drove slowly up to the aircraft without incident or challenge.

The three climbed out and Mould drove back the way he had come to wait for developments.

As the three climbed the aircraft steps, Rodney leading, followed by Sharky and then Caroline, a pilot appeared at the door of the plane and said hello to them. Caroline answered in Spanish, "Nice machine you've got; better up there than waiting around all day in this heat." He noticed Caroline and was immediately relaxed.

He volunteered, "My friend's not so hot, being a flyer. As you know, we are just an air taxi and I can tell you for nothing, we spend more time hanging around for clients than people realize. In a word it can be as boring as hell."

"Don't we know it; our aircraft should have been in to pick us up two hours ago. So we got bored too and thought a fellow crewman might take pity on us for a while. We wondered if we might bring you a little excitement!" Caroline smiled up at him; the pilot laughed and Rodney and Sharky took up the mood.

"Not a chance," retorted the pilot removing his well-worn cap to reveal a clump of dark unruly hair; he wiped the sweat from his brow, "Anyway, look at this lot." He indicated the soldiers and thumbed across to the south, "Going to have a go at the Belizeans at last I shouldn't wonder."

Sharky shrugged his shoulders, "Don't think so; more like an exercise; something up in the capital probably and the president just wants them out of the way for a while, I shouldn't wonder. Where are you flying to?" Sharky asked his question casually.

The pilot laughed, "I told you this was a waiting game. They hired us to fly in from Mexico and wait while they went off for a meeting. I expect them back sooner or later, but no matter; come and have a drink and cool down," he ducked back into the aircraft and they followed.

Once inside the aircraft, Rodney swept the space quickly. Two of the crew were asleep in the second row of seats, either side of the aisle; another behind them at the back of the aircraft; a third man, his head down working on something with only the dome of his head showing. The pilot had disappeared behind a curtain leading to the flight deck and galley. Sharky placed his bag on the first seat and drew his gun. Rodney gently drew his and with a hand on Caroline's shoulder pushed her down into the front seat on the other side of the aisle to Sharky. Rodney motioned to Sharky cover the aisle.

The pilot arrived with the drinks; he saw the guns and indicated his acquiescence to the inevitable. Rodney took out his radio and called Mould whispering, "Get yourself back here now. I want you to change places with Caroline, her task is done." He looked at Caroline, "Sorry, from here it may get messy. Take the car, go back to Staff and he'll get you home. Thank you for what you did but it's now up to us." She smiled back and left the cabin, walking back down the stairs as Mould drew up and Mould appeared in the doorway seconds later.

"Now Captain, we will take those drinks and then let's get your companions up."

Rodney, Sharky and Mould took the drinks from the tray the pilot was still holding out to them. They toasted him. The last thing Rodney saw before his head exploded was Sharky and Mould being covered by the two crewmen holding automatics. They had been feigning sleep and had come out of their seats like coiled springs. They cracked Rodney over the head and had then each pointed their weapons on Mould and Sharky who with drinks in hand were powerless to react in time.

Rodney stumbled forward and fancied he felt the floor of the aircraft come up to meet him.

Colonel Tsygankov uncoiled his large frame from his seat at the rear of the aircraft. "Well done, I hope you haven't killed him." He was serious.

The crewman shook his head, "No sir, he will not be out for long and will suffer no ill effects, maybe a little headache."

"Good, he and I have a lot to discuss," the Spymaster commented, holding the confiscated radio in his good hand.

He looked at Mould and Sharky, both of them nonplussed as to where the Spymaster had come from; he was the last man they had expected to meet again.

"Surprised, I think; and I am not sure what I should do with you. For the moment, sit," he indicated seats a few back from the front. "Tie them up and gag them." The crew moved, pushing Mould and Sharky into the seats. While one of the crew covered them, the other moved cautiously to bind them, never coming between them and the man covering them with the automatic.

Den looked at his set then put it back to his ear, "Who's that?"

"Rodney's busy."

"Just tell him the Russians are on their way back."

"Will do, thank you," Tsygankov smiled and turned off the radio. So they had a man observing the house, how clever. He called the pilot, "We will be leaving in a few minutes, as soon as the others arrive and we have concluded a bit of business, so start your checks please."

Five minutes later Polyakov and his party, along with Saied, clattered up the stairs of the jet into the cabin. "Success," he started to say and stopped, seeing the two men bound in the seats and Rodney still flat on the floor but stirring, "What's been going on here? Ah, Major Rodney Brown?" he looked at the colonel.

"Indeed it is; thankfully my crew were prepared for unauthorized boarders and they were easily overpowered. However, they do have others in the area so we need to get out of here now."

"My crew? I thought this was a private charter," Polyakov questioned.

"The plane, yes, the crew are ours; didn't I tell you, General? Now," he turned to Saied, "can we drop you off somewhere?"

Saied listened to flight checks going on; he was tempted but, not trusting the colonel, he rasped, "No, I have my own transport." Saied was in the entrance with his hand in his pocket; the pocket everyone knew was not empty. Any thoughts the Russian colonel may have had of not paying or of disposing of him were checkmated. Saied's lips curled in contempt; he sensed their disappointment. "The device checked out, therefore I need the money for the engineer and the locals. My money, now, please; the third payment for the job done."

Tsygankov eyed the man, "In view of your work and involvement we were hoping you might consider renegotiating the price and coming to work for us. Clever and professional people are difficult to come by."

"The money, please; when you have another task for me you know how to contact me," he jerked the gun in his pocket, "and please be quick."

"Pity." Tsygankov turned to Polyakov and the technocrat colonel, "You are happy?"

They confirmed the device had passed its tests. Colonel Carl Tsygankov, code name Blue, took a case from the rack and passed it carefully to Saied.

"Open it," Saied snapped.

The colonel shrugged and spun the lock dials, opening it to reveal a case full of dollars, tied in three large bundles.

"Empty it on the seat in front of me, so I can see all the notes and then repack it."

"Really, Saied, you are not being very trusting."

"Humour me," and then as an afterthought, "Please."

"Oh very well," snapped Tsygankov impatiently. "Major," he handed the heavy case over to Valeria Gershuni and she did as Saied had instructed.

"Thank you; now pack it up please." The tension in the tight space of the executive jet's passenger compartment was overwhelming and the heat was stifling. Rodney began to groan. He was still in the same position. He blinked and could see the shapely leg of Gershuni close to his face as she struggled to replace the money into the case. As she was kneeling to carry out her task, Rodney suddenly had the mad impulse to bite her calf. His mind was still a little muddled but he knew somehow she was involved. He gently lifted his arm a few inches and clasped her calf. She let out a whoop and straightened up. The distraction startled Saied for a moment, along with everyone else. Her reactions were fast as she chopped out at Saied. He easily caught the blow in his free hand and clamped his hand round her wrist and pulled her towards him. He then reversed the pull into a push and propelled her into the knot of people in the gangway. Without stopping he piled the remaining notes into the case, clamped the lid on tight and disappeared from the aircraft.

By the time order had been restored on the plane, he was long gone. The plane engines were now running up, and one of the crew had squeezed past to retract the steps and close the door.

"Damn, damn, damn! Excuse my outburst, General," Colonel Tsygankov was momentarily angry. "Your Major will be the death of me and has cost us a lot of money," he said to Mould and Sharky pointing to Rodney, now recovering and getting to his feet; Tsygankov added with the hint of a grin, "But you have to admit he has style." He said, looking at the KGB Major Gershuni, "I'll bet that's the first time a British agent has grappled with your leg and lived." His dry humour brought a smile to everyone's lips.

Rodney, shaking his head to clear it, added, "Felt great."

"Thank you, Major," Gershuni countered. All Rodney could manage was a weak smile as he cradled his head which felt as though it was splitting in two.

The revelry was cut short by the captain of the jet calling, "Colonel, there is something up. The soldiers appear to be excited about something out there. I think we had better get going before they come this way."

What had happened was that Caroline, instead of driving direct to the border, had stopped to watch the aircraft and to make sure the team were safe. When she saw the Russians enter the plane and then Saied leaving it and the door close, she just knew something had gone wrong. It took her seconds to decide; running to the eating area she found the captain and the warrant officer eating their supper after having set up the guards and patrols. Her Spanish was fluent so she had no problem convincing them that there was something wrong and that her crew had been kidnapped by the guerrillas; time for explanations and apologies later. The officer, alert and tense because of the situation, was on his feet and shouting. Caroline decided that this was the time to leave while confusion reigned.

Mould and Sharky looked at each other; the Guatemalans had obviously got their angst up about something. It wouldn't help any of them if they were boarded. "Take off now," the colonel ordered the pilot. "We'll have to decide what to do with these British later."

The captain, having completed his checks, must have done the quickest power-up flight of his career, for in moments they seemed to be rolling down the runway. He turned the jet for take-off, began to run up the engines to full power and then applied the brakes, throttling back, causing the aircraft to rock on itself.

"What's up, captain?" Gershuni was the first to react.

"They are blocking the runway with jeeps," was his worried reply.

Tsygankov rushed forward into the cabin. "Can't you get round them, man?" he asked, bent over and bobbing up and down trying to see over the pilot's shoulder. "There man, to the right, try to get your run down the road that leads off the airfield."

Soldiers were now deploying around them, and the jeeps closed the gap between themselves and the aircraft.

"You mean the main road to the border? I doubt I'd get airborne before I hit the custom post," the pilot said hopelessly.

"Do you want to spend the next twenty years in one of their filthy jails, or even worse?" the colonel's voice was calm.

"No," the captain stated, "I don't."

From his observation post at the ruin, Staff had a full view of the events and was relaying minute by minute developments to Belize HQ.

"Then do it. The road is fairly straight and it's clear on either side bar a few shanty structures."

The pilot took a deep breath. He rammed the throttles forward causing the colonel to topple against the empty co-pilot's seat; he manoeuvred himself down into it and strapped himself in. He sat tight-lipped as the pilot spun the jet and, with the engines roaring, accelerated along the rest of the short portion of the runway, then passed between two native houses before bumping up on to the road, where he picked up more speed. Tsygankov could see the buildings and trees flashing by faster and faster as they sped along the road. The pilot stamped on the left brake to slew the plane round, lining it up, then held the brakes at speed for a moment, while the engine roared and the vibration threatened to destroy the plane. Releasing the brakes, the plane catapulted forward, pushing everyone back into their seats.

The passengers, both Russian and British, gripped the sides of their seats and prayed. In the cockpit, the colonel and the pilot watched the road roll up in front of them; a chink to the left, a car driven off the road, several cyclists and civilians running for cover and others closing in on the side roads to see the spectacle. Then the customs post came into sight and the bridge over the river leading into the state of Belize. The customs post loomed large and then disappeared below them as the aircraft lifted. They were airborne. The pilot busied himself trimming the plane and easing the screaming engines out of the red to an acceptable climb thrust, turning half left at the same time.

Staff, from his observation post, immediately called up that the plane was in Belizean airspace. He sent a Land Rover to intercept the hire car to secure Caroline as soon as she was over the border and get her back to him. "What a mess; bloody civilians," was his take on the developing situation.

Tsygankov let out his breath slowly. "Well done." The pilot glanced quickly at him and nodded then returned to his instruments.

"What now, sir? We are in Belizean airspace." The pilot's eyes never left his flickering dials. "That's better," he said, almost to himself, "the port engine was overheating slightly but it seems to be coping now." He sat back and looked about, and then back to his radar screen, "Two small jets closing on us fast," he looked at Blue for instructions.

Major Collins and the commander were in the force command centre listening to the radio traffic and Staff's reports. "James, I've asked the Wing Commander to try to shepherd the jet on to our airfield; more than that we can't do. Now get yourself off. I need you fully functional now as my force ordnance officer. I will let you know how it goes."

Staff had watched the whole incident from the ruin. What he didn't know was who was in control. He had seen the runway blocked and the aircraft dive between the houses, which had saved those on board for the soldiers were unable to open fire without killing their own civilians. The guards on the customs post had been too startled to react. The airfield was returning to normal and the jeeps and soldiers stood down.

By radio, Staff passed the information to the force intelligence officer; he then left his vantage point and made his way down the hill to his Land Rover for refreshment and to await Caroline and Den, the South African, who, he felt sure, would make his way to him soon. He had decided, as he drank his over-sweet tea made with condensed milk, to drive back to Belize HQ as soon as they joined him.

Through all the excitement the Russians hadn't given the British on board the jet a chance to move. Colonel Ivanovich and Major Alcksandrovich had trained their guns on them steadily. When the plane levelled out, Major Gershuni bound them tightly to their seats with seat belts cut from other seats.

In the cockpit, Tsygankov concentrated on the radar screen. In moments the two illuminated bleeps developed on the display and began to close on them from inside Belize; the British! His thoughts echoed the pilot's who had also seen them.

"From the flight pattern and their speed, they have to be fighters," the pilot groaned; he waited for his master's orders.

"Take her as close to the ground as you possibly can; pick up the Belize River to your right and try to fly down it; it will take us to the sea." The pilot pulled the craft round and down.

Soon they were flying down the rapidly flowing, wide river, a silver phosphorescent streak in the night, between the monstrous mangrove and redwood trees and palms that fringed its banks.

In the Harriers, the radar picture of the jet disappeared and both planes slowed up and dropped low to try to see if it had ploughed in somewhere. They were over the site in three minutes; they swept the area, and on one of their circling sweeps the leading plane picked up a bleep on his screen away to the east as the pilot of the jet had to pull up to negotiate a tight river bend. The chase was on again. The two Harriers rocketed away to overtake the civilian jet.

Blue, watching the screen, was oblivious to the flying foliage and tumbling river that threatened to drag them out of the sky at any moment; the screen picked up the two jets on their intercept course and he grabbed the pilot's shoulder, "They are on to us again. Take her up and run for it." He waited for the craft to lift and to gather speed, "How long before they intercept us?"

The pilot studied the radar picture, "They are closing at about two hundred miles an hour and we have about twenty miles lead on them so they will be on us in about five minutes," he looked helplessly at the tall man in the co-pilot's seat.

"How far to the coast?"

"It will be coming up soon. The country's only sixty or so miles wide and we have been hitting three and four hundred knots at times since we took off."

Tsygankov sat for a while and then looked at his watch, "We've been flying for..." He didn't get to finish, for they burst out of the jungle and over the sea. With relief, he said, "I don't think they will pursue us now and even if they do, what can they do?"

"Shoot us down."

"Don't be silly, they're British. We are an unarmed civilian jet and they must know by now we have their people on board." He smiled, slapped the pilot on the shoulder and told him, "Heading about thirty degrees should fetch us up in Cuba. Carry on." He went back to see the others.

He found the British tight-lipped and his own team expectant. "I believe we are going to get away," he began. "I expect the British jets to buzz us in a few minutes or so but by then we should be far enough away to avoid anything more serious. Now, what are we going to do with our uninvited guests?" Colonel Tsygankov pondered.

"It looks as if we have little choice but to take them back to Russia with us," Polyakov said languidly, raising an eyebrow in the direction of Rodney who had looked up when the colonel had posed the question.

"What then?" it was Rodney.

"Difficult to say from this distance and at this time," Polyakov dismissed Rodney curtly.

"There is going to be hell to pay. You don't think that our people don't know that we are on board this plane?"

"If they do, all to the good, they are even less likely to shoot us down. Your masters are going to have enough trouble satisfying the Guatemalans that they didn't have anything to do with our escape." Polyakov laughed. "What do you think happened to make them attempt to block the runway like they did?"

"It was probably the Arab that arranged that, Colonel Tsygankov," Rodney commented, "Didn't exactly endear himself to you, did he? I take it that was Saied?"

"Yes, it was. Huh, you could be right, he was angry before today concerning another matter." Tsygankov slumped into a seat opposite Rodney, "Now, I hope you and your men are going to behave. We have a long way to go and I'd rather we did it in a civilized manner."

"If you mean a parole then forget it. But, tell me, what are you going to do with the device?" Rodney put in lazily.

"Study it, I expect," answered Tsygankov, "and what would you have done with it?" Tsygankov asked rhetorically. "Given it back to the rightful owners, of course. I don't think so, Rodney."

Valeria Gershuni, listening to the exchange between the two, giggled. Tsygankov and Rodney looked at her and at each other; it was a change to meet such a woman who also had a good sense of humour.

"Major Gershuni you could do better if you arranged for refreshments for all," she pouted but got up to go to the rear galley.

"Would you like a hand?" asked Rodney as she passed.

"Regrettably, Major, as you have refused to give us your word that you will not try to escape or make trouble, there you must stay, tied and trussed like a chicken," the way she emphasized the word 'chicken' made Rodney blush and he was not sure if it was from embarrassment or anger, but he knew if he had been free he would have slapped her.

As he was powerless to do anything his attention returned to Tsygankov, "What happened to the South Africans, I wonder?"

"The Guatemalans think they killed someone in Guatemala City so Saied fixed it for the local police to pick them up as soon as they got to Menchos. Actually it was the other way round. They will no doubt be releasing them as soon as the mix up is realized," Tsygankov said tiredly.

Rodney thought he had aged and looked weary and, above all, bored. "So, they knew they were coming?"

Before the colonel could answer, two shock waves hit the jet. It was the Harriers. In a flash they were back and seemed to the passengers so close alongside that they appeared to be extensions on either side of the jet. They could see the pilots clearly.

"Time I spoke to them, I suppose," Tsygankov lumbered out of his seat, "They are behaving very irresponsibly." Polyakov made a move to follow but realized he could not add gravitas so he relaxed back and sipped his drink, seemingly untroubled.

The captain's voice came over the intercom, "Colonel, the British pilots want to talk to you."

"I'm coming," shouted Tsygankov. "I'm coming," he added for a second time almost to himself. He had been apprehensive about this exchange. He knew it was important to keep them talking for as long as possible until they were forced to turn back to refuel. He knew that the Harriers' range was considerably less than theirs and they would have to break off the attack sooner rather than later. All they had to do was to get to Cuba and that was not too far away. Another 15 or 20 minutes and they would be safely into airspace that could reasonably be termed as within the Cuban sphere of influence. He settled back into the co-pilot's seat again; took the mike from the extended hand of the captain and spoke into it.

"Hello Royal Air Force, you appear to be very close; stand off, please."
He could almost hear the flight leader say to himself, "Cheeky sod."

A tiny disembodied voice floated from the speaker, "You have violated
Belizean airspace and you must return to Belize."

As if to emphasize the command, the Harrier to their right pulled
forward and the left Harrier throttled back a few feet; the fighter pilots
were turning them. The captain looked at Tsygankov hopelessly and he
looked with consternation as the compass needle began to swing.

"Don't let them turn you, damn you," said Tsygankov fiercely to the
captain.

"If I don't, we'll have a mid-air," the pilot spat.

"They wouldn't dare, they need their aircraft more than they need us.
Resume your course."

Try as he might the captain couldn't. The colonel's respect for the
Harrier pilots was grudging; they were good, too good he thought.
Tsygankov threw the transmit key again. "RAF you are violating our
right of way. Let us pass."

The calm voice came again. It was chilling to Blue's ears. "I am
ordered to bring you back. Your plane is now in our envelope; if you
attempt to gain or lose height to get away you will incur a collision."

"RAF you are acting illegally. We intend to resume our course in one
minute. The consequences after that time are on your head." Tsygankov
knew he was bluffing and so probably did they. The compass was almost
fully turned now; they were flying back to Belize. "RAF, for the last
time, will you let us resume our course?"

"Negative," was the reply and the Harriers closed up even tighter.

The jet's captain was good but he was in a cold sweat. He had to
fly for his life. In the distance, Blue could see the dark coastline of the
Belize coast appearing in the far distance against the curve of the earth.

"Reduce your speed to two-fifty knots and drop down to five thousand,"
the voice of the flight commander intoned, "and do it gradually."

Tsygankov sat back in frustration, he was beaten. His clever brain
began to compute all possibilities.

"Give me your Belize map set."

The pilot pointed to the map rack behind the co-pilot's seat and
indicated that the colonel would have to get them for himself as he was
too busy. From the back of the jet, Tsygankov heard a cheer from the
captives; he took no notice, the game wasn't over yet.

During the next five minutes they flew on in silence and Tsygankov pored over the maps of Belize. He spoke to his team and then to the jet's captain, then he settled down in his seat and watched out of his co-pilot's windscreen at the Harriers' silent escort. The Harrier pilots could be seen clearly and once or twice as the pilot glanced over to the Learjet, Tsygankov fancied the Harrier pilot was as nervous as his own.

"November 7L49," the Harrier's commander cut through Tsygankov's thoughts, "Change frequency to Belize International Frequency; acknowledge." The pilot picked up the microphone and looked at Tsygankov. The colonel nodded impassively, "Roger, wilco." The pilot relaxed back into his seat; he was to be taken in.

The voice of Belize air traffic control came floating over the ether and into the Learjet, startling them. "November Four Niner," the Belize control shortened the full jet registration for speed, "this is Belize; we have your radar contact, one four miles east. Turn right on to 270. Descend to three thousand feet on the QYE 1012."

The captain repeated the air controller's instructions routinely.

"Clear to and maintain three thousand feet on the QYE 1012, November Four Niner now."

"Leaving five four three," the pilot confirmed.

Control came through with the next set of instructions. "Belize, call level three thousand; you are cleared to join for an ILS approach to runway One Six Eight."

The captain checked his instruments and trimmed the craft, "November Four Niner copied and level three thousand feet. One Zero One Two, set."

"Roger, call out and establish on the ILS," Belize responded. "November Four Niner established." The Learjet was now following in the signal generated from the runway, down which it would travel to land.

The Learjet captain put down his undercarriage and Belize control came up immediately, "Roger check. Three greens," which meant his landing gear was down and locked. "Remain on this frequency for ground control."

A new voice clipped and military made Tsygankov sit up, "November Four Niner this is Belize Ground. After landing turn right at the first intersection. Follow the military vehicles to your designated parking area."

The jet was now fully committed to landing and as it swept down on to the runway that ran between the jungle on either side, the Harrier jets peeled off before beginning to let themselves down on to their landing pads using their revolutionary side-thrust vectored jets.

James and his colleagues, now clustered on the airfield, could only watch what happened next in horror. The jet's wheels screeched on to the tarmac throwing up a miniature dust storm. The waiting military and immigration officials waited for the noise of the reversing of the fan jets. It never came. The jet's engines roared and it accelerated along the runway until it attained take-off speed and then it completed a perfect roller, lifting off the ground to loop over the control tower and away.

James would have run for the communication rover to order a chase but the restraining hands of the local air commander and intelligence officer stopped him in his tracks.

James looked at them in puzzlement and annoyance and tried to free himself, "That's it, it's over. The Harriers need to refuel," ordered the intelligence officer, implying that they had tried but that was as far as they would go.

"But there are our people on board!" James was angry.

The British commander had come to the airfield and now stood in front of James, "James, we appreciate that, and that they are colleagues of yours. God knows how, but in case you have forgotten there has been a mini-coup or something in Guatemala this morning and other priorities have been allocated, not least your job responsibilities." The commander was sharp but then suddenly softened, "Look, James, we were prepared to have one try at getting your friends out of the mess they got themselves into but now we have to think about the sovereignty of this part of the world and I'm afraid until we know which way the General's successor is going to jump, then it's 'stand to' and be ready for anything. And that means all resources. And you are one of them. They were screaming for you back at the base to do your logistic bit when I left them, so off you go. The intelligence officer and I will deal with this now. I will talk to you later."

James just shrugged, "Thank you for trying, sir."

The commander and the air chief walked off. They were right and anyway Rodney was a big boy and had got out of worse scrapes than he was in now.

"I suppose they should be grateful we didn't shoot them out of the sky," James said out loud.

The intelligence officer, Captain West, with his unruly black hair, gave a little chuckle, "We did consider it but it was decided that it might cause all sorts of a stink and anyway we need, or may need," he corrected himself "all the missiles we have or should I say my ordnance officer has."

"Thank goodness for small mercies," replied James squinting into the sun and listening to the fading engines of the jet.

His frustration began to ease, "Will you or the Commander tell London?"

"That, regrettably, is my task and one that I am personally not looking forward to one little bit," replied the intelligence officer ruefully. On the airfield, the soldiers and airmen who were to have secured the jet and its occupants wandered back to their other duties. The local immigration officials, after their initial chagrin, trudged, hot and bothered, wearily back into the terminal building, disappointed at the loss of the jet and the bounty they might have had, had they been able to confiscate it.

Soon James was left alone with the intelligence officer; they watched briefly the preparations being made around the airfield should the Guatemalans decide to come. They watched the Harriers being refuelled and extra armaments being fitted, then they both realized that they had other tasks to attend to.

"Come on," said James "Did you say that they wanted this intrepid logistic officer at HQ to work his magic on ammunition, tables, food, fuel, aviation and ground miscellaneous, not forgetting the oils and grease," he paused smiling. "Socks, battle batteries, vehicles, trailers, tyres, weapons, equipment, defence stores, tents, rations, beer?"

"Stop for goodness sake, we know you supply people are needed," the intelligence officer laughed, all earlier tensions dissipated, "My car I think."

"So do I, my warrant officer took mine." When James got back to the office that he shared with his technical and specialist officers, he thumbed through the latest signals. His team of specialist warrant officers and their clerks were poring over papers, answering phones, and questions from staff and regimental officers who in large numbers squeezed in and out of the office. He worked fast clearing his desk and in fact, after a while, he felt for a moment a little surplus to requirements during a lull. After studying his wall map of the operational area kept up to date by a clerk, he delved through the latest resources states to make sure he knew how much he had of anything if he was asked. Then he returned to his desk, cleared a space and put his feet up. His staff saw him leaning back in his chair, an amused smile on his face.

"Where have you been, sir? The engineers and the whole of the G staff have been screaming for you all morning," the ammunition technical officer, noticing James for the first time, was a little rattled. Unlike the RAF who seemed to have unlimited manpower to out-load their munitions, his ammunition technicians were flat out, loading army needs from the theatre ammunition depots.

"I've been around here and there. Let's see how far we have got, shall we?"

"But they want you in the corridors of power, now."

"A few more minutes won't hurt at this stage. Come on boys, could a bunch of highly paid, highly trained and acknowledged experts tell me what you have done so far, so that when I do go and see the masters I know what I'm talking about and also what's yet to be done."

"Not a lot," was their combined reply; for a moment James thought they meant that they had done nothing, and then he saw them nudge one another.

The force warrant officer took over, "Fact is, sir, everything that can be done has been done," he then launched into the detail while James listened, going from planning table to planning table. He scanned the logistic planning document to operational plan and back to the maps. The warrant office rattled through the remaining logistic tasks ongoing on the ground.

James was very impressed, even though he worked with these men day after day, in crisis they shone. "What can I say to you all except you're worth your day's pay; very well done. Are you sure you really need me? You seem to have covered everything."

The sergeant major was the warrant officer that replied for the room, "We need you, sir, to keep us amused, to give us adventures and, of course, your wallet in the sergeants' mess when this is over. Right now, we need some tea if you wouldn't mind." The warrant officer handed him a briefing file with all the latest states and actions, "Your script, sir."

"Thank you very much. Now I know I really am surplus; just a mouthpiece." After he had made and poured the tea for them all, he left them grinning as he made his way to the main operations centre to find the latest on deployment that he and his team might need to make adjustments for and to answer any questions.

Far away now the Learjet cruised leaving vapour trails in the night sky. It had been a tense time for them over the airfield; they didn't know if they would be chased in again or shot out of the sky. After about ten minutes they had begun to relax. They were puzzled at the lack of response but nevertheless relieved, although a niggling doubt still lingered. The pilot and the colonel searched the radar screen for signs of pursuit but all was clear. Rodney, Mould and Sharky although relieved that they had not been shot down began to think about their fate. Rodney was relieved that Caroline had not been caught along with them but he could not help wondering if she made it back safely.

In the jungle, Caroline had changed back into her jungle greens and boots and sat round with the Gurkha cook in the base camp. He had prepared for her a mouth-watering chicken curry. It was hot by her normal standards but delicious and welcome. She would have liked a stiff drink but settled for a refreshing drink made up from army lemon powder commonly known as jungle juice.

After their escape, Tsygankov had had the pilot reset his course to Cuba, once it had been confirmed that he still had the range. When they were well on their way, Tsygankov left the cockpit and joined the others aft. The British were being shepherded one at a time to and from the toilets and then fed in a similar fashion.

Tsygankov joined Polyakov sitting opposite, "Well, Colonel, what is the latest?"

"We should be landing in Cuba within the hour. I took the initiative to call ahead and we will be treated with diplomatic courtesies; so we will be able to stay on board until a plane is made ready for us to fly direct to Moscow. The embassy even offered to bring us some food and anything else we required. I'm afraid I used your rank, General, to impart the necessary sense of urgency."

"I have to say Colonel that I had my reservations about you, but seeing you in action this little while I must tell you I am grateful to you and I will do all in my power to get your rank back."

"I confess this mission was important to me. It has been a long time since I was able to get back into the field. Yours and the Director's trust is all that I want."

"Nonsense, my dear Tsygankov, I have been little more than a spectator. The success of this mission is down to your detailed planning and foresight against contingencies," Polyakov was deadly serious.

"Thank you, General. I always thought the rank of Brigadier General would be a good rank to retire on, not to mention the pension." He smiled and added, "I did say I was not a vindictive man but I do find myself feeling slightly self-satisfied to have got Major Brown into a bit of a fix. I expect we will swap him and his men for something as the British will no doubt be pleased to have them back."

They both turned in their seats to look at Rodney.

Rodney was eating his plastic airline meal and washing it down with a very fine wine. He raised his glass as Tsygankov appeared in his vision. Although his mouth was curved into a smile of greeting, the Russian noticed that Rodney's eyes were cold.

Tsygankov studied Rodney for a moment and remembered again that this man was the cause of his demotion some five years ago. Tsygankov had of course seen him operate in Cyprus when Rodney had taken him prisoner. Events there had moved so fast that he hadn't had the time to really get to know him and to understand what made him tick; perhaps this time he would. Tsygankov for all his coldness was interested in people and he was good at his job as an arch-manipulator who took care to develop the people that were needed in the service. Like Rodney, he was a fixer with a good organizational brain. He smiled, not to Rodney but at their nicknames, himself the Spymaster and Rodney simply, the Major.

"Salute, Major," Tsygankov raised his glass.

"Salute, Brigadier," Rodney echoed.

The moment between the two men was broken but their eyes and minds had locked on the past.

Not brigadier yet, thought Tsygankov, but soon. He settled back into his seat and let his mind race back in time to the Cyprus affair.

In his seat Rodney sipped his wine closed his eyes and also reran the last time they had been tested against each other.

Part Two

THE CYPRUS AFFAIR

Chapter 20

THE CYPRUS AFFAIR

It had begun when the duty officer's phone rang and Graham Swain had clambered out of the camp bed, stretched his long body and checked the time by squinting out of one eye at the electric clock staring at him from above the operations desk.

"3 am, who the hell can this be? Bloody nuisance," he thought, reaching for the phone. "Swain."

"513 duty desk?"

"Yes," Graham was wide awake immediately. The voice on the telephone was heavily accented; nobody outside the five or six departments should be coming in on this phone, especially with an accent like that. It shook him. He grabbed his log sheets and pen, and then switched on the tape machine connected to the phone and quickly put on his glasses almost dropping them in his haste.

"Fetch your director, Brigadier Robinson; I will call again in one hour. Tell him it's Chekhov," the man added, almost as an afterthought. The line went dead. Graham took the handset away from his ear and stared at it nonplussed and somewhat bewildered. He automatically reran the tape and listened carefully. Did he call out the director or not, or a section head? As Graham had only been with the department for a few weeks and had transferred with promotion from Special Branch, he did not want to make a mistake.

He reached his decision in his usual way, "Sod it, if I am wrong, I am wrong." He looked up the director's number which would be rerouted to wherever he was.

It rang for a few moments, "Robinson."

"Sir, it's the Duty Officer. I've a message for you, sir," Graham said in slow measured tones, once the director had grunted into the phone and ungraciously identified himself.

"Well, get on with it," snapped Robinson, "or are you going to keep me up all night?"

Touchy, thought Graham, "Chekhov phoned and he will be calling again in exactly fifty-five minutes from now. He wants to speak to you."

"I'll be there." And after a pause, "You did the right thing, ringing me, well done." The duty officer let out his breath. He had not realized how nervous he had been. Still, you didn't get your boss out of bed at three o'clock in the morning every day and get away with it, especially if your boss was a man like the brigadier who demanded a great deal of his staff, whether they be in the field or desk-bound at base. Graham started to update his log, recording the events of the night and then tidied the duty room.

"Well," he thought, "at least cleaning up will pass the time until the Old Man arrives." He also realized that something quite exceptional was about to happen. It had to be very important to get the boss out of his bed at this time in the morning. He finished his tidying up, sat down at the desk at last, and looked at the clock, quarter to four, 15 minutes to go. He became aware of someone else in the room; his scalp crawled and he threw himself round in his swivel chair, ready to spring. He found himself looking into the dark intense eyes of his chief who had noiselessly let himself into the room and was standing over him reading the log.

"Bit jumpy aren't you, Graham?" said the brigadier derisively. Praise does not keep you in good stead very long here, thought Graham thinking back to the "Well done," of 50 minutes ago. Need to remember that.

"Sir, just startled; I confess that I had assumed you'd ring to get me to let you in."

"If you never assume anything, you may, and I do say may, live to a ripe old age," smiled the brigadier, although Graham could see from the look in the old man's eyes that he meant it. "Otherwise you're going to die before your time. Now, I would like a cup of coffee and then I want you to wait outside until I've finished talking to friend Chekhov."

"I can get you a coffee but my orders do not allow me to leave the desk unattended until the day officer takes over," Graham said with some trepidation.

The brigadier looked at the duty officer and was about to let loose but stopped himself, instead he said tiredly, "Don't be an ass, Graham, I made that order and I can also break it, now just get me a coffee, there's a good chap."

"Aye aye, sir, sorry," Graham conceded. He disappeared into the alcove to make the coffee. On second thoughts, he made one for himself too; he gave the brigadier his coffee and then withdrew.

Brigadier Robinson was well over 60, however, he was well built and still hard despite his years. He sprawled in the chair, his left hand stirring the coffee with a pencil and the other cradling the hand piece of the phone, his grey hair stuck out over the curled up collar of his British warm, officer pattern greatcoat. Really must get a haircut tomorrow or rather later today, thought the brigadier to himself, then he turned his attention to the coffee and thought of his first meeting with Chekhov. It had been just after the surrender of Germany. He had been an intelligence officer and Chekhov, his younger counterpart in the Russian army. Despite the intervening years it seemed like only yesterday

They had met often at the War Trials and it soon became apparent to Robinson that, for a price, Chekhov could be bought and was prepared to be useful. Despite his youth, the Russian was sensible enough to insist that his only contact would be with him. Chekhov, according to tradition, was given the code name 'Red Five'. Over the years, Chekhov had grown rich, his spoils logged away safely in a Swiss account. In all fairness, despite his mercenary side he had given good value. He had once explained to Robinson that money was his country now. He was clever and had seemingly remained undetected all those years. Why, therefore, now, wondered the brigadier. Had he been compromised by declaring himself tonight using not only plain language but a public telecommunication system instead of coding a message, he must be desperate? It could only mean that he needed to come over to the West and soon; just how soon, Robinson was shortly to find out. He was already beginning to mentally compute the means of getting Chekhov out when the telephone rang, cutting off his train of thought and jerking him back to the present.

"Robinson?" said a voice in his ear as he lifted the receiver; he recognized Chekhov immediately.

"Chekhov, how are you?" the Brigadier responded.

"My old friend, never better, but I've got to come out, it's time. I am no longer fully trusted." No surprise, thought Robinson.

"No doubt you have something to sweeten your retirement?" It was not an idle question and Chekhov knew it.

"Of course; a complete list of our people in western Europe including the UK and all that goes with it, and a sprinkling of US deep cover etc. Do not ask me where it came from. I do not have long, I am phoning you from Turkey and I will be in Cyprus later today. I'm part of a small team sent to meet certain Turkish gentlemen sympathetic to Mother Russia." The brigadier's eyes closed to slits. Another link in the intelligence coming in that the Turks were preparing to make a move against the Greek Cypriots, he wondered.

"For my information," went on Chekhov, "and my retirement, I want £250,000 in diamonds and the same in US dollars and of course a British passport; on receipt of it, I will disappear. I have been planning my disappearance for some time and will cause you and your government no embarrassment. Is it agreed?"

"Wait," the brigadier sat back and thoughtfully watched the second hand of the clock tick over 15, 20 seconds. "No, Chekhov, make it £150,000 in each product; I can authorize that myself and it will be quick," Robinson thought coldly, with luck I may even make a profit out of the Americans, French and Germans; they would certainly contribute.

"OK, you tight-fisted capitalist," retorted the Russian without rancour and the brigadier allowed himself a chuckle at the Russian's expense.

"I'll be in front of the Hilton Hotel, Famagusta this evening, a hundred metres offshore. Send your man, make it Seabrook, I know him by sight."

"You are not giving me much time."

"I do not have much time my friend, nor does that beautiful island before it explodes into chaos. The Turks and Greeks do not realize what they have, such a shame, and for what? A few miles of beach and years of misery for their people." He swore and then got back to the meeting plan, "Seabrook should be on the hotel patio facing the sea at seven o'clock local time this evening, I know you can arrange it; got to go now," Chekhov rang off. There was nothing else to say, thought Robinson; it was time for his department to get moving.

Despite what he had told Chekhov, he still had to get clearance from the minister for an out-of-country operation. He looked at the clock. Still a bit early to call him but he could sort the team out in the meantime. In addition, there was the matter of how he would put the proposal to the minister, after all, in this financial climate, even at the knock-down price of £150,000 it had to be justified. Of course the 'friends', the Americans and even the French and Germans, could be persuaded to contribute handsomely, he thought again, he might even make a profit.

"Graham!" Robinson called him back in.

"Yes, sir," Swain appeared at the door.

"I want you at six o'clock to call the following, so take some notes please. But first, more coffee and then tell me how you're settling in."

They sat at opposite sides of the duty desk, sipping their coffees. Graham had made the usual noises about enjoying his new environment and now they were getting down to business.

"Call Major Brown at six; tell him to come in to see me and to be in my office by 0700 hrs latest or he's sacked. That is all you tell him. If he asks, you do not know why, which, incidentally, you do not. Then call Mould, Sharky and Seabrook and tell them to get ready to go somewhere hot, today, and to be here with their kit for 0800 hrs. In the meantime get me, as soon as possible, any flights to Cyprus from 1100 hrs today onwards. At 0730 hrs call the minister and patch him through to my office. Got all that?"

Graham repeated the orders back, word for word.

"Good, now get one of the messengers to go out and get you and me some breakfast. Full English, nothing else will do. In addition, do not go off duty today without checking in with me. I will be in my office if you want me. Don't forget to impress on the messenger that the breakfast request is from me and that a sense of urgency would be appreciated." Robinson took out a ten pound note and passed it over. He was ravenous; whether it was the excitement of the situation or comfort food he did not know and did not care.

By seven o'clock Robinson was fed and the arrangements, thanks to his duty officer, had been set in place. The brigadier had decided to keep Graham on the inside team, he thought it would help his integration into the squad and give him the sort of experience it would take years to acquire otherwise.

A meeting with the team he had chosen to carry out the exchange had been set up in his large dusty wood-panelled office for eight thirty. Robinson looked up at the picture of the Duke of Wellington in full uniform and mounted on his charger; the Iron Duke seemed to be looking at him with a look that said you are too old for all this; Robinson smiled slightly, you, old soldier, were still active when most men would be in their bath chair.

Getting back to the present, Robinson was feeling somewhat miffed; for some reason the minister had insisted that he be present at the briefing and this had concerned him. He felt that this was still an in-house operation until the list of agents was delivered. His gut reaction was to object to outsiders seeing too much of the way he operated and especially the machinery that set it up. He was resolved to get rid of as much routine of the action for the operation as he could before the minister arrived; he'll never know the difference anyway, he thought. He quickly went through his operations procedures and by seven thirty he was ready to proceed. First, he called his aide, the deceptively jovial Major Rodney Brown, known to his peers simply as Rod the Bike because of his passion for high-speed motorcycles, although, due to a leg injury, he was no longer able to ride competitively and the brigadier had begun to hear people simply refer to him as the Major; Robinson thought this was a sign of maturity and it pleased him.

Because of the unique position of the section, they were not housed with the two main secret service branches but had a secure suite of offices in one of the corridors of Northumberland House, much to the annoyance of the RAF who thought the building their special preserve.

He looked at his clock and thought his section leader should now be in and rang for Rodney; when he appeared, he began quickly, "Morning Rodney, everybody here?" Rodney nodded. "Good, Rodney I have some tasks for you and they have got to be carried out quickly."

"Sir?" Rodney was intrigued; it was not often he had a summons at this time of the morning.

"Firstly, this is for your ears only," he summarized the situation in a few curt sentences, "Now, are you ready?" he concluded before going on with his orders.

"Yes, sir." What an incredible scoop for the old man and their department, was all that Rodney could think until he realized that if something went wrong then, conversely, the old man's head would be on the block; therefore, whatever he was asked to do, he had better get it right or his head would roll too.

The brigadier shuffled his papers until he got to his task listing, "Rodney I want you to carry out the following tasks in the order I give them to you." Robinson paused, "Firstly, make sure Seabrook, Sharky and Mould are in this office at five minutes to nine o'clock. Secondly," the brigadier went on without a pause, confident in Rodney's ability to take instructions and to carry them out accurately and without question, "get three places on the 12 o'clock flight to Larnaca and have a Consular Q car waiting for Seabrook et al with small arms and field kit, scopes etc., you know the score. Yes, they're going to Cyprus, and then book them on the midnight flight back, got that?"

"Yes, sir."

"Lastly, for the moment anyway, get security to get a messenger to take this order across to the Bank of England to collect the diamonds and the money. He won't know what he is being given, so just tell him to bring the packet to you unopened and," he added, "he had better not lose it, for it'll be his pension and mine, which also means yours, Rodney, down the drain, do I make myself clear?"

"Most clear, sir," said Rodney with a grin; he had been with the brigadier long enough to allow himself a few liberties now and again and, clearly, the old man must be under some pressure to carry this one off; Rodney knew he would appreciate a little humour making light of a difficult situation. "Just leave these tasks in my hands; if I experience any difficulties I'll let you know immediately." Rodney left Robinson to work out the rest of his briefing for the minister and the rest of the team. He did not actually expect to have any difficulties in fulfilling his boss's requirements. He was the department's best fixer, but he appreciated that time was bloody short.

By five to nine the agents were in the brigadier's office, their flights and transport fixed, and the messenger had gone to collect the diamonds. He calculated that they would be back before ten, when the agents would be flown by the stand-by helicopter to Heathrow in good time to catch the flight to Cyprus. Lucky sods, he thought.

Rodney knew that the leg wounds he had received in Borneo barred him from many field jobs. His pet theory was that any army officer like himself brought up through the army system with a little bit of espionage training could leave the prima donnas of the department standing. He was determined to try it one day, despite his gammy leg. Little did he realize, that day was not far away. It was just before nine when he entered Robinson's office. The briefing had not yet started. Robinson was making the introductions of his men to the minister, The Right Honourable Ronald Peter Lawson. Rodney nodded to the brigadier to indicate that all was well and the brigadier's heavy head moved perceptively in acknowledgement.

"Minister, I believe you've met my deputy during your national service days in the Far East?" the brigadier's voice sounded almost vindictive. When the minister turned, he found himself face-to-face with the man he had left to die in the jungle more than 12 years ago. How the old man had managed to tie the two men together, Rodney did not know, but he had. The brigadier turned half away but continued to watch the two men as they faced each other. He saw the blood drain from the minister's face as his shoulders drooped and he saw a series of emotions move over the face of his deputy.

Then Robinson saw Rodney regain his control almost instantaneously and imperceptibly; good man, thought Robinson and he saw Rodney step forward smiling, hand outstretched to the minister.

"How nice to be working for you minister after all these years," Rodney had followed the minister's career but never expected to meet him again.

"Err, Brown!" began the politician and then more confidently, "How are you?"

Smooth bastard, thought the brigadier as he saw the minister regain something of his aplomb and the man's high colour return.

Rodney countered, "Couldn't be better; we must have a talk about old times sometime, sir." That's it, thought Robinson, turn the screw.

"Yes, we must Rodney and let's make it very soon. How about lunch today? But I expect you will be too busy with this mission."

"I'd be delighted, sir, if the brigadier doesn't need me?"

Well done, son, turn the screw. The brigadier did not think the minister had expected Rodney to take up his offer so this was worth giving his deputy a few hours off, god knows he would be busy soon enough, "Not at all, the prep work's done, team's ready to go and Rodney will be free after this meeting until this evening. You both go and have some fun." The minister looked at the bland expression on the brigadier's face and decided that he couldn't be sure if the head of the department was having a joke at his expense or not, but he nevertheless had the decided feeling he was being put down.

The minister decided to take charge of the situation and said, "Shall we get on?"

"Yes, shall we? Please be seated. With your permission, Minister,

I will begin." The rest seated themselves in old battered leather chairs strewn around the room but all facing the brigadier's heavy and overlarge mahogany partners' desk. Sitting down, Robinson began and it took five minutes only for him to summarize the situation and give the background on Chekhov. As Chekhov's current position was in a post not unlike the minister's, it was a possibility that Chekhov could deliver what he claimed. He covered the necessity for 'need-to-know', confident that his team would not leak; he was not sure about Lawson. He not only instinctively did not like him, there were disquieting rumours among his fellow directors. Finishing on actions so far, he called for questions.

Seabrook made a comment, "Interesting he called for me by name. This must mean I am compromised. Not really a shock at my age and my years in the field. Looks like you will need to find me a desk after this, sir. As for the task, it's straightforward on the face of it, so no questions," Seabrook sat back, job done.

Mould and Sharky, the terrible twins, looked at each other and shook their heads.

"Let me say," the minister said, making an attempt at humour, "there had better not be!"

"I have every confidence in my people," countered the brigadier seriously. "I think I can guess why you were chosen, Seabrook; I rather think Chekhov knows you are a middle-tier agent who the Russians would not associate with anything as devastating for them as the list. In other words they do not see you as a threat and will assume you are intelligence gathering on the Turkish/Cypriot situation if they spot you at all. Now if there are no more questions, off you go with Rodney who will sort the money end and other matters. Good luck and I will see you all when you get back." Adding as an afterthought, "And so I suspect will the minister."

"Indeed and please make sure the package arrives here seals intact."

"That would be normal procedure," assured Seabrook, all the while thinking that the old man would want them to have a look at the exchange to ensure they were not being sold a pup.

After the team had left the brigadier and the minister in the office, it soon became clear to Robinson that the minister was nervous and worried and it was all he could do to settle him down. It transpired that he had not referred the issue upwards which was very unusual for such a potentially important intelligence catch as there appeared to be on offer. The test of the man's strength of character, Robinson decided it would be if anything went wrong, and in these jobs something could always rise up and bite you. Still, he mused, the job is well set up despite the shortness of time and he was not overly worried provided the team was not mixed up in the Turkish/Cypriot problems; unlikely, but you never knew.

After he had got rid of the minster he called his contact on the Middle Eastern desk. What he heard did nothing to ease his doubts that simple jobs can go wrong. His contact told him that there was a lot of military activity on both sides, not only in Cyprus but also on the mainlands of Turkey and Greece. Worse, the Turkish navy was at sea. His contact told him, "If things stay the way they are, it may blow over, but I will let you know, if you're interested, if matters deteriorate." The man was fishing and he knew it; Robinson asked him to do so immediately. His contact pressed him for information and for why he was so interested and gave him a gipsy warning of the consequences if he found Robinson or his men playing in his part of the world.

Hell, thought Robinson, looking up at the Iron Duke staring down at him, I don't care what you say, it's time I handed over to somebody, but to whom? He rang for his mid morning tea from his secretary.

Not far away, an hour later in a high-class bistro, the minister was talking animatedly into a telephone. He was reporting into his Russian handler. Lawson had belonged to them for some time and was now frantic, for if the Chekhov list had his name on it he was finished.

If my name was on the list, it would probably head the list, Lawson thought as he was negotiating with his handler, "Best they stop Chekhov in Turkey if it's not too late. Failing that, they need to meet him in Cyprus at Nicosia Airport and do the necessary. God forbid that fails, then we would need five men at my disposal from twelve tonight to intercept the list when it arrives in the UK. Should it all fail, transport must be available to get me out to East Germany. Understand?" There was nothing nervous about Lawson now; he was in control and apparently capable. Lawson had made his high office with every help his Russian masters could afford him. They would be disappointed if all the money and effort they had put in was wasted, especially as he had only held his present post for a few days and their payback had not yet begun. He realized this and he had to do everything he could to avert a disaster at this early stage of his ministerial career. His masters would want him to progress higher and higher, so he could count on their support to head off this issue.

The other issue that he now had to face, and he had thought was buried, was when he and Rodney had been members of the Special Forces on the Borneo border duties. They normally put in three men at strategic points along the top to spot the insurgents' movements over the border. When the insurgents were sighted, the regular army and Gurkha strike groups would ambush them. The technique was very effective.

Early one morning, when they had been in place for a few weeks, they were attacked by a small section of six insurgents who had tracked them in the jungle. In the resulting fight with the insurgents, the third man of the party was killed and Rodney took fire in his legs before he and Lawson killed their attackers. In the firefight the radio had been shot up and their only contact with the outside world was lost. With relief still two weeks away and no radio contact, they were on their own. No radio contact to base would mean no activity as radio traffic was only used for contact with the enemy; the procedure in this case presented a major problem. Lawson was left with Rodney badly wounded and probably dying and him safe, untouched but in a compromised location.

Although they had successfully dispatched the insurgents, others would not be long in coming to look for them. When Rodney passed out, Lawson calculated he would eventually bleed to death and he decided to leave and try to get back to his own lines. For the sake of appearance, he bandaged up Rodney's legs and gave him a shot of morphine before abandoning him. There was another group he knew ten miles to the east and he decided to make for them. Rodney was fortunate; when Lawson left he, Rodney, did not know that he was under observation by two of the indigenous Iban natives who were out hunting for food. They pulled Rodney out of the death area, stopping his bleeding with leaves and mud. They then carried him gently down to their village in the interior. The shot of morphine had probably saved Rodney's life in those first few hours but Lawson thought it unlikely that act would go anyway to absolve him in Rodney's eyes for leaving him in the jungle to die.

Rodney spent three months with the Iban as they skilfully but without ceremony removed bullets from five wounds. He did not remember anything for several weeks after they fixed him up. Initially, through a red curtain of pain as he recovered, he shared the Iban's primitive environment, food and fear of the visiting insurgents. During these visits, he was hidden in a jungle hide at the back of the kampong. Why he was never handed over to the terrorists, he never found out. He could only suppose that the natives were loyal to their code that a man given hospitality meant more to them than a few pieces of silver or whatever the going rate was at that time.

When he was eventually returned to the British by the natives, he found that he was not only listed as killed in action but also that his team report indicated that he was dead at the time he was abandoned. However, as his commanding officer pointed out to him, yes, he may have been left too early and Lawson may have been able to do more, but as Lawson was no longer in the theatre of war and was on his way home to be demobbed, why make waves; the CO reminded him that at least he had his life, the third man in the team did not.

Rodney was still in recovery and weak. Under normal circumstances, he would probably have made a fuss about his abandonment but he let the hurt lay. Another time, he promised himself. As a young captain, his active career was over, or so he thought. Once back at the regimental headquarters in the UK he had found some sympathy but also the knowledge that he was not going anywhere ever again. A few years later, fed up with the regimental job he had been given, they offered him the rank of major, a pension and a desk job in the Home and Foreign Office security services.

At one o'clock, Rodney entered the bistro, walking strongly to hide his limp, approached the minister's table where he eased himself into the chair opposite the man who had left him to die alone in the jungle all those years ago.

"Minister, I hope I am not too late and I have not kept you waiting too long. Regrettably, I had a few details to sort out before I could escape the office."

"Not at all, I had a few calls to make anyway and it gave me the chance to look at today's menu which I commend to you. I am not in a rush, no appointments till three this afternoon, so let's enjoy what they have to offer, not to mention some very fine wines." Lawson passed the menu to Rodney and called the wine waiter over. While Lawson selected an expensive red, Rodney quickly scanned the menu and chose spaghetti bolognese with garlic bread. He reasoned that in such a fine Italian as this, the meal would be excellent. He passed it back to Lawson indicating what he would like and the minister ordered for them both.

The waiter bought the wine and poured it. After they had sampled it, Lawson began, "I wanted to talk to you Rodney about that incident in the Far East, sort of clear the air really. I should have contacted you years ago but with work and the passage of time, well, you know... I want to put my side of the story before you say anything. I know it will have been on your mind since we met this morning. I did not just run out on you, although in a way I did."

Rodney found himself tensing his leg, it still gave a twinge from time to time, and he felt the familiar tremor. He was surprised at his reaction and clamped his fist on his legs under the table. The minister noticed Rodney's pallor; he had gone quite grey.

"I say, are you all right?" he appeared concerned enough for Rodney to find himself apologizing to the man he blamed. He realized for the first time since the incident that he may have judged the man too harshly. He had, Rodney acknowledged, fought bravely in the firefight. It was a fact he had been left but, after all this time, did it really matter? Would he have done anything differently? He didn't know; it was another life, another time.

Rodney realized that he was left with mixed feelings of contempt and pity for Lawson and that the trembling in his legs had stopped; the hate he had been carrying for Lawson all this time had completely dissipated. He grinned to himself; of course the man did not know how Rodney was going to react. Certainly, he could not afford a scandal in his position. He made up his mind that as far as he was concerned the incident was closed and he said so. Nevertheless, he wanted to hear what Lawson had to say.

"Please call me Peter," said Lawson relieved, "After all, we were friends once and shared the same room in the mess for nearly two years."

"I am fine about it," Rodney's colour had returned. "It occurred to me just now that you must have thought over your actions as many times as I had thought of them, albeit in a different way. Anyway, tell me your side of the story; I really would like to hear it." Rodney noticed a waiter who kept looking their way; he recognized him as one of Robinson's undercover men who flitted in and out the office. He ignored the man but wondered why the old man had seeded the restaurant; he would no doubt have his reasons.

"I will tell you," Lawson swirled his glass, looking at Rodney through the thin area of red liquid. "After the shoot-out when, by the way, we did the lot, I did not even get a scratch. I checked out you and Dave. Dave was dead; he caught it in the head. I checked you and you were unconscious, bleeding like a stuck pig all over your lower body. Your pulse was weak and I assumed you were dying. You were, in any case, way past any help I could give you. Nevertheless, I did what I could to make you comfortable and tied rags round your wounds. The radio was shot to pieces so we were stymied. No way to call for help. I gave you a massive shot of morphine – not enough to kill you but enough that you would feel no pain if you regained consciousness. Then it was time for me to get going to the next post some ten miles away. But, as you know, in the jungle that mileage is multiplied many times. I did contemplate putting you out of your misery but couldn't do it. Rightly or wrongly, I decided to leave you just in case. And, against all the odds, that proved to be the right decision." He paused, "It took me two days to find the other group. It took another two days to mount a helicopter into our hide. You had gone, but everything else was as I left it. There was some evidence of animal attack on the bodies. The bodies had been stripped and our kit was gone. We assumed the headhunters had found the site and taken what they wanted. And you with your golden hair had gone the way of many heads in that part of the world."

"Didn't the fact that my body had gone alert anyone to the possibility I may be alive?"

"Afraid not, Rodney. We assumed that they had buried the remains somewhere to avoid awkward questions from the authorities as headhunting was frowned on, although I am told it still goes on today."

"Jesus!" was all Rodney could say.

"Yes, I know, I'm sorry. If there is anything I can do to make up to you, just say. I know it's a bit late but I can make life very easy for you now."

Rodney was silent for a while. "As far as I'm concerned, the whole incident is just a bad memory. I may have done the same as you in the circumstances. Then again, maybe I wouldn't. Who really knows until they're in that position?"

"That's the way," beamed Lawson, obviously delighted.

Rodney did not want him to get off that lightly so he plunged in once more, "But just tell me one last thing, what did you think when I turned up alive and kicking?"

"I didn't know what to think; I waited for you to come ranting at me and when you didn't, I decided to sweat and wait it out. I should not have, I know that now. I should have gone to see you then. As the years rolled on, the incident began to fade; I was busy building a career, but the incident was reawakened every time I read of the death of a soldier in some part of the world. You were right when you said I had relived the incident many times. The meeting today was a complete surprise. I had no idea that you were actually working in my department of the Ministry. All I can say is that I'm glad you've taken it in the spirit you have. I shall be eternally in your debt."

"Supposing I hadn't, and decided to make a fuss, what then?" asked Rodney mildly.

"I would rather not contemplate that," grinned Lawson, "because I don't know what I'd have done. I would not wish to give up what it's taken me such a long time to acquire."

"I can understand that. Anyway, Peter, enough of the past horrors; I see our food is coming, so let's enjoy it and talk of the future. I personally would like to run my own department."

"And so you shall, dear boy, and so you shall." said Lawson with a wink. "And I dearly want to be the prime minister, and shall be," stated Lawson, beaming from ear to ear.

Rodney could see that while Peter's face was smiling his eyes told another story – that the man was in deadly earnest. Therefore, he raised his glass and said, "Shall we drink to our mutual future? Good fortune, should it ever happen."

"Rest assured, dear boy, it will, it will." Lawson downed his glass and called for more wine. By the time the two men left at three o'clock they were both in high spirits and the bistro owner was pleased to see them go.

They sauntered down the road for five minutes to sober up and arranged to do the same thing again the next month, little knowing that the date would never be kept. They took separate taxis to their places of work and both received news that would sober them up very quickly indeed.

Chapter 21

THE MINISTER

Lawson arrived at Westminster at a quarter past three, paid off the taxi and ambled his way cheerfully to one of the offices he used for his constituency work and where he intended to sit quietly and await the news of Chekhov's demise, he hoped.

He was not unduly concerned for, like the brigadier, he had complete confidence in his own operatives to take out one man who, although an ex-soldier, had spent the last 25 years going soft in a clerical environment, although that environment had been at the very nerve centre of the KGB. Goodness, suddenly the minister was unnerved, what Chekhov could tell would be nobody's business, never mind the fact that he could destroy Lawson completely.

As he walked back into his ministerial office, he could hear his secretary packing up to go.

"Hello, just off?" he said as his fussy but efficient secretary looked up from the task of putting her things in her bag.

"Yes, Minister, I was, but as you're back would you like me to stay to clear some work with you? Today's red box came for you about an hour ago. It is in the secure cabinet. Shall I stay?"

"No, that will not be necessary. I've just got a couple of things I want to attend to then I'm off too. See you tomorrow, OK?" He went past her and into his office. He stood behind the door listening for her to go then nipped back into the office and locked the suite door. On returning to his office, he switched on his answerphone and ran through a number of calls until he got to the one he wanted. He plugged in the earphone and listened. It was a woman's voice.

"Mr Lawson, I've a message from my boss who is in charge of collecting the consignment you ordered. He would like you to call as he requires more details." The minister erased the message from the tape. Damn, he thought, something's gone wrong. It was now only a few hours from the time of the exchange.

He had to act now and risk calling his contact. He lifted the phone, dialled a Fleet Street number and announced himself by his code name when the phone was answered.

"The party was missed at Nicosia Airport. He was spotted again at Kyrenia but was able to elude them and to take a high-speed boat out to sea. We are trying to locate him again, if we cannot, we should certainly meet him when he gets to Famagusta."

"You had better," said Lawson.

"We rarely fail," said the voice evenly.

"You mustn't fail on this one, too much depends on it," Lawson's mood was changing to one of anger.

"Don't worry, extensive preparations have been made. Should all fail in Cyprus, thanks to you, we will meet the parties when they arrive at Heathrow."

"OK, I will call you again at eight o'clock. By then you will know what the situation is and what action is to be taken."

"Very well, then. Goodbye for now."

The minister cradled the telephone on to its base. What he had heard did not please him; still there was nothing he could do so he decided to go to his apartment and sweat it out until eight, then he would authorize the necessary and go and wait at the department.

* * * * *

About this time, Rodney was receiving very conflicting reports from the Middle East desk. It seemed that the Turks were invading Cyprus and Turkish planes were in the air. He rushed the news to Robinson who was speaking to his wife on the phone, explaining yet again why he would be late for dinner. He took one look at Rodney's face and hastily concluded his call.

"Well?"

"Cyprus, sir, I think the Turks are invading, or are about to," Rodney reported.

"Damn, damn, damn," the brigadier exploded. "It's always the simple jobs that somebody or something fucks up." Rodney was surprised at Robinson's outburst.

"Shall I inform the minister?" Rodney rode over the outburst.

"No, don't do that just yet or it will be all over the news in no time. I think there's something you ought to know about your chum Lawson and I think this is as good a time as any to tell you, because I think I'm going to need your help," Robinson had calmed down and was back to normal.

"Yes, sir; please go on," Rodney was intrigued.

"He is one of theirs," he let the fact sink in. "I intend to take him to the cleaners and, if possible, I want these Chekhov papers in my possession, as confirmation to convince any disbelievers."

"You're joking, surely? He was only saying at lunch that he might be the heir presumptive to the Prime Minister." Rodney was shocked; whatever he thought of Lawson, this was far from it.

"I am not joking; never been more serious. We have been able to feed him information up to now that he's passed on for us, unknowingly, of course, but if the fools unwittingly vote him in as they might, I'm afraid we can't allow that, now can we?"

"Who are the 'we' sir'? And I think I need some proof."

"The 'we' doesn't matter, but proof you shall have. For now, let's not waste any more time, we have a very tight schedule to keep." The brigadier turned on his tape machine and Rodney heard the telephone conversation that Lawson had made to his contact a short time ago.

Chapter 22

FAMAGUSTA – CHEKHOV'S RACE IS OVER

About this time, the Boeing 727 carrying Seabrook, Mould and Sharky banked for its final run into Larnaca Airport. Seabrook was having difficulty clearing his ears and sat with one hand on his nose, alternately pinching it and blowing until his ears cleared and everything suddenly seemed unnaturally loud, while Sharky pressed his head firmly into the headrest and gripped the armrests of the seat; he was not a good traveller and did not believe in hiding the fact.

Mould was simply bemused by his companions' antics; he said in an exasperated voice, "For goodness sake, just relax; we'll be OK." Just then fighter jets rocketed over them and the civil airliner shivered from the shock waves.

"Jesus!" the other passengers seemed to say in one voice as the aircraft intercom came alive and the reassuring voice of the pilot addressed them.

"This is the captain. Please keep calm; there is no cause for concern as far as this aircraft is concerned. It does appear that since we entered Cypriot airspace the situation between the Turks in the north of the country and the Greek population has deteriorated, and hostilities have opened between them. We have been ordered to land in order to clear the airspace for military aircraft."

The aircraft touched down and every neck strained to look out of the windows to see what was going on; in fact, it all looked very quiet. The captain's voice came on again, "I just received a message from the tower; they've told me that the normal customs procedure has been suspended and they have requested that you make your way as quickly as possible to the airport entrance and clear the area. Thank you." Almost as an afterthought, he added, "The cabin staff will direct you; good luck." He then threw the engines into reverse thrust and the aircraft began to slow its headlong rush towards the terminal buildings.

The plane came to rest at the airport main entrance. The agents looked at each other; they knew without speaking that the mission was not now just an easy exchange task as they had been led to believe. Moreover, even if the exchange was achieved, the return journey was no longer guaranteed. They made haste to get clear of the aircraft and made their way at the double through scurrying anxious crowds that seemed to be rushing round aimlessly in every direction.

They found their car after a little difficulty, or rather the driver from the British consulate found them. He took great delight in telling them that they had come at a most inconvenient time and he had better things to do at this time than babysit them. Seabrook shot out a hand, grabbed the front of the man's shirt around the neck and twisted; a few choice words put the man straight before he was released. He straightened his clothing and was visibly relieved when he realized that he was not expected to accompany them. Once they had got him to show them the equipment they had ordered, they thanked him and climbed into the car. The consular man was nonetheless put out when the men shut the car doors and waved goodbye, leaving him to make his own way back to his office.

As they sped off to the east towards Famagusta 20 miles away, Seabrook was the first to speak, "Bloody hell, what a mess. What's the time Sharky?"

"Five to five local, that means we have got about two hours to get into position for the meet."

"We should do that easily if there are no hold ups," said Mould with some authority since he had served in Cyprus during his army days.

"If there are, we will just have to deal with them," Sharky commented.

"Won't we, though, my friends," drawled Seabrook as they passed through the top of the Sovereign Base Area of Dhekelia. They observed that the British soldiers appeared to be moving purposefully to prepared positions. Army vehicles were noticeable, moving stores and personnel from one location to another. As the men passed the base a military policeman operating a checkpoint flagged them down.

"Good evening, sirs, I see you are driving a British CD plated vehicle;

I must tell you that reports reaching us from the Famagusta area are not encouraging; I would advise you that if your journey is not essential, you should return to Larnaca and up the back road to Nicosia, if it's still open."

"Thank you, officer, regrettably we must proceed, but thank you for the advice," said Sharky as he engaged the gear lever and accelerated away at high speed. "Right," said Sharky, "I'm not stopping again until we get to the hotel, so hang on." He pushed the Granada up to 60 and held it there or as near as possible for the next 30 minutes along the narrow twisting roads typical of that part of Cyprus.

The road took them along or close to the brilliant blue sea of the Mediterranean and then through orange and lemon groves, at other times through small villages with houses covered in bright flowers with old men sitting outside drinking from small coffee cups. Olive groves were infrequent but patches of land cleared for melons and potatoes were not. As they got closer to Famagusta and the new border between the Turks and the Greeks, things began to change.

Now they sped through villages where nervous and frantic Greeks were already loading personal belongings into already overloaded vehicles. These villages had been unpleasant places to patrol in the high days of EOKA but the sturdy peasant stock were used to the emergencies and turmoil of political and military manoeuvring.

Greek soldiers in their blue commando berets, so often confused with UN troops either by accident or design, screeched by them, squeezing by on the narrow roads in their light jeeps and old-fashioned trucks. Fighter planes buzzed overhead and the occasional helicopter signed with large UN markings circled in and out of their view. As they approached Famagusta, they saw their first Turkish soldiers scurrying down the road in platoon strength. Then another group made a half-hearted effort to stop them but they ducked and kept going round the next bend and into the outskirts of the city.

They could hear sporadic shooting and the three men, by now tense, looked at each other and then away. All were thinking, should they abort the mission when, with a shrug, Mould grunted, "It's too late now, let's get it finished." He was navigating and gave the final instruction to Sharky, "Second on the right, drive for twenty yards, park; the hotel should be on our right."

It was now ten minutes to seven. By the time they were in position at the front of the hotel on the seaward side it was two minutes to seven. Chekhov was not there. He was in fact just entering Famagusta Bay. He went in as close as he could to the shore and with his binoculars picked up Seabrook and his men immediately. Only 50 yards of shoreline and beach separated them.

His boat was a high performance craft capable of 60 knots. He had had her nearly flat out at times and cruising at others for the last five hours, covering the distance from Karenia on the north side of the panhandle, round Cape Apostolos Andreas and down again. His passage had not been without incident for Turkish patrol craft had twice fired at him but his tremendous speed had enabled him to leave all obstacles behind.

The boat had handled superbly and although he had had to stick at the wheel, he did not feel tired, only elated. He was on his way to freedom. Chekhov had been planning this escape for some time and it looked now as if it was going to pay off.

He dropped the anchor over the side. He jumped from the boat into the warm waist-deep Mediterranean Sea and waved to the Englishmen who had by now also seen him and they began to walk towards the wading figure.

"Chekhov," called Seabrook.

"None other, yes. You have my retirement money with you?" he said cheerfully.

"Yes, do you have our goods?" Seabrook questioned.

"Of course," Chekhov spread his hands in an expansive gesture, "Come, let us retire to the boat for a drink and do our deal; the town doesn't look at all friendly."

"That," said Mould, "is the best offer we have had all day." So saying, the three men waded through the water and clambered on to the boat. On board, they laughed as they realized that they had just walked into the sea in their London suits. Chekhov brought them ice-cold beer. The beer was drunk in silence.

Finally, Chekhov looked at Seabrook and addressed him, "You were surprised at my choosing you for the exchange, I think, yes?" His English was good and the Russian accent was surprisingly slight, "Well, it's not so strange; in my position I have had to be very careful and I know you to be reliable but not on our top lists where you would be under surveillance all the time; so you were my choice." He laughed, "I'm afraid that after this your standing in the eyes of the KGB will be very much enhanced. Sorry about that."

"It's OK, it's time I put my feet up. So let's make the exchange and get out of here," growled Seabrook.

"Agreed," said Chekhov, holding out a waterproofed package the size of a small paperback to Seabrook.

As he stretched out his arm to pass the package, his white shirt front became stained with red. He grunted and grabbed his free hand to his chest. His eyes looked towards the shore and as he slumped forward on to the little deck table, through bubbling, frothy blood that was now pumping out of his mouth, he wheezed, "KGB," and slid over the side of the boat.

The agents picked out two men on the beach who were moving towards them, making for the shoreline. Sharky was hit by a stinging blow, searing hot on the top of his shoulder. Momentarily shocked, he spun and tumbled gracefully backwards into the sea. Seabrook was hit in the arm and the shock whirled him on to the deck of the boat, the parcel flying from his hand into the sea. Mould reacted immediately and followed the parcel by jumping over the side.

The shooting roused a group of Turkish soldiers on the beach and they raced towards the Russians, shouting. The Russians halted, undecided, weighing the odds; then turning their guns on to the Turks, they scrambled for the sea, struggling through the surf.

Two of the Turkish soldiers dropped to the sand as a man, in a classic shooting position, took quick aim and fired a volley at them. The two Russians, both hit several times, catapulted into the sea and floating face down leaked lifeblood that carried and spread stain into the sea. The blood attracted a myriad of small Mediterranean fish to investigate the possibility of an easy meal.

On the cockpit floor, Seabrook raised himself painfully to see what was happening. He had seen the two Russians hit the water and not reappear and could see that the soldiers were still a hundred or more yards away on the beach. Mould was scrambling aboard with Sharky who was unhurt apart from a bloody furrow on his shoulder. Seabrook felt that if he delayed now, all would be up; with his team safely on board, he reached over his head and switched on the engines. The hot engines roared into life immediately and Mould grabbed the wheel spun the boat round and threw the throttles full ahead. The two 250 h.p.

engines virtually lifted the 25-foot craft out of the water; it pulled out the beach anchor and roared out of Famagusta Bay leaving the astonished soldiers gaping at the spectacle on the beach.

Chapter 23

MOULD AND SHARKY

Seabrook, supporting his injured arm, pulled himself into the seat next to Mould, while Sharky nursed his shoulder, tying a rag over the wound. Mould glanced over his shoulder as the boat roared its erratic course out of the bay. As he did so, he could see the soldiers recover their initial astonishment and level their rifles at him; puffs of smoke flashed from their rifle barrage and instantly the bullets started to crack around him.

Mould ducked automatically but Seabrook was not so quick and one wild bullet ricocheted off the metal of the windscreen and struck him on the temple. The shock spun him out of the seat and back on to the cockpit floor where he struggled to remain conscious, alternating between worlds of black and white. His head whirling, the last thing he would ever see was the coast as they travelled south towards Cape Greco.

Sharky, feeling sick, bleeding heavily and in pain, went to Seabrook but he was past saving and he shook his head at Mould.

Mould slumped in his seat; he had known Seabrook and his family a long time. He turned his attention to matters he could control. He calculated from the fuel indicator that he must have something like 60 to 80 miles of fuel left if he feathered the throttle; he calculated this should get them back to Larnaca easily.

"Sharky," he called, pulling back on the throttles, "we need to discuss the stuff we have on board, so get up here."

"Go on then," said Sharky, joining him on the seat left vacant by Seabrook, his shirt now pressed tightly on the shoulder wound to try to staunch the blood.

"You all right?" Mould seemed to notice Sharky was wounded for the first time, Sharky nodded. "You don't look it, but you'll have to 'man up' as we used to say, we need to move on; first, we need to say goodbye to Seabrook."

"What, you mean tip him overboard? No way!"

"We don't have any other choice; if we're stopped, we won't be able to explain a dead body; it's got to be this way. Seabrook would understand."

"You going to explain that you tipped his body into the sea to his wife?" Sharky quizzed him.

"Well, yeah, if needs be," Mould said unconvincingly. "All right, we'll do a burial at sea; grasp the beach anchor to weigh him down."

"Have a heart, mate, I've only got one arm," Sharky retorted.

"Wimp," Mould remarked but throttled back just enough to keep them under way and left the wheel to help Sharky sort out Seabrook. Mould then stopped the boat and it gently bobbed on the swell. As Seabrook went over the side, Sharky said a few words of farewell.

Mould broke the silence that had grown between them, "We have enough fuel to get to Larnaca but if we get chased I just can't guarantee it. I think we must hide the pay off money and diamonds and the information. If we got stopped and searched we would be in queer street."

"I agree, but where?" Through half-closed eyes, Sharky scanned the rugged coastline leading away from Cape Greco and could see the fishing village of Ayia Napa in the distance. The pain in his arm seemed to be getting worse now the first shock was wearing off.

"I know a place, I've been here before. Get the stuff together and find a waterproof cover for it. The list is already protected but we can't be too careful; don't want any chance of it getting wet," said Mould.

"Give me a minute," Sharky was glad to have something to distract him from his comrade's sea funeral and the pain in his shoulder. He ducked into the cabin. Wrenching open the first-aid box, he rifled through its contents until he found paracetamol and swallowed two. He took the dressing packs which he stuffed into his pocket to treat his wound, some antibiotic powder and a roll of waterproof tape. In a cupboard he found a roll of large freezer bags, black bin bags and a roll of string.

Returning to the deck, he retrieved the diamonds, money and Chekhov's list. Fumbling, he carefully double packed each in to the large freezer bags making sure all the air was expelled. Then he double wrapped the three packs into two black bags. "OK, genius, where are we going to stash this lot?"

"Be there in a minute," was Mould's muted comment as he entered the Ayia Napa bay before hooking round to the right. He nursed the boat between some rocks and entered a small, deep lagoon, some 40 metres in diameter and five metres deep. The bottom of the lagoon was white sand that reflected back at them even as dusk settled into blackness; Sharky had the impression there was nothing between them and the sandy bottom and that they were suspended in the air over it, so clear was the water.

Mould stripped off his shoes, trousers, jacket and shirt. He took the two black sacks from Sharky and let himself over the side of the boat into the lagoon. Taking a deep breath, he receded into the depths, disappearing under the left shoulder of the horseshoe ring of cliffs that protected the bay.

When he reappeared some time later, having been gone long enough to cause Sharky concern, and returned to the boat, the bag was gone. Sharky helped Mould back on board, "That should hold it until it can be retrieved." Mould gulped for breath, "There is a small cave down there that goes in for a yard and then up and there is a ledge high up in an airlock, about three metres up. Bugger me, if there wasn't a fair-sized octopus in there, nearly gave me a heart attack. Plus, the place is infested with spiny sea eggs so I had to be careful how I went." He was breathing more easily now, "I used to dive this area when I was a young soldier out here and found it one day."

"Just hope nobody else knows this place," Sharky was impressed.

"With all this going on, I don't think anyone will be out doing anything else but serious fishing for a few months, and that's not going to be here, fingers crossed." Mould put his clothes back on, drying himself as he went.

"What now?" asked Sharky.

"Don't know about you but that harbour has a bar and restaurant. A Greek named Charlie used to be the owner and he has a phone." Mould looked at the boat and bloodstains, "Need to swab the boat down first and sort out that wound of yours."

After ten minutes, Sharky looked at their clean-up work and Mould's first aid on his wound. "Good enough, let's get out of here."

Mould backed the boat out of the lagoon with Sharky's help. They covered the mile across the bay and slid into the small harbour, tying up at the restaurant quay among the colourful traditional fishing boats.

Charlie, the stocky cheerful Greek, came out of the restaurant to meet them as they disembarked, smiling as he half recognized Mould. Behind him, a squad of grim-faced Greek soldiers emerged and covered the two British agents with their rifles. Mould and Sharky smiled at them and raised their hands.

Chapter 24

ROBINSON

In Brigadier Robinson's office a few hours later, Rodney had just finished reading the dossier on Lawson. What he had read had filled him with horror. The brigadier had sat quietly behind his desk, his seat swivelled round looking out of his window and out over London; he had watched Rodney's face for a time as he had absorbed the detailed intelligence reports collected over 15 years on the activities of Lawson but having seen that Rodney appreciated the seriousness of the situation, he had turned away. Pigeons flew on to and off his window ledge, squabbling over morsels brought up from the street below. Robinson could have watched them for hours but he sensed when Rodney had finished from the sound of the file snapping closed. He swivelled back to the desk. Rodney sat very still in his chair, the Lawson file closed on his lap, and looked at Robinson.

"You're going to ask why we haven't pulled him before now," said Robinson seriously.

"No, Brigadier, in fact, I wasn't. I was going to ask why pull him now; and why did you bring Lawson into this operation when he could jeopardize the whole thing?"

"For two reasons, Rod." Robinson rarely shortened Rodney's name but the familiarity pleased Rodney when he did, "One, is the fact that he is about to become too powerful. As a minister under the control of the PM, who incidentally knows all, we have been able to manipulate him, as I said before; reason two: the complete list of the agents operating in the West. We have decided to give our opponents in this underhand war

of ours a very bloody nose, at the same time drawing out Lawson's back-
room boys in this country. They are going to have to surface, under the
circumstances, and may not be named on the list. I want the lot. We also
felt the time frame would prevent Lawson and his people intervening
quickly enough, a risk we were prepared to take. And, of course, to bring
a minister down, we needed more than we had."

"It's still high risk. So where do I come in?" Rodney was now pacing
the room trying to rationalize all he had read and been told.

"From now on, you are to be his shadow until told differently,"
Robinson responded.

"I noticed in the restaurant that he was already under surveillance.
Incidentally that man Jones makes a very good waiter."

"Jones is part of an eight-man team of watchers with Andrew Harrison
from Five as the team leader. Think you know him; he has been told to
report to you from now on."

"We go way back, Andrew and I. Five must be OK with us borrowing
their men. Anyway I will look forward to working with him again. Good
choice."

Robinson raised his eyebrows, "Yes, I thought so; the director of Five
is in on this, so he doesn't have a great deal of choice." His demeanour
was reflective, "Rodney, I know you're not as active as you might like to
be, therefore I intend to ensure that I give you a very good team who can
do your legwork for you. Harrison and his men, of course, are not fully in
the picture and have not been told about the reason for the surveillance,
and that's the way it has to stay unless circumstances dictate otherwise.
Right, Harrison will be here any minute so go and get your team set up
and I'll see you in an hour."

The brigadier stood up, took the dossier from Rodney and added, "A
word of caution, Lawson is dangerous and, I suspect, has on call a small
army of agents and riff-raff that will be at his disposal in this country,
plus other activists and fifth column sympathizers through them. Make
sure your men are armed and that goes for you too. Don't underestimate
the man or it could be he will complete the job he didn't do in Borneo."

"Don't worry, sir,' said Rodney bitterly, "I don't intend that he should
get the chance. I think on this one I would like a few more men so that I
have a rapid reaction team to handle pickup etc. Say, another four?"

"All right, you have them; tell Harrison to fix it. Good. All the same,
watch out for him. See you later," said the brigadier gravely.

When Rodney went out, Robinson allowed himself a smile. He had no fears that Rodney would not carry out his task well. At that moment the telephone rang, cutting across his thoughts, he picked the instrument up, "Robinson."

"Sir, this is the Middle East Section. The local informer in Famagusta that you had monitoring the situation there, and looking out for Seabrook and the others, has just called in. The news is not good, I am afraid," he paused to give Robinson an opportunity to interrupt but he did not. He went straight on to describe to the brigadier the events on the beach, as the agent had seen them. The fact that the agent had tried to follow the boat in his car along the coast road, but had been delayed by the Turks at a checkpoint and by other people fleeing from the fighting, had not mattered. The agent had eventually caught up with them at Ayia Napa. "I am sorry to tell you, Brigadier, that Seabrook was killed in an action. Sharky is wounded but alive, shot in the arm. Mould is fine." He went on to explain how his man had taken over from the locals there and got the Greek soldiers to let him take Sharky to the British Military Hospital at Dhekelia, but they were keeping Mould as a guest for the time being and he could not change their mind. "Our report is that the wound Sharky has sustained, whilst not life threatening, has caused him to lose a lot of blood. The doctors in the hospital expect Sharky to be there for a week recovering; they emphasized that there was no chance of moving him before then." The man paused, "What do you want us to do now, sir?"

"Who is this agent we have out there?" Robinson asked, hoping it was someone to be relied on.

"Expat retiree from 'Five', went out there to live a few years ago; you would know him, he worked for you at times."

"Oh yes, do you mean Fred Costa who was a section head?" Brigadier Robinson was pleased he had at least someone competent to work with.

"Yes, sir, that's it, our Fred; still does freelance for us now and then."

His manner was altogether too cheery for Robinson's liking, and he brought the conversation to an end with, "That's good news. I'll call you back in a few minutes. But now I would like Fred to call me immediately on my number and to stay with our man until I can organize a relief. I don't want anybody else out there involved, he'll just have to do the best he can." The brigadier ended the call and went to Rodney's office where he found him surrounded by a group of men; he was briefing his team. When he saw Robinson's face, he quickly concluded his briefing and tasked his men for the immediate future, he then dismissed them. They left hurriedly, they knew something was up. Robinson did not come to his officers' desks; he sent for them.

"Back to my office," Robinson spun on his heels and strode down the corridor, Rodney following him.

"Rodney, we've got a problem," began the brigadier and proceeded to outline the situation. "I want two of your team out to Cyprus now, and I want them to relieve the agent there. I will get on to the consulate and get Mould released as soon as possible. I want the location of the lists and diamonds. If I know your lot, they will have dropped them somewhere safe. Get them to look at the boat at Ayia Napa, as well, just in case."

"Yes, are you going to tell the minister?" Rodney asked, concerned for his boss.

"I'm not sure yet. I will of course have to tell the PM and the other directors but I think he will let me continue with whatever course I decide."

Just then the phone rang. Robinson indicated Rodney should stay. He put the phone on speaker.

"Sir, Fred Costa here," Fred's voice was weary.

"Fred, how is Sharky? Can you get a phone to him? I need to speak to him urgently."

"Sharky is sore but he will be fine. The answer is yes to the phone although he is pretty woozy; they had dosed him up so I don't know how much sense you will get out of him."

"Can you stay with him, Fred, until I sort this mess out?" Robinson asked hopefully.

"Not a problem, sir, nobody is going anywhere; the whole area is a no go. There are Greek and Turkish soldiers thrashing it out and, until they stop, I'm marooned here," Fred said with resigned acceptance in his voice.

"What about Mould's situation?"

"He is not in any danger from the Greek soldiers; they were joking and laughing with us. I think they just wanted to keep him for a while, I think more as a shield and peacemaker against the Turks if they broke through. Anyway, I have asked the local police chief, who is a friend of mine, to go and get him. The soldiers will not mess with the police chief even now. I hope to see him here in an hour or two," Fred chuckled.

"Thank you, Fred, good job; I am so grateful to you," the genuine gratitude in the brigadier's response came over the line to him clearly.

"Don't thank me yet, sir, wait until you see my bill; this is going to cost the department an arm and a leg!" Fred did not hang up and he was not joking now, "Sir, if you just handle what you need to, leave Sharky to me. I'll be here if you need me. I think when you do get people on the ground, they ought to check over the boat just in case they left anything on there that's incriminating or important and, yes, as quickly as possible. I did have a word with the bar owner, Charlie, I trust him; he will keep an eye on the boat but he can't oversee it 24 hours a day and I assume you consider it HM property now?"

"Thank you, again, Fred. I will get some people in as soon as possible and, yes, the boat's now ours," Robinson said seriously.

"Thought so; first refusal, please, if the department wants shot of it later. You can get me on this number until you release me." The brigadier heard the phone cradled and he put his down thoughtfully.

Rodney broke the silence, "I will go and sort the situation on the ground in Cyprus. I may need a lift from the RAF now the situation is so fluid."

Robinson nodded his approval. He watched Rodney walk back to his office, racking his brains for a plan to keep the minister in the dark but at the same time stop him from panicking and skipping out of the country. He had no illusions that the man would run if he thought they were hiding something. He would automatically assume that the brigadier and his men had already read the list and found his name on it, right at the top, as the KGB number one plant. He could not immediately think of a way through but when he looked up he saw the minister impatiently pacing up and down outside his office.

"Ah, Minister, I thought you were coming over around eight."

"I had a few things to do." I'll bet you did, thought Robinson, like organizing your thugs that murdered one of my best men and getting your escape route organized.

"Well, Minister, I have little to tell you except that the situation in Cyprus is in turmoil and that I have not yet heard from my men. It may be that they have become caught up in the troubles and are having difficulty contacting either Chekhov or us, let alone getting back," Robinson's heavy eyebrows were raised in innocence.

"What a mess. Well, what you are doing about it?" Lawson attacked. He, too, was at a loss as the information he had had from Cyprus was simply that the authorities had reported to the Russians that two nationals had been killed by Turkish soldiers for resisting arrest and a dead man from a fast boat was floating in the bay. Apart from that, he was completely in the dark. He had asked his contacts to get the full story but did not expect a reply for some time, if at all.

"I've decided to send a backup team," Robinson was thinking furiously, and decided that that remark should satisfy the minister for the moment.

"It's a pity that you didn't send a spare team with Seabrook and the others," Lawson rebuked the brigadier. "I can see that I'm wasting my time here anyway; I might just as well go back to the office and you can contact me as soon as you have any news," snapped Lawson.

"Of course, Minister, immediately I hear anything." Robinson stood, dominating the room.

The minister collected his briefcase and coat and, with a curt nod to the brigadier, was gone. Robinson let out his breath and summoned Rodney.

"Sir?" enquired Rodney as he entered the office.

"Lawson just left; think we are OK for the moment. Are your men active yet?"

"Indeed. He is being followed and at this moment we are enhancing an already very sophisticated bugging system in all the places he is likely to be in the next few days." He added, "We are linking with Special Branch who will keep tabs on any known agents and activists in this country. Special Branch doesn't know why, but their chief has agreed to do it for me for the next 48 hours without questions, but after that he expects a full briefing from you. Until then he will keep mum."

The brigadier laid back his long frame in the leather desk chair and rested his head against its back; he said, reflectively, "Good, if we can't crack this in that time then I don't think we ever will. Of course, it depends on our men in Cyprus, who aren't saying anything to anybody at the moment."

"How did you fob off Lawson?"

"It was easier than I expected; he believed me because he wanted to believe me. He accepted that we had lost contact with our men and that I was sending a backup team to extract the original team." The brigadier leant forward placing both hands flat on the table, "I rather suspect that he left to get his operatives organized. The point is, or rather the question is, which way is he going to jump? If I were him I'd have a team activated in Cyprus to cover our man and risk an attempt at getting the list from our people before they return to this country, so we need to be one step ahead of him and I think I have the answer. It will be a gamble but I think it's worth it." Rodney could see that the old man was working out the final details in his head and stood respectfully at the desk waiting for him to continue. A full minute passed before the brigadier gently raised his left hand and smoothed his large domed head, he looked at his aide down his long aristocratic nose, grinning, "I've got to clear this with the PM but in the meantime this is what I want you to do..." he paused, "but before we start, where is the backup team?"

"They are down at the equipment section being kitted for the operation; why is that, sir?"

"Will they be reporting back to you before they fly out?"

"Absolutely!"

"Right, Rodney. Mould and Fred can look after Sharky but I will brief the backup team that they are to carry on with the flight but, on arrival, they are to go straight away to the Nissi Beach Hotel at Ayia Napa and await our call. They can check out the boat while they are there. I take it they are going to fly from RAF Northolt?" Rodney nodded, "Well, I am sure Lawson will have them followed in this country and in Cyprus, so I want them to give the enemy every opportunity to follow them. In the meantime, get on to our contacts in RAF Special Ops. I want the fastest plane they have available to ferry you and me over to Cyprus. I want to be gone from these shores before the backup teams have left. In other words, they are to act as decoys and I want our team to tie up the other side's assets while you and I go to see Sharky and Mould. Got it?"

"Understood, I will make the arrangements immediately. Need to get us flown to the RAF base in the south, Akrotiri, and then have us choppered into Dhekelia. OK, sir?"

"Fine, I'm off to see the PM; I'll be ready to fly in an hour."

Rodney was pleased to be able to get into the field but slightly disappointed that the old man was coming. He shrugged the disappointment away; if the old man felt he had to come, so be it. He started to number off the matters he had to attend to. However, priority number one must be to fix up the flight for himself and Robinson. And for that he knew a desk in the building that could fix that for him.

Chapter 25

LAWSON AND THE RUSSIAN

Over the last hour Lawson had been busy. He had first contacted his head of operations again and arranged for agents to pick up and follow the brigadier's backup team as they left the department for the airport and had taken the additional action to ensure that the men would be followed once they arrived in Cyprus. At the present time he was in animated conversation with his Russian chief of operations again, "But look here," said Lawson, "I do feel we should try to retrieve the list in Cyprus and not wait until they get it back to this country. It's far too risky."

"I couldn't agree more," said the calm cultured voice at the other end of the phone with only the slightest hint of a Russian accent.

"Couldn't we at least meet and discuss this situation in some detail," interjected an angry Lawson, his voice gradually rising in pitch.

"Do try to keep calm, Lawson, we won't let you down. As I just said, I also believe and concur with you, that we should lift the list over there, but there are obvious problems. Firstly the whole country is in turmoil and, secondly, our network over there is by no means as in depth or as well placed as it is here. Nevertheless, I am going to try to set up the Cyprus Russian team to sort out the problem from that end, if they can. By the way, it has just been reported to me that, along with our two men that were killed, was an Englishman who was drowned, a minor agent we knew called Seabrook. There is no doubt about his identity. He was with Chekhov, who is also dead, along with two other British who escaped out to sea on the boat and they were possibly also wounded."

"Good grief!" this news did nothing to lessen Lawson's panic.

210

"Yes indeed. It does seem to me that we can assume the worst; that some sort of exchange was made and that the wounded, if that is the case, English agents are somewhere with the documents. All we have to do is find them and the documents before their own side do. If Robinson's men get to them before we do, we will rob them. If you monitor the developments this end then I will attend to the recovery of the list."

"Yes, yes of course, very well; anything else?" Lawson was irritated.

"Yes, I've assigned two men to you, twenty-four hours a day. They will be very discreet and will have orders to be within calling distance of you at all times should you need assistance. I think that's all for now."

"Thank you," said Lawson gratefully; he was strangely calm all of a sudden. Traitor he may be, among other things, but he was no fool and realized at that moment that the KGB machine had taken over and that he was no longer in control of even his own destiny. The shedding of responsibility was, he realized, welcome. Conversely, the two helpers that had just been assigned to him probably had orders to safeguard the good standing of his chiefs and would not hesitate to liquidate him if the need arose.

After digesting his new situation he called Robinson and asked him if he had any news.

"Not yet I'm afraid," lied the brigadier who had recently returned from the PM's office, "Things do appear to be very confused out there. However, my backup team should be leaving in the next hour or so and should be out there within the next twelve; I really do not expect to hear anything for a while, so I am going home to sort some domestic administration and, most of all, get some sleep. I will however return to take charge of the operation as soon as the duty officer calls me and I suggest you do the same, it could be a long night once it all kicks off." The brigadier was enjoying the deception and the innuendo offered in the most innocent and bland manner to a man he intended to crush as soon as he had the key and only Sharky and Mould could give him that. Thank goodness Lawson called when he did, Robinson calculated that their conversation would hold Lawson for at least eight hours and by then, he assessed, he should be at Sharky's bedside and the operation could well be tied up, bar the shouting.

"You're probably right, Robinson," he never called the brigadier by his Christian name, Alex, and this unaccountably niggled Robinson in the extreme.

Lawson, feeling placated for the moment, concluded with, "Thank you. I will be off to my London residence, then. Please call me immediately anything happens, if not I will see you in the morning, say about ten."

"Certainly, Minister, good evening then. It does seem to have been a very long day," the brigadier closed the conversation and put the telephone down. He suspected, and was right as usual, that friend Lawson was in a state of considerable nervous consternation despite his apparent calmness on the phone. He did not feel any sympathy for the man at all. He made his way to the duty room and found Graham Swain, the duty watch officer who had roused him many hours earlier that day, still on duty.

"You still here?" said the brigadier lightly.

"Yes, sir, Major Brown asked me if I would see this operation through to the end. He said the less people who knew about it the better. He thought it expedient that as I have all the facts relating to the operation so far, I might just as well stay on. Always difficult for someone to come in cold and carry on with as complicated a case as this is turning out to be. Also, I'm supported by Williams who seems to know how to sort most things."

"Jolly good; I just came up to say that, if anything happens, contact me. Tell anyone who wants me that I am at home or I am on my way back here or I am delayed at a meeting, anything, just convince them. If you have any difficult customers who will simply not go away, it is always best to bounce the nuisance up one, so get Williams to handle them. He will delay until he has to bounce them further up or I am found. Right?"

"Of course, sir," the desk officer chuckled.

"Right, see you later, much later." Well, thought Robinson, that should hold off anybody for hours. Graham was, from what he had seen, a past master at delay. He walked back into the department office complex and found Rodney stuffing a diplomatic bag with an assortment of items that might be useful to them on their quest.

"Are we ready?" asked Robinson.

"Yes, all packed, ready to go. I've even got a phial of stimulant in case we decide to bring Sharky round if the army doctors get difficult in the hospital and will not play ball; of course if Mould is there by the time we arrive we will not need it." Rodney finished stuffing his old battered black leather briefcase and snapped the lock. "Shall we go? I've got rather a unique aircraft to take us to Cyprus." Robinson raised an eyebrow but as Rodney gave nothing away, he decided not to pry.

As the brigadier turned to lead the way, Rodney said, "I've got the car at the rear of the building, so we need to go through the basement and out into the next street; I thought we ought to take that precaution in case they are watching, don't you?"

"Quite right, Number Two, and I've left the watch officer, supported by Williams, with an instruction to create a smokescreen should anybody try to contact me," added the brigadier who was obviously pleased with himself. Truth be told, he was looking forward to this foray into the field, he had not been active for many years. The PM was a little put out as he relied on Robinson's clever organizing brain for difficult matters of state and expected the brigadier to coordinate everything from base. Whilst Robinson enjoyed his work, he reckoned that this would probably be his last chance to be active before he hung up his bowler for good. As it was the big one, he was going to make it his swansong and enjoy it. They made their way down to the basement and through a labyrinth of passages that housed other parts of the organization behind their walls, from a miniature firing range to well-equipped laboratories. He reminded himself that he really must make a tour of inspection of his domain when he got back. "Don't spend half enough time walking round my department, you know. When we get back, I'll inspect the lot," mused the brigadier aloud.

"What is that, inspection? I did not quite catch all of what you said."

"Oh nothing, just thinking out loud," said the brigadier. Amazing, Rodney thought to himself, here we are on our way to a country at war and all he can think of is an inspection. They came up to the rear door and Rodney punched a code into the electronic lock. There was no doorkeeper here, the door only opened one way and only opened to a complicated combination. It was also monitored by TV cameras that were viewed continuously by the department's security men.

Outside, an old car was parked, "Wait here, sir, just going to check the alley is empty." The brigadier looked questioningly at his aide. "Just a precaution; I don't want to let any more in on this than is absolutely necessary, or to see us drive off," Rodney explained. "You and I, plus the necessary immediate staff are the only ones who know we are on our way to the island and I think we should keep it that way as long as we can."

"Not quite, the PM does; he didn't like it one bit, I have to admit, but he saw the sense and capitulated," responded his boss. "OK, so what're our movements from here on?"

"Well, sir," said Rodney letting the boss into the car, "It's a very quick ride to the back field at Heathrow and then a flight by helicopter to RAF Waddington. From there we travel by one of their faster planes available for the job, a Vulcan."

"Well done you, what a marvellous aeroplane the Vulcan is. I'll look forward to that! Let's go before something happens to delay us." Robinson climbed in the car and settled back in his seat as Rodney eased in the gear of the Q car and roared off into the night. They arrived at Heathrow half an hour later and after flashing their cards to the customs man drove directly to the helicopter pad at the far end of the airport. Rodney threw the keys to a security man and asked him to call Graham and get the car picked up.

They were met by one of two RAF crew members who hustled them on to the waiting Puma helicopter. As soon as the airman had them strapped in, he gave the pilot the all clear. The pilot had the machine engine turning over and in seconds they were wheeling away from the ground in a steep climb. Both men experienced the strange feeling one always gets in a helicopter, of being jumped into the air, and that initial sense of disorientation as the machine whirled round to the direction of flight. From the vibrating, incredibly noisy military aircraft, they could see the twinkling lights of Greater London as they now sped quickly over Hounslow and off to the north-west. Conversation was impossible so they both settled down and relaxed. The crewman smilingly tried to communicate their route by drawing in chinagraph pencil on a bespattered air map with incomprehensible circles and triangles superimposed on it. However, it did not help them much and the brigadier thanked him and shouted to the man to rouse him five minutes before they landed. He leaned back in his seat harness and was soon dozing.

Rodney wanted to relax but could not, he had too much to think about and the added responsibility for the brigadier's safety was just another thing on his plate. The day had started like any other, if there was such a thing in his life, but was developing into a thoroughly unexpected one. He had met an old enemy, made up with him only to find out he was probably the most dangerous man of this era; he had lost an agent and had another wounded, now he was about to enter the field with an old man who he believed was past this sort of thing, as Rodney's old wounds should also have precluded him. You could say, thought Rodney, that my world has been turned upside down in no small way. It makes a change, though, and a change is as good as a rest, they say. He shrugged his shoulders, what comes, comes. He would just have to manage the situation every step and as it developed. He looked out of the window to see the lights of London falling behind them. One thing I'd better do though is to make sure that the brigadier is not exposed to any danger. The PM would never forgive me, and nor would Robinson's old lady.

He sat back and racked his brains to make sure he had not forgotten anything and to see if he could foresee any other problems he might have overlooked or that he may have to overcome in the next few days. As he turned his head, he could see the pilot's boots on the half-deck up and to his right, making deft corrections to the craft's flight by working the rudders and the control stick. The rest of the man was hidden by the structure of the cockpit and Rodney found himself imagining what the pilot may look like. He found he could not, but didn't think that the position the pilot had to hold could be that comfortable for a long period and that the vibration must get on their nerves eventually. Still, he thought, the job must be rewarding or they wouldn't do it. He must have dozed off about then because the next thing he knew he and the boss were being roused by the airman.

"We are just about to land, sirs," he said shaking them gently with his leather-gloved hands.

They could feel the tempo of the engines change and then they seemed to sweep towards the earth. At the last moment, the craft seemed to flare nose up and then dance upright, before settling gently on to the ground. When the pilot cut his engines, the silence was profound, with only the swish of the blades as they slowed to a stop. They were both helped to the helicopter door and on to the ground. They felt a little shaky after the hour-long flight but they soon recovered their equilibrium when they were met by the station commander who offered a flask of coffee liberally laced with brandy.

"Well, Alex, it must be twenty years since we served together, you old campaigner," said Air Commander John Williams.

"My God, John, I thought they would have pensioned you off ten years ago."

"Not a chance. Takes experience to run a place like this and where are these college graduates going to get that in these settled times, eh?" he laughed and took the brigadier's hand in a firm handshake of comradeship. He was suddenly serious, "Listen, my old friend, this plane you are going on is not a commercial airliner, it is a beast, are you sure you are up to it?"

"Not really, but needs must and the old ticker is fine," Robinson sipped his fortified coffee.

"Anyway, I wish you luck. Got some special suits for you to struggle into to make the journey a little more comfortable and the plane is all ready and waiting. Despite what you say, I have told the pilot to take it easy on take-off so as not to give you a heart attack," he smiled. "I still think you are too old, much too old, to go buzzing around in one of my Vulcans."

"As I say, needs must. Anyway, I couldn't miss a ride in one of these things, could I?" chuckled Robinson, sweeping his hand towards the dark menacing shape of the aircraft 50 yards away on the tarmac. Its generators were running and it was making that very individual noise that aircraft do just before they come to life.

"No, I don't suppose you could," said the station commander. "Come on then, I'll help you into your kit and then see you on-board."

When they were both kitted up, the air commodore and the two men walked over to the Vulcan where they met by one of the crew.

"Good evening, sir; we are now ready and waiting to go."

The huge aircraft seemed to dwarf even the brigadier who was a very tall man. He turned and thanked the air commodore one more time for laying on the plane at such short notice.

He reminded the brigadier that all of the RAF fleet of Vulcans were ready to go at very short notice and in fact this task fitted in very nicely with a sortie they had to do anyway. He also pointed out that his bottle of duty-free sherry was in need of replenishment so they were not to give it a second thought, it was his pleasure. Waving farewell, he and an aide who had appeared at his side moved away from the plane. The crewman led the men into the aircraft. Once inside, each was given instruction to don helmets. The crewman helped them sort out their dress needs and connected the various systems that would keep their environment at a constant temperature and pressure during the flight before leading them into the cockpit. The crewman indicated that they should take the two vacant crew seats at the back of the cockpit; he then connected them and strapped them in.

Up to now, the preparations had been made in silence. The crewman checked that their helmets were linked into the intercom system and at once the buzz and hubbub of radio transmissions setting up the Vulcan for take-off exploded into their headphones. The aircraft captain turned his head and gave them the thumbs up. Their position was a little cramped but not uncomfortable; they were surprised how small the cabin was in comparison to the size of the aircraft. The brigadier and Rodney almost involuntarily gave the unaccustomed gesture to the captain by returning his thumbs up. The captain nodded and resumed his original position and completed his conversations with the crew and the control tower.

By now the engines were running up to the point where the Vulcan would begin to roll along the ground turning into the runway. Rodney could see the old man was mesmerized and that although he tried not to be, he was enthralled and totally fascinated by his surroundings. Rodney himself felt like a kid on his first encounter with a flying machine, so he could understand the brigadier's feelings. This was a privilege very few got to experience. The craft seemed almost alive; it seemed to hum and the array of on-board computers and instruments with their flickering lights in the dim ethereal green light of the cabin seemed to bathe everything, even themselves and the crew. This is an alien environment, was Rodney's fleeting thought. He shook himself free of the feeling as the Vulcan began to roll down the runway and gather speed. He and the brigadier were pushed back into their seats as the Vulcan roared down the airstrip. The noise was deafening inside the aircraft and it seemed to penetrate their helmets as a deep vibration that they felt throughout their bodies. Suddenly they were tilted back in their seats at an impossible angle as the machine lifted, thundering into the sky. Still accelerating, the plane continued its upward thrust. The roar of the engines shortly afterwards began to diminish as the craft left the earth and the speed of sound behind. Quite suddenly, all seemed quiet as the aircraft levelled and seemed to float on its way.

"Welcome on board, gentlemen," said the captain through the intercom. His voice had an echoing, metallic quality, "I trust you are both still with us and in good health?"

"I am not sure my stomach would necessarily agree with you on that, captain," said the brigadier, "How about you, Number Two?"

"Agreed, definitely, but I wouldn't have missed that for the world. Tell me, captain, what happens on landing?"

"I'm afraid you will not notice much difference to a commercial flight this time around. But I can promise you an unforgettable experience before that point, when I take this kite up to the roof of the world you will see the curve of the globe. Later, when we descend to low-level flight over the Mediterranean and on into Cyprus it will be another experience for you too. I presume you two have a fairly hectic time ahead of you so I suggest you enjoy the ride and relax for a little while. We shall be there in a few hours' time," said the captain. He obviously was being diplomatic and returned to his instruments. However, he must have had second thoughts about his guests so he said, "I'll just patch you two into the discreet mode so you can converse with each other in private through your intercoms, OK?"

"Thank you," said the brigadier. He really did want to go over matters again with Rodney and try to see the way ahead. Very often, talking out this sort of problem with colleagues produced the best results in the long run. So the brigadier and Rodney once again scratched out the likely courses together and the solutions to any problems they saw that could possibly arise.

The captain buzzed them halfway through their conversation and said, "We are about to take our machine all the way up, so hang on." He clicked his connection off and they felt the Vulcan tilt upwards; they felt the power surging the craft forwards and up into near space. The sights were spectacular from this height and both had their fill.

They flew at this high altitude for another hour and continued with their deliberations when the captain cut in once more to inform them that he was about to descend to sea level and that they should once again hang on to their stomachs, although their flight suits should help with the sudden change in pressure. However, he added, should either of them feel distressed, they should sing out. He would be leaving the communication channel open this time so if there was anything they didn't want the rest of the world to hear, they had better not say it. The brigadier and Rodney glanced at each other, both thinking that this pilot was no fool.

The aircraft tilted over and down. Looking over the pilot's shoulder, they could see the earth far below; they were so high that the curve of the earth's surface could again be clearly seen. They felt their stomachs lift as the powerful, but ageing V bomber dived headlong towards mother earth. The plunge seemed to last forever and both their heart rates increased in anticipation of something going wrong, but they need not have feared. At 10,000 feet the aircraft began to slow its dive and straightened out in a gradual banked curve until they were flying at great speed almost at wave level. The captain banked once to show them the rapidly approaching Cyprus mainland and explained that they would shortly be sweeping round from the south coast of the island to the north-west and on to the RAF Akrotiri runway in the Sovereign Base Area.

They felt the machine bank once to the left and felt the captain just touch the power to take the craft into its final approach. Quickly the plane flipped into level flight and they felt the aircraft touchdown. Seconds later, they were taxiing to a pan at the far end of the runway where they rolled to a stop.

The captain's voice broke into their thoughts again, "I've just had a call to say that the helicopter taking you on is waiting over on our left and a representative from the hospital is waiting to convey you to the Dhekelia Base British Military Hospital."

"Many thanks to you, Captain, for all your efforts and an unforgettable flight. Please pass our thanks again to the Commodore when you get back." The Vulcan captain acknowledged with a thumbs up.

The captain called out, "The Commodore said that if you need to move out and want a lift back within the next twelve hours, you are to get the RAF tasking officer here to call us with the code name 'BEACH' and give the local time you want to be picked up. OK, sir?"

Rodney acknowledged him with a wave; he also acknowledged by speaking into his helmet communication set. "Yes, got it, thank you."

The brigadier also confirmed, giving the captain a thumbs up, "See you again, then, and thank you."

The pilot simply gestured in a way that indicated it was a pleasure.

The crewman came forward to uncouple the two men from their umbilical cords and to help them off with their flight suits. Once they were ready, the crewman helped them from the Vulcan and directed them to the helicopter which stood on the tarmac with its rotors turning. The July heat of the island hit them immediately and it was daylight too. As they walked over to the waiting knot of people by the helicopter, another sound blotted out the clatter of its engine. It was the Vulcan running up and they turned to watch it for a moment as it thundered down the airfield and climbed into the sky.

"Hmm," said the brigadier, "so much for a shopping trip to get the Commander's duty-free flagon of Cyprus Sherry; commandeer, I think it's called. I always knew he was an old bluffer," and allowed himself a little chuckle.

At which Rodney said helpfully, "Perhaps, sir, he meant for you to bring it back with you."

"Ah, you are probably right. Come on, my boy, let us get to the hospital and see what sort of mess Sharky has got himself into. He really should know better at his age and I'll tell him so if he's in a state to take a joke."

Sharky was in no state to take anything in as they were soon to find out from the hospital administrative officer who was waiting for them at the helicopter. He was a serious man and he informed them that Sharky had a fever, "Probably brought on by shock and the wound; touch of pneumonia, I am afraid, he's resting and full of antibiotics, so he's not too coherent at the moment." He apologized for the CO not meeting them but he knew that they would understand that he was busy at this time, with casualties of all sorts arriving from the conflict areas.

As they climbed through the helicopter door for the last leg of their journey, the heat from the engine turbine seemed to intensify the natural temperature and both men gasped as they were temporarily engulfed in a heat bath. As they rose into the air and started the flight, the temperature soon dropped and the constant stream of air coming into the body of the helicopter from the open door then cooled them.

They flew off to the east with the Troodos Mountains on their left and the twinkling Mediterranean blue sea on their right. They followed the Limassol-Larnaca road for some time and then they were flying over smouldering oil tanks at the BP refinery just outside Larnaca; they followed the road to the Dhekelia Sovereign Base Area. During the flight, Rodney had asked the captain if Mould had surfaced; the captain did not know but confirmed that Fred was at the hospital.

Minutes later, they were landing at the base, touching down on the helicopter pad at the rear of the British Military Hospital. The administrative officer led them from the helicopter at a crouched trot until they were clear of the rotor blades, he then turned to give the pilot the thumbs up and he took off immediately.

"Sir, follow me please." He ushered them the 50 yards or so into the rear emergency entrance of the hospital. "I will take you up to the ward and you can speak to the doctor in charge of your man before you see him."

Chapter 26

LAWSON

Back in London, Lawson had just finished actioning his constituency correspondence and turned to his briefcase to get out more files on which to work for the next day's sitting in Parliament; he stuffed them back in the bag with a dismissive gesture; his heart was not in it as his mind dragged him back to the day's events.

With a sigh, he snapped his briefcase shut. There was finality in the action. He went to his desk cupboard and drew out a whisky bottle he had been hitting and poured his sixth of the night. Although he knew that drink was not the answer and he did not drink whisky regularly, the golden amber liquid soothed him. If he were to sleep tonight, he would need something to anaesthetize him. He collected his jacket from the peg and shrugged into it.

His ministerial car was waiting for him in the underground car park at the Houses of Parliament; his usual driver was not in attendance. "George not on duty?" Lawson's remark was casual.

"George has a domestic issue so I am driving you for the next few days, Minister. I will try to live up to George's standard, though; he briefed me so I hope you will accept me for the moment. Home, sir?"

"Yes, straight home please. What do I call you?"

"Roberts will do, sir." Lawson smiled; he would have his first name out of him on the next run; right now he was too tired to play games.

Lawson had a penthouse flat overlooking the Thames on London's South Bank, downriver next to the new Tate gallery. On most days, he enjoyed the stroll home but not tonight; the car dropped him and he thanked the driver. Letting himself into his apartment, his eyes roved over the luxury and the high standard he and his Russian masters allowed him to live in. Modern paintings and the comfortable furniture made his flat a space in which he could both relax and entertain; a gilded cage, he thought. Throwing his briefcase on to one of the two four-seater settees, he went into the bedroom, undressed and showered. After drying himself, he collapsed on the bed, took a book that he was reading from the bedside table and opened it at the page he had marked. Within minutes he was asleep and the book slipped from his fingers on to the floor. The bedside light shining on the minister's face showed cruel lines that appeared on his face as he relaxed into deep sleep. He woke once in the night but otherwise slept undisturbed until eight o'clock.

His first act on waking was to call the duty officer in Robinson's department. Williams answered, telling him that all was quiet and there were no new developments, he added that the brigadier had not yet arrived. Relaxed, he put on his dressing gown and went into the kitchen to get breakfast. His morning routine was to take breakfast on the balcony of the flat and watch the ships on the river plough back and forth. Not today, the weather was miserable for the time of year and anyway he was in a hurry. Nevertheless, one routine he would keep was to review the headlines of the day. He flicked on the television and went to pick up the papers that were delivered to the flat every day.

What he read and heard on the news channel did nothing to allay his underlying anxiety about the whole affair. He was acutely aware that the Turkish and Greek authorities would not appreciate a clandestine operation on their land. He was also aware that the brigadier would be in the firing line if anything went wrong. On the debit side, he mused, he did have great confidence that, if anyone could see the task through to completion, it was the brigadier. His doubt and nagging worry was that his KGB masters would not be as effective. On the other hand, Tsygankov was the best there was and a worthy opponent to his British counterpart.

Finishing up with the newspaper headlines, he switched off the TV and rinsed the breakfast things. Hurriedly he showered, dressed, and took the lift to the ground floor. A new man was on the building security desk. He nodded to the man.

"Good morning, Minister," the man said respectfully. "Your car is not here, do you want me to call a taxi?"

"Thank you, no, I will walk. New here, are you not?"

"Higgins is the name, sir. Charlie is sick; luckily I was available or there would be complaints from the residents of the building. Have a good morning, sir." Higgins was one of many of the brigadier's army of watchers. The man noted the time Lawson left and phoned it through to Williams who was now manning the duty desk.

Lawson turned left past the Tate and got on to Blackfriars Bridge which led to the brigadier's building on the north side of the Thames. Lawson was a complex character, a man of contrasts. He had attended public school and had gone to university. At university, he had explored the ideas of socialism and they held a fascination for him. Only later did he realize that what really attracted him to the ideology was the possibility of wielding total autocratic power if you were in the right position of power.

He believed the ideology could be a shortcut to all the good things in life. The idea consumed him and it led to him courting the right people in the college societies until one day he was contacted by the local recruiting communist agent. The man, to Lawson's surprise, was a rather dowdy professor at the college. Lawson had inherited enough wealth from his stockbroker father to realize he did not have to sell himself cheaply. Politely but firmly he declined to join and pay subs to the discussion groups who simply wanted to discuss high-flown theories. He left the door open by hinting to the professor that really he was looking for something more than he could offer. The man was not dismayed, quite the reverse, as he realized he had a star in the making and promised to put Lawson in touch with a more active member of the organization.

A man did approach Lawson a week or so later. Lawson again explained that he was really looking for perhaps a long-term relationship; he wanted some position that had purpose and direction. The man questioned Lawson for some time and despite his Oxbridge accent, Lawson was convinced he was a Russian. It was some time before he was contacted again and Lawson had by then assumed he had been dropped and had buried himself in his studies. One morning on his way to a lecture he was stopped by an exceptionally tall man, not quite a giant but heading that way. The man was Tsygankov, who in a quiet and slightly accented voice had told Lawson that he was his contact and would be the only one he would ever have. Tsygankov gave him a contact number and instructed Lawson to make himself available for a week in a month's time.

The week of the initial indoctrination took place in a house in a quiet seaside village on the east coast. For the first two days Lawson was psychoanalysed and tested. After that, for another day, he was taught simple fieldcraft, enough for him to contact his minder in the confidence that security would be robust. The fourth day he learnt about the opportunities open to him and on the last day a lifelong game plan was discussed and an action plan agreed. The plan was simple in outline. Lawson was to complete his degree then join the army special forces for a few years, leaving to become a politician. The Russian explained that the army was for him to have fun and to create a background of loyalty; he could leave his political career to his masters.

He needed to ensure that there would never be any skeletons in his cupboard to round on him in the future. He cut himself off from his friends in college societies, scorning their naivety, and became a fervent right-wing advocate of the Conservative agenda.

At the age of 22, he joined the army with a first-class degree. After six months as an officer cadet at Mons Officer Cadet School, he passed out into the Intelligence Corps. After training as an intelligence officer and a posting to Germany, he volunteered for the Special Air Service. He was bright, fit, and physically well suited. However, despite the considerable physical and mental attributes he possessed, he was basically lazy and was almost found out when he tried to buck the system by finding a shortcut in one of the early selection tests. The test was one of those long walks to be done within the allotted time, carrying a modest 50 pound load in his bergen. Bergens had been weighed before the walk and he and his fellow candidates were surprised when they found a manned checkpoint halfway through with a set of scales to check bergen weights as each man arrived at the checkpoint. The scales were 20 out and each student was giving another 20 pounds to carry, making the rucksack a respectable 70 pounds.

Lawson, twigging the ruse, jettisoned the extra weight. 20 pounds lighter than his colleagues he made good progress and was about halfway down the field when the final checkpoint came into view. Bergens were again being weighed. As he was in sight of the finish, he realized he was in trouble. He reached back and undid the straps of his rucksack. As he approached the knot of staff and potential SAS men, many of whom were taking a well-earned rest, he stumbled and went down, much to the mirth of his fellows. The bergen rode up his back and the rubble in the bag spilled out and mixed with the other rocks and rubble already deposited from the bergens of those potentials that had finished legitimately.

The staff were obviously suspicious but being unable to prove anything was amiss put Lawson down as a pass. He realized he could not give them any future cause for suspicion, so laboured through the course for the remainder of the year. He served, in all, for three years with the regiment. Even the incident with Rodney did not affect him and he left on a high note, very fit and ready for the world.

Initially, civilian life seemed very dull and he soon had itchy feet. After a month of resting, he called his contact. The help he got was significant; first he was ordered to move and live in a suburb of London and then to join the local Conservative party branch. He was fed information and speeches that got him noticed by the local press and branch members. First he won a local council seat within weeks and then the local MP died unexpectedly. He won the party nomination and then the local by-election. Nothing was spared; he was well funded and his campaign was very professional.

With resources behind him far greater than any of the other new MPs and his mystique of having been in the SAS, he soon moved up the party ranks. It was his faster than normal acceleration towards the front benches that first drew the attention of Robinson and his peers. Anything out of the ordinary attracted these men like bees to a honey pot. In their way, they wielded great power and initially looked at Lawson with the curiosity of cats. He got his first junior ministerial post in the Ministry of Defence; they began to notice that he was far too well briefed and they saw a dangerous situation developing. Snippets in his material, when carefully analysed, could only have come from one source, the Russians.

They were in a quandary; he was the government's pet and the Prime Minister's favourite. He was everywhere in the papers, briefing far above his level.

Robinson and his colleagues had a dilemma, they realized they could gather enough evidence to challenge him or they could use him, and this is what they decided to do. This was five years ago now and since then Lawson, fed by two sides, had gone from strength to strength. The problem was that they had been too successful and Lawson was now a danger to the whole country.

Robinson and a circle of friends who were seen as the guardians of the realm had decided he had to be culled. It was by good fortune that Chekhov had decided to come over at this time. It was believed the information he was bringing would not only rid them of Lawson but also put the other side back for years to come if the list enabled them to roll up the spy network in the West. It would also give the West a little elbow room to use on the Russians for a few long outstanding agreements.

At the brigadier's building, Lawson squinted up at Robinson's office on the top floor; there was no indication it was occupied. He went through the high, solid wooden doors into the reception area. A guard saluted the minister and went to meet him.

"Good morning, Minister, can we help you?"

"Could I speak with the Brigadier, please?" Lawson smiled warmly.

"I'm sorry, sir, but the Brigadier has not yet come in and neither has the Major, but it's still only just after nine. Can I get one of them to ring you when they arrive?"

"That's a problem. Can I use your phone to call the duty desk, they may know if they have been delayed."

"Of course, please use the phone in the booth on the right. Just lift the phone and the switchboard will put you through."

"Thank you," Lawson hid his growing annoyance while making his way to the phone. He was quickly put through to the ops desk, Graham Swain was back on duty and he introduced himself immediately.

"Graham, can you tell me how I can get hold of the Brigadier or even Rodney. No news I suppose?"

"They are both late in, sir. Think they may have been working late somewhere last night and have slept late; very unusual for them not to call. If they don't surface by ten, I will start ringing round. As for Cyprus, nothing, sorry; not even a call to say they are all right. Worrying, I know, but it is not so unusual considering the circumstances."

"Thank you, Graham. But please, immediately you trace one or the other please call me." Lawson thought Graham was genuine; he had not detected anything out of the ordinary but still, it was a situation of which he was not in control and that worried him.

His finger drummed the telephone table in the phone booth. He made a few calls and then made his way out of the building. His KGB shadows followed him and Rodney's men followed them.

The KGB men had been identified the night before purely by accident when Rodney's driver had noticed the two men hanging around Lawson's flat. In the morning they had noticed that Lawson had spoken quickly to two men who had caught up with him when he left his flat and had then

walked off, but had followed him across the bridge. They disappeared
when he entered the brigadier's building and then reappeared from a
side street as Lawson made his way to Parliament. The night before,
Rodney's men had watched the two men meet a third one in a car and had
the car checked out. It confirmed their suspicions, the car was registered
to a man on the prohibited list.

The watching team realized immediately that Lawson was now
under protection and that they were up against possibly very dangerous
opponents. As a precaution they had themselves relieved and another car
took their place in a better position, where the new team could see not
only the entrance but the enemy as well. The original team had been too
close and would certainly have been spotted and compromised had they
held their position.

The original team had consisted of experienced agents Reid and
Avery, both recruited by Rodney for the initiative shown during their
time with the forces. They were both conscientious and capable men
who realized that it would not hurt to have an edge on their opponents.
Once back at base they headed for the laboratories; after a little while
they emerged carrying a homing device that they intended to attach to
the KGB car and for good measure they had a miniature, electronically
detonated, magnetic mine that they would also affix. Heading back to
their car, Avery was the first to question their actions.

"OK, so the boss isn't here and we've taken a decision he may have
made anyway but how are we going to do it?"

"Hmm," said Reid screwing up his face, "just wait here a minute," and
he disappeared back into HQ. He was back shortly with a policeman's
uniform under his arm. "Right," he said, laughing, "the old policeman
and drunk routine."

"The what?" questioned Avery.

"You're the policeman and I'm the drunk; you approach from up the
road from the bandits and I from the other, we meet close to the car and
you arrest me, a little scuffle and I go down. Whilst I am down I fix the
devices on to their car. Easy," explained Reid. "Easy!"

"Why do I get the job of policeman and therefore run the risk of
bumping into a real one; what then, my friend?"

"Firstly, the suit's your size and you've got short hair and, secondly, if
you do bump into a real copper, fat chance, you just have to spin it out.
Tell him you're on your way home from work and your car broke down

or something," essayed Reid, waving his hands around implying that it was the easiest thing in the world to do.

Avery was not impressed and snorted his feelings but agreed to do his bit, adding, "Listen, Reidy boy, you're lucky I am in a good mood, or I would have done what you did when that old commanding officer told you to, 'fuck off,' and you did, for two weeks," they both laughed at the memory.

They carried their exercise out successfully and even managed to get a good look at the enemy without arousing their suspicions, although Avery thought Reid overdid the drunken bit especially when one of the men got out of the car to help Avery lift him off the ground. Reid kicked the man in the shin, and then fawned over him saying, "Sorry, sorry," in the way only a drunk can.

It was fortunate that Reid, true to form and professional, had sprinkled a few tots of whisky over himself and drunk a few more. Avery had had to drag him off the man and put him, still professing apologies into a half nelson. Avery had felt obliged to ask the man if he wanted to make a complaint against the voluble Reid but the man had just shaken his head, waved and got back into the car. Avery kept the overacting and noisy Reid in a restraining hold until they were well out of view of the car and its occupants.

"What the hell did you kick him for?" demanded Avery sharply as he released Reid and took off his police jacket which was in some disarray after the scuffle and he was sweating profusely in the thick blue serge.

"I just wanted to see if he was armed, he was, and I wanted his wallet to see who he is, which I got and hereby produce," and with a flourish he produced the man's wallet.

"Christ, you're a mad, crafty bastard. Let's get the hell out of here and have a good look at it." They headed for their car and then down to the department. Avery and Reid went to the duty room.

At the desk, Avery was handed a message that had been radioed in from the surveillance car, it said simply, "Thanks for the cabaret; you two have missed your vocation."

"I'd forgotten about our guys out there, they had a ringside seat," said Avery laughing, much relieved now that they had successfully completed their little exercise. "That reminds me, I'll just get this radio control for the mine and the receiver for the bug down to the guys on watch. I'll get one of the backup teams to take it over to them. I'll be back in a few minutes; you see what the wallet has to offer while I'm away."

When he returned, he found his partner relaxing at his desk drinking a coffee and with one waiting for him. He picked up the cup and looked at Reid expectantly.

"I've checked the name in the wallet with our friend in records. He's Russian and he's suspected of being a hitman. He normally works in this country and with a partner who answers the description of the other man we saw in the car tonight. If we have to blow him and his mate it will not be any loss to the system. Once this caper is over I'll inform Special Branch that they can put their suspect fifth column man on to the definitely suspicious list or whatever they do. Strange, though, the tall man we saw talk to them briefly, although he is on their list, there is nothing actually known on him. He's been seen sometimes briefly with groups that the Special Branch have under constant surveillance. Even where they have somebody in a group and he's been seen, they say he just seems to turn up, moon about a bit and leave quietly. He never speaks but is recognizable by his height; he's almost 6 foot 7 inches. They have him down as a weirdo. After tonight I think I'd class him as a talent spotter. In fact I think we ought to pull his file and get it over here just in case he can actually be tied in to the present operation," voiced Reid thoughtfully. "But for the immediate, old friend, let's get a few hours shut-eye, what do you say?"

"Good idea. What time do we relieve the surveillance team?"

"How about eight o'clock? I'll radio through and tell them to expect us about then. OK?"

"Great, six hours kip, I need it. See you later." Avery couldn't help chuckling as he left the office with Reid bending over his notebook busily recording the night's events. Reid looked up and smiled, and waved goodbye to his partner.

"Always gets you right there," said Reid thumping his chest, "when there's a possibility of a little excitement."

Avery just raised his eyes to heaven and left. It was Reid's task to get his notes up to the duty officer and logged in. Williams is now on duty, thought Avery; he would wonder what he had let himself in for with mad bastards like Reid running round the place.

At eight o'clock the next morning, Reid and Avery relieved a stiff and bored team.

At nine minutes past nine they followed Lawson and the two Russian hitmen as they left Lawson's apartment for the Commons. They were both still in high spirits from the previous evening's activity, which was not a feeling shared by the brigadier and Fred as they waited at the Cyprus RAF airbase for their return flight.

Chapter 27

ROBINSON AND RODNEY

The brigadier and Fred Costa sat in the airport VIP lounge, if you could call it that, a soulless white box, waiting for their plane back to the UK. It was now early morning; Robinson, tired, his age catching up with him, felt nevertheless invigorated as the cool of the morning streamed through the open windows carrying with it the scent of eucalyptus.

The staff had been very helpful and had shown Robinson and Rodney every kindness, but the situation raging on the island meant that they had had to leave them to their own devices, which in many ways suited the two intelligence men admirably. After the interview with Sharky they had discussed the way ahead and had actioned their decisions using the military-secure link on the base to alert their office in London.

On their arrival, they had met the doctor in charge of Sharky's case on the third floor of the military hospital at Dhekelia. He had been open and explained the situation to them.

"Good morning gentlemen, I am Doctor Sainsbury in charge of Mr Sharky's rehabilitation and care."

"Let us introduce ourselves; I am Brigadier Alex Robinson and this is my second in command, Major Rodney Brown," responded the brigadier, shaking hands with the army doctor. "Perhaps you would brief us on the position of my officer."

"Yes, of course. Despite the apparent simplicity of the wound, Mr Sharky has suffered a loss of blood and some minor bruising. He developed a bad infection in the wound and that led to a high fever which very quickly developed into pneumonia. However, he has responded well to the antibiotic drip, otherwise he would already be dead; he was a very poorly man indeed. I am frankly staggered that he is doing as well as he is and I can now say that I believe he is fine but needs time to recover."

"He is as tough as an old boot," commented Robinson quietly. "Is he conscious? I really need to speak to him urgently." His voice held that smooth and authoritative tone he adopted for such occasions. Rodney could see the doctor wrestling with his duty as a doctor who wanted to protect his patient and the clear necessity to allow access.

"Tough he may be, sir, but I do not recommend you tax him unnecessarily. It is of prime importance that he gets as much rest as possible to rebuild his strength. He has only just fought off the fever and infection a few hours ago and is still a little groggy. I am not sure you'll get a lot of sense out of him, but you may."

"Thank you, Doctor, I will be very brief and at the slightest sign of distress I'll leave his bedside." Robinson put a paternal hand on the doctor's shoulder, "If you'll lead the way."

They followed the doctor through the swing doors into a corridor that had private single wards off it. In the distance, they could see Fred nodding, apparently asleep in a chair outside what they assumed was Sharky's room. Next to Fred was a ward sister sitting at a desk writing up her notes. As she saw the men coming down the corridor, she stood up to meet them. Rodney noticed she was elegantly tall, very pretty with a golden tan and light brown hair, a rare beauty.

The doctor, to Rodney's disappointment, waved her back to the desk, "I take it," the doctor said by way of explanation, "that you will not want too many people with you on the visit, so we will dispense with the services of the ward sister."

"Absolutely correct," said the brigadier, "and I think that I should tell you that it would be in your interest not to be in the room when I question my man. It could be highly disadvantageous and possibly dangerous for you to become involved."

The doctor was shocked; he had assumed he would be in the room to safeguard his charge. "I don't know if I can allow you to be alone with him, no matter what I happen to overhear," said the doctor. "Certainly not in his state."

"My dear Doctor I hasten to assure you that all will be well. I take full responsibility for anything that may happen and I again assure you that I shall not distress your patient in the slightest. Indeed, I can promise you that Mr Sharky will rest much more easily when he has passed to me the information he has taken such pains to acquire and risked so much to carry to safety. Now, don't you think that I am right? He only has to unburden himself to me for a few moments and his anxiety level will drop tremendously. You must appreciate that until he passes the information to me he will be in a very distressed state indeed. The intelligence he has is not for your ears."

The doctor knew he had to give way and capitulated gracefully. He was no fool and realized that, despite the man's charm, no matter how much he protested, the brigadier would eventually get his way. So why create a situation he could not win? In addition, on the anxiety front, the man had a point.

Not completely capitulating, he said seriously, with a twinkle in his eye, "Very well, but only for five minutes and not a moment more or I send in Sister," he threatened. "She may look pretty but you'd better not cross her." He opened the door to a darkened room to let the two of them in then closed it quietly behind them.

It took them a second or two to adjust to the gloom but then they could see the outline of Sharky's arm swathed in bandages and, trailing from his body, several tubes and drips.

As they approached his bed, Sharky's eyes fluttered open. "Is that you, nurse?" he slurred.

"No, it's your boss and Rodney," said the brigadier gently.

"Oh, thank God," sighed Sharky with a grin, "I knew you'd come." He was obviously still weak and his eyes burned a little from the after-effects of the fever. Sharky's state shook the brigadier when he looked at his battered agent.

Robinson wasted no time for he could see that Sharky wanted to get the information he had off his chest. "Sharky, listen to me; I know most of what has happened so at this stage all I need from you is to know if you got the list and, if you did, where it is."

Sharky smiled weakly, "Your damned list and the money and diamonds are safe." He gave them the location of the package, describing the cove and the rock by which they had hidden the loot. When he had finished he was tired, but managed to tell them how Seabrook had bought it.

"Yes, I'm sorry, he was a good man. Just so you know, Mould is fine and should be released back to us soon," said Robinson gently. "Now you must rest. You can safely leave the rest to Rodney and me."

Sharky closed his eyes and his face lost its tense appearance. He seemed to drop off to sleep. The boss indicated to Rodney with his head that they should leave quietly. As they reached the door, Sharky's voice carried to them, "Make sure you make the bastard who was responsible for Seabrook's death get his desserts."

"He will, now rest, we need you back at work soonest. As for those responsible, I'll see to that, never fear," promised the brigadier as he and Rodney let themselves out of the room, closing the door quietly behind them.

As they emerged, the sister was standing outside the room with her arms crossed and feet firmly planted in a defiant attitude. She gave them a look calculated to shrivel the stoutest heart and then pushed past them to see her patient was still OK.

The doctor was waiting with a now wide awake Fred and they stepped forward to meet them.

"Ah, Doctor Sainsbury, thank you, I think your patient will settle now. Fred, good to see you again and thank you for what you have done," smiled the brigadier. "Doctor, I'd rather like to go somewhere where I can have a few words with Fred to discuss some matters with him and the Major. After that, I'd like to see the commanding officer in, say, an hour. Possible do you think?"

"Not a problem, you can use my consulting room on this floor, one on from your man's, then I'll collect you later and take you to the Colonel. I'm sure Fred knows the catering arrangements by now and can supply coffee."

"Fine, thank you. One more thing before you go about your duties, what information does your hospital have about my man in there?"

"Nothing at all; as far as most of the staff are concerned, the man in there is simply a casualty from the war zone. Further, we don't even have a name for him yet, although Fred mentioned the name Sharky, and I could add that all the admin officer and the CO and I know is that he is someone special because Fred, you and the Major are here, but that's about it."

"Please make sure that's all that's known for the moment. I'll brief the CO and you later but now, if I may use your room, we have a lot to get through and time is not on my side." The brigadier took the doctor by the elbow and propelled him to his consulting room to unlock it for their use.

Chapter 28

DHEKELIA

Once in the consulting room, with Fred out the way, sent off for refreshments, Rodney was the first to speak. "All is not lost then, on the face of it, the situation appears retrievable. Do we use our men at Ayia Napa?"

"Definitely not. Good grief, Rodney, they must be compromised by now and may well be under surveillance. After all, that idea was just to seed doubt about our knowing where the stuff was. I want those two to make a great play of going to the place where the boat ended up, Ayia Napa, and searching it. If they've done it already they can do it again. Even if they were allowed to retrieve the stuff, as you call it, I doubt that they would be allowed to get it out. No, we need a fresh approach. Do you realize that the war has now been underway for two days and I suspect that the line between the warring factions is stabilizing. For all I know, the hiding place may now not be accessible. And if the hiding place is close to the front, then we really are in trouble." The brigadier relaxed into the doctor's chair and began to think.

Rodney followed his example and sat in another chair; for a few minutes neither spoke as they both thought of the courses open to them and racked their brains for a solution to the problem.

The brigadier broke the silence and issued an order to his aide, "Get on to the local intelligence corps here, they must have a few people we know, and get a situation report on the position." He added, "And, without giving anything away, find out about the area we are interested in; what's the name of the place?"

Rodney looked into his notebook at the notes he'd taken from the interview they had had with Sharky, "It's the area west of Cape Greco, a mile east up the coast from Ayia Napa."

"Ah yes, well get on with it, my boy, and then we'll decide what we are to do."

Rodney picked up the telephone and the hospital exchange answered. It took him a further three minutes to get the right contact, an officer of the rank of major they had worked with in the past. Eventually, the intelligence major gave him a brief report on the situation as it was known and could be forecasted to be in the next few days. When he had finished Rodney thanked him and replaced the telephone on its rest.

"Right," began Rodney slowly, "The situation is as follows: the area we are interested in is in effect fluctuating between Greek and Turkish hands and this situation is likely to remain hot for the near future. Positively, at the very least, it's going to be no man's land should things stabilize on the present line. We have no access. The only people who will be able to get in and move around with relative freedom, in time, will be the UN troops, once things settle down in a week or so. In the end, the intelligence people don't see the Turkish army settling forward of the Cape as that area houses an installation, something to do with NATO, so in time we should get access."

"OK, clearly we have a few days to get the list and the diamonds before anybody is likely to be swimming in that part of the sea for pleasure and might just chance on our property by accident, which sounds like it's well stashed. So let's see what we can do in the meantime. It also looks like the two men we sent to the area may well not have got there. We need to find out soonest; perhaps Fred knows," the brigadier was thoughtful. Summarizing, he went on, "Sharky is vulnerable at this moment. I don't suppose the security is very tight here and that means that if someone on the other side should learn that he is here, they will almost certainly try to get at him and that must be avoided at all costs. Any suggestions?"

"Well, sir, a solution and the safest is to eliminate him and Mould..." Rodney paused and looked at the brigadier for a sign that this course was unacceptable, but the brigadier remained impassive.

"Alternatively, we could get some more security and button that up with the military police."

"No, he and Mould have to die," said the brigadier. "Clearly Sharky is in no state to be moved, so he has to die."

"What! You can't be serious?"

"Never more so dear boy, never more so, and you are going to arrange it with Fred." The brigadier looked at Rodney's horror-struck face and began to chuckle, "I don't intend he should really die, only that he should appear to."

Slowly it dawned on him that he was to arrange a charade and Rodney beamed back at his boss.

"OK, sir," his mind was now racing, "I'll need to involve the doctor, the nurse and, I suppose, their commanding officer, but that should do it."

"What about the trusty Fred who brought Sharky in? Fred is still at hand in case anybody tries to get at our men."

"Aye aye, sir, you can leave that to me from here on; I will fly in men and between them and Fred they will be a strong team to guard our charges."

"Good, now the next problem, how the hell do we get the list and the loot back without causing an international incident and do it quickly?"

"I've been thinking about that and how we get round the difficulty of reaching the stash as the whole island from here to the target is a no-go area for anyone but UN Blue Berets," said Rodney. "I believe there may be a way."

"Yes?" said the brigadier eagerly, his mind alert and his eyes fixed intently on his aide.

"Just let me talk out loud for a minute, sir, whilst I order my thoughts. It has to be a Brit, yes, and he will have to be a legitimate UN soldier. Now, that area is traditionally policed, if that's the right word, by the Scandinavians, but the supply people, the ordnance, travel freely between the various United Nations contingencies delivering materials, rations, fuel, ammo etc." said Rodney enthusiastically. "They also have officers that visit the contingents sorting out problems and complaints. They have a, damn, what's he called? Oh yes, a FOO."

"A what?" interjected his boss.

"A FOO, a Force Ordnance Officer."

"I see; anybody else?"

"Yes, I'm trying to remember; got it! An Ordnance Detachment Commander in command of the supply base up in Nicosia. The man we want has to be genuine. I don't think that any other regiment or corps has that sort of access. He needs to be an Ordnance Officer who is a little out of the ordinary, a maverick, but I'm sure Ordnance will have somebody on their books that could do this job for us."

"It's a little risky, but I confess we don't have a great deal of choice in the immediate. But we have got to be damned careful we don't cause an international incident with the UN and our allies."

Fred rejoined them with a coffee jug, cups and a stack of egg and bacon sandwiches. The London men realized for the first time that they had not eaten since leaving the UK. They were hungry and as they demolished the food mountain Fred told his story. The best news he left until last and was that Mould would be with them in about half an hour; not only that, but his friend in the police force had been handed another two Brits who had wandered into the area posing as journalists. They would be coming in with Mould.

The two London men spent the remaining time before the doctor came for them, sorting out the fine detail of their plan and briefing Fred who was all for the idea.

The decoy bodies of Sharky and Mould would be flown back to the UK for burial. The ploy would give the scheme credibility and buy them time. They agreed that the minister would be told simply that Seabrook was on the bottom of the sea somewhere after having been shot and both Mould and Sharky had died of their wounds not long after they arrived in the hospital, frustratingly, before they were able to tell anyone anything of use and the list and the diamonds were not on their persons. The inference must be that the men must have hidden them en route, if the exchange took place at all. They did not like admitting that point to the minister in case the Russians began a search, although it would be an almost impossible task, under the circumstances, to find the secret location, so it was decided in the interests of authenticity as an acceptable risk.

They also agreed that while Rodney was making the arrangements with the CO of the hospital, the brigadier would speak to his contacts and arrange for his and the bodies' journey back to the UK. Once back on home soil, Robinson would use army records to find their man to recover the document and diamonds.

There was a knock on the door and Doctor Sainsbury entered.

"CO is free; he will see you now if you are ready. We suggested you might like to join him for an early breakfast, not quite late supper, as he suspects you may not have eaten since you left the UK." He sniffed the aroma of egg and bacon and observed the empty plate, "Whatever."

"That, Doctor, sounds like a very sensible idea," said the brigadier. "Will you be joining us?"

"Indeed. And I thought it sensible to have the Sister along as well."

"Well done, good idea. Lead on. I don't know about the Major but I'm suddenly very hungry again. Fred, will you keep an eye on Sharky till Mould and the team get here? And then I am sure they can find you a bed."

"No problem. The room next to Sharky is empty and I think that should do fine if the Doctor has no objections."

"None at all, see you later." The doctor led the two men back through the hospital and over to the Royal Army Medical Corps officers' mess. It was a new building, light and airy with fans whirling on the ceiling, driving a cool breeze of air down on to them when they crossed through the anteroom to the dining room. Inside the dining room at the end of a long table sat the commanding officer smoking and drinking a cup of coffee. When he rose to meet the party, the brigadier could see from the man's demeanour and movements that the colonel was not going to be difficult; he had about him the air of a man who was quite capable of doing most things easily. The brigadier prided himself on being able to sum a man up from his appearance and presentation, and he was rarely wrong.

"Welcome!" the CO called, his blue eyes twinkling. He was a stocky, medium-built man, fortyish with sparse, sandy hair; his distinguishing features were his broken nose and his massive hands, which he now held out in welcome. "I believe you own and are interested in our mystery patient, as I am; first, let's get you your breakfast."

An orderly appeared and food was ordered. Whilst they were waiting, the sister joined them, introductions were made and the preamble with the Official Secrets Act was given by Rodney. His gently persuasive voice stopped when the food arrived. The men from London ate theirs in silence with the three hospital staff looking on. Once finished, the five moved to more comfortable chairs in the anteroom and Robinson outlined the problem and what had to be done.

The local contingent listened in astonishment and when the brigadier had finished, the commanding officer allowed himself a little chuckle. "Amazing, I'm trying to cope with a war and you want me and my staff to play games; why, is not important," the commanding officer shook his head. "Nevertheless, I know what to do and appreciate it's essential to do as you wish," he sat back.

"Go on then, what's your plan, sir?" said the sister looking at her boss who she obviously held in the highest regard.

"With your permission...?" The commanding officer sought Robinson's agreement, who inclined his head. "I will contact Thomas Cook's who will deal with the shipment of the coffins to the UK, and there will be bodies in them. You see," he explained, "I just happen to have a few unidentified bodies that have been placed in our morgue, casualties of the invasion. We'll obviously choose those resembling your people, as far as possible." He added quietly so that the others had to strain to hear, "All the dead tend to look the same when they have met violent ends," and then he seemed to be through his sadness and resumed his briefing. "The bodies will not stand up to an autopsy or even close scrutiny when they get to you, so you'll have to make sure that doesn't happen," he added looking at the two men.

"Naturally," said Robinson and Rodney simply nodded.

"And I want them back. They belong to someone, so they are only on loan, say a week at the most. Someone will want to claim them eventually." Robinson agreed. The colonel went on, "Rodney, you will have to fill in some forms for me, identifying them, next of kin forms, that sort of stuff."

"No problem," agreed Rodney.

The commander looked at his staff. "Sister, you get our mystery man booked as a Greek national. I've seen him and he could easy pass at a pinch and anyway nobody's seen him cleaned up, he could have been a Martian as far as anybody knew yesterday under all that blood. Rodney, you will have to speak to your agent, Fred, or whatever he is."

"No problem. Technically, he's an assistant, a friend on a retainer, not an agent," broke in the brigadier. "I've decided to take Fred back to the UK with me when I go. He has a little job to do for me there, like convincing someone else that the men are dead. Anyway, two of us came out so two must go back; I've just finally decided to leave my able aide at your disposal."

Rodney looked at his boss questioningly.

"No need to worry my boy, I'll handle the London end and the other matters we discussed; you can handle this end. We have Mould and two other men arriving shortly; I'll send others, so there is someone to guard

Sharky and, with the Sister's determination to ensure his well-being, all will be quite safe. We will need to be here for phase two anyway, so enjoy yourself," said the brigadier with a wink at Rodney.

Rodney groaned and the others laughed. He knew it was foolish to argue and anyway what Robinson said made good sense. The prospect of spending a few days with this tanned army nursing sister also held some attraction.

The meeting broke up and the hospital team left the men to themselves in the anteroom to finalize their plans, then they too parted when an officer arrived to tell them that the brigadier's helicopter was ready to take him back to the RAF base. Rodney went first to get Fred and then on to the commanding officer to sort out the paperwork for the removal of the bogus bodies to the UK.

Rodney saw the brigadier off and then returned to the hospital where he adopted the guise of a hospital orderly. When Mould and the two other agents arrived, after a brief meeting to bring them up to date and to hear their tales, they too became orderlies, albeit well armed, and they formed a 24 hour guard for Sharky based in the ward corridor and the adjacent room. It had amused Mould greatly when he found his sidekick was officially dead. He said he couldn't wait to tell him. The grin came off his face when Rodney told him that he was dead too. Rodney grabbed a few hours of sleep but was up and running by mid afternoon.

By evening, Sharky had brightened considerably and was threatening to get up. Rodney, with Mould's help, and with the aid of a large-scale map had been able to pinpoint the hiding place of the objects. Mould had also confirmed that there was absolutely no chance of anyone who was a stranger getting out to the place. So what he needed now from the brigadier was a man who could get in and out legitimately. Rodney was talking with the sister when the call came through from the brigadier and he was summoned to the commanding officer's office to take it.

He took the phone from the CO and covering the mouthpiece said to the colonel, "Sir, I think the less you hear of this conversation, the better it will be. I don't want to compromise you or your position. Could you excuse me for a while?"

The CO nodded and left Rodney to take the call alone.

"Rodney," it was the brigadier, he sounded tired but satisfied. "Our man will be there by morning and has orders to report to the hospital before heading for his post at Nicosia with the UN. Lawson appears to believe the story of Seabrook's death and the death of the other two. Fred was brilliant and convinced him, but he is not amused at us going off without telling him. Any questions?"

"The name of the officer who is to report to me?" enquired Rodney.

"Collins, Captain James Collins."

"Thank you, sir. I suggest that you get yourself off home and get some rest. Didn't Lawson ask about me?"

"He did, as a matter of fact, but I think he was too shaken by the loss of the list and trinkets to register my mumbled explanation that you were looking after the arrangements. He doesn't realize you are doing that from Cyprus and I don't intend to tell him. I've dispatched Reid and Avery to assist you; they have become too hot here. They can explain. Fred will be with them. I'll call you tomorrow if anything changes. Goodnight." The brigadier rang off and Rodney was left staring into the silent earpiece.

Now the brigadier had gone he felt alone but, with Reid and Avery joining the team, life would not be too bad and until they arrived he had the sister almost to himself. When he arrived back on the ward the team was around and Mould was in with Sharky. The sister was in the ward office with a coffee waiting for him.

"Thank you, that's just what the doctor ordered," said Rodney taking the mug and eyeing her over the rim. "Aren't you going off to rest?"

"Not until Doctor Sainsbury relieves me in the morning, what about you?"

Rodney leaned wearily against the wall, "I'll wait until more relief arrives. They are sending me a couple of men to help. I just hope they, along with the others, can carry off the guise of orderlies without attracting attention."

"I shouldn't worry, it's going to be busy for a few days, if not weeks, before the chaos sorts itself out; anyway, there are new staff arriving all the time and a few extra at this time will not be noticed." The sister fiddled with the papers on her desk and it was obvious to Rodney that she was making up her mind to say something but didn't know how to start, suddenly she looked at him and smiled, "By the way, my name's Sue."

"Ah," said Rodney. "I'm called by many names, but you can call me Rodney."

"OK, Rodney, good name. What made you get into your line of service to queen and country? You're the first spook I've met."

Rodney suppressed a chuckle and just succeeded in preventing the coffee he was drinking from going up his nose. "First, I'm not exactly your James Bond and as to joining, l suspect that, like you, it seemed like a good idea at the time."

She laughed and then said seriously, "Come on, then, Rodney; let's get Mr Kristos prepared for the night."

"Mr who?"

"Your man has been renamed."

"I see," said Rodney as casually as possible. "And just what does this task entail your temporary attachment doing?"

"Well, you get to help me change the plasma bottles, prepare his injection and things like that. Also, to change the bed and dressings and lastly you get to wash out the bedpan."

"Ugh, lead on Miss Nightingale," Rodney bowed and swept his hand before him and Sue glided past him. Inside the sickroom she was all business, dismissing Mould who had become a fixture. Rodney just watched the calm professionalism she displayed in changing Sharky's bandages and attending to his other needs. Sharky was awake and apart from a little discomfort declared himself fit; he was not too ill to give a knowing wink in Rodney's direction to which Rodney found himself, to his surprise, blushing. When they had finished and had returned to the sister's office, Mould went back into the room to keep Sharky company. They could see his door and his attentive guards through the glass panelled walls. Rodney stared at the door and then asked her what she thought about Sharky.

"Tell you the truth, when they brought him in yesterday and the pneumonia set in, I would not have given you a fiver that he would have lasted through the night but a few hours after surgery his condition stabilized and now, with rest and treatment, I see him in no danger at all. He didn't go into shock or if he did he came out of it. But he was full of morphine and other stuff so I suppose that helped him."

"Hmm," Rodney thought back to the time when the drug had also saved him.

"What was 'hmm' for?" queried Sue.

"I'll tell you sometime, but it's a long story, perhaps when this is all over."

"I have all night and so do you, so get on with it."

"OK, you asked for it," Rodney settled down.

It was late when he had finished telling his story and he could see it had touched her for she leant forward and stroked the injured leg and he suddenly felt very vulnerable; then they were in each other's arms. She pushed him away gently, took his hand and led him to an empty room down the corridor, on the opposite side to the one the team were using.

Rodney was worried about leaving the observation point in the office but Sue put her finger to her lips and indicated the door to Sharky's room. Sue went and opened it a few inches. In the gloom of the room, they could see Mould, sleeping now in a chair and Sharky well away too. Rodney could see her smiling. They returned to their room, leaving the door ajar. They spent the night together until reluctantly they made themselves respectable and wearily took their posts back in the office. Mould was around and told them the other two had gone for breakfast.

Surprisingly, when their own relief came, it was not the doctor but a boisterous Reid closely followed by a sleepy Avery. "Hi, boss, how's our patient?" Reid was attired in the hospital whites of an orderly with sergeant stripes on his arms, "And may I present my assistant, Corporal Avery."

Mould muscled in, grinning, "He's fine this morning; wants out. What are you two reprobates doing here?"

Reid said seriously, "Slight problem of overexposure. And watch your mouth when you are talking to a senior rank," he used his index finger to indicate his stripes.

Rodney put a stop to the banter, "Good to see you guys. Now, let's get sorted. Sharky is in that room and you have a team base in the room next door up the corridor. For clarity the rooms run: Doctor's room, which I will use as and when, then Sharky, then your team base. OK? Reid, as you are the senior rank anyway, goodness knows who gave you those new stripes, but there you are, you're the Guard Commander. Sharky is bed-bound until the Doctor says he can get up and Mould also needs to be hidden, so he and Sharky need to stay in the room and your job is to make sure that no one that isn't authorized goes in or out. OK?" Mould pulled a face. "Sorry, Mould, but you too are at risk, as both of you are now officially dead and dead men don't walk around disproving carefully crafted plans. Got it?"

"Got it, sort of forgot for a moment that I was dead."

Everyone laughed.

"Rest of your team is at breakfast," Rodney continued. "So that makes four of you to keep two safe and hidden from prying eyes. There is a serious aspect. The other side has already tried to kill them and these two hold knowledge that the other side would not hesitate to do whatever was required to retrieve it."

"Got it in one, boss; leave this to the lads now. You get off to sleep," Reid characteristically thumbed over his shoulder. "Mould, you in there and kip," he directed his other thumb towards Sharky's room. He left no room to argue and both men nodded compliance. It did not do to argue with Reid, his slightly sadistic sense of humour was legendry and to buck him could mean you could come in the office and find your desk nailed to the ceiling, at the very least.

"OK, OK, two minutes, just waiting for the Doctor to come to relieve Sister and me and then we are off. He should be here any minute."

The doctor walked in shortly afterwards and the handover was effected. Rodney and Sue left the medic and crew to their task and after a shower and breakfast they both stumped tiredly off to bed.

Sue promised to get him back in time for him to get his dinner and to take over the night shift.

Later, after he had showered and crashed for a few hours of much needed sleep, Rodney sat on his bed in the officers' mess and thought through the events so far. Having decided that there was not a damned thing he could do until Captain Collins arrived, he again was laid full stretch on the bed watching the lazy fan circle above him, which was the last thing he knew until he was aware of someone else in the room.

"Rodney," Sue sat on his bed. "It's half an hour until lunch finishes. You've slept for the last five hours and I thought you might like to take a shower before we take cocktails on the veranda and we can eat there."

"A shower yes, to wake me up, but why don't you go and shake up half a dozen brandy sours and we can have them here?" said Rodney in a low voice with a wink. "I'm told until you drink a brandy sour made from Keo brandy in Cyprus, you have never really lived."

"True it is, sir; I'll be back in ten minutes so get into the shower with you."

Rodney was savouring this pleasant interlude in the middle of the operation that every soldier knows so well, when the guns fall silent and the battlefield seems to go to sleep for a while.

A very mystified captain on the other hand was just arriving at the hospital, which was really going to mess up any plan Rodney had for after the brandy sours.

Chapter 29

COLLINS

Robinson had little difficulty in finding a suitable candidate for the recovery job. A call to the right quarter and an old friend quizzed had turned up a Captain Collins who not only, his friend had said, enjoyed the, 'out of the ordinary,' but for a while had been in Cyprus training soldiers on exercise in assault boats in the south-east of the island and was a true water baby if ever there was one. He was dependable and could keep his mouth shut. The only difficulty had been persuading the general to put an extra officer out with the UN at this time for some undisclosed reason. Robinson had eventually persuaded his old pal by agreeing to accept full responsibility for any comebacks.

The first thing Captain James Collins knew was a roar from his commanding officer in the next office.

"James, get yourself in here at once."

He raised his eyes to the heavens, "What now?" he thought. He was stuck in this supply job in one of the depots in Germany and although the job was interesting and totally absorbing it was not entirely his cup of tea. He threw the pile of papers he was working on back into the pending tray and wearily got up from the desk.

"James!" the officer commanding shouted again.

"On my way, sir."

"Now, not tomorrow," the CO had just finished bawling when James's stocky frame filled the door entrance. "Ah, there you are. What have you been up to this time? You are to report to a Brigadier Jones at Corps HQ immediately. Take my car."

"What for, sir?" James was not worried just curious.

"I haven't the faintest idea; his PA just phoned and that was all she'd say, except to bring kit for a week in a warm climate; so get moving."

He left the CO, for whom he had the greatest respect, mumbling to himself about losing his staff again, and then the call for the sergeant major rang out as he was leaving the building.

James had collected his hat and had found the German driver of the boss's little Escort staff car, they headed off to the mess to get a bag of basic kit and then drove to Corps HQ, on arrival he was bundled into Brigadier Jones's office by an excited PA.

James saluted and stood at attention in front of the officer's desk.

"James, got a bag packed? Good, I've had a call from London. It's a little brief but basically you're on your way to a destination-unknown job. I have been asked to say that it's not a volunteer assignment, so you're on your way whether you like it or not. My view is that it may be a job that could help to redress the balance over that fiasco with the air rifle."

James blinked – he hadn't realized that the brigadier was aware of his brush with the military police. He had introduced the idea of the duty non-commissioned officer carrying the unit air rifle on his rounds to knock off any vermin that had found its way into the food storage area of the supply depot. It had been a good idea and effective until one clown, after a few beers, had taken a potshot at the intelligence section, with which they shared the barracks, and broken a window. The next thing James had known was the OC pulling him out of his bed wanting to know why the depot was surrounded by military police. After an embarrassing half hour with the MPs he was let off further action after a thorough dressing-down and a warning.

"I..." began James, by way of explanation.

"No one can be in our business and not find himself foul of the norm at some time. Why, I remember the..." the brigadier's voice trailed off, his eyes crinkled at the edges. "Hmm... forget that. Good luck with whatever it may be that they want you to do. I know you will not let the Command down. I'll see that everything is squared here. They estimate a week's trip at most. I'd like to see you on your return, see the PA on the way out, she has your travel arrangements."

James was no further forward when the still harassed PA led him to a waiting helicopter in front of Corps HQ. He was whisked away to the nearby RAF base and flown to RAF Brize Norton, where he was met by a tight-lipped civilian who supplied him with fresh lightweight clothing and a suitcase full of the necessary kit. James at least got a chance to repack some of his own kit amongst the new. The civilian took James's unwanted kit and said he would get it back to him later. The man kept James confined in a VIP lounge at the back of the airport until he was emplaned, still with the civilian in tow.

"OK," said James as the DC-10 took off into the sky. "How about a hint of a briefing; to start with, who are you?"

"I'm what you could call a policeman, of sorts; the name's Pollard," said the man relaxing into his seat. "That, Captain, is all I can tell you, except that I've been told to get you safely to Cyprus and then to the British Military Hospital to meet one of my bosses. Oh, and to make sure you don't give anything away that you're not exactly on a routine posting," he added in a quiet, comforting voice. "Your legend is: you're to say that you're part of a small reinforcement to the lads out at the UN Base at Nicosia, in these troubled times. Things are a little hectic at the moment and they're having trouble coping with the situation. Got it?"

"Sounds very reasonable to me," said James acerbically. "You policemen think of everything." He was starting to realize that someone had pulled a fast one on him.

Suppose he had said no to Brigadier Jones, what could he have done? Probably given him a lecture on any refusal being career limiting. Still, on the bright side he was off to the island he loved and, who knows, it might even be exciting. So he, like Pollard, settled down into his seat and dreamt of those happy days he had spent on the island, gently burning under the Mediterranean sun and lulled by the rolling of the sea, while consuming Cyprus wine by the bottle for pennies a bottle.

The flight was uneventful and James felt his heart rise as they approached the coast and he could look into the clear Mediterranean Sea. They were down. The door of the aircraft opened and he suddenly realized just how much a war can change things. There seemed to be soldiers and civilians, stores and vehicles everywhere and the airport seemed to be crammed with transport planes disgorging stores and people. Long lines of people, obviously civilian, clutching precious belongings, were being shepherded on to waiting planes. James, in his sleepy backwater in Germany, had not really appreciated what was going on out here and he said so. Pollard's remark was typical of the man who James had summed up as being a cold–hearted, miserable, bureaucratic bastard who, despite his almost frail figure, he would not like to meet on a dark night.

"There's a war on and you're a soldier, so earn your money and be damned."

James's response, however, brought a flicker of a smile to the man's dark features. "Aren't our policemen wonderful? So full of humanity."

Sleepy Cyprus was awake. On the pan they were met by an RAF flight lieutenant in full flying kit who led them quickly to his helicopter.

As they flew from the base at Akrotiri to Dhekelia, they could see from the open doorway of the craft, fleeing refugees jamming the roads with their overloaded cars, carts and buses of every sort. Everybody seemed to be heading in the opposite direction to James, which was somewhat disconcerting.

The pilot's voice came over the intercom, "What you see below are the Turkish and Greek refugees making for the base and protection, fleeing from the war in the north. They appear to have somewhere to go. Some are to be evacuated but the people I feel sorry for are the Greeks now trapped behind the Turkish lines; they have nowhere to go at this moment. I believe they are forming into enclaves but I don't fancy their lot. Still, the UN does seem to be coping with that problem and it's reported that the UN refugee organization is to swing into top gear so at least their basic needs will be met."

James looked at Pollard for a reaction. He got none. The man was as hard as nails. When they landed, Pollard stayed on board and James found himself in front of the hospital feeling a little lost. As he picked up his kit, a figure emerged from the hospital complex and waved to him. The man was about his height and build and despite a limp moved quickly to meet him.

"Captain James Collins, I presume? I'm Major Rodney Brown and directly responsible for you being here. Any complaints, any questions?" Rodney flashed a smile, studying James.

"Nothing sensible at this time. Well, yes, sir, what the hell am I doing in Cyprus when I should be in the officers' mess in Germany about now, getting changed for dinner?" James grinned.

"You'll do." Rodney put his arm round James pointing him to the mess, having made his mind up that this young officer would work out just fine and fit in with the team. "All in good time; what exciting lives our soldiers do lead these days; here one day and gone the next. First, a bath for you and a drink, food and then I'll explain all. It's nothing to worry about and I think you may even enjoy the role you are about to play." Rodney led James into the mess.

James satisfied his immediate needs, got dressed in his new uniform and tried on the UN beret before rejoining Rodney in the mess anteroom.

Rodney, who had decided that James was a good choice for the job, felt completely at ease and indicated that James should join him and take a seat. He waited for James to settle into his chair and when Rodney was sure he had his attention he began. "Ostensibly, you are here to help out your hard-pressed brother officers up in Nicosia and as far as they are concerned, that's exactly what you are doing."

"But really?" It was a question James again began to get the feeling that it would have been better to have said, 'No,' to back in Germany.

"But really your sole task is to get something that's been dropped by one of my men, well hidden, here." Rodney unfolded a map and indicated the place where Mould and Sharky had placed their cache. "What it is doesn't concern you and I caution you against being inquisitive. The packages, two of, are relatively small, say each is about the size of briefcase, and they are double wrapped in black plastic."

James nodded in acknowledgement.

Rodney described in great detail the location of the hiding place, even the depth and cave characteristics.

James looked straight at Rodney, "I know the area well, the blue pool is a favourite spot of mine and probably even know the cave to which you refer, but if I'm based in Nicosia how the hell do I get there?"

"You have to work that out, but obviously as the supply officer you will have the opportunity to visit the units being supplied from the detachment and that includes the UN contingent in Famagusta, and that's not too far from the point you have to reach."

"Hmm, could say one of the reasons they sent me out was to beef up the unit liaison to leave the detachment commander time to concentrate on the business, when I meet the Force Ordnance Officer that may fly." James smiled, "Yeah, that very well may fly." He paused. "OK, suppose I can get there and retrieve your packages, how long have I got? Is there a time penalty? And what do I do with it after I get it, assuming I can? Most importantly, what's the opposition I am likely to run into? As important, who is on my side?"

Rodney put his hand to his forehead and scratched it, then looking

James in the eye admitted that he didn't have long, in fact, he wanted the packages in his hand here by yesterday or this time next week at the latest. "Getting it to me is easy once you have it; you take the coast road past here, nip in and give me the stuff before heading north to Nicosia. As for the opposition, apart from the indigenous population and the nervous Turkish soldiers who may be in that part of the island you should meet no other." He went on to explain that although the Russians were involved, that should not bother James as his cover was, as far as Rodney could tell, completely watertight.

James, for his part, was already running his plan and calculating the risks involved. He didn't see that it should be too much of a problem but you could never tell. He looked at Rodney, "You forgot to say who was on my side."

"That's a bit difficult to quantify. There is me, of course, and I have a couple of lads with me but we can't leave the Sovereign Base, we are gated, at least for the time being but things do seem to be easing."

"OK, I'll have a go," said James making up his mind. "But first I'll have that drink you promised me to seal the deal. I take it I can't bring anybody else into it?"

"Definitely not; this operation is already known by too many people, that is, more than one, so if you need help or advice you speak to me. This is the local number and they will find me if you call," Rodney handed a slip of paper to James. "Now those drinks, brandy sour OK for you?"

"My absolute favourite! Then I need to hightail it to Nicosia and meet my new boss or they are going to wonder where I have got to."

Chapter 30

LAWSON IN LONDON

Back in a dreary, wet London, Robinson was trying to control the pace of things during a difficult interview with Lawson who was being tiresome and Robinson wished Rodney was back with the list.

Lawson had been in contact with his KGB handler who had ordered him to get back to the brigadier and find out more. They were not satisfied with the report of Seabrook's death and the others and they wanted proof. They had initially relaxed for a few hours with the news from Robinson that the list had been lost. Tsygankov was not convinced and he persuaded Lawson to see sense and to realize that it was just too much to hope for. Lawson was frustrated and fearful, and he vented his frustration on Robinson who remained calm throughout the interview.

Despite Peter Lawson's personal anxiety of discovery he wasn't particularly worried; he could ride any situation now as he had the whole resource of the UK KGB network behind him. The Russians had obviously done their appraisal and realized that he must be saved at all costs. He was so close to the top of the tree and he would soon be in a position to provide them with a mole at a level that would be right at the centre of NATO decision-making. And, in addition, be in a position to influence future policy and Britain's world position for the foreseeable future. The minister was too good to give up without a fight.

Lawson wanted to meet Fred Costa and the brigadier called for him. Fred was convincing and Lawson was left in no doubt that Sharky and Mould were dead and that Seabrook had been lost at sea. Lawson thanked him for his work and Fred excused himself.

"Good man," commented Lawson and then asked the brigadier when the bodies of the two agents were likely to arrive in England.

"We expect them to arrive from Cyprus within the next few days after which they will be going to one of our special plots once a post-mortem has been carried out."

"Why a post-mortem, I understand they were shot, surely that should suffice?"

"It's standard procedure, in case either of them swallowed anything; after all they may have swallowed the list or the diamonds before they died. It's a possibility we can't overlook, although hardly likely."

"Surely then the bodies should be guarded?" said Lawson questioningly.

"Oh yes, they will be, Rodney will be dealing with them all the way. You may remember that I did say Rodney was dealing with the arrangements. He is with the bodies at this very moment."

"You mean he is in Cyprus at this time; I thought I had not seen him around," said the minister in a surprised voice.

Blast, thought the brigadier, that's really torn it, how stupid of me. Too late to retract now, just have to bluff it out; it might mean that Rodney and his team need to get a move on. The brigadier continued responding to Lawson, "Oh yes, I thought as he was on the spot he may as well have a few days of sunshine before he returns and he could marshal our men back here. Think a few days out there will suit him to escape this miserable weather. Don't you think?" Robinson said seriously, looking directly at the minister. He thought, "That should make you sweat a bit more."

The minister gazed back and said curtly, "An excellent arrangement. When did you say they would be back exactly?"

"I didn't, but I believe arrangements have been made with the RAF and Cook's to get the bodies back probably on this Thursday's flight, subject to space."

"Three days from now. Very well, Robinson, I will be available to meet the plane with you and then let's get the post-mortems carried out immediately. I may as well be in at the death of this ill-fated adventure as I was in at the beginning."

You will most certainly be in at the death, that's a promise, thought Robinson to himself.

"What about Seabrook? How did he die and where is the body?" questioned Lawson.

"Wish we knew; all we do know is that he was shot dead by, we believe, KGB thugs," Robinson said with feeling for the first time. "Which led to him going over the side along with poor Chekhov. We have to assume the bodies, or what's left of them, will be washed up sooner or later. What perplexes me is how the KGB knew our men would be there at that time," he looked questioningly at Lawson.

Lawson felt himself colouring which, although it was noticed by the brigadier, Robinson was careful to keep his face bland.

Lawson said coolly, "We must assume that they were tailing Chekhov, don't you think?"

Robinson twisted the knife, "But how could they have followed him in that powerful boat of his? How did they come to be there? It has me beat I can tell you."

Lawson just grunted, "Perhaps we will never know, anyway, what is past is past; the priority now is to find the list if it is still around. I suppose Rodney is at the hospital in Dhekelia with the bodies of the two hapless agents?" He made to leave the brigadier's office casually whist keeping eye contact. The look on Robinson's face told Lawson what he wanted to know but he let Robinson confirm it, pausing by the door for the answer.

"Yes, that's correct, why do you ask?" said the brigadier reluctantly.

"Oh, no matter, an idle question, that's all," with a smile he was gone.

Robinson was furious with himself. Although he didn't see any way of avoiding the minister's question, he felt he had made it very easy and now his men were in danger. Robinson returned to his desk and slumped into the high-backed swivel chair. He closed his eyes and relaxed. He knew that Lawson would want his people to carry out a search; they may even try to get at the bodies and cut them open. He wished he hadn't embellished his explanation about the autopsy; reluctantly he reached for the phone. He put a call through to Rodney.

He had to wait some time for them to fetch him and he reflected on what he would say.

"Rodney, sir." It was a statement.

"Listen, Rodney, I'm sorry to say that I've probably just made your life more difficult." He explained the Lawson interview and the facts that he had let slip, not only that Rodney was in Cyprus but at the hospital with the bodies.

"Oh dear, if we do have uninvited visitors, that could stretch Colonel

Matthews' hospitality. How long do you think we have?"

"Not long. If at all possible I think you need to meet Collins at the recovery spot to save time, might be safer too, that's if you can move, although Graham tells me that now we have a tentative ceasefire, the curfew is not strictly enforced by the Greeks in your area." Robinson told Rodney again to be especially careful as he believed that the KGB men would soon be snooping round, so Rodney had better be ready and should revert from his orderly disguise to that of simply a retired officer waiting to escort bodies back to the UK, even if in realty he was going to stay and support Collins. Avery and Reid with the other two would have to take care of Mould and Sharky's security on their own now.

He told Rodney to give Colonel Matthews his apologies but to brief him on what to expect. Lastly, he asked about Sharky. Rodney assured him that his progress was excellent and that he was almost fully recovered.

Rodney pushed back on part of the brigadier's plan; he argued strongly that, as the link with James Collins, he needed to stay and support him until the mission was accomplished. He would keep Reid and Avery to make sure Mould and Sharky were safe and hidden until then. He suggested he send the other two agents back with the decoy bodies to make a show at the reception in the UK.

"It's a sound plan, sir," Rodney waited for Robinson to respond.

"Oh, bollocks!" Robinson responded.

"Err, what is?" Rodney was surprised, the old man rarely used expletives.

"Thing is, I told Lawson you would be coming back with the decoys. We have a few days yet. What are the chances of James getting the job done before the flight back on Thursday?"

"Honestly don't know. He seems OK to me and I am sure he will complete at best speed but he is not a free agent and has to wriggle to get out of Nicosia. Don't expect they are in 'lock down' like the Sovereign Bases but I expect movement is restricted. Our Turkish and Greek cousins are still probing at each other in some places despite the ceasefire."

"Do your best. If you don't make the flight make sure the boys have a note from you saying why you decided to stay a little longer. Fallen in love with Matron," Rodney almost burst out laughing, "or broke a leg, or recovering Seabrook's body or some such nonsense. I leave it to you."

"Do my best, sir," Rodney replied.

"Sure you will. By the way," Robinson added. "I almost forgot to tell you, you will no doubt have heard the story from Reid of his escapade with the Russian watchers, well, I decided to dig a little as the tall figure seen around the watchers was niggling me. I got the Russian desk to dig deep. It appears the man was high profile to them and disappeared off the face of the earth about ten years ago. But they did some more research for me and called in a few favours, tapping a source in the KGB. The tall man is called Tsygankov and he is a ranking KGB brigadier. I think the rank and his involvement could mean he is Lawson's handler, so I am going to trace him and put full surveillance on him."

"My goodness, Tsygankov could be something of a coup."

"Just thought you would like to know, but now, back to the list. Tsygankov is my problem and I just hope he doesn't become yours, as by all accounts he is a ruthless professional and a worthy opponent." Robinson killed the call.

Rodney was thoughtful; he knew the boss was not happy, clearly under pressure to close this out and he could feel for him, on the other hand the brigadier was an old hand; Thursday really was the crunch day for Rodney and he thought about how he could get James to move just that bit faster, still, he didn't want to acknowledge he was worried after the call. He knew deep down that Lawson was now on their trail and that his KGB masters were not going to leave a stone unturned, they could be very persistent. He was of course right in his appreciation of the situation.

After his interview with Robinson, Lawson was soon on to his handler who, after criticizing him for not getting the information sooner told Lawson to leave the rest to him. Tsygankov told him coldly, "You are to stay firmly in the background until advised otherwise, except for your trip to the airport with the Brigadier when the plane arrives carrying the bodies."

Tsygankov activated two Greek freelance agents working for the Nicosia Soviet Mission, brothers, Nikos and Joseph. These agents were notorious for the work they did fomenting unrest in the country. It was believed that they had been instrumental in helping to further the EOKA cause and had arranged mines and explosives through intermediaries. They had been implicated in the present troubles, but little proof existed that could bring them to justice. Both were large, violent men and generally considered to be out of control. There was little doubt in the minds of Special Branch or of the Cyprus police, now temporarily disintegrated due to the split in the country, that these two were the local hitmen for their Russian masters.

After the undersecretary at the Russian embassy, a contemporary of Tsygankov, had briefed the two brothers, the hired men left immediately for Dhekelia.

Chapter 31

COLLINS JOINS THE UN TEAM

James had arrived and had settled himself into the mess at Nicosia. The UN Headquarters and many of the units were based there and to the south of the airport runway. He had received a warm welcome from his brother officer who was only too grateful for his help and a little surprised, disappointed even, when James explained that he didn't think he'd be there long and that his help was very temporary indeed, just until the situation settled down he explained. No one could tell how long that may be. Needless to say, after James had put his kit away in one of the tin huts that made up the officer accommodation, he was then led to the HQ for his briefing on the situation and his introduction to the UN culture and rules of engagement.

A tired intelligence officer, giving his fourth briefing of the day, really didn't want to be bothered. He had enough on his plate just keeping track of events, from plotting minefields to Greek and Turkish deployments that were weaving around the front line like a field of corn blowing in the wind; then there was the refugee problem, etc., etc. He had the standard prepared talk about being part of an international force and to be careful not to show any nationalist leaning or to show favour to the British outside the UN organization.

The intelligence officer, a Canadian, took James a few doors down the corridor to meet the Force Ordnance Officer, a Major David. David followed a briefing with a rundown on the unit and the dependency and units they served, as well as the refugee camps.

James was able to tell Major David that he had been briefed to support the detachment commander and particularly to take the strain off the team by visiting as many of the units as possible.

"Interesting that they picked up on that aspect of our mission; they must realize that one of my responsibilities is visiting but with all that's going on my time is taken up with other matters. So that's an area you can get straight on to. The other area that could take the pressure off your brother detachment commander is for you to help with the refugee supplies receipt and out load of essential life-maintaining stores. We are expecting a particular large drop of tentage for the enclaves." He ran his hand through his thinning dark hair. James realized he was with a man who had so much on his plate that James would have a pretty free hand to do what he wanted, providing he got the refugee supply sorted and moving.

"OK, James, got you a UN car outside, a Mazda, for your use while you are here. You can drive me down to the detachment. We will see Paul and then you can drive me back to the mess for dinner. Come on." He grabbed his blue beret and led the way, throwing the car keys to James.

It was a quick one mile drive to the ordnance detachment, ORDET for short, at one end of Nicosia's bombed-out runway. James noticed the wreckage of several aircraft that had not made it off the runway before the Turkish Army had overrun the place.

"What a mess," exclaimed James out loud. "You must have had a difficult few hours until the situation calmed."

"You can say that again, we are still manning the trenches as you can see," said David. "In fact one priority issue, now I come to think of it and why I and Paul are particularly grateful to see you, is that sleep has not been exactly the easiest thing to get around here. So, as it happens, I was rather hoping you would take on a bit of the load and volunteer to do the liaison bit with the outstations to see that they have all they need. I normally do it as I said, but as they have obviously understood, I am tied down with other issues."

"I'd be delighted, and it would give me time to orientate myself. So the Turks, I take it, are to the north and the Greeks to the south of here, but that's about as far as I can go apart from the briefing, which scared the pants off me."

Major David laughed, "Nothing to worry about, it's all over bar the shouting and a bit of line adjusting for tactical reasons, hills and valleys and that sort of thing. So relax, get stuck in and enjoy yourself."

As they pulled up in the UN car they were met by the company sergeant major, "Good evening, sirs, all well; the trenches are manned and the observation post crew is just about to change for the next shift."

"Thank you, CSM, can I introduce Captain Collins, he's come to give us a hand for a while."

"Where's the observation post?" said James looking round.

"Look to the right and you'll see a dirty great water tower, one of our men caught a stray Turkish bullet up there the other day and it was only the timely action of one of our seniors that got him down to safety."

"I can see you are carrying out an infantry task as well as the technical one."

"Exactly, sir," said the sergeant major. "The days when the support troop could expect to be protected by the infantry are long gone, as you know; as ever, soldier first and tradesman second."

With that, he saluted and left the two officers surveying the scene. From their vantage point in the Nicosia valley they could see mountains and hills around them in the middle distance.

"It has a beauty all its own don't you think?" said David.

"Yes, I do. I confess that I always feel at home in Cyprus. They say it was the birthplace of man, I always feel as though I'm coming home. Crazy, isn't it?"

"No, not necessarily, after all it is the island of Aphrodite, the goddess of love." With that David led James into the large hangar that housed the ordnance detachment to talk to Paul, the ORDET commander and was then introduced to the rest of the team. They were all weary, but he could detect the thrill and enthusiasm in the men as they felt they were doing something special and that was sustaining them. How long before they complained about the attrition? Probably never. He met the Force Ordnance Warrant Officer known to all as the FOWO, in the same manner the Force Ordnance Officer was known as the FOO. The FOWO, it was soon decided, would shepherd James round the island on his first round robin visiting the various national contingents of the UN. The small British logistics group supported the whole force with backup from the sovereign bases at Akrotiri and Dhekelia. They discussed the units they would need to visit, spotting them on the map one after the other and discussing what would be the best route. James was pleased to see that whichever way you travelled, Famagusta was either at the beginning or the end of the circuit.

"Fine," said James when they had exhausted the subject. "Let's start tomorrow early, first light, and do the lot."

"OK, nay problem with that, I will organize the transport; I'll get a chopper if one's spare. For the Greek side at least, not sure they want to overfly the Turkish lines just yet. We may have to do the Famagusta visit by UN car. That will be a bonus as we can call in on Dhekelia and I will introduce you to the ordnance company that supports and supplies us either before or after the visit," replied the FOWO, his Scottish accent becoming strong.

"Good," said James trying to hold in his excitement; with luck he would be able to get the packages for the major tomorrow. Now he was with his own kind and he could see that they needed him and his help. He wanted to get rid of the spook mission for the men from London and then get stuck in with his own people.

"Do you think we could do Famagusta and then the Dhekelia stop last?" he enquired.

The warrant officer cocked his head to one side. He had a natural distrust of junior officers until they proved themselves, coupled with the fact that they were either up to something or they could drop you right in the mire with the greatest of ease without even trying. Both scenarios could be generated by a young officer at the same time without them even realizing they were doing it.

"We can, but why?"

"Oh, I just thought it might be nice to see that part of the island as night begins to fall; memories you know, stuff like that," James said to the warrant officer with a wink.

"Oh yes, I can believe you. OK, sir, but no high jinks, eh?"

"Absolutely not; I can see that you have a situation here and the last thing you need is a passenger," said James raising his hands in mock horror. Nor did he think he could mess with this FOWO, who was both taller and clearly stronger than James. In fact, James thought, built like the proverbial brick shithouse.

"Sir, just remember life is a little difficult at the moment and the areas where you may have sown your seeds in the old days are not open for business at the moment." The FOWO nodded at the officers, saluted and left them to their work. "I will call for you at five o'clock at the mess, so don't get to bed too late, there is a lot to do," he added as he went on his way.

"I'll be ready," James called after him.

David gave James an old-fashioned look, to which James simply drew a rueful face and opened and raised his hands in the manner of complete innocence.

Major David shook his head, smiling and said, "He is right you know; now is not the time for high jinks, the commander here bucks no nonsense and would have your balls if anyone stepped out of line, especially at this time."

"Don't worry, sir, I have no intention of bringing the wrath of the UN on our heads or getting our corps a black mark." James was serious and Major David nodded his understanding. At this moment James almost decided to confide in Major David but thought better of it. Major David was a good officer whom he could have trusted, but he realized that he could get the major into a career limiting situation. Major David's loyalties would be torn, he may even order James not to carry out the mission and put him on the next plane off the island if he confided in him, and so he held his peace.

The two ordnance officers took another hour to brief James on the operations and duties of the detachment and the FOO's staff duties. They showed him round the various sections in the complexes and James's mind was soaking up the layout and what each section did with ease. It was standard worldwide so he had little trouble fitting in. They settled, as they had previously agreed, that James would do the liaison duties outside of the base and the odds and sods that took focus away from the main task. James would deal with unit queries. Paul would do his stuff supplying items, mainly of British origin, to all the units with his fleet of trucks and in liaison with the Army Air Corps detachment.

They worked until around six thirty when the major declared a halt. Paul would work on, James would take the major to the mess and get himself sorted out and they would all meet for dinner at seven that evening.

They left the cool of the main stores hangar, stepping into the brilliant sunshine. James's practiced eye reviewed the trenches and the two men in the OP. "Guarding oneself does eat manpower," the major grunted agreement. They got into the UN car and wound down the windows to release the heat that had built up inside. Arriving at the mess, Major David told James to be in the bar just before seven and he would stand drinks. James made his way to the third tin hut away from the mess, grateful it was only a short distance. Once inside, the cool of the room pervaded him and he fought off the desire to lie out on the bed and get some sleep. He sorted his kit and then went to the shower block which doubled as an ablution and sauna block. First he joined a crowd of officers in the sauna. A Scandinavian entered and declared it was time for a Finnish-style event and threw a tumbler of vodka on to the coals. The heat was overwhelming and the vaporized alcohol entered James immediately and he felt his senses reel.

The other occupants cursed the officer in a good-hearted way and the sensation of instant drunkenness soon vanished; but the heat beat James and he had to abandon the room. Taking a cold shower he let out a chuckle, this place could be fun. Returning to his room he changed into a clean uniform but with sleeves rolled down as it was after six, this being the order of the day pertaining to the dress of the mess at night.

He passed a group of Australian Commonwealth Police drinking beer and taking the last of the daylight on the small mess rattan-screened patio. They waved to him as he passed and he nodded a greeting.

The mess had that indefinable air of expectation and excitement. The bar throbbed with a mill of people from many armies and police forces. The array of uniforms was of interest to James; he spotted a dozen different nationalities in as many seconds. Most conversed in English, the official language. There were a few civilians in the mess who mainly kept to themselves. He saw Major David who excused himself from the Canadian engineer he was talking to and made his way to James with two beers in his hand.

"Let us head into the anteroom, it will be a little quieter." Major David led James into another room simply separated from the bar by a large central brass fireplace. He noticed James's disorientation, "Know how you feel; a blizzard of nationalities and uniforms; on the other hand they all work well together and believe they are doing something quite special and worthwhile. For many, like the Finnish, it's the first time they have been out of their homeland, let alone worked with other nationalities. It never fails to intrigue me the way we all get along together. Ah, I see Paul has arrived. Come on James, I'll show you around and introduce you to some of the officers. You need to meet them anyway. They are the people you are going to have to deal with on a day-to-day basis."

In the next hour James met Canadians, Danes, Austrians, Australians, Fins, and Swedes; they all seemed to have a great sense of humour, more

English than the English. There were some Americans in civilian clothes and a pretty green-eyed blond from the British embassy, an attaché perhaps and a real beauty. To James's disappointment she was being hosted by an American who turned out to be a major in civilians.

A Republic of Ireland colonel joined their ever-changing group of people. He looked at James over his whisky glass sternly. James guessed the whiskey was a Jameson. The colonel surprised James by asking him what he was going to do about the Irish problem.

James was out of his comfort zone and began to explain that there was little he could do personally about the situation and that he thought it was up to the people and the politicians to resolve the issue. He saw the glint of humour in the colonel's eyes.

"Oh, you mean that Irish problem, Colonel. Would it be another Jameson that could resolve this Irish problem?"

The colonel roared with laughter, "Ah, David, they have sent you someone with brains at last!" He turned to James, surrendering his glass, "Away with you, boy, got it in one. Recharge the glasses and tell the man on the bar to bill me."

Shortly afterwards with glasses recharged, the major decided James could take some more of what the mess had to offer. He and Paul led him into the dining room where a hot buffet of meals from various nations was being served by a battery of cooks. James, along with the other officers, fell on the food, sampling dishes from many different lands, all on the one plate.

Much later, dinner over, they took coffee on the veranda. By now it was dark but the large Mediterranean sky was filled with stars and the Milky Way. Major David talked about the Cyprus situation.

He began, "It's a damn shame. Cyprus or Aphrodite's Isle is the third largest as well as being the most eastern of the islands in the Mediterranean. It covers 3,600 square miles and its population must be closing 700,000; about 80% Greek and 20% Turkish, with a few other minorities. The minorities are calculated to increase with the turmoil over the water in the Middle Eastern countries, Lebanon being a case in point. The climate is fabulous, very healthy. You can swim all year round and ski in the Troodos Mountains in the winter. OK, so they suffered from a trading imbalance but with expanding tourism and the fruits and wine, life was sweet. And now look at this mess. All because the Turkish Cypriots wanted a few concessions in the way of a little more autonomy than the Greeks were prepared to give them. Personally, I think the writing was on the wall since the death of General Grivas. So there you are," he put his coffee down and slapped his thighs in a sign he had finished. "Tomorrow is another day." He then excused himself as he still had work to do.

James sat back in the old rattan chair obviously purloined from an old colonial British mess somewhere, and relaxed, trying to work out exactly what he was going to do tomorrow and how the hell he was going to complete his mission without the UN people finding out that he was not all that he seemed. He would have the FOWO with him unless he could dump him somehow.

Chapter 32

KIDNAPPED

Dhekelia was an open base with only nominal security fences separating it from the surrounding area. The base covered many acres and was open to the sea on one side. Dressed as fishermen, they had tied up at the Dhekelia quay in their small fishing boat. They were challenged, but with a basket of fish supposedly for the officers' mess and needing to see one of their cousins in the hospital, the sentry bought their story, which was good enough to get them into the base even in these troubled times.

Once in the British Military Hospital they had found it easy to mingle with the afternoon crowds moving around the hospital and casually made their way to the morgue. Apart from a local Greek laboratory assistant who was just leaving and whom they met at the entrance, the morgue area was deserted. Puzzled, but unsuspecting he asked the brothers what they wanted.

"We have been sent by the relatives of the two men, Mould and Sharky, to make the identification and finalize any details and also so that the relations can begin to wind up their estates," lied Nikos easily. "Can we see them?"

The man hesitated; he looked at the two brothers and instantly knew that they could not be turned aside but he tried, "Is it possible you could come back tomorrow, when the Doctor will be here?" suggested the assistant.

"That's not possible, we need to see the bodies now, please." Nikos was insistent.

"I am only a technician; I can try to get the Doctor for you, it would be better if he showed you."

"Time is not on our side, now, please." Nikos held out his hand to shepherd the man into the building.

The assistant could see he had nowhere to go, they blocked his escape. "Come on then, but this is most irregular and I could get into trouble." He led them into the morgue.

He opened the two doors to the refrigerated body compartments and respectfully pulled out the two plastic covered bodies of the decoys.

The assistant had been briefed to inform the commanding officer the moment that anybody made any enquiry about the bodies, and that he was to delay until he had somehow contacted the CO so that he could take any necessary action. He therefore suggested that the two brothers might like to be left to make their examination while he sorted his work for tomorrow. His nervousness obviously showed because Joseph blocked his way, "No, please wait here with us."

"Here, see the tags on each with their names; if you would excuse me for a few minutes," the assistant mumbled.

"I would like you to wait, we will be but a moment," said Nikos forcefully.

"I'm sorry but I simply must go," and with an impatient wave of his hand the assistant made for the door. As he passed Joseph, he was hit on the head from behind by a hammer blow from Joseph's clenched fist.

The man winced, let out an oath and stumbled to the floor. Joseph pulled the stunned man to his feet and hissed, "Now you wait and be quiet or it will be the last sound you make." The man nodded, his eyes shut tight from an effort to ease the pain.

Nikos quickly took out a knife from somewhere in his sleeve and slit the plastic bags holding the bodies.

Looking into the first of the body bags, the sightless, watery eyes of the corpse stared up at him. For a moment Nikos swayed from the effect of the formaldehyde fumes that emanated from the bag then recovered himself. Ignoring the stench of the body that hit him he studied the corpse's face for a moment and then straightening said to Joseph, "This is not either of the agents."

"Are you sure?" questioned Joseph disbelievingly.

"Absolutely, come and see both of them and bring the technician with you."

"You're right, the descriptions don't match either of these men; they look like locals to me and are far too old anyway. They have done a switch somehow."

"Then where are our men?" questioned his brother concerned.

"They must still be alive, that is the only logical explanation. If the reports are to be believed they were wounded and therefore must still be here in Cyprus recovering and where better, my brother, than right here in the hospital," reasoned Nikos, while advancing threateningly on the luckless attendant. He reached forward and grabbed him with one massive hand round the man's scrawny neck. The man struggled in the vice-like grip on his neck that threatened to throttle him. While Nikos held him immobile, Joseph took the man's hand and twisted it inwards towards the wrist and continued to apply pressure until the man submitted. They let him go and he slumped to the floor like a beaten animal.

"Where are they?" demanded Nikos.

"I'm not sure, they are here somewhere in the hospital. There are men on the third floor who have their own nursing staff, they may be the men you seek," gasped the man through his pain.

"Anything else?" questioned Joseph grabbing the man's hair and bending his head back so his Adam's apple bobbed up and down.

"Please, I was supposed to tell the officer if anybody asked about the bodies," the man squeezed out tearfully.

"Tell us about the nursing staff, please," Nikos was relentless in his enquiry.

"All I know is what a friend told me. They do not seem to know much, and are under either the direction of the Sister or Doctor Sainsbury. There were four of them and another stays in the officers' mess most of the time. The men are normally looked after by two of the strange orderlies at any one time," the technician finished in a rush.

"Describe the Sister; what time does she come on shift?" Joseph twisted the man's arms.

"I think she is on night duty, she is tall and has light brown hair."

Nikos gave a nod to his brother. Joseph delivered the blade of his hand with speed and deadly force down on to the man's neck, crushing his throat and then gripped the man's head in his two hands, whipped it round and broke his neck.

Nikos considered the situation for a moment only, "We need a car. See if he has any car keys on him."

Joseph rummaged through the technician's pockets and brought out a set of keys with a Mercedes fob. "They pay these boys too much," he said grinning. "Should be easy to find on the staff car park, eh?"

The men worked quickly tidying the two plastic shrouds; they picked up the dead assistant, laid him on top of another of the shrouded corpses nearby and stuffed him back into the refrigerated compartment. They made sure the morgue, at least to the casual observer, appeared undisturbed.

Leaving the building, they went to find the car in the staff car park at the front of the hospital. It was easy to find; it was only a few yards from the hospital front entrance. With the advantage of the vehicle, they made a quick plan and by the time they had reached the reception desk, they were ready.

A medical corporal in charge of reception looked up as they approached him.

"Yes, can I help you?" He was busy but the two large men caught his attention.

"Indeed you may. My brother and I are from the village Dherynia just down the road where we had several casualties the other day and your Sister helped to treat our people, so our village mayor has sent us to thank the Sister. She is the one on the third floor, we think. Could you ask her to come to the desk if it is not too much trouble?" explained Nikos with his brother smiling and nodding over his shoulder.

"Certainly, sir; I'll just see if she is on the ward." He spoke briefly on the telephone and then returned to the desk, "I'm sorry, she's not on duty but she's expected any minute, the night shift starts at 2000 hrs. If you can wait, I will point her out when she arrives."

Nikos was annoyed but did not show it. "OK," still smiling, "Thank you, sir," the brothers softly withdrew just out of earshot of the soldier.

The brothers discussed the situation and the risk they were running but decided in the end that they would wait for half an hour.

Almost immediately they were hailed, "Here she comes, just walking through the car park," called the corporal to the brothers and they turned to see the sister heading in a direct line towards the entrance hall, her nurse's cape swishing from side to side. The brothers waved to the desk corporal and then moved to meet her to head her off before she entered the building.

"Sister," Nikos waved and called out in a friendly way, greeting her with an enthusiastic smile, "We have been waiting to see you."

She stopped suddenly, not suspicious at this stage as they were all just outside the hospital. "Yes? Do I know you?" she said enquiringly, looking up at the two large men.

"No," said Nikos laughing, "but you and your fellow sisters have been helping some of our people from the village and the headman has sent us to say thank you and also to give you a gift for you all."

"That is very kind, but there really is no need, it has been a pleasure to help anybody in these difficult times." She had not the slightest idea which village the men were from but obviously they represented some of the injured refugees that had been brought in over the last few days.

"Please, please you just come to our car over there by the gateway, we give you the gift, yeah?" said Nikos taking her arm gently and leading her away from the hospital reception.

Her initial lack of suspicion was evaporating fast and she looked dubiously towards the hospital entrance and the staff at the reception desk. Feeling safe enough as she was on home ground, she allowed herself to be guided towards the waiting car. However, the increased speed at which she was now ushered brought a rising sense of danger. Nikos, with the other arm behind, urged her forwards.

She tried to shake the man off but he held her tighter. A few yards from the car she was now certain the men meant her harm and were not what they said they were. Realizing she was in danger, she struggled against Nikos, but the man held her fast, he was too powerful to break away from. She started to scream as she was bundled unceremoniously into the car.

Fortunately her plight had not gone unnoticed. The desk corporal had seen the men meet her, then walk her to the car and the last minute struggle. He could not believe his eyes and it was a second before he reacted, his shouts attracting other members of staff who looked on in horror.

By the time he had leapt the desk and sprinted out of the hospital building to rescue the nurse, the car was moving, reversing out of the parking bay as he closed on the vehicle. It completed its reversing movement and shot forward at him, bowling him over and under the wheels. The last thing he saw before he died were the grinning faces of the brothers and the horror on the sister's face. Nikos held her by her hair as she stared wide-eyed through the windscreen. By the time anybody else in the hospital reacted to the commotion outside, the car had gone.

Nikos knocked the nurse unconscious and slid her below the level of the seat. At the barrier, they were waved through. The guards were interested in people trying to enter the base not going out. They drove through without stopping.

Minutes later Rodney, reading the papers in the officers' mess to pass the time, received an urgent summons from Colonel Matthews, delivered by a soldier who ran into the mess to get him.

"Well, Rodney, what do you think?" after the Colonel explained what had happened, "What's the form in a case like this? I have to make this official and let the military police know."

"Sir," Rodney was rocked to his soul; his growing fondness for the sister meant that he had to consciously shake off his own distress after hearing of the abduction. "It is likely we will get a call from them after they have settled themselves in wherever their hide may be. I'm so sorry about your corporal, he must have tried to stop them." Rodney could see that the colonel was worried but was trying desperately to remain calm and detached in the circumstances. His personal courage was not in question but he, like Rodney, was seething with rage and frustration over the murder of one of his staff and the abduction of another.

"What I cannot understand is how they knew," continued the colonel.

He's thinking now, rationalizing the situation and that's a good sign, thought Rodney.

"How the fuck did they find out and how did they know which sister to lift?" questioned the colonel.

"One thing is sure, they could only have found out here in Cyprus, that fact I'm sure of, therefore somebody has leaked the story, or enough of the story for the enemy to deduce that Mould and Sharky are not dead," Rodney countered. "Are you sure nobody else knew, apart from our group?"

"Nobody except the technician in the morgue and all he knew was that I wanted to know of anybody who came sniffing round the bodies. Oh no, I thought I was being clever," both men looked at each other and exclaimed together. The colonel rang down to reception and called for the keys to the mortuary. Collecting the keys from the desk, they hastened out of the hospital and headed for the building on the other side of the car park. The colonel tried the keys but the door was unlocked and as he made to rush into the building, Rodney held him back.

"Let me check the building first," Rodney cautioned him.

Rodney inspected all the rooms, which were clear of any living being. He returned to the entrance and waved the colonel in.

"No sign of the technician," it was a statement from the colonel, Rodney simply shook his head.

Once inside, the colonel moved quickly to the body room and pulled out the drawers. He saw that the body bags had been disturbed. Looking round as though distracted he suddenly started pulling out the other body drawers. He did not take long to find his man.

"My God, they've killed him," the colonel recoiled and had to support himself against a dissection table.

Once again Rodney's heart went out to the man who had so willingly given his help. "Sir, leave this to us, we will get Sue back and I'll give you my personal guarantee that they will pay for this." He led the colonel back to his office; by the time they got there, the CO had recovered his composure and was ready for action.

"When do you think they will call us?"

"I would think in the morning."

"You say that they will not call till the morning that gives us about twelve hours to do something. But why the morning?" He added, "You're the expert, what's to do?"

"The morning for two reasons, I do not think they would want to do anything in the dark hours and, more importantly, they are going to have to speak to and get further orders from their masters. I don't think the kidnap was pre-planned before they came here, therefore, the situation has changed for them and they are going to have to get instruction, which will take time."

"I think I agree with you. The technician must have given them enough information for them to link Sue and the third floor. Despite our cover all, the staff know that there is something odd going on up there. Now what do we do for the next twelve hours?"

"Clearly, they are going to their hide and although our need for secrecy is still extant, we could, in fact should, put it out to the police, both military and civil, about the kidnapping. At least they might be able to give us leads that will help to identify the men responsible. Secondly, if we are not available tomorrow to take any calls they will have to contact us direct somehow and that could give us a few more valuable hours. So we need to brief the telephonist well." Rodney looked at the colonel. He could see the man wrestling with the need, on the one hand, to find out quickly what the men wanted and, on the other, the logic of manoeuvring them into a direct contact situation.

"What is the chance that they will reveal their identity and location if they have to contact us direct?" queried the colonel.

"Most unlikely; they will use an intermediary and from their work so far they appear to be very professional, so will choose him or her, I suspect, from a totally different locality to where they are holding up. That has got to be somewhere between here and Ayia Napa." Rodney briefed shrewdly, eyeing the colonel.

"Why do you say that?"

"Consider, the first incident took place in Famagusta and our men ended up in Ayia Napa, therefore, perhaps they assume the list and loot are hidden somewhere between here and there and perhaps out to sea. Secondly, the men know that we do not have the loot because if we did they would have heard about it by now, that's for sure. They will deduce quite logically that we're waiting for information. The only thing they do not know and, thank goodness, neither does Sue, is that we have its location and are acting on it. They are unlikely to hurt her once they satisfy themselves that she does not know anything. They will use her simply as a lever to get at us."

The colonel looked hopefully at Rodney, "At least the news just in about the ceasefire means we can move out of the Sovereign Base if needs be."

Rodney paused, nodding, "And now, sir, I need to call London. Would you please call the police and report the kidnapping and the death of your corporal. You can say that the victim and kidnappers were, we think, seen heading east."

"Suppose you are wrong, won't we be putting the police on to a false trail? Wouldn't it be better to let them search all points east, south, north and west?"

"I have worked with men like these before, on our side and against them, when I had to; believe me, sir, I know our enemy." Rodney saw the hope in the colonel's eyes and hoped to God that he was right for Sue's sake. "I am right, sir," said Rodney seriously.

After he had phoned London, he got his team together. They were by now aware of what had gone on and were as angry as Rodney was. Sharky was sore but fighting mad and it was good to have him back on board.

"Orders," Rodney said to the men. "First, as you know, the news is of a fragile ceasefire in place between the Greeks and the Turks but we can expect everyone to be jumpy out there, so there is good reason to be cautious. Reid, you are the quartermaster. I want us tooled up."

Reid nodded, "Still got friends around, give me a few hours to get what we need."

"Avery, you are with Reid; make sure he doesn't do something I will come to regret. Be a steadying influence." Rodney switched his gaze, "Mould, Sharky you are with me, wherever it takes us."

Mould and Sharky grinned and gave the thumbs up.

"What about us, boss?" said the other two.

"You are both assigned to the Nissi Beach Hotel, where you should have been from the beginning. It is only a quarter of a mile from the harbour at Ayia Napa. Get down there now. Have a look at the boat and keep your eyes open. I am convinced that the area will become the focus of our attention. We are being or will be watched. Clearly we are compromised, so we can't stand James Collins down; he has to get the stuff for us. He is independent of us, so we make ourselves visible, be tourists. Go with Mr Reid, get something to defend yourselves with and I want you to call me from the hotel in not more than two hours." Rodney swung back to Reid. "Mr Reid, you deputize for me, so make yourselves usefully visible. You are all under command of Mr Reid when I am not around. Any questions?" There were none.

After the briefing, Rodney took Reid with him to meet the colonel who he found being interviewed by the senior military policeman of the Sovereign Base Area. He was flanked by a military policeman and plain-clothes army special investigation officer. Rodney and Reid waited until they had finished taking the colonel's statement and were making reassuring noises before they left to interview the other hospital staff that were around the scene of the kidnapping.

Rodney introduced Reid as his anchorman and the colonel's conduit for all matters if Rodney was away. The colonel shook Reid's hand. He was stilled by the man's obvious strength. "The police seem confident enough. What did your people in London say?"

Reid excused himself and left them alone; he had work to do.

"The Brigadier sends his profound regrets and is holding off the world. He was disappointed with me and wants the matter cleared up yesterday."

Chapter 33

NIKOS AND JOSEPH

The brothers and their captive, as Rodney had predicted, had driven east. They stopped briefly in the village of Xylophaghou for Nikos to make a telephone call through to his bosses in Nicosia, to pick up food and drink and to decide where they were going to hide out. He told them why he thought the agents must still be alive. He was convinced that they were getting care and protection in the British military hospital. He explained his reasons for taking a captor for leverage, if needs be. His masters needed to consult and they would contact him later.

They had then driven on to Liopetri and then south into the Sotira Forest avoiding troops and police that were scarce in this area, in any case. They hid themselves and the car in some old crumbling ruins in a wild, sparsely forested area surrounded by low rolling fields. Surrounding the ruins, citrus and olive trees had been left to grow unattended.

They had travelled around twelve miles from the Base Area to their hide and only six or more miles would take them to Ayia Napa.

Joseph took up guard duty on a small wooded hillock that commanded the approach to the hide. He settled himself down to wait. With bread and cheese and a bottle of local red wine, he was happy enough.

Nikos made a round of the ruins and perimeter to make sure that their presence could not be seen by the casual observer from land or air. He disturbed a herd of local Shami goats. The goats scattered into the citrus orchard at his approach; they looked uncared for, so perhaps they were not minded, and that was to the good.

Nikos was satisfied that the location they had chosen was off the beaten track and, therefore, reasonably secure. He shrugged; it was time to begin his interrogation of the nurse.

"Pretty one, there is no need to be frightened," he began gently, "Nothing will befall you providing you cooperate, just tell us what you know." His heavy accented voice, a few inches from Sue's ear, was quiet but threatening.

Sue was tied to a rusting ring in the wall of the ruin which was low enough to allow her to sit comfortably on the rubble strewn and vine covered floor. She was convinced that she would never see the base again if she proved difficult, but at the same time she knew that she could not betray totally the confidences of her people. She needed to find a middle way. They obviously had most of the story so whatever she said needed to be credible.

"Well?" said Nikos, as if expecting an answer; drawing back from Sue he pulled up an old orange crate and sat down looking at her with unblinking eyes. He was very still looking down at the nurse, prostrate and bound at his feet. Sue could see that he was weary now that the adrenaline rush from the events at the base had subsided in the man.

"The questions I have to ask you are few and not difficult. I already have most of the answers. You must realize that you are simply an object to me that I hope to trade for something more valuable, attractive though you certainly are," Nikos stated flatly.

Sue saw in that moment that he didn't intend to harm her. She was more valuable as a live hostage and she believed the man only saw her as an object to trade. She allowed herself to relax a little.

He eyed her and seemed to read hope in her eyes. "You are quite right that I do not mean you harm but unless you cooperate, my brother..." he raised his eyes to the sky, "...God help you, he doesn't like women. He is not as civilized as I. His methods are primitive and you have the added disadvantage of being a beautiful young woman. Be sensible." His threat was implied but not pressed.

Sue shuddered. It had been Joseph who had run down the orderly who had tried to come to her rescue. She raised her head and said, "What is it you want to know? I really don't know why you took me or what I can possibly tell you that would be of the slightest use to you. I'm only a nursing sister and not an important person or anything like that."

"Oh, but you are important. The men you nurse on the third floor, Mould and Sharky, are they well enough to travel?" He saw her eyes open slightly and knew he had the answer. The rest was academic.

"I don't have patients by those names under my charge."

"Forget it, Sister, I know you are lying." Nikos didn't raise his voice which made his response all the more dangerous. "Let us both forget you said that. And answer truthfully in future. Answer my questions and you need have no fear. Are they fit enough to travel? If not, can they talk?"

Sue thought the questions through. The reason she was there was that they knew somehow that the agents were alive so it was no use denying that. Did it matter if she told this man that they were conscious? She reasoned that it didn't because whatever he had to tell he had already told to his colleagues earlier when they had stopped to telephone.

"They were wounded and were sedated for some time but they are on the mend and out of danger now but not yet ready to travel. Yes, they can talk but they only talk among themselves when the hospital staff are not in attendance." She looked at him wondering if he had believed her.

He looked at her with half-closed eyes and with a grunt stood up and went to the open doorway of the ruin. He lit a Turkish cigarette and the strong acrid smoke drifted back to Sue. Nikos leaned on the door frame and smoked calmly. She watched him. She could see he was thinking through the situation and weighing up his options. He ground out the cigarette with his heel and turned back to her. He was a tall man, something over six foot, very broad and, she judged, exceptionally powerful. He sat down again and smiled at her.

"Very good, Sister, last question and then you must get some sleep, for tomorrow you will need all the strength you have as we will be doing a lot of walking. How many men are guarding these men? Who is their leader?"

Sue again realized that this question did not really matter because Nikos had to have a contact name to talk to and she could inflate the guard numbers to scare them from any attempt on the hospital.

"The man you want is Major Brown. As to the guards, there seem to be ten or more in shifts, twenty-four hours a day. It's difficult to say, they come and go."

"OK, thank you. You have played your part well, although I think the number of guards gives concern. Now you must rest. I'm going to put you in the car with the seats down so that you can sleep in relative comfort and also because I can keep an eye on you more easily."

He left her for a few minutes and returned with bread, cheese, water and wine. He untied her and indicated that she should sit on the orange crate and that she should eat and drink. "Simple food, but nourishing." He ate with her. For her part, Sue ate as much as she could to spin out the time.

When they had finished, he led her out to the orchard and told her to do whatever was necessary to make herself comfortable before he put her in the car. Sue found privacy in a bush and then allowed herself to be walked back to the car, collecting a few ripe oranges which she plucked from the trees. He put the seats down and tied her hands to the wheel. She made herself as comfortable as she could and tried to sleep. He had wound down the windows halfway so the heat would not build up; he then went to the front of the car and removed the distributor cap and, with rope from the boot, tied the doors so they would not open.

He called Joseph from his post and she could hear them talking in Greek. Nikos returned to the car and told her that he had sent his brother for more food and water and for more help. He didn't tell her that she had confirmed his thoughts about the agents and that his brother would be relaying this information to his bosses in Nicosia for onward transmission to the people in Moscow and in England.

Nikos was privately angry with himself. They had acted in haste. Taking the nurse, he realized, was a stupid thing to have done. Admittedly, she was a bargaining tool but not, he thought, that powerful a one. And it raised the risk of being found out as the pursuers would be all the more determined to find them. He cursed himself for not trying for the agents, even though they may have been well guarded. Nikos now realized that all they had really done was to bring attention to themselves. He had taken a decision and in view of the very limited confirmatory information she had given him, it was the wrong one.

Nikos broke open another bottle of the local wine and toasted the stars as they appeared.

Chapter 34

MOULD DOES WHAT HE DOES BEST

The base was cloaked in darkness. In the officers' mess, where Rodney and the colonel had decided to mount their vigil for the night, all was quiet and subdued when the duty phone rang. It startled the mess members. One of the officers answered the call and called to Rodney that it was for him. Both he and the colonel rushed to the phone. Rodney identified himself and when the colonel saw Rodney's face relax, he realized it was not about Sue.

"Rodney, we spoke earlier today, you may remember?" James had left the United Nations officers' mess later than he had intended and had got into bed before finally deciding that he was going to go for the task tomorrow.

He wanted to make plans to deliver the items and thought he had better brief Rodney, so he had dressed quickly and gone back to the mess where he used the office phone to get through to the British military hospital switchboard. He had been put through quickly but the line sounded hollow, rather like it did when somebody is on an extension, so he decided to play it clever and disguise the call.

"Ah yes," said Rodney catching on to James' conscious manner.

"You were asking about where fruit bats can be seen in Cyprus at this time of the year."

"Err yes, so I was. Do tell," Rodney had to stop himself chuckling.

"The best place is a little cave just round the point, along from the beach at that place your friend's boat got beached the other day, do you remember? Well I am going to have a look tomorrow night; could be midnight, probably an hour later, whatever fits with you."

"He means Ayia Napa," thought Rodney.

"By the way, I expect to see you the day after tomorrow about those stores you ordered," James added.

James wondered how he was going to get the rest of the message across to Rodney without compromising the task. Rodney came to his aid; he had had lots of practice over the years.

"Good, much sooner than I had expected, but I do need them desperately, as the situation has changed and time is running out for the operation." Rodney was pleased, "It's got to be done as soon as possible or the patient may suffer." Rodney added, "No chance you can get the stores in tomorrow night, say, if we meet you at the cave location?"

"Always willing to serve, I'll do my best. See you soon, Major." Right, breathed James, I've committed myself now and I'd better deliver or somebody's in trouble, by the sound of it.

When Rodney got back, he could see Colonel Matthews was curious to know what was going on. He decided to tell him even if it cost him his job. The least he could do for this man who had helped them so much was to let him know what was going on.

"That was the man who should be bringing the items we have been waiting for, the reason for us being here, and I hope to be collecting them from him, all being well, possibly early morning the day after tomorrow is now the firm plan."

"How will this affect the return of my nurse?"

"Sir, I don't know. I truly wished I did. But it may speed her return. They would have no reason to keep her longer. Anything that has to be done will be done in the next day and a half, of that I'm certain."

The CO looked all in. Rodney was aware that the buck stopped with the colonel. He and his men could fade into the background when this was over, the colonel could not. He must have been thinking that he may well never see his nurse again. Her captors had already killed twice that day and the only use she was to them was as a bargaining tool which was, in view of what was at stake, as the Greek had reasoned earlier, not a very powerful lever as far as London and the Russians were concerned.

The colonel was also coping with an unprecedented number of patients as a result of the Greek and Turkish conflict and now the ceasefire was in place more patients arrived every hour of the day.

Rodney took the colonel gently by the arm and said, "Sir, you look like you could do with a break. Why don't you go and rest. We will do everything we can, you know that. You can't hope to carry out your job at the hospital and worry about this other thing. I don't have to tell you how fond I am of Sue; that is why I intend to do all I can to see she is returned safely to your care."

"Yes, you're right, I can't help now. Damn, it all seemed so simple when we started." The colonel yawned, "I'll take your advice and get some sleep, I may well need it." He sank what was left of his drink and said goodnight. Rodney did the same and then went up to the ward to see his men. As he approached the ward he could hear Sharky and Mould laughing.

"Hello, what's going on with you two?" he said as he came round the corner of the ward. The joviality of his two men cheered him up and lifted his tension slightly.

"Good evening, no, morning, boss, just," said Mould cheerfully looking at his watch. "It's our man here; he's all right now, he's been making overtures to a staff nurse and she said as soon as he can catch her, she'll think about it."

"Well, it's good to hear he's better. We've got to go back eventually and that means him too. I wouldn't give either of your chances of surviving as very high if we stay here, now the enemy knows where we are," Rodney said running his hand through his hair.

"Where do we stand now, no news of the sister, I suppose?" Mould enquired, leaning back in his chair.

"Not a damn thing, I'm afraid," returned Rodney, looking round the ward. "As we are alone," he continued fixing them with his gaze, "I expect that tomorrow will be a long day, so I want you, Mould, to go now to join the other two at the Nissi. My gut says things are going to pop and I want you to lead them to whatever happens, OK?"

"Now means now, right?" Mould queried, Rodney nodded.

"Transport?"

"I got Mr Reid to get us some hire cars and they have been delivered to the hospital this evening, three of them. Here is the key to one of the Datsuns. It's downstairs in the hospital car park. I'll stay with Sharky until you get back or until Avery turns up."

Mould caught the keys neatly as Rodney tossed them to him and moved to go. He stopped and looked at his boss, "Why don't I phone our men?" To which Rodney simply gave him the look that said all. "Oh, I see," said Mould dumbly. "They haven't got transport, they went by taxi, and they don't know the way, which I do. You have been reading my file and remembered I've been here before in the EOKA troubles and you think that their phone could well be tapped, and they may well be under observation, is that right?"

"You're a cheeky sod, I don't know why we keep you on, but yes, you've got it," laughed Rodney.

Mould made the Nissi Beach Hotel inside an hour. He had no delays and apart from a few missed turns he had no trouble in finding his way there. As a precaution, he had turned off at Xylophaghou and followed the dirt road to Nissi Beach just below and to the west of Ayia Napa. At one point he was only two miles to the south of Sotira Forest where, unbeknown to him, Sue was being held.

As he travelled towards Nissi, threading his way through the village of Xylophaghou, he had seen the first sign of soldiers, thankfully Greek. He knew the area very well from his previous time on the island when, as a young soldier he had been posted to Cyprus, the EOKA troubles although not at their height, were still of concern. He had crawled all over this area and knew it was good ambush county for shoot and scoot tactics which EOKA had adopted.

A sixth sense of trouble ahead made the hairs on his head stand up and he shivered involuntarily. He pulled into a field about two miles from Nissi Beach and the hotel. Switching off the car lights he waited for his night vision to kick in. The night was chill and the starlight was enough to navigate by. He got out of the car and jogged cautiously forward under the cover of the tall grasses that lined the road and eucalyptus trees that ranged the sides of the road. The moon and stars gave him all the light he needed. In the cool, noises carried far and he had not gone more than a few hundred yards when he heard raised Greek voices.

Three men were in the field to his right. Talking excitedly and gesturing freely with their hands, Mould could make out a car under cover of trees on which the tallest man was leaning and smoking. The party consisted of Joseph and two other men who had been sent to watch both the hotel and the harbour at Ayia Napa. They were discussing the situation and every so often one of the group would go over to the front of the car, lean in and make a call over a radio. All of this Mould could see clearly. He knew a little Greek although a little rusty and was able to follow the gist of the conversation; along with their body gestures he was able to piece together enough to understand what was going on. Coupled with this, whoever it was on the radio, the Greeks were speaking to them in English. The man who seemed to be more senior than the other two, from the conversations Mould had heard, was called Joseph. He understood that a man called Nikos had sent Joseph to this contact point for a number of reasons. Firstly, to make contact with the watchers and to call headquarters in Nicosia from their radio and, secondly, to get stores and a backup crew organized. He had been there for some time now; he was waiting for instructions and more men to arrive, that much was clear to Mould. They were discussing things in general and the other two were complaining of boredom, that all the two Englishmen had been doing was eating, drinking and walking on the beach and rocks, as well as searching the abandoned boat several times. They obviously thought that this watch was a complete waste of time. There was obviously some anxiety from the bosses when they were told that they had a hostage. Joseph complained to his two companions that he and his brother were not appreciated by those bastard Russians.

For Mould, the news that the nurse was close gave him something of a dilemma, whether to get to the men at the hotel to support them, and then get back to Rodney, as per his instructions, or follow up the information on the hostage, at the same time getting as much information as possible. He even now had a line on the location of the kidnapped sister which he knew his boss would want him to do. Clearly, the man Mould had identified from the conversations as Joseph was now also waiting for more instructions.

Mould was unsure about the risk of getting hold of his two colleagues in time to support him in his pursuit, against losing the opportunity to follow up this lead. If he left now, he might lose the initiative. He knew Sue was in the forest but that was a large area to search. Clearly, wherever the sister was being held, it was close by; in fact it was a little over three miles across country from where they were.

Mould made his decision; he must leave his colleagues and get to them later if he could. Joseph was here – a bird in the hand, he thought, was worth some risk to himself; he would follow him when he left. He was satisfied with his decision and settled down to wait.

The men at the car were obviously weary of standing around and as they seemed to have exhausted their conversation all three had climbed into the car and were either dozing or smoking.

Mould had himself begun to doze when, at around three o' clock, he heard a truck approaching and was instantly alert. It pulled off the road and up to the car, disgorging eight men and a lot of stores.

They impressed Mould in the way they cleared the truck and then moved into the undergrowth on the opposite side of the road in a most professional manner. He realized that these men were well trained and that he had better be very careful.

Joseph left the car and joined the group. After a short, muffled conversation, too low for Mould to get any sense from, the group carrying the stores moved off to the north-west across the potato fields. They left two men, one for the car and another for the truck, and both men immediately drove off towards Nissi. Mould waited a few minutes to allow Joseph and the eight men to get over the first ridge of the skyline. He followed the group, checking all the time that they had moved over the next ridge as he made his way after them. He took the extra precaution of counting the party as they outlined themselves each time they were silhouetted against the night sky. It was just as well he did because after about three miles they dropped their first man at the entrance that led into the forest. He had no choice but to stick to the north and skirt the man's field of vision. Almost into the security of the forest he nearly stepped on a pile of fur that stirred and cried out in a sleepy voice in Greek to mind where he was walking. His heart thumped in his chest until be realized it was an old Mesaorian shepherd that was tending his flock of ragged Shami goats that were grazing at the edge of the forest. He whispered a word of apology and hurried into the forest heading off to intercept the group.

He picked up the sound of their movements after about five minutes. They were coming his way. He only had time to throw himself to the ground before they were on him. They passed within a few metres and he hugged the ground and prayed. As they passed him talking in low tones, by turning his head slightly he could see that two more men were missing. Odds getting better he thought. He suddenly thought back to the village he had passed and wondered why he had seen soldiers so close to the front and realized that he was, although not on the ceasefire line, probably close to a no-go area.

Cautiously following the sound of their voices, Mould kept close behind them but out of sight. Presently, he heard Joseph call out Nikos's name and for a moment he thought he had been discovered so he scuttled into some undergrowth. Seconds later, he heard a reply from a man who was outlined as he emerged from an orchard with the white stones of a ruin at his back and to his left a car parked under a tree.

Realizing he was now at their camp, he circled round and got himself into a position to see the car and the ruin, although still close to the camp. He had chosen by chance the spot where Joseph had kept guard earlier in the day when he and Nikos had first brought the young woman to the camp.

As he concentrated, he was gradually able to make out the layout of the camp. It was an open clearing of about 50 metres in diameter, fringed by trees with a road, more a rough track, leaving to the north. In the clearing was an old crumbling shepherd's house pushed into the east side and parked alongside this was the car that held the nurse. It took him a little time to pick her out and it was only when she moved did he see her white face against the car window looking at the recently arrived party of men. His heart gave a jump as he recognized her. He now had to make the decision to try to rescue her or to go for help. He relaxed and decided to see how things developed.

Nikos redeployed his men, including the three they had dropped off, to cover all the approaches to the clearing but he kept Joseph and four men behind and they lounged by the car. Mould realized that rescue without help was impossible and only just managed to get away before one of the men moved towards him.

He struck due east past the Sotira Dam and towards Liopetri. It was now just after four in the morning and he knew that if a rescue was to be made, it would have to be launched in the next hour and a half or it would be too light. In the village, he encountered the soldiers he had seen earlier, they were tired and nervous.

He held up his arms as he approached them. He convinced the corporal in charge of the section that he was English and not Turkish and that it was imperative he be taken to the officer in charge or the local policeman.

Irritably, the corporal led Mould to the coffee house where a captain was stretched out on one of the café tables and at another the local policeman slept on a chair with his head on the tabletop. Other soldiers not on duty littered the floor, asleep on their packs with their rifles crooked in their arms; been there done that, thought Mould to himself.

The corporal warned Mould emphatically, before he woke the captain, that his business had better be serious or he was in big trouble; then he shook the officer awake. The captain, Mould could see, was quite old for his rank, in his middle thirties, and as he shook himself and shivered from the morning cold he swung his feet round and blinked at Mould and the corporal who now stood to attention before him and said, "Sir, this Englishman says he requires your help and that it is very important."

The captain looked at Mould and jammed a blue Greek commando beret on his head. He saw Mould's eyes widen slightly when he saw the beret. The captain kicked the chair of the policeman who moved but didn't wake.

"So, Englishman, you know the Greek regiments," the captain spoke in perfect English. "My name is Captain John Ramos; who are you and why do you need my help so urgently at this time of the morning, when every God-fearing man should be in his bed, unless he is, of course, a soldier?" The captain gestured to the corporal to wake up the policeman.

Mould told the story of the kidnapped nurse and the death of a man who tried to stop the kidnappers. He told them how he had stumbled on the camp but not why he was there in the first place. The local policeman was useful and was able to confirm that a nurse had indeed been kidnapped yesterday. The policeman, initially surly when he had been rudely awakened, came alive as he heard, through translation by Ramos, the part of Mould's story concerning two men he named as Joseph and Nikos. Mould gathered that the policeman was excitedly explaining to Ramos the credit of at last getting these two notorious villains against whom nobody to date had been able to make anything stick. They spent five minutes with the map of the area until the captain and another older corporal were satisfied they had all the facts.

The captain roused his 30 men and within half an hour of Mould entering the village, he was heading back to the forest.

As they trotted along, Mould asked the captain for one good man to go ahead with him so that they could work their way round to the car and, when Ramos stormed the camp, he would get the nurse out.

To Mould's surprise Ramos called forward the older corporal that Mould had first seen at the map recce.

"Meet Corporal Mamas, he is the best I have, so don't get him killed, Englishman," Ramos grunted. "He is my other half, when he sleeps, I work and vice versa."

The corporal did not seem remarkable. He was as much the runt as the captain was the pick of the litter. Mould would wait and see, he knew appearances could be deceptive, Reid was a good example, he reflected, short, stocky and lethal.

Halfway to the forest Ramos found an orange grove and pulled his men over and under cover.

"Now, Mister Englishman, who has not given me his name yet, I brief my men. After this little trot out they will be awake."

"Good trick," remarked Mould. "Must remember that one. They call me Mould."

When Ramos had his section leaders around him, he made Mould go over the detailed points of the camp's layout and where the men from Nikos's force were distributed. When he was satisfied, he said to Mould, "My friend, it is now fifteen minutes before five, we will make our assault from the south," he paused looking at his watch, "in exactly one half hour from now, so you and Mamas must move. Go now and may God be with you, my Englishman."

Mould wanted to say something but Ramos waved him away. "Time enough later," he said and turned back to brief his team again.

Mamas pulled on Mould's arm and gave him a pistol with two spare clips of ammunition and an unsheathed bayonet.

In halting English he said, "I know the place, you follow me." He led Mould round to the south and by instinct went to the right of the re-entrant as Mould had done. He motioned Mould to the ground 50 yards from the forest and went forward. Mould saw him approach the shepherd who still slept, strike the prone form and move over him in one smooth motion. He waved Mould forward. "He is not dead," he said in a whisper, "just asleep for a few hours. Good, yes?"

Mould nodded and they made their way into the forest which soon enveloped them.

When Mamas stopped again, Mould estimated they were around a quarter of a mile from the camp.

Then Mould realized what the shuffling just ahead of them was, the noise was made by two of the men that had been set as guards, their rifles slung lazily over their shoulders, alternately disappeared and reappeared as they moved in and out of the trees like dark malevolent shadows.

Mamas pulled Mould quietly to the ground and indicated that he should reverse the grip on his pistol and use it as a club, Mould nodded.

What next occurred seemed to be in slow motion, taking forever, but in reality took only seconds. As the men moved within striking distance of the two figures huddled on the ground, Mamas touched Mould and then leapt up and drove a knife that appeared from nowhere into the heart of the first man. Mamas then dragged him to the ground, his free hand clasped over the man's mouth so he could not make a sound or cry out.

The second man was bringing his rifle off his shoulder in a reflex action but the suddenness of the attack left him momentarily frozen in thought and conscious response. Mould struck him with all the force he could muster and the butt of the gun hit him squarely on the top of his cranium. Mould felt rather than heard the skull bone give way and, as the bone splintered, the man gave a deep sigh and his legs folded like liquid. He died instantly.

Mamas, extracting his knife and wiping it on the ground, looked at the Englishman and gave a satisfied appreciative nod.

They dragged the two bodies a few feet along the forest floor into a depression and covered them quickly with some debris.

In a moment of panic Mould looked at his watch. He need not have worried, they still had 15 minutes to get into position.

Both men sensed that the way was probably clear to move on. The fact that a two-man patrol was so close to the camp indicated that, apart from the posted guards that Mould could easily circumvent because he knew roughly their positions, the rest of the camp was probably asleep.

Nevertheless they moved cautiously; the night sky was giving way to dawn. They crept forward and manoeuvred until they got to within ten yards of the car at the spot agreed with the captain, when Ramos started his assault.

When the attack came it was sudden, noisy and aggressive, even though Mould was expecting it. Mould and Mamas went to ground immediately to avoid the scatter of waist-high rounds and huddled under a bush.

The four men sleeping around the car staggered to their feet, sleep deprived, befuddled and confused. Mamas shot the four in quick succession.

Joseph and Nikos appeared from the ruin both holding machine guns, cocking and triggering immediately letting rounds fly to the left and right as they ran for the car. Mould rose between them and the car and shot them at close range, double tapping each man. Joseph and Nikos, their nervous systems conditioned by years of fighting, in death swung their machine pistols towards Mould who emptied his magazine at them, turning them and pushing them backwards as the machine guns they held arced harmlessly upwards into the sky, their dead fingers holding the triggers down until the magazines were empty.

The guard on the mound in front of the clearing stood up when the shooting stopped to see what had happened. As he did so a burst from a machine gun wielded by one of Ramos's men cut him down.

Suddenly all movement stopped and the silence that followed was unexpected. Ears ringing Mould was the first to react and dashed for the car. "Over here, Captain," shouted Mould.

Sue, unhurt and grateful to see Mould, cried out with delight, "Thank goodness, please get me out of here."

Mamas pushed Mould aside and attended to the ropes that bound the doors closed and fastened the captive to the steering wheel. "You go and see the Captain; I will look after this lady."

While the soldiers swept through the clearing, the captain came over to Mould. "So you survived and Mamas too. Good," he looked round. "You did well. Now," he countered, "we don't want any loose ends." He turned over the dead bodies of the six men Mould and Mamas had killed and said, "Six here, one over there, and we dealt with another, that makes two missing."

"No, Captain, we dealt with them earlier on our way here," said Mamas quietly, helping Sue out of the car. The captain eyed him and smiled.

"So," he said. "A complete success and here is the lady we came to rescue."

"But how did you find me?"

"All in good time," said Mould, "for now we must get to the hospital."

"I know." Then as she became aware of Ramos and his men for the first time, "Who are these soldiers?"

"They are your rescuers," explained a smiling Mould.

She went over to the captain and Mamas and kissed them both on the cheek, thanking them profusely.

Ramos coloured and Mamas looked embarrassed. The soldiers, now moving back into the clearing, collecting weapons and bodies, laughed at their boss's blushes and Mamas's bashfulness. One look from Ramos soon quelled their amusement.

"Now, my friends, you are to take the car and go. I am going to have to explain what has gone on here to my colonel who is a very bureaucratic sort of chap and if he gets here before you leave you will be here for some considerable time, until you've made statements. You may be here for the rest of your lives!"

"Thank you, Ramos. I don't know if we will be able to repay you, but you must consider that I am in your debt." Turning to Sue, "Who's got the keys?" She indicated Nikos with her hand, quickly looking away, shivering; shock was setting in.

Mamas searched the body and soon found the keys; he handed them to Mould together with the distributor before taking it back and getting one of his men to fix it back in place.

"You come and fight for me again," Mamas nodded to Mould who could see that Mamas's eyes were slightly moist. It was amazing how danger could bring people together in so short a time; he knew he had a friend for life.

Mould squeezed the shoulder of the wizened corporal and waved to the rest of the soldiers before turning to get into the car. He called out to Mamas and his captain, "For the record, my name really is Mould, just Mould." It was six fifteen and dawn was on them.

It was half past seven when Mould and Sue walked into the dining room and as the bulk of the mess were at breakfast their entrance caused the sort of stir that only happens on very rare occasions. Spoons were suspended in the air between breakfast bowls and the mouths of the diners and all eyes stared incredulously at the two, drawn and tired, dust covered figures at the door. The moment was soon broken and the other nursing sisters left their seats and swarmed round Sue and the men were surrounding Mould clapping him on the shoulder. Only Rodney and the CO stood back not knowing which one to go to first.

In the end, both Mould and Sue emerged from the melee and came over to them. Rodney put his arms round both of them and laughed aloud with delight. The colonel was beside himself and, despite the early hour, ordered a bottle of champagne from the bar to celebrate.

Chapter 35

COLLINS GOES FOR A SWIM

To the north, in Nicosia, Captain Collins had been picked up from his mess by the warrant officer, Mr Anderson, and conveyed to the helicopter pad from which a small flight of Army Air Corps operated on behalf of the UN. In the crew room he met the pilot, a young sergeant who was obviously looking forward to getting airborne. First, though, both he and James had to hold back while the warrant officer went painstakingly over the details of the locations they had to visit.

When the briefing was finished, the pilot left to log his flight plan and warm up the aircraft. Mr Anderson motioned the captain over to the map and then began to describe what had to be done at each of the three locations they had to visit, ending up at Famagusta for an overnight stop, he pointed out, eyeing James questioningly.

"Works for me," said James as blandly as he could. He felt a sense of relief that at least phase one of his plan was effective and that he stood a real chance of keeping his word to the major, from whichever branch of the intelligence service he came, it was all one to James. Then he could really help out his busy corps brothers.

Just then the corporal from the flight came in and told them that the helicopter was ready for them and that the pilot would like them to board.

Outside the sun was already gaining its strength and the crystal-clear freshness of a Cyprus morning was already in danger of being overtaken by that hot and dusty heat of the Nicosia plain.

The two men were signalled aboard; both bent to walk under the rotors and tipped their daysacks aboard before clambering into the seats.

Belting themselves in, Anderson gave the thumbs up to the pilot. The engine revolutions rose to a scream and the rotors flashed overhead faster and faster until they were a blur and seemed to be going backwards.

The small craft bucked and vibrated and then lifted off. As they rose and flew off to their first stop, the country began to unfold before them. At the height of their climb, James imagined he could see the whole of the island laid out before them.

Their first port of call took them to a British infantry outpost at a box factory slap in the middle of the Greek and Turkish lines. They stopped only for an hour to sort out ration and ammunition problems. The major in charge asked James to send up some glass marbles.

"You are joking?" But the raised eyebrows of the major and the tilt of his head showed he was in earnest. "Forgive me, sir, but whatever for?" asked James showing his surprise.

"Come on, I'll show you," the major grinned and led James to a sangar, in this case a three-man sandbagged observation post, where the three soldiers were watching the Turkish side. He led James into the OP and the soldiers moved over to make room for them.

"All quiet, sir," one of OP staff commented.

"Johnny Turk still awake," said another.

"That, Captain, is the problem. Look to your front. See that bump in the ground fifty feet, slightly left?" the major indicated, pointing. "See it? There's a Turkish soldier there."

Suddenly James felt that uneasy rush of adrenaline. A feeling he was no stranger to and everyone gets the first time they are face-to-face with an unknown in the middle of two warring enemies.

"He's alone?"

"Yeah; our teams operate in threes so at least they can spell each other. That poor beggar can be out there all day and night without relief and if he falls asleep and is caught by his officer he is likely as not to be summarily shot."

"You're joking!"

"No, I'm not, not at all," said the major seriously. "But we keep him alive. Every time he falls asleep, the team catapults a missile at him if he doesn't respond to a call, and that is why we want those marbles, they will increase our accuracy."

"You'll get them or something equally effective," James was astounded.

When he related his story to the warrant officer, all he said was, "They can't have run out already, the workshop still haven't forgiven me for diverting the last lot of ball bearings to this lot." With a sigh he made a note in his logbook, and they were off to the next location.

The flight westward had the Troodos Mountains to their left and the sparkling Mediterranean Sea to their right. The sun was now high in the heavens and the shadow of the helicopter raced beneath them.

They flew on to the town of Morphou to see the Danish and stayed for lunch while the helicopter was refuelled.

Their business concluded they waved goodbye to their hosts. Retracing their route and past Nicosia, they banked south-east which took them over the Green Line at times and James was able to see both the Greek and Turkish lines. A few bored soldiers waved at them from both sides; it seemed more than a little surreal to James.

Looking through the plastic bubble of the helicopter, James saw the city haze of Famagusta emerge. They flew along the seafront where deserted and empty hotels basked in the stark white of the afternoon sun. The mile-long beach, almost deserted, gave the illusion of a ghost town.

A UN flag was fluttering, heralding the headquarters of the Swedish contingent to the United Nations Force in Cyprus.

When they had landed and climbed out, they were met by the Swedish quartermaster, like James a captain although a bit longer in the tooth, who introduced himself as Rolf. It was now nearly five and he offered Anderson and James refreshments. Anderson declined, he needed to sort out the helicopter and he needed to get the pilot accommodated after the helicopter was refuelled. Mr Anderson suggested to James that, as he would visit several of the outstations tonight, if James could look after the quartermaster's needs, he would see James in the morning, to which James readily agreed. Mr Anderson added that if James needed anything later he could get hold of him in the seniors' mess. Saluting, he and the pilot left James to his own devices.

"Great location you have here." James started looking round the base.

"Not bad, could be worse," Rolf laughed.

"Heard last night in the Nicosia mess that the contingent here is called the Beach Patrol; as you are so close to the seafront I can see why."

"How right you are; but I wouldn't let the others hear you say that, it's not popular with our commander. He sees it as a term of derision implying we are playboys, when in fact we have plenty to be proud of, and he feels it derides us. He is the sensitive sort." The old quartermaster smiled, "It is not true, we work hard and we play hard. Until recently that was not difficult. The beaches were packed and the hotels full of people enjoying themselves. The young soldiers had a ball," Rolf laughed. He was a big jolly man with thinning white hair and a nose all but flat against his face; disfigured from some past encounter, of that James was sure.

Rolf ushered James into his office and into one of two easy chairs, calling to the clerks to bring two beers.

"Well James, from your pale colour I take it you have just arrived?"

"Yes, got in yesterday. And I do feel a little bushed, especially after today's gallop round the island in that bone-shaking chopper. I must say, the sea looks inviting for a refresher," James indicated out of the window, waving his arm in the general direction of the shore.

"Hmm, look James, I've got some issues to settle with the company commanders later tonight. So, what say you, we do our work for half an hour now and then finish off after breakfast tomorrow? There is not a lot to go over anyway." He added by way of explanation, "There are some of your soldiers from Dhekelia around for the next hour, collecting kit left behind when they moved out pre invasion. They had stuff in houses so now the ceasefire is effective, they are repatriating their kit. It would not look good to be enjoying the Med while they are around. So, to work and then I will take you for a swim. After that, an early dinner and then the night is yours to sleep or drink, while I sort out the company commanders. How is that for a plan?"

"Sounds good to me, thank you, that would be great. Any spare snorkel kit, knife and a speargun going begging? I would like to try my hand."

"Sure, no problem, but you will find few fish. In this part of the Med, as in most parts, it's fished out. These people catch and eat everything. Until recently they dynamited the fish; this form of fishing is indiscriminate and kills even the fish eggs too; it is, as you will appreciate, completely unsustainable. Just maybe this stretch of water funnelling out of the Green Line from the land may allow a corridor of fish to regenerate itself. I have seen it before in other parts of the world; I hope so anyway."

"It's crazy. Now, how can we help?" James was keen to get on with the task.

"Basically, we don't have any problems over combat supplies, rations, fuel and ammunition. What we are really short of are creature comforts, barrack stores, and we are having major problems with our Land Rover spares. I'll get out the unsatisfied demands in a moment and show you what I mean..."

The two worked on and finished by six; by six thirty they were floating in the Med. James saw only a small silvery coloured fish, nothing worth chasing down. At just after seven they had showered and changed and were sitting down to the evening meal in the mess. At dinner, James asked Rolf if he could hang on to the kit for a swim before breakfast. Rolf readily agreed, it was not a problem.

In the mess, James met most of the other officers and it was eight before he could feign tiredness and make his excuses.

Once back in his bunk he opened his daysack, taking out his black hooded cotton shirt, lightweight black cargoes and black canvas jungle boots. He put them on with his UN uniform over the top. He tucked his green uniform trousers into the boots and, satisfied with his appearance, he let himself casually out of the room and on to the beach road. With his snorkel kit in his daysack he sauntered along the beach, throwing up the odd salute and smile to any Turkish soldiers he saw. They seemed pleased with the gesture and responded with grins.

He needed to be at the end of the Famagusta beach heading for Cape Greco before the light faded. He calculated he had about eight miles to go overland to the point where he could enter the water. He wanted to be at this point before last light. He could do it if he hurried. As the hotels and beach began to be left behind, he met the rocks fringing the sea. The rocks gave concealment and he struck inland to cut off the cape to his left. Safe in his environment, he jogged at an easy lope following old worn animal paths; jogging was a pace he could keep up for hours.

As dusk began to fall he continued unchallenged. He thought that both sides may have pulled back from the confrontation line now the ceasefire was agreed to prevent any unfortunate incident from overenthusiastic troops. Sweating slightly from the jogging, he found his way to the point he had chosen from the map; a mile plus round the point of the cape leading to the Ayia Napa bay, only a mile or so further on. The location of the target was half this distance and as the light faded he was confident in himself that he could locate the mission materials.

He slipped out of his uniform and hid it under a mass of pebbles high on the small beach on which he found himself. The beach was little more than a tiny cove and he could see the phosphorescence of the wavelets that gently lapped the edges of the cove.

Sitting half in and out of the water he put on his swimming fins and wetted the glass of his mask. He spat on the inner glass to stop it misting and after running his snorkel through the sea to wet it he jammed it in the strap of the mask as he put it over his head. With his diving knife strapped to his chest and the harpoon gun looped over his shoulder, he slipped into the water. It was like getting into a tepid bath. Free of the land he floated for a moment, enjoying the feeling of weightlessness, before turning to his task.

He swam cautiously out, turning his head to land. He constantly surveyed the side of the cove as he broke out from it and swam towards the target. At times he felt the tug of the current flowing from Ayia Napa to the cape, but by swimming closer to the shore he easily broke out of it. He sensed the odd fish, squid and spiny crustaceans, but let them go. No time to hunt.

He made the blue pool that had been described to him and even though it was nearly dark now, the silver sand at the bottom of the pool reflected what light there was. He had little difficulty identifying the area where he needed to dive to retrieve the hidden items.

Taking a few deep breaths he flipped his way down and in moments he located the subterranean cave. Pulling himself inside the cave, he felt rather than saw a spiny lobster move backwards away from him, deeper into the darkness. Drawing himself upwards inside the funnel, he felt round and grasped the two bags he had come for. As he pulled the bags towards him and began to reverse his way out, he felt the momentary silky wrap of an octopus tentacle round his forearm. The octopus, sensing the size of the man, let go but James nevertheless felt his heart rate jump. Once outside he kicked for the surface until his head was free of the water.

The night was fully set. James orientated himself and floated for a moment, listening to the sounds around him. It would be another hour before he was expecting to meet up with the major.

Despite the relatively warm water, James knew he would begin to chill soon if he didn't get out on to the rocks. He found a place just above the waterline where he could observe any approaches. First he needed to secure the packages. Diving down again, he tied the bags to a rock and then finned back to the surface and shook himself off. He stretched out on the rock's surface and curled up.

When he opened his eyes, the silent environment he had been enjoying had changed. He heard oars and voices from at least two boats. Gathering and donning his kit, he slipped off the rock and under the water. He armed the harpoon gun and made his way to a rocky outcrop in the cove where he surfaced so that he could see what was going on around him from deep cover. Against the light of the star-studded night sky, he could see two craft close into the cove and picked out the voice of Rodney from one of the boats.

He waited to see what was developing as it was clear even now that the two parties were not as one.

Chapter 36

LAWSON'S RACE FOR THE LIST

Earlier, the information of the nurse's kidnap had reached Lawson, with the news that whilst Seabrook was dead, the others were still very much alive. The news was fresh, only hours after the brothers had informed Nicosia that they were going into hiding in the forest.

He had felt the blood drain from his face as he realized that the brigadier had been lying to him.

He felt shaken to the core and lay back in his chair at his office in Westminster in shock. For some moments he could not bring himself to speak into the phone that hung limply in his hand. It was only when he felt it slipping from his grasp that he shook himself back into action. With a trembling hand he put the receiver back to his ear; he could hear the man with the soft voice calling his name urgently into the receiver.

"Yes, yes, I'm here."

"Listen, all is not yet lost, but you must meet me at the emergency rendezvous, take care you are not followed. Be there in one hour, now move." The phone went dead.

Lawson was galvanized into action. Pushing the work on his desk into the top drawer and locking it, he grabbed his briefcase and hat, looked round his office to make sure he had left nothing of importance on view and rushed from the office, leaving his aides startled by his haste. He ordered them to cancel his appointments for the rest of the day.

"But sir, you're due to see the PM with the Leader of the Opposition in a few hours time," his PA was horrified at his behaviour.

"Tell them I am sick, tell them anything, but make it good," Lawson snarled slamming the door.

His PA, a lady of mature years and sound reputation in the corridors of power, told the rest of the staff to get back to work and that she would be back in a while. It was time she had a discussion with the Cabinet Secretary about her minister.

Lawson was an anxious and angry man as he slammed through the door. He hurried along the corridors of the Palace of Westminster that led to the rear of the complex.

His mind was working at a furious pace. His immediate thought was that anybody on his tail would not be expecting him to make a break at this particular time. He was right; the brigadier's men were covering all the front entrances, not the side and rear.

The communications centre in the duty room of the brigadier's section monitoring Lawson's phone were already relaying the latest exchange between Lawson and Tsygankov. Robinson cursed as he realized that Lawson was on the run and he was now a loose cannon.

Robinson sent out an immediate alert to his people knowing in his heart it was too late.

Once into the open, Lawson crossed the gardens and stepped on to the slipway that led to the Thames. As always, at the river's edge was a police launch. They knew him and he had no trouble persuading the officer in charge to ferry him to the other side. Once in the launch, he had time to compose himself and, by the time he reached the other side, he was outwardly his normal self.

"The short trip seems to have brought your colour back a little, sir," remarked the officer holding the boat steady while Lawson clambered out.

"Yes, I was feeling a little peaky," Lawson responded and thanked the man for the trip. He hurried off to find a taxi. A Tube train later and another taxi found him entering one of those seedy overseas clubs that proliferate along Finchley Road in North London.

He was there within the hour making the rendezvous. Adjusting his eyes to the gloom in the club, he went to the bar. He ordered a brandy from a surly barman and then retired into one of the cubicles lining the edge of a circular copper dance floor. Shortly afterwards his contact appeared.

"Mr Lawson, it's a great pleasure to meet you after all this time," the soft, slightly accented voice floated down to him, and he looked up into the gloom. The man that faced him was very tall and thin, almost Dickensian in looks and dress.

"Blue," it was a statement, not a question. Lawson added in a resigned voice, "Well, what's to be done? It looks as though I'm finished in this country."

"Probably, possibly, but no, not absolutely necessarily so; consider, evidently the secret service have their suspicions about you and have lied to you, but surely if they had had enough to hang you... forgive me, they don't do that here anymore, do they? A pity, in many ways, it did get rid of messy business effectively." Lawson shivered. "Anyway," Tsygankov continued, "apparently they don't have enough on you to pull you in, so let's not let them get anything else, shall we? You are to come with me."

The man's voice was suddenly firm and authoritative. "We are going to fly to the continent, to a little private airstrip in the south of France to await events and how they may go in Cyprus. We will see. If all is well, then you will return, if not, then you won't. It will be Russia, pensioned off, not a bad life," Tsygankov finished almost casually. "I for one am looking forward to going home anyway."

"Do I have a choice?" Lawson asked, resigned to the answer.

"In this instance, no, anyway, have we ever let you down?"

"No," smiled Lawson, shaking his controller's hand for the first time since they had met. "Whatever, your private plane will surely have better brandy than this watered down dishwater."

The man put his hand round Lawson's shoulders as he rose from the table, "Brandy, no, but excellent vodka." Tsygankov led him out the back through the kitchens and into a waiting car with tinted windows.

As Lawson got into the car, he looked round; his companion laughed, declaring that any watcher from Department E4, the envy of many a secret service, had been lost way back.

The car sped them to an executive jet that waited for them at a small private airfield to the north of London; there were no customs, no security.

Two hours later they were already crossing the Channel and heading for France.

Tsygankov and Lawson sat back in the rear seats looking at each other. Blue raised an eyebrow and brought his hands together to form a sort of tent in front of his face as he studied Lawson for a moment. "You don't seem to have much to say; I'd have thought that, after all these years of contact with me, but never actually being able to spend time with me, you would have had a thousand questions. Like, who am I?"

Lawson leant forward. "Yes, you are right, I do have a lot of questions for you, but frankly I need to address a few to myself, for the moment, in the context of our position. I've been weighing things up and trying to piece together the situation. I tell you, quite frankly, that the step we are now taking is wrong, so wrong."

"Really, how so?" asked Tsygankov interested.

"You, or whoever it is wants us to go to the south of France and just sit it out," Lawson paused. "I must ask myself why? It really doesn't make any logical sense, if something does go wrong, surely it would be better to be closer to home, say Austria, for a flight into Eastern bloc airspace?"

"I think I should tell you that I, and only I, am in complete control of this phase of the operation until it is resolved, one way or the other," Tsygankov smiled. "So if you have a suggestion to make, please do so."

"If we are serious about saving the list for our eyes only and possibly salvaging my career, I believe we should go to Cyprus and see the operation through."

"Are you serious?" said Tsygankov looking down his nose at the minister. "For if you are you'd better have very good reasons for suggesting that course of action."

"I haven't cracked, if that's what you think," rasped Lawson testily. "We know that they may have their suspicions, but they couldn't have enough proof or I'd be in their custody by now, as you said. Therefore, you must also surmise that they don't yet have the list. We know they intend to return to the UK from Cyprus on Thursday and that is tomorrow. Therefore, it must mean they are going for the list possibly tonight. I believe we should be there to take it off them, not just wait for them to recover it unchallenged, whether or not I am named on it." And then vehemently Lawson burst out, "For goodness sake, it's the only course to take!"

"I see," said Blue thoughtfully. "Possibly, perhaps you are right. But there are risks to you, have you thought about that?"

"Yes, but at this point it seems to me that the list is more important than me as an individual. Being pensioned off is not my first choice but it has some appeal in other ways."

Tsygankov nodded with a smile; he rose and went forward to the cockpit.

It was some 20 minutes before he returned and, when he did, he was serious; he eased his long frame into the seat and strapped himself back in again. As he did so the plane turned a few points to port and he nodded.

"You convinced me, and I've spoken to my people and to Cyprus. Here is the current situation and what I propose to do. I would like your advice on a few points when we start to get into the tactical detail of the course proposed."

He went on to tell Lawson that they should arrive in Larnaca about seven in the evening and that a backup team and car had been arranged. He briefed him on the disastrous events in the forest and appraised him of the fact that Nicosia had put another man in the field who was monitoring the developments at the hospital.

Lawson listened impassively, only interrupting to go over a point of detail when Blue expressed himself badly. When the Russian had finished, both men made out a detailed plan of the steps they would take when they got to Cyprus. As usual, the intellect of Lawson took over and slowly Tsygankov allowed himself to become the minor partner in the relationship, especially when Lawson took over the operational planning of the task ahead.

The hours flew by as they considered every angle. When they had exhausted every possibility they could think of, they rested, dozing fitfully, each imaging his future if anything went wrong.

They arrived ahead of the forecasted time at Larnaca Airport. They had to circle for a while as the airspace was very congested with civilian and military aircraft; once permission to land had been granted, they were quickly on the ground and disembarked.

At the terminal, the airport staff, supported by soldiers and police, were busily processing passengers, many of whom were refugees with no papers. Lawson and Tsygankov, with their papers in order, were waved quickly through the immigration and customs counters. Lawson's diplomatic passport barely drew more than a raised eyebrow. Normally, he would have had the VIP treatment but, after all, there was a war on.

They moved to the concourse of the airport reception area and found seats amid the sea of people and baggage. The impression they received was one of organized chaos, which it clearly was at this time.

By half past eight, they had still not been contacted and both of them began to worry. Finally, Tsygankov went to try to phone Nicosia. He had only been gone a few minutes and was waiting in the queue for the telephone when a hand touched him on the shoulder. He turned to see a man of average height, dressed in a tropical suit, looking up at him.

"Yes?" inquired Tsygankov as he looked at the face of the man and decided he was Russian. The man looked uncomfortable, clearly intimidated by the senior officer of the KGB.

"Sir," he said almost bowing, "you are expected and I am your contact. I am the junior attaché from the embassy. Sir, we don't have a great deal of time. Where is your travelling companion? We should not stay here too long or the authorities could become interested."

"Of course, where's the car?"

"In the car park, in a row at the rear."

"Return to it, I will bring my friend to it immediately."

The attaché, a man in his mid thirties, nodded and withdrew. Blue headed back to Lawson and indicated that he should follow. They made their way to the car park and soon picked out the car when the attaché waved to them from an open window. Although the evening was well advanced, the two men from the UK were sweating in the warm air; both felt like a shower and were tired and irritable. They held themselves in check and didn't berate the Nicosia man for being late, which they were sorely tempted to do simply to vent their frustration on someone.

There were two men in the car, the attaché that Tsygankov had spoken to and another man of broad-shouldered and rugged appearance who was obviously the muscle.

The attaché introduced himself as Nicolai Borchev and his companion as Dmitri Nikoliavich. Borchev ushered the two men into the rear of the car and got into the front passenger seat so that he could direct and work the radio. Nikoliavich started the car and they pulled out of the car park into the traffic.

The attaché went over the situation and explained that they had put a man at the British hospital and that they were in radio contact. He had just called in to say that the main team, comprising a man who appeared to be in charge and two other men, had gone to the officers' mess with a nurse. A car had been brought up to the mess and one of the men with the leader had stopped by the car to take the keys from a man who had left the car and gone away.

"Where is your man, for goodness sake?" said Lawson, somewhat impressed.

"He is actually at the Base but over the road from the hospital, in the bush, as it were. We couldn't get any nearer as those two idiots yesterday really made a mess of things and security at the hospital has been reinforced. Still, with a good pair of binoculars he appears to be able to see most of what is wanted." The attaché turned back to the road as he had to concentrate on the traffic which was heavy and erratic to ensure the driver didn't go the wrong way.

The driver picked up the story; his English was more heavily accented than his companion. "He is a Greek who works for us and is related to the dead agents, so he has a score to settle. Right now, we are driving to the area on the road out to the base. Once he sees that they are on the move, we will be able to link up and follow them."

"What about the curfew?" Lawson said suddenly, leaning forward and tapping Nicolai on the shoulder.

"We have diplomatic plates and I have a pass that will get us through any roadblock we come to. After the British base, I don't think we will encounter any obstructions anyway."

The base was now only about two miles away and while the car sped to the area, Dmitri talked to the men and tried to describe why the confrontation between the Greek and Turkish elements had taken place. It was the old story, the people of Cyprus, whether they be Greek or Turkish, were, for the most part, happy to live together; as usual it was the power seekers who had forced the situation, supported by politicians in each of the respective countries. Sadly, it was not the men in power that would suffer but the ordinary man in the street. In the days to come, families would be split and their lands, their houses and possessions confiscated by the other side. Many people would find themselves homeless, forced to live the life of refugees. He went on to show how the country, only just beginning to get on its feet in regard to tourism, would now be put back economically for a decade or more. His belief was that the Greeks had simply pushed the Turks too far and when this happens to a proud and warlike race, when a Turk sees that you are overstepping what might be reasonably acceptable, a quick retaliation can be expected.

Tsygankov, surprised at the bodyguard's insight and opinion given so freely, thanked the man for his information.

They were stopped briefly by a roadblock outside Larnaca city and then on an entry road leading to the British base. Both were manned by Greek and British military police respectively. The diplomatic plates and passports gave easy passage to their progress.

They made their rendezvous point by just after nine and settled down to wait. The lookout at the hospital reported that all was quiet. The car still stood outside the officers' mess; the men had been out to it a couple of times, once to check it over and another time to stow some gear in it. The occupants of the Russian car took this as a good sign that what they expected to happen, would happen, but how, they had no idea.

The two men from Nicosia had come well prepared with food and wine and the men from England were grateful for their foresight; in addition to the sustenance they had brought weapons. Lawson accepted the automatic pistol and two spare clips he was offered.

Tsygankov declined. He rarely carried a weapon, preferring to rely on his wit to get him out of trouble, the two Russians simply shrugged; there would be four of them against possibly three and they had the element of surprise, so they were not too worried that the senior officer appeared to be no more than a passenger or at best an interested party. The two Russians and Lawson felt a certain excitement as it was out of the normal run of their daily lives for any of them to become involved abroad in a mission like this. For the Russians, it would normally have been third parties carrying out such work but their Greek mercenaries had spectacularly failed in this case.

Chapter 37

GAME SET AND MATCH

The time passed on to nine thirty, about the time that Captain Collins was nearing his entry point, having circumvented Cape Greco.

The watcher at the hospital noticed movement in the forecourt of the officers' mess. Three men got into the car and were waved off by the same nurse he had seen earlier and a man in a full colonel's uniform. He radioed his Russian masters immediately and then ran the quarter of a mile to where they were waiting.

As he reached the waiting car, Rodney and his party drove past, oblivious of the presence of Lawson and the other men who had crouched down to avoid being seen. Lawson's party watched the other car disappear round the bend and turn right towards the village of Xylophaghou and out towards Ayia Napa.

"Get in, get in," Tsygankov hastened the Greek contact. "Quick," Tsygankov tapped Dmitri on the shoulder, "Follow them!"

Dmitri moved off smoothly, "Sir, we know they are headed for the Ayia Napa area, we will follow at a good distance, their lights will show us the way." After exiting the British base he speeded up. "See?" he said pointing. "They are climbing the hill to the village." Their car tail lights could be seen clearly against the night sky. "Now we follow." He added to the carful of people generally, "Have no fear, after the village, the country is mainly flat, only two roads to speak of, we will not lose them easily."

In the car containing Rodney, Mould and Sharky, there was an air of expectation. Mould was driving as he knew the area better than anybody else, and he was quite at home throwing the car around the twisting roads.

"Hey, slow down, I want to make this trip in one piece!" shouted Rodney laughing and thumping Mould on the back. Rodney had been thinking about the call from Robinson earlier, warning that Lawson had given him the slip. They had agreed together that they could wait no longer or risk Collins failing. He had been working out all the probable issues and had only been brought back to the present by Mould's racing driver tactics.

"Sorry boss, just getting the feel of this pig of a car, so to speak," explained Mould, concentrating on the road ahead.

"Fine, but just don't kill us."

As they swept out of the village, Rodney, looking at the map open on his lap, told Mould to take the dirt road along the coast and told Sharky to keep a sharp 'look out for bandits'.

As they turned on to the dirt road, the Russians entered the village. Dmitri automatically took the coast road once he reached the far side and the other car's lights could be seen clearly a mile ahead of them. Dmitri slowed down and allowed the other car to just get out of sight and then followed at a steady pace.

Despite his caution, Dmitri was not clever enough to fool the trained eye of Sharky who picked up the bouncing headlights of the Russian car.

"Hey boss there is another car on this road and it's keeping its distance constant from us."

"Let me have a look," said Rodney turning in his seat. After a few moments, he picked up the lights too. "Blast, who the hell can they be? Look," he spoke to Mould, "let's lose them. At least let's get to Ayia Napa with a little time to spare, don't make it too obvious."

Mould immediately put his foot down and the car shot forward bucking and shaking over the rough road while he clung to the steering wheel. "Sorry, boss, there is only one way to do this." The other two clutched the backs of the seats and anything else they could to stop themselves being bounced about in the car. Even so, both banged their heads on the roof several times and cursed. The road was potholed to a spectacular degree and the car was airborne more than once.

"Dmitri, they seem to have picked up speed," Nicolai commented.

"Seen that, they may have spotted us; how far to the next turn off so we can rejoin the inland parallel road?"

"One coming up leads to the village of Liopetri. That will get us back on the other road."

"Give me a 100 metre warning."

"Coming up soon; get ready, turn left now."

Dmitri swung the car left and accelerated to the north. The village of Liopetri was only a mile away and the Russian car was soon lost among the houses.

Mould, looking in his mirror, was the first to see the other car turn off. He slowed down much to the relief of the other two who looked over their shoulders and Sharky asked, "What's going on?"

"They have turned off," Mould said picking up a little more speed, which at least was controlled.

The men looked over their shoulders again; both were tense. The events of the last few days, including Mould's excursion the night before, meant that they were all keyed up. Rodney realized he should now take no chances, so that the other two would simply have to follow orders, without thinking.

"Good," said Rodney in a forced relaxed voice. "Just keep the speed to a moderate pace so that anybody who may be about will take us for locals that would be driving at an easy rate on this road." Turning to Sharky, he ordered him to return to his task of watching the road behind.

Rodney let his gaze fall to his right. Because they were on the coast road and only a few yards from the shoreline and the sea, he could make out the black lava rocks clearly and the phosphorescence as the sea lazily bubbled over them. Further out, the moon shone on the sea and he realized that it was a very clear night that could aid them but would also give them little shelter from the enemy wherever they were.

He was astute enough to realize that the other side would by now have regrouped, but he didn't know and nor could he guess what they could offer in the way of further disruption. He reasoned again, as had Lawson earlier that day, that the enemy must realize that they either had the list by now, or that they were about to get it. They had advertised that they were due back tomorrow. Rodney felt uneasy, but couldn't quite put his finger on the reason why. A cold shiver went down his back and it was noticed by his two agents.

"What's the matter, sir, you all right?" enquired Sharky, concerned.

"Just got this bad feeling; can't explain it, so best forget it," Rodney said suddenly brightening. "What comes, comes. Nevertheless, let's be on our guard." To Mould he added, "Try to drive without lights for a while and let's see if our friends appear again."

Mould doused the lights and found after a few minutes that he could drive quite comfortably by the light of the stars, moon and the reflections off the sea.

The other car did not reappear as the Russian party had decided to go round on the high road through the village of Sotira and then turn right through the Sotira Forest. Although their journey was a few miles longer, they were able to make good time and were at Ayia Napa harbour a good ten minutes before Rodney's party arrived. They parked their car, hiding it a few yards off the crossroads that Rodney and his people would have to drive down, and waited.

The café, 40 yards or so to their right, was, despite the loosely enforced curfew, in full swing. The Russians and Lawson from their vantage point could see a few Greek soldiers sitting outside the café, eating and drinking wine, and an old beaten-up truck belonging to them was parked by the side of the café. There were a few other cars in the car park. Half a dozen Greeks inside the café were mixing with the soldiers at their tables, the civilians looked like they were local fishermen, some were trying to decide if they should venture out to fish in their boats.

As Rodney's party approached the village crossroads, they switched on their lights and turned into the café car park, stopping alongside the army truck; in the shadows across the other side, the Russian party watched and waited.

The locals and soldiers looked up suspiciously at the British as they got out of the car and made their way to the front of the café which formed one side of, and overlooked, the square, rock-built harbour.

In the harbour itself, brightly coloured fishing boats rocked gently on the swell of the sea.

The eyes of the three men swept the area and in the far left of the harbour, run up on the harbour beach, they saw the boat that Mould had driven into the quay area only a few days earlier.

They viewed the damage from a distance and saw the numerous bullet holes scattered through the hull and superstructure. Smiling to each other with low whistles and raised eyebrows, they suddenly realized just how lucky they had been not to end up like Seabrook.

Rodney led the way to an empty table just under the canopy of the café, facing the sea. There was some slight hostility around them but in the main it was just curiosity from the others around the café.

This area was not only close to the ceasefire line but was historically nationalistic and terrorists had been very active in the area in the old days. It was not a place in which a British soldier would chose to be alone.

"Act naturally and be friendly," whispered Mould. "Just chill and follow my lead."

The other two knew that Mould had spent a fair amount of his time in this part of the island in his service days and had brought Sharky safely to shore here, so they were happy to follow his lead.

The occupants of the café were now huddled over their drinks, glancing occasionally at the group. There was a general hubbub that threatened to turn noisy. One of the fishermen waved meaningfully in their direction.

A stocky man in his middle thirties rose and came over to their table; his unruly curly black hair covered most of his eyes. "My friends!" he opened his arms welcoming them. "I am Charlie, the owner of this restaurant," he added quietly and conspiratorially, leaning over the table, "I do not think that tonight is a good night to be here." His voice was almost apologetic and his manner genial. Clearly, he did not want trouble at his place and as diplomatically as possible was asking them to move on.

Mould broke into his best Greek and explained that they were in trouble and needed the assistance of a fisherman tonight and didn't know where else they could go for help.

Charlie was at first taken aback by Mould's Greek and then grinned. "Perhaps after all you have come to the right place. I know you now. You two are the men escaping from the Turks earlier in the week, my God, you look better now. What a mess you were in when you arrived, like drowned rats, and shot up." He put his hands on Sharky and Mould's shoulders. "And you," he looked hard at Mould. "I remembered you after they had taken you away. You were here many years ago in the old troubles. You were one of the soldiers who came to the church at our Easter celebration. You were given Easter candles and joined in with us that night long ago. I was just a young man then, but I remember it well; we were surprised just like tonight. Eh?" He laughed and spoke rapid Greek to the fishermen and soldiers who were now taking an interest in the exchange. As Charlie went on and explained the reason for the visit, the tension in the restaurant eased.

Mould had turned to Charlie in surprise. The memories of that night in the old village monastery and its church built into the rock began to flood back from the past. He and his partner had been on patrol in their

Land Rover when they had run into Ayia Napa one evening. The village had been empty, but they had heard the singing from the almost ruined monastery just to its south. They had driven down, dismounted and walked into the monastery courtyard, which they found full of people in their Sunday best. The men were in black suits and the womenfolk were in black dresses and black cotton stockings with their heads covered. The whole courtyard was ringed with people facing the church. It was an unusual church as it was built into the wall of the monastery and carved into the rock on the monastery's northern side.

Like tonight, they had been met with hostility until one of the children had come up to the two of them and offered them a lit Easter candle as was being carried by everyone at the service.

Mould remembered he had been very touched and had picked up the child and smiled at the villagers. The spell had been broken and for that one night they had been accepted like village locals. They had sung the Easter songs with the villagers and afterwards had drunk wine with them in the café.

It was one of those unforgettable events in a person's life that returns in quiet moments. Just for an instant, a man can relive such an experience with pleasure many times but always with the private regret of a moment lost.

Mould stood up, "Charlie, I ask that you give me a lighted candle tonight." He put his hand round Charlie's shoulders, "That Easter night was a good night, no enemies, just people, friends. I give you my word that we are here for a purpose that has nothing to do with the present troubles, nor does our problem involve anyone in this village. It is to do with the day when we came in that boat."

Charlie looked at him for a long time and then he turned to the men and soldiers, who were all now looking at Mould and waiting for their host to give a sign. They returned to their conversations when Charlie announced that here were friends and that they were welcome. First, he brought them drinks and salted nuts, "Enjoy your drinks, I need to speak to the men." He left them to go to speak to the fishermen in the café who all wanted an explanation.

"OK, Mould," said his boss, when the man was out of earshot. "What did you promise them, the Queen's jewels, the Bank of England?"

"You wouldn't understand if I told you," said Mould, smiling quietly to himself.

"Try me."

"I will tell you but not now, it's too long a story. Just accept that I asked them for help and because of something that happened a long time ago, I think they will. We must just wait."

"For how long? It's close to eleven now and that means we only have a few more hours to get our hands on a boat and a driver, leave the harbour and get over to the cove and the cave. As Lawson is on the loose, anything could happen. I've had this bad feeling all night that the Russians are closing in, that car that was following us, perhaps."

"Give them half an hour. I am sure they will help us in one way or another." Mould paused. "If not, it means an hour and half walking and swimming to get to the cave and I am sure we should be able to do that easily."

"That's all right then, let's relax and take in the sea breeze for a while," Sharky intoned yawning.

Lawson and his companions, in the meantime, remained in their car which they had pulled back silently into the shadow on the other side of the car park, where they were more able to observe but not to hear what was going on at the café and they had seen the exchange between Charlie and Mould. It was clear from this exchange and from the attitude of the locals that the British group had been successful in gaining the confidence of the locals.

Lawson was worried. "Look, it's clear that they have come to the end of their journey, by land at least. What if they now go off in a boat? We are going to be stuck here on land."

Just then the soldiers in the café got up, waved goodnight to the locals and made their way reluctantly to their truck to carry them back to base. Tsygankov held up his hand for silence until the truck had moved off, its headlights lighting up the harbour restaurant as it pulled out in a wide circle.

"Do not worry, even if they go somewhere by sea they have to return to their car here," offered their driver. "Don't they?"

"I expect so," said Lawson hopefully. "But what if they don't?"

Tsygankov stirred and pointed out that at the moment there was nothing they could do to follow until they saw them move out of the harbour, the locals were obviously sensitive. He advised everybody in the car to calm down and await developments; it was now late and he thought that soon the people at the café would start to drift away to their homes or boats for the night.

The occupants of the car subsided into a restless vigil.

* * * * *

In London, the brigadier was having an interview with the prime minister. The disappearance of Lawson and Tsygankov had been discovered but no leads had been unearthed to suggest their whereabouts.

The river police had by now been quizzed; the taxi driver that had driven Lawson had been found and questioned and the club where Tsygankov and Lawson had met had been turned over.

From that point the two men had been lost from sight. What particularly annoyed the brigadier was that his team should have lost both men, the error was unforgiveable. He could not offer anything but failure to the PM.

"How on earth did he give your men the slip?" The PM was annoyed, not so much with Robinson's people or even the brigadier, he was angry with himself for not exposing Lawson earlier. He smiled wryly, "It appears Alex, old friend, that I've been a bit greedy. I wanted the whole of that rotten crew and now we may not get anything."

The brigadier noticed the royal 'we' had crept in. He was not too naive to recognize that the PM, being a political animal and not that popular, would be looking for a scapegoat and that could well be the brigadier's organization. It was nothing new and all part of life's rich pageant, he thought to himself. The brigadier realized that he could be asked to resign to pacify the populace. It was ironic that past service and an outstanding record did not sway in circumstances like these. He would not be the first good man to hit the dust to the political machine.

The PM was speaking again, this time to his Home Secretary, who was a worried man and kept looking at the brigadier in the hope he could suggest a way out of this mess. "I want this thing kept out of the press and Cabinet until Thursday; we should know by then if Alex's men have recovered the list of agents or not."

"And the money and diamonds!" interjected the Home Secretary.

The PM's Private Secretary looked down his nose at the man as if to say, "The man's a fool."

The PM banged his pipe out on the desk and put his thoughts into words. "Sod the money and diamonds, the only thing that will satisfy

Parliament and our own Cabinet colleagues will be the list. With that, we may ride out the Lawson affair, if we tell the truth that we have been manipulating him for years."

"Oh, I see, sir, how right you are." The man was nervous and ran his hands together, "But do you think it will work?"

"It will damn well have to!" Turning to the brigadier, "There is nothing to be served by you hanging on here, and I expect you want to get back to your people, eh?"

"Prime Minister, all may not be lost yet," Robinson was cautious. "I don't believe it would serve any purpose to bring in the police at this stage; far better to leave this to my people."

He saw the Home Secretary look uncomfortable. Yes, Robinson thought, if you had your way they would be in it now. Robinson didn't mind that he had probably made an enemy, politicians come and go, he didn't care. He knew he was right and, anyway, he may have to retire tomorrow and then it wouldn't matter, would it?

"Absolutely right, keep this in the family. Now, let me see you out," the PM waved the Home Secretary and his Private Secretary back into their soft green leather armchairs from which they had risen. He took the brigadier by the arm and steered him out of his office in Number 10 and into the hall where portraits of the past men of power glowered down at them.

"You obviously have something you wish to say, Prime Minister."

The prime minister was short and stocky and, instead of looking up at Robinson, kept his head down looking at the tiles. "Yes, Brigadier, I do. We have known each other for a good few years and I know you are good at your job or you wouldn't have lasted for so long. But, if you and your people don't come up with the goods tomorrow, I may not be able to protect you from the wolves. I give you my word I'll try and on that you can rely. Now, for goodness sake, get out there and for both our sakes get Lawson and his contact, dead or alive. On balance, I think dead," the PM's cold eyes rose to meet Robinson's and held them for a long second.

The man's power came through to the brigadier like a sudden shock to his system. He means it, by God, he wants Lawson dead.

"You will not be disappointed, Prime Minister, if it is within my powers to complete the task."

"Good, good evening, then," he waved Robinson out and returned to his private study.

Outside, the policeman on duty saluted the tall man with the air of command who had just been in to see the prime minister. He wondered who he was but didn't ask.

The brigadier smiled at him, reading his thoughts, and hailed his staff car parked down the street. As the car drew up, the driver leapt out and reported to Robinson. "Sir, a report from Major Brown; he's gone to get the stuff himself."

The brigadier got into the car quickly and ordered the man to take him back to HQ. The driver raised his eyebrows to heaven; the old man would be at the control centre for the rest of the evening and night and, if necessary, the next day as well, until the job was done. He, the driver, would not be getting away early that night. He shrugged and let in the clutch, he would just have to phone his wife when they got to the office and tell her.

Chapter 38

ADAGIO

Charlie, teeth flashing and carrying a bottle of the local Commandaria wine along with four glasses, approached the table and set the refreshment down with a flourish. "My friends, you are welcome; we will help if we can. Tell me exactly what you want," he sat down and leant on the table with his arms folded.

The three let out a breath together and tucked into the wine and salted peanuts that always grace café tables in Cyprus. "Charlie, we need a boat to take us to the little cove over there," said Rodney pointing into the bay.

"That's no problem," said Charlie, opening his arms and hands wide.

"It may be that, after that, I will also ask the boatman to go as far up the coast as he dare, to drop a friend off."

"That's no problem either," said Charlie repeating his throwaway gesture, "We go as far as the point, Cape Greco, maybe even further, who knows?" He paused, drained his glass and then refilled all the glasses, "What time you want to leave?"

"From here, as soon as possible. Yesterday would be fine. Is that OK?"

"Sure, no problem; you go with my father in about ten minutes, OK? You do a little fishing and then he takes you in." He left the bottle on the table and excused himself to attend to the last of his customers who were waiting for their bills. Only a few fishermen were left now. The soldiers had piled into their truck and departed five minutes ago and the bulk of the fishermen were down on their boats making their preparations for the night's fishing. It was suddenly very quiet and a peace settled on the harbour with only the occasional spluttering of old diesel engines chugging the wooden-hulled fishing boats out of the harbour. A few flies buzzed round and the occasional large beetle crashed into the side of the café as it was temporarily blinded by the light.

The three men relaxed and sipped their wine whilst staring out to sea. The wine warmed and relaxed them; they occasionally glanced at a table where two old fishermen drank their Keo brandy and told or retold stories of the ones that got away. The men were the salt of the earth, uncomplicated people, weather-beaten and, like fishermen the world over, a special breed who respected their fickle working environment and kept their own special fishing grounds a close secret. The last of the fishermen made their way to their boats leaving the three Englishmen alone.

Charlie soon appeared from inside the café with his father. Leading him over to the group, he introduced him to the table and each man rose to shake his hand. His father was a big man of about 60, weather-beaten, lean and physically very fit and strong for his age, as his firm handshake had proved. He didn't speak any English and Mould came into his own again. After a few words with the older man, Mr Rambosides, Mould motioned the other two men to follow him.

The party made its way to the boat moored to the right of the restaurant at the harbour edge. Only Charlie now remained to clear up the glasses and to prepare for the next day's trade.

The Russians had observed the group's departure and had filtered cautiously out of the car as soon as the old man had nosed his boat towards the harbour entrance, ensuring that the interior light of the car did not come on. They circled the café and moved on to the sea wall of the harbour so that they could see what was going on.

They saw Rodney's party sitting in the prow of the ancient fishing boat and the old man coaxing the single-cylinder diesel engine's revolutions as the boat cleared the harbour entrance.

Dmitri moved quickly to get a better view and to note the direction that the boat had taken. He watched for a few minutes while the boat, a few hundred yards out from the harbour entrance, laid down several lines of hooks and then cut towards the shore with the tilley lamps throwing a ghostly light on the water while the crew appeared to be having a great time with the long spears trying to pin octopus and squid that had been attracted by the lights. Dmitri was going to return to the main party but stayed longer than he had intended, watching them. After a while it seemed to him that the boat, now half a mile from the harbour, brought in the fishing lines and lamps. The lights went out.

He instinctively knew that the British party were near to the end of their journey. He retraced his steps to where the rest of the party waited impatiently for him.

"Where the hell have you been?" began Lawson but Dmitri cut him short.

"Listen," hissed Dmitri holding up his hands for silence. "They are near a cove about half of a mile out from the harbour entrance, they look as though they are waiting for something or somebody. They have put out their lights so they can't be searching, can they?"

Tsygankov looked at Lawson for comment.

Lawson fixed Dmitri with his gaze. "Light enough to see what they want once they have their night vision. And they could have a torch, so who knows. Well, there is another boat in the harbour that we could use. Could we get to them undetected or at least unsuspected?"

"It's possible," smiled Dmitri, brightening at the thought of action. "We could use the rowing boat with its outboard motor. Drive close to the shore, protected by the outcrop from their line of sight. With the outboard for most of the way, we can be there in minutes and then steal up on them. No problem."

"What about the people at the café?" queried Lawson.

"All the people have gone now except for the owner; the place is otherwise completely deserted, and the owner is sitting out on the front, obviously waiting for their return," put in Tsygankov.

Lawson contemplated the situation for a second. "Right, first we will take care of the owner, then Tsygankov, Dmitri and I will go to our friends and sort the other matter out. Let's move. You," he said, turning to the Greek, "stay with the car and make sure we are ready for a quick getaway." The Greek nodded.

The four men crept up on and then rushed the owner. Charlie, for all that the four of them came on him quickly, was the first to react. He was at a table close to the rocks leading to the harbour.

He saw them from the corner of his eye a second after he had sensed other presences moving towards him. He swept the brandy bottle from the table into his hand, reversed it and let fly at the first shape that came within his reach. He felt the satisfying crunch and a man slip away from him, then he was on his feet roaring. He charged into the remaining body of attackers.

His unskilled, bull-like attack, which would have sorted most of the local lads, failed before it began. As Charlie charged, Dmitri struck him on the back of the head viciously with his gun and Charlie crashed to the ground stunned.

It was Nicolai that Charlie's wild swing with the brandy bottle had caught high up on the chest and he was struggling to his feet, trying to get his breath.

"Are you OK?" asked Tsygankov helping Nicolai into a chair.

"Yes, I am fine," Nicolai was having difficulty in breathing. "I've just been winded a bit." He kicked Charlie's prostrate body with his foot, swinging at him from his chair. "You three go, I will have no trouble with this one now."

The three others moved quickly on to the harbour wall then along it until they drew abreast of a small rowing boat. Dmitri was the first to climb in, he helped the other two aboard and settled them down while he released the painter from an old rusting mooring ring. He pushed the boat off from the low wall, started the outboard and settled himself to concentrate on the short trip. Lawson checked and then cocked his machine pistol with practised ease.

Dmitri paused just outside the harbour entrance to get his night vision working; soon he pointed out to the others the shadowy outline of the near shoulder of the cove to which Rodney and his party now made their way.

Lawson considered the situation and his position with an experienced eye. He felt all the old special skills a soldier picked up when reading the land terrain and the best form of approach to an obstacle.

"Dmitri," he whispered, "run along the shore, as close in as you can. We will not be detectable over the sound of the waves running on to the shore. When we reach the near shoulder of the cove, if that is what's it is, switch off the engine, and then we will row round quietly and see what's to do."

Dmitri cut to the left, running the boat along the shoreline. The sea was almost flat calm, only the rustle of the waves rolling the stones on the beach disturbed the night and the current curling along the beach was in their favour, enabling them to cover the distance in what seemed hardly any time.

When they approached the near shoulder of the cove, Dmitri cut the outboard and pulled out the oars quietly.

In the boat, Lawson readied himself and signalled for silence as they glided to the cove entrance. He strained to see if he could see Rodney's party. In the darkness that seemed more intense on this side of the cove shoulder, he could just make out Dmitri's nod.

Lawson held his breath, along with his companions, as they floated the last few yards to the point of the rocks and looked round. He withdrew his head quickly; he had found himself staring into the face of Rodney Brown.

They were separated by ten yards of sea in the moonlit cove. The contrast of the bright moon-filled cove over the other side of the rock shoulder on which Lawson now appeared was marked. Lawson's position was distinctly in his favour, they would be black against the background, near invisible.

Lawson had absorbed most of the cove's features but he now cautiously took another look to confirm that the idea that was forming in his mind was plausible.

The old Greek's boat was being anchored in the middle of the cove just to the far side of the rock bridge that began above Lawson's head and curved, forming an arch, to meet a large rock that rose from the seabed almost in the middle of the cove.

Because of the column, some of the old Greek's boat was hidden from Lawson's view, but it didn't matter, he could see the crew quite clearly. They were sitting quietly all looking out to sea. Behind them, the sheer rocks rose into the night. The cliffs were scarred with black holes in places. These holes housed bat colonies and streams of bats flew in and out of them swooping to the sea to pick up moisture before winging into the night.

It was obvious to Lawson that the men in the cove were waiting for someone to arrive.

He motioned to Dmitri to pull the boat back behind the rock shoulder. When Dmitri had accomplished this, taking care not to make a sound Lawson, whispering, explained the situation to Tsygankov and Dmitri. They decided amongst themselves that the best plan of action was to simply row round the shoulder of the cove, sheltered by the column of rock, and surprise the party on the boat. This, they reasoned, they must do before whoever they were waiting for arrived, otherwise the chances were that the visitor might see Lawson's party and leave.

Lawson's position could well be compromised then by anyone

approaching from the land or sea. He was too late; Captain James Collins was already astir.

Some sixth sense had warned James to hold back from warning Rodney whom he had now identified; the others could be friendly, maybe not. He realized a dangerous situation could be developing and his silence might just tip the balance or there could be a total fuck up.

He cast his gaze round the cove to satisfy himself that all was well; the small boat a few metres from him was the only other presence, along with Rodney's boat.

Staring seaward from the boat, Mould thought he saw something out of the corner of his eye, he thought it might be Collins, but when the movement came to nothing, he dismissed it from his mind, deciding it was a small dark wave that had curled round the mouth of the cove.

It was silent now except for the high-pitched squeaking of the bats and the flutter of their wings.

When Mould had detected the movement in his peripheral vision, he had begun to rise and the others had followed his gaze. In this moment, unprepared for an attack, the Russian party struck.

So suddenly had Lawson come on them that at first they simply stared at the occupants of the tiny rowing boat; Tsygankov was now rowing and the other two, Lawson and Dmitri, had Rodney's party covered with their guns. Sharky was the first to react, but not quick enough, and Dmitri shot him even as he rose and tried to pull his gun from the back of his waistband.

"Fuck, not again!" was Sharky's cry as he clutched the wound; the bullet had hit him high in the shoulder, taking him half over the gunwale of the fishing boat with its impact; the other three in the boat turned instinctively to pull him back.

The old man caught Sharky's collar and dragged him back into the well of the boat in a flash. By the time they had Sharky safe, Lawson and Dmitri were on board. Tsygankov remained in the smaller boat, holding on to the side of the larger craft looking over the gunwale.

James, from his vantage point at the entrance to the cove had seen the exchange. The sound of the shot had been deafening as it was amplified by the walls and caves of the cove, its noise rebounding out to sea. For a millisecond he considered recovering and then fleeing with the target goods, his next thought was to instantly and coldly plan his attack. Only he could rescue the others from their present predicament which he reckoned would be fatal if he did nothing. They would want no evidence left behind.

On the boat, Rodney looked into Lawson's eyes, not trusting himself to speak; he knew that the traitor and his professional killer were on short fuses and would kill them now rather than later; Rodney had to play for time.

Mould was sitting down looking at his feet. He knew now that the dark movement he had seen was Collins. He didn't dare look up or he felt he would betray that fact, so out of the side of his eyes he looked again to the spot he had seen the movement minutes ago. He saw the movement again and waited. What would Collins do to create a diversion? Whatever it was, Mould needed to be ready to react. He tensed, coiled like a spring.

The old man sat near to Rodney's right, cradling Sharky's head against his knees, he wrapped a rag around the flesh wound.

Lawson stepped calmly past Mould into the cockpit, with Dmitri covering from the shallow open fish hold, the skull-like head of Tsygankov between them, still holding on to the gunwale and looking over the scene.

"Well Rodney, we meet again in combat, however this time on opposite sides."

"Under the circumstances, I am not certain we were ever on the same side, Minister," replied Rodney quietly.

Lawson's eyes flared and then grew cold, through clenched teeth he said, "You could be right, but that is not important now."

"What is? You are obviously going to kill us so what do you want?"

"I think you know damn well what I want and it's no good bluffing now," Lawson said quietly. "We are all going to sit here calmly and await your contact."

Lawson put his foot against Sharky's shoulder and pressed. Fresh blood appeared and the injured man groaned with pain. The pain and loss of blood was sending him into shock.

"Enough," it was Mould, still looking down. "I'll tell you what you need to know." Rodney knew Mould well enough to realize he was making a play and was duty-bound to follow him up. He slapped Mould across the face with the back of his hand rocking Mould back towards Lawson.

"Say nothing or you'll be as big a traitor as he is," Rodney stood over Mould convincingly. For his trouble, the cold pistol barrel swung by

Lawson struck him across the mouth and he felt sudden pain and tasted blood from the blow. Right, you bastard, Rodney promised himself, you'll pay for that.

Lawson was confident. "Shut up, Rodney, you are becoming a bore. Your time is nearly up so enjoy the minutes you have left. No beating the clock tonight for you." Beating the clock was an old expression from their days in the army; it meant if you could not beat it, you were dead.

Rodney made much of his injury whilst Mould wove his story. "It's like this, we are waiting for a contact."

"We have worked that out for ourselves. Tell me quickly and be brief or you'll wish you hadn't opened your mouth," said Lawson tartly, putting the barrel of his pistol to Mould's temple. "Who, what, when and how?"

There was no more time. Collins was under the boat holding Tsygankov. He had his borrowed diver's knife in his left hand and the harpoon gun in the other. He could see Tsygankov's arms stretched between the boats. He kicked upwards hard. As he rose above the water between the two boats forcing them apart, his arm holding the knife swung in an ever accelerating arc. He drove the knife burying it deep into Tsygankov's nearest hand, his left, the momentum of the power of the drive pinned the hand to the fishing boat.

Tsygankov screamed and this faded into a chilling moan; Dmitri turned to see the black-clad figure hold the hilt of the knife with Tsygankov's pinned fingers outstretched in pain. Collins was fast; holding on to the hilt of the knife to steady himself, he wielded the harpoon gun with his right hand. He shot Dmitri at close range. The harpoon entered the Russian's neck and at that acute angle travelled up into his brain. Dmitri was dead before he hit the deck.

Lawson hesitated and found himself pushed back and an arm went around his throat carrying him backwards. Lawson let go of his gun to try to release the stranglehold on his throat but found himself dragged from the boat and into the water.

The surprise attack and the devastation had stung Rodney's party, experienced as they were; the retaliation had taken the fight out of Lawson and Tsygankov. Dmitri was dead.

The arm had belonged to Charlie's father and he, now with Collins' help, kept Lawson underwater until his struggles stopped, then they pushed him back on board, coughing and spluttering. The old man heaved himself back on board followed by Collins.

Rodney covered Lawson while Mould found some rope and bound his arms and legs. Lawson grunted as Mould pulled the ropes tight making sure there was no way he could get loose.

The old man was the first to move to Tsygankov. He removed the knife from the wounded hand, none too gently. He handed the knife to Collins before he pulled the long frame of Tsygankov roughly into the larger boat; Mould was ready for him and bound him also.

Collins sat on the side of the boat and collapsed, breathing hard. "Jesus, I thought you lot were the experts at this sort of thing, I'm absolutely knackered," he grinned.

"Yes, yes, crap hat to the rescue. I'll never live this down," countered Mould also grinning, looking up from Sharky to whom he was now giving first aid.

Sharky managed a weak smile, the bullet had hurt him and he was in some pain. "Yeah, nice one, mate."

Charlie's father covered Tsygankov with Dmitri's gun and spat at him menacingly every time the man moved to ease his hand, which now throbbed like hell and was bleeding heavily.

Rodney rolled Lawson alongside Tsygankov.

James stood up, shaking himself to loosen up. He was beginning to stiffen. "Major," he spoke to Rodney. "Just going over the side for a minute to get the bag of goods."

Rodney told Mould to wrap up Tsygankov's hand. Rodney studied him. He thought he was Lawson's contact and, from his age, Rodney guessed he was a senior KGB officer. He had been contemplating what to do with him. He didn't want to take him with him, unlike Lawson, and thought he could use him to get away from the area. Rodney was sure that there would be others in support of these three men back on shore. Making his mind up to use Tsygankov as a hostage in case he was needed, he settled back to the problem of Lawson. For sure, he probably needed to get him back on to the Sovereign Base but after that Lawson's fate was above his pay grade.

James slipped back into the boat with a bag in his hand. "This is what you want, Major?"

Mould took it and opened the package, searching the contents; he nodded to Rodney. "Thank you, Captain, well done. I am sorry, I had intended to give you a lift back up the coast but, under the circumstances,

I don't think that would be a good idea," he glanced at the prisoners.

"That's fine, the current is with me now and I should be on my way. Time is not on my side." James collected his gear and extracted the harpoon from Dmitri with some difficulty. "The kit's only on loan and I need to get it back," James said to no one in particular. "Right, I am ready. Sure you don't need me anymore?" he addressed his question to Rodney.

"No, thank you. Think you have done quite enough damage for one day." Rodney shook his hand, "Thank you, I owe you."

"Going to collect one day, for sure." Collins slipped back over the side of the boat and was soon lost in the night.

Rodney took the gun from the old man and motioned him to take them back.

Their troubles were not yet over. When they were 200 yards out from the harbour entrance they could see Charlie's slumped body in the chair, the man, Nicolai, covering him from another chair pulled up to face him. In the bright lights of the café, Rodney knew that the two there were bound to be blind to the boat out on the sea.

He gave a quick order, gesturing to the old man who, along with Rodney, had seen the situation at the café, to turn the tiller to shore. He mimicked getting off the boat on the seaward side of the harbour wall. The boat turned into the shore and ploughed its way close to the seashore side of the harbour wall. As it passed close and before he was forced to turn to avoid beaching, Rodney leapt for the wall of boulders landing on his good leg.

Nicolai could hear the boat engine but from his position could see nothing, nor could he risk leaving Charlie who had now recovered from the blow to his head.

Rodney having made his landfall, circled in cover to the left as fast as his damaged leg would let him.

As the boat made the harbour entrance, Rodney was round at the café, Nicolai with his back to him. Nicolai's attention was fixed on the entrance to the harbour as the boat made its way in and Rodney was able to surprise him easily.

There were no dramatics when Rodney came up behind Nicolai; he wound one arm round his neck while in the other he pressed the barrel of his pistol into the side of his head. Charlie was on his feet in an instant and took away Nicolai's gun.

The Greek agent waiting in the car could see enough of what was happening to realize his position was untenable and there was nothing he could do to rescue the situation. He left the car and stole away into the night.

When the passengers and prisoners were out of the boat, Charlie's father spoke to his son and then left them to take his boat out to sea.

"Where has he gone? I needed to thank him," Rodney asked Charlie.

"My father liked your Captain; he was reminded of when he, himself, was young. And he has gone to pick him up and take him up the coast, maybe even to Famagusta. Don't worry, my father will soon find him. Remember, even in this water, after a period one gets chilled and the currents off Cape Greco at this time of night can be treacherous and contrary."

"What can I say but thank you? But what about the body?" Rodney suddenly thought of Dmitri.

"My father thought he should be lost out to sea. Good idea, no?"

Rodney was not shocked and secretly pleased; it did away with one problem at least. "Good idea, thank you."

"No problem. If you my friend, I kill you for nothing! Now, what are you going to do with these live bastards?" Charlie spat out the words and waved his pistol at Lawson and the two Russians.

With Charlie's father gone after Collins, the remainder fell to discussing what was to be done with the prisoners. Charlie wanted the Cypriot Russian agent to be left to him and his friends to find and then to deal with; he reminded Rodney that it was a smaller island now and there would be no escape. Rodney only told him he wished he would as this would solve a difficult situation, one that was likely to have political implications.

He told Charlie he would take the Englishman back with him but asked if Charlie could get some men to hold the other two for 48 hours to give him and his team time to get away and refer back to the UK. In reality, Rodney wanted this time to enable the security services to roll up those on Chekhov's list. He didn't think he could stretch the time any further with Charlie or he would want to know why.

Charlie readily agreed but asked Rodney and his team to look after the Russians, giving him half an hour to get some support from the village.

Mould was puzzled. "Why not let them go?"

"Can you imagine the fuss and political fallout if we kidnap these two? They have lost one man which they will have to swallow, but three? Besides, those forty-eight hours may well be crucial to us."

Mould caught on quickly, "I understand what you mean. Now, where is that cold beer? I think we have earned it."

Charlie was as good as his word, returning with four men who took the two Russians away with them without a word being spoken.

Charlie said his men had offered to hold the two with the aid of some of the men from the village until he was told to release them but in any case 48 hours from now, as Rodney had asked. He also promised in his characteristic manner that not a hair of the men's heads would be touched, with his hands in the air, clapping them to his chest. "Believe me, I still not hurt them. They will be returned to Nicosia completely unharmed. This I promise. Unless you decide you might want them later." Rodney looked at the man and Charlie smiled. "You see I do this for you, you saved my life. If you had not returned victorious, he said they would have killed me, for I was the only witness left. Is this not so? But now I know that they can do nothing now or hereafter for if they do we will take our revenge. I am safe and so is my family, you have nothing to fear. It is important that you and the others get away safely back to England, yes?"

"You make very good sense, my friend, and it will be today we return to England." Rodney looked at his watch; it was now four in the morning. They still had to get back to the hospital, get Sharky patched up, phone Robinson and transmit the names on the list. And, just as importantly, get instructions about what to do with the minister.

"Charlie, you are an honourable man, so I accept your offer. Now, is there anything we can do for you?"

He hunched his shoulders. "Just come back one day when this is all over and our island is at peace and have drink with me and my family."

"That's a promise," Rodney shook Charlie's hand.

They put Lawson, bound and now gagged, into the boot of the car and Mould helped a very pissed off Sharky into the front seat.

Sharky was getting increasingly uncomfortable and moaned as he strapped himself in. The wound was not serious but it ached.

It was time for the party to move, though all were weary and would have given anything for a few hours sleep. Waving goodbye, they drove out of the car park. Charlie shouted as they went by, he would call Rodney at the hospital or get a message to him before mid morning and tell him how the trip went with his father and Collins.

They drove, retracing the route they had used a few hours earlier. Dawn was breaking and the morning, still cool, kept them alert as they ate up the last few miles to Dhekelia. As the car bucked along the coast road, the occasional muffled grunt could be heard from the boot of the car.

"He is still alive, then," said Rodney with a suppressed giggle.

"That's not the way you should treat a senior Member of Parliament, boss," said Mould in mock seriousness.

Sharky managed a weak smile and Rodney laughed, "Serves him bloody well right."

Chapter 39

LAWSON'S LUCK RUNS OUT

They passed a local shepherd on the side of the road who waved his hand at them and broke into a toothy grin, his herd of Shami goats just stirring for their repetitious day of scratching food from this sparsely-grassed coastal plain; then suddenly they were on the Dhekelia road and they arrived at the military hospital a little before six.

They drove into the forecourt area and were met by a corporal from the reception desk. He had been tasked to watch out for them and inform the commanding officer the moment they arrived. He had seen them drawing up and had already called the colonel and summoned assistance for Sharky.

From reception Rodney called the rest of his crew together. Reid and Avery extracted Lawson from the boot of the car and took him upstairs to secure him.

Rodney sent Mould with the Chekhov list to the signal centre to have the message encrypted and sent to the brigadier's control centre in London.

His men sorted and the list on its way to London, Rodney met the colonel and went with him to his office to talk on the telephone to Robinson.

The colonel left Rodney alone to speak to his brigadier while he arranged for the RAF helicopter to pick up Rodney and his party mid morning.

In London, Williams dozed at the duty desk. He had hoped that this operation would have proved exciting but virtually nothing had happened for days and he had long ago wished he had handed over to Graham instead of hogging the watchkeeper job, although he knew Graham was busy keeping the routine of the section going.

Even the brigadier had given up waiting by the phone with him and had retired to his study to work on his envisaged letter of resignation.

Williams was therefore startled when his telephone suddenly rang and for a second he stared dumbly at the instrument before he snatched it up. "Duty Officer."

"Get the Brigadier."

For a moment Williams thought to challenge the caller to provide more information before connecting the call but there was something in the tone of the voice, which he now recognized as Rodney's, that made him act without delay.

"One moment, sir." He reached across the desk for the internal phone and called the brigadier who answered as though his hand had been resting on the phone. "Cyprus, sir."

"Hold them," the brigadier slammed the phone down and was in the operations room before Williams had finished replacing the receiver. Robinson snatched up the duty phone.

"That you, Rodney?"

"All is well," said Rodney.

Robinson, although elated at the news, recognized the signs of fatigue in his second in command. "You've got the consignment?"

"Yes, it's being encoded and sent to you. You should have it within the hour. You have forty-eight hours to roll up the names on the list, I'll explain later when we arrive. And I also have Lawson under guard. I've put his handler in quarantine for forty-eight hours, after that he is back on the street."

"Lawson, he's alive?"

"Yes."

"Listen very carefully, Rodney. I appreciate you're all very tired but we don't want Lawson. Nobody wants Lawson, he is an embarrassment; I repeat, we don't want him. On the other hand we would very much like to speak to his handler."

"But..." interjected Rodney incredulously. "Do you expect me just to lose him in cold blood?"

"This is not a secure line," said the brigadier roughly and then in the same tone, "You have your orders, do it. I'll see you later today." With that he replaced the receiver and leant on the desk his eyes closed for a moment.

It was rare to give the order for an execution and each time it affected Robinson, but that was his duty, that's all there was to it. He turned to see Williams watching him covertly. When he caught Williams' eye, the man looked away and busied himself with some papers on the other duty desk.

"You don't record that conversation, because it never occurred."

"Yes, sir, it never happened."

"And what else?"

"There was no call from Cyprus at this time, sir."

"You're learning; you will probably therefore fit in very nicely," mused the brigadier, patting Williams on the shoulder as he left the room. He closed the door and then reappeared. "Arrange for the VC10 from Cyprus to be met by two cars and an ambulance, one of ours. Put together a team to carry out the job. Drivers plus bodyguard for each car; drivers and guards to be well armed with spare guns for Rodney's party."

"Do you expect trouble at this late stage, sir?"

"I always expect trouble. There will be a list of names and addresses coming through soon, I need them brought directly to me." Robinson's mind was working overtime; he needed now to alert the directors of the two main security services to be ready to call a meeting as soon as the list arrived. Rodney had indicated they only had 48 hours to take whatever actions they thought appropriate. And he needed to appraise the prime minister's office of the situation.

Rodney sat in the colonel's office in the hospital with his head hanging down on his chest, his eyes closed and his arms resting on the desk either side of the phone. He sat there thinking for a few minutes about the order he had been given. He was in two minds whether or not to carry it out. He could simply ignore it and take Lawson back to England and let the brigadier carry out his own dirty work. His eyes drooped, he couldn't keep them open and he began to doze and had to grip himself to stay awake.

He rose from the desk and went to the window. He opened it and let the fresh morning air play over him. He rubbed the stubble on his chin and then his face vigorously. Yes, he would carry out the old man's orders. He was dog-tired and not in any condition to make a rational decision himself. He would let others direct him until he could get some sleep and begin to think normally again. He went to find his men. Mould was down at reception waiting for him.

"Where have you put Lawson?" his tone told Mould that his boss was under stress quite apart from his obvious fatigue. He had tried to make the question casual but Mould guessed that Rodney didn't want a fuss and his past experience told him Lawson was on his way out.

"He's on the top floor with our people, in the ward office. Do you want me to see to him, sir?" Mould held his boss's eyes steady. "He was clearly a friend from the past and therefore you are involved. In your condition, an outsider might be better. I owe him for the rough stuff in the boat and the bullet wound he gave Sharky."

"No," said Rodney, purposefully. "He is mine." He gave Mould a reassuring pat on the shoulder, much the same as the one the brigadier had given to Williams a short while ago. "No, I must take care of it, but I'd rather you didn't say anything to the rest of the team."

"Won't they know anyway?"

"No, I don't think so; watch and learn. But I did screw up last night; the toffs want Lawson's tall Russian back in London. Tell Reid and his sidekick to get to Charlie and I don't care how they do it but be at the plane for twelve with the Russian; take a medic to treat his hand too." With that Rodney went to the lifts.

When he went into the ward office on the top floor, Lawson was asleep, slumped at the desk and Reid sat at the other end of the room covering him. Lawson didn't stir as Rodney entered the room. He was fast asleep.

Rodney put his fingers to his lips and motioned Reid outside to the corridor. As Reid slipped past, Rodney said, "Go and see Mould, he is downstairs."

Rodney took Reid's gun. He closed the door quietly and lit a cigarette. He smoked it quite calmly as he watched Lawson. He was a miserable sight; for a moment Rodney almost felt sorry for him but immediately dismissed the thought; the man was a traitor. When he had finished the cigarette, he stubbed it out with his foot; Sister Sue would not be pleased.

Lawson had not moved. Rodney went to the window and opened it to its full extent.

He put the gun in his pocket and then with both hands free he crossed behind Lawson.

He put his right hand through and between Lawson's right arm and chest, grasping Lawson's right wrist, snapping it back through and putting Lawson's into a half nelson hold.

At the same time with his left hand he grabbed a handful of Lawson's hair, forcing Lawson's head back.

Before Lawson could properly react from his deep-sleep state, he was halfway out of the window.

Rodney released his hold to get a purchase on Lawson's legs to tumble him completely out of the window. Lawson, his hands free, tried to twist for a hold on the window frame, but he was too far out. He paddled frantically at thin air. He was completely out the window and falling before the full enormity of his situation dawned on him.

He was falling to his death. Rodney saw the terror-stricken face staring up at him as Lawson fell away from the building and to earth.

Rodney was held for a moment by the sheer terror on the man's face and then began to retch and he kept retching as he heard Lawson hit the ground below.

Rodney went to the door and called out to the other agents on the floor. "The man's jumped," he said as the men ran into the room and with that, Rodney found himself slipping away.

He came to in the chair with his team and the hospital's commanding officer leaning over him, the doctor was injecting him with a stimulant.

"What's going on?" mumbled Rodney, shaking himself. "My God the man jumped. Is he alive?"

"I am sorry, he is dead. As for you," said the doctor seriously. "You're just exhausted. Against my better judgement I've just given you something," he added looking at Mould who was worrying in the background, "to keep you going for a few more hours, but then you must rest or I will not be responsible for the consequences."

"Thank you Doc, what's the time?" Rodney felt suddenly alert, the drug was quick acting.

Mould said, "Half nine, you've been out of it for a couple of hours. Everything's ready. It is all arranged, the helicopter will be here in an hour at half ten so you've time for a shower and some breakfast before we go." He added, "We had a call from Charlie. James is safe in Famagusta and Reid's picked up the other man so we should all be going home together. Oh yeah, all the kit we borrowed is signed back in. I called the Brigadier about Lawson's suicide and he told me to tell you the list arrived. We are ready to go, boss."

Rodney's brain was alive. "Good. Care to take breakfast with me, Colonel, or brunch? I'd like to thank you and tie up any loose ends with you before I leave."

"Good idea, I'll give you half an hour to get changed and then join you. I've got some things to do, not least arrange for the body of the man who jumped to be expatriated. I will need some statements on that matter."

Half an hour later, Rodney was sitting down in the mess dining room with the colonel.

"It is all but over. I need to thank you for your cooperation and your forbearance," Rodney suddenly felt embarrassed. "I hadn't intended to turn your hospital into a battlefield but that's the way it seems to have turned out. I'll get the Brigadier to clear everything with your superiors and you shouldn't have any trouble with any overzealous redcaps or the like." Rodney paused, "Is there anything that's worrying you that I can clear up before I go?"

"I understand you had to do what you did, but I find it..." the colonel seemed to be searching for his word. "Find? Yes, find it difficult to grasp the situation completely. Why did he jump for instance? It just doesn't make sense."

"As you say, it doesn't; and I can only apologize again for the trouble we have put you to." Rodney found he couldn't meet the colonel's eyes and even felt himself reddening; he added quickly, "Perhaps he decided that he couldn't face his situation anymore, stressful job and all that. We don't know that he didn't fall out of the window by accident. That, by the way, is what the official line is likely to be and it is the story that you will read in the papers."

"But surely you were in the room too?" said the colonel slightly exasperated.

"Indeed I was; one moment he was at the window and the next he was gone." That's true at least, thought Rodney. "You may as well know that he was a cabinet minister and I expect that there will be a bit of a stink. However, I can assure you that none of the flak will come your way."

"That's reassuring at least," the colonel was not quite convinced. "I still don't have an explanation for what you were all doing in my hospital to give to my bosses here."

"That's easily fixed. I will get London to put in a call to the garrison commander before I leave."

"Now, that would be helpful," the colonel smiled at last, his good humour returning.

With relief and some pleasure Rodney saw Sue enter the mess. She came straight up to them and looked with concern at Rodney.

"You do look terrible," she started, her face showing concern.

"I know, I know," laughed Rodney throwing his hands up. "But it's over now, so we can all relax."

"I've just seen your lot and a fine sight they make; there's hardly any of them that's unscathed and," she went on breathlessly, "they say you're all off in a few minutes. Sir," she said turning to her CO, "surely, you're not going to let them travel in the state they are in? They need a few days rest, at least."

"They know what they have to do and it appears that our hospitality is no longer required," the CO said with a smile. "But I should think the Major will no doubt wish to visit for a holiday," he winked at Rodney and Sue felt her colour rising.

"Well, will you?" queried Sue.

"The very first chance I get. You have such a peaceful environment." They all laughed. The colonel made his excuses to leave; he wished Rodney well and hoped to see him again in the not too distant future, but not on duty. He also would like to know if the whole business was a success and worth all the trouble. Rodney promised the colonel satisfaction, on that matter at least.

Sue went with Rodney to the waiting helicopter minutes later. The crew was on board waiting for him; he said a fond farewell and promised to see her either in England or on his return to Cyprus for his next leave.

Inside the helicopter, it was surprisingly gloomy after the bright sunlight outside. Tsygankov, his hand now bandaged and splinted up into a sling, was bracketed by Mould and Sharky while Reid and his team were strewn around on the cabin floor.

Reid gave Rodney the thumbs up and Rodney nodded back. "Good morning all; and what do we call you?" Tsygankov just looked down at his feet. Rodney shrugged, nodded to the crewman who gave the order over his throat microphone to the pilot to take off.

The remainder of the journey to England, including the transfer to the RAF DC-10, could not have gone more smoothly. Rodney even had time to call the brigadier before he left Cyprus to ask him to call the garrison commander and get the colonel at the hospital off the hook.

Reid had procured handcuffs from somewhere and Tsygankov was chained up for the flight, which meant the team could sleep for the whole of the journey. A slightly more rested and alert team landed at the RAF station and everyone without exception was pleased to be back.

Chapter 40

GENERAL POLYAKOV

The Greek agent, who had escaped from the scene when he witnessed Borchev being overwhelmed by Rodney, had assumed victory by the British in the fracas at Ayia Napa. He had, by the time of Rodney's arrived at Dhekelia, been able to contact the Nicosia Soviet Mission.

He passed on the news to them. The Soviets now realized that the British had the Chekhov list and their man.

They were faced with a fait accompli. A frontal assault on the team would be the only possible approach and they didn't have the immediate resources to mount such an operation. Indeed, it would be crude and quite unacceptable to do so anyway. Nor did they have the contacts in place to tamper with the party at Akrotiri.

The only choice left to them was to contact Moscow direct and let the centre coordinate any action. With trepidation, Arbuzouhov, the head of the Cyprus Mission, put through his call to Moscow's Dzerzhinsky Square, headquarters of the KGB.

The Cyprus news caused an angry stir in Moscow's corridors of power and the few people privy to the finer points of the situation were hastily ordered to a special meeting.

The Soviet system, though extremely slow and ponderous under most circumstances, when needs must, could move very fast indeed.

The men at the table masterminding the operation were very good at what they did. To aid them, they had a computer system that was the envy of the Western alliance. They fed into the machine the facts they were offered to work out options and solutions to the problem.

The solutions came fast. One was to shoot the aeroplane that was ferrying Rodney's party to the UK out of the sky. Or solution two was to meet the party in the UK and attack them.

The machine worked out the probability of achieving either and the second was heavily favoured. They asked it how they should attempt course two. The machine told them.

This plan was passed to the Russian embassy in London; London was told not to fail or else. In truth, they were worried that if the list did reach London, years of valuable work would all be for nothing. They knew it would be embarrassing to have networks uncovered that they had never acknowledged existed.

They desired respectability in the Third World but they also wanted to build up credibility within Europe.

The head of the KGB chaired the meeting. When one of his subordinates mentioned political embarrassment, he quelled the man's fear by paraphrasing Golda Meir. "What do you mean they won't like us if we do that, they don't like us anyway; so send in the men." He was deadly serious. "Who do we have in London at the moment?"

"Colonel Polyakov is our man there currently," one of the directors said.

"Bit of a playboy," said another.

"Ah, yes," said the KGB head, "but brilliant, nevertheless." His support for Polyakov closed the discussion.

The meeting then focused on the very real issue that the British may have communicated the list of names already. Damage limitation strategy for both Russia and their agents in countless countries was the next item on the agenda.

The head of the KGB rose; he could safely leave his directors to sort out the damage limitation exercise. He needed to go to the Kremlin and report to the Soviet.

Chapter 41

TSYGANKOV RETRIEVED

A waiting ambulance took Sharky and Tsygankov off the plane first and then the other passengers were allowed to disembark before Rodney and his party left the plane.

Men were waiting at the plane steps with a customs man who looked the party over and then waved them to the waiting cars, but not until he had spoken to Rodney who walked away from the group with him, so the rest of the party could not hear them talking.

When Rodney returned they were all crammed in the cars and Rodney got into the leading car.

"Any problem, sir?" enquired the driver.

"No, no, just wanted me to sign some customs' declaration, holding them blameless etc. usual bullshit."

The man grunted.

"You're not from our section, are you?" Rodney quizzed the driver.

"No, sir, we are from the pool. They had your section committed elsewhere, chasing shadows if you ask me. Some flap or other. I might add it was all a bit of a rush. Eh, George?"

The bodyguard in the front seat turned to Rodney, "Right flap on, sir, the whole place is buzzing and Special Branch stood up too. Must be planning to arrest a large cell or something."

"Yeah?" Rodney was suspicious.

"Are we in radio contact with the others cars?" he asked the driver. The driver confirmed that they were and also that they had a relay to London. "Good, pass the microphone." The driver passed it back to him.

Mould looked at his boss, "What's going on? George, got a spare shooter?" Rodney looked at Mould and thought, he's reading my mind again.

"I thought you would never ask." George opened the glove compartment and picked out a 9 mm and two spare magazines and passed them over, "A full magazine is in the gun already."

"Hello all call signs." Rodney waited for cars and ambulance to answer. "Switch to scramble," he waited again for their confirmation. "Our troubles may not be over yet. When we leave this road at the T-junction, I want each car to go a different route, we will stay with the ambulance." They were just east of Oxford. "Car one, go south of the city; car two, I want you to go north and enter London on these coordinates. We will be going through the town and then down the motorway, so stay clear of us." The other stations broadcasted their agreement, one asked for clarification on the threat. Rodney simply told them that if there were bandits about, why make it easy for them.

As they accelerated away down the country lane, bound on each side by trees, Rodney felt distinctly uneasy.

Tsygankov, in the ambulance, heard the exchange with the car and he perked up. He now sat attentively looking out of the ambulance windows like a man who had lost everything suddenly realizing that he may yet get a reprieve.

Rodney's car and the ambulance split off together, from the remainder of the convoy at the junction. A hundred or so yards further on, the road on which Rodney's vehicles travelled began to snake in tight curves. Another hundred yards and the junction was lost from view. Another hundred yards and they were in deep country.

It was on the next turn that things began to happen. As they came round the corner, they could see the ambulance carrying Tsygankov and Sharky slide into a ditch at the side of the road to avoid a crash scene of two cars, one on its side. Two police cars were in attendance. They could see four police officers busy round the overturned car.

Two more ran to the ambulance to help. By the time Rodney's car had come to a stop and George, Rodney, Mould and the driver had got out the police were helping Sharky, Tsygankov and the attending medic out. The driver was leaning on the door of the ambulance obviously a little shaken.

The artificiality of the situation suddenly hit Rodney with force. Why should the ambulance suddenly go off the road? Oil slick, yes, possibly, but the crash area showed none and how did the police get to the accident so soon?

"Set up," Rodney warned his team.

"Be still all of you." A policeman covered Rodney and his team with a semi-automatic.

Four other bogus policemen surrounded Rodney's group and took away their weapons.

The leader of the other group emerged with Tsygankov. "Put them all in the back of the ambulance and handcuff them together and to the vehicle." Rodney's Russian was not perfect but he could pick up an air of quiet authority and understood most of what was said.

He had a quick word with Tsygankov before turning to Rodney, "The list, please."

"You're too late, it's already on its way to London." Just then a helicopter raced overhead, Rodney looked up, "A ruse, you see."

Tsygankov looked at Rodney, "We underestimated you, Major." It was a statement of fact and he turned away.

The leader headed to one side of the attack group and gave a casual salute and left with Tsygankov, moving into the overturned car, now righted. Later in the day, Rodney thought through the incident and was sure that the group leader had had the hint of a smile hovering on his lips and a twinkle in his eye. Rodney thought to himself that it would be interesting to meet him again sometime.

As they had sped away, the remaining captors hurried the British into the ambulance where they were secured and the doors shut and locked.

Rodney noted that apart from the group's leader and the tall Russian not a word had been spoken by the others.

When they were alone in the ambulance Mould said, "The customs man, I suppose?"

"Yes."

"Brigadier's idea, I suppose?" Mould pressed.

"No, mine actually. Now Mould would you please put that brilliant mind of yours to getting us out of here," Rodney pushed back. Everyone laughed, despite their predicament.

"No problem," he turned sideways offering his jacket pocket. "If one of you could just reach inside the pocket, there is a handcuff key in there." He winked at Rodney, "I kept it after we unlocked the Russian from the plane."

Some hours later, Rodney and his men were back at base and welcomed by all the team; Robinson was in his office but didn't come out. Rodney left the backslapping and went to see the brigadier to report in.

When Rodney entered the office, the brigadier was behind his desk and there were three other men seated in easy chairs, one of whom was the new minister now in control of the department, the other two men Rodney did not recognize.

"Welcome back," the brigadier rose to meet Rodney. He indicated an empty chair and Rodney, after shaking hands with all, sank into it. "I trust that you are not too exhausted from your break in the sun to hear the results of your labours; pity about the loss of the Russian but no matter."

"He never did give me his name you know, I have no idea who he really was apart from his association with Lawson," Rodney reported tiredly.

The American within the trio frowned and said, "He is Brigadier Tsygankov of the KGB and given the code name, 'Blue'. Whilst he would have been a coup, I think you may have trumped that, Major."

"Thank you," Rodney said, almost to himself. He didn't feel friendly towards the brigadier or his guests at this moment, reflecting that the brigadier quite seemed to have forgotten that he had very recently ordered him to kill a man in cold blood. He would have to have that out with his boss later, when his guests had gone.

"Good, I'm just about to hand over a complete copy of the Chekhov list to our colleagues here. They have already had the sections that relate to them but it is thought that there may be merit in this." He indicated the two men who Rodney still didn't know. "Later you can brief my two counterparts here, from America," the man nodded but didn't volunteer his name, "and the Federal Republic of Germany."

The man grinned at Rodney, "Good job, Major, I, for one, am in your debt and won't forget it."

"Thank you, sir, that's very kind of you to say so, but it was a team effort and not forgetting the back-room team here," Rodney surprised himself by feeling pleased for his team.

The minister clearly thought he needed to say something. "Is there anything they wish to know on the operation?" The brigadier frowned at the minister and cleared his throat.

It was clear to Rodney that the brigadier did not approve of the minister being there but the minister had obviously pressured him.

The minister did not meet Robinson's eyes but touched his tie instead in a nervous gesture. No doubt the man had got some deal going, thought Rodney. This really was a dirty business, he thought, maybe it's time to get out. He wondered if Charlie would like a partner to develop the beach area of Ayia Napa; it would make a great resort; fat chance!

The old man looked at the audience and beamed. He really could turn on the charm, thought Rodney.

"Now gentlemen, let us see if the trouble my worthy second in command and his party was put to was really worth it. As you know, Chekhov was my contact and, I think, a friend, for many years. He claimed that he was going to give us a complete list of agents in Western Europe and some in America. You have your sections already, from the list transmitted to me, so let's see if he was as good as his word."

The brigadier lifted the waterproof packages and broke their seals once again. The tension in the room could be felt. The men in the chairs were on the edge of their seats, craning forward to try to catch a preview of whatever was going to come.

First, the diamonds and money cascaded out, as the brigadier shook the contents of the packs on to the table. An inner envelope fell out of the oilskin. The brigadier deftly took off the outer oilskin covering. A fat oiled envelope appeared in his hand. The envelope had been resealed by Mould so the brigadier took his paper knife and slit it open again.

Inside was a thick fold of photocopies and a letter. The photocopies he leafed through and then passed them to the minister.

He withheld the letter and by way of explanation, "The letter is to me from Chekhov, you will understand that I would like to read it first before I give it to you." He stood up and went to the window. The minister and the men from the allied countries poured over the lists.

Rodney felt out of the circle so went to the brigadier's cocktail cabinet and poured a drink for everyone; he placed the drinks on the guests' table in silence and the brigadier's on his desk. He retired to his seat and let the fiery whisky mellow him.

He watched Robinson carefully reading his letter and could hear to his side the excited comments of the other men as they recognized names of men on Chekhov's list that they knew of, but had not seen on the information they had had so far.

The brigadier read his letter in silence.

"Dear Friend,

It has been many years since we met and now we may never.

You and I are old men and I don't see you coming to my refuge somehow.

The Chinese seem to think I may be of some help to them to understand the Russian mind.

I don't.

I never understood the Russian mind myself and I'm one of them.

I think however they are like everybody else, a little frightened, confused and overawed by our place in the world and their pace of change.

Anyway, the diamonds are not for me but for my family who will be in England by the time you read this.

You can find them through your investigative people. Look after them like they were your own. Your country owes me this much.

When you read this you will either have the diamonds or I will and I'll need them although I don't really expect to get away.

I have enjoyed the years we have working together. I am sure you will appreciate that it could not go on forever. I was bound to be found out eventually. They were closing on me but a friend not unsympathetic warned me off. I had been amassing that data you now have for some time in the event that I needed a nest egg for my family's future.

The friend I mentioned will be contacting you. He can be trusted and will carry my code name Chekhov. I suggest you have the same deal we had reporting to one man and one only. In fact I know he will insist on it.

Be careful, you're too old to take chances. – Chekhov"

Rodney could see that the brigadier was clearly upset. He beckoned Rodney to him, "This letter is for you to read and then destroy." Rodney read the letter quickly. He realized that the boss was giving him the new Chekhov to run. No time to think of leaving now and anyway, Rodney thought, you don't retire from this business even if you want to, never truly. They simply put you in cold storage until they want you again.

The brigadier left Rodney to join the animated men in their easy chairs.

When he had reread the letter, Rodney went to the brigadier's desk and, using the brigadier's large desk lighter and holding the letter at an angle, lit the bottom edge. He watched the letter flare and then ground the ashes into the square glass ashtray.

The minister looked up and frowned but the others ignored Rodney's action. It was the way of it; they understood that Rodney had just been appointed to the succession when the brigadier was no longer in command.

Part Three

THE SPYMASTER'S VENDETTA

Chapter 42

THE RUSSIANS AND THE BRITISH

Tsygankov's laugh was harsh; he pushed the Cyprus affair to the back of his mind. He gently swirled the wine in its glass, looked at the 'oily tears' as the wine tears slid slowly down the sides of the glass and then drank in the aroma, before sitting opposite Rodney. He studied Rodney for a moment through the wine glass that he held out in front of him to toast their escape as much as to examine its clarity.

"We all appear to have had a miraculous escape."

"Don't 'we' us, though," Rodney clicked his glass against Blue's. "Here's mud in your eye, Brigadier Tsygankov. Somebody must love you, for your black guardian angel must have been working overtime today, that's for sure, damn you."

"Hasn't he, though?" replied the Russian brigadier paraphrasing Rodney, not drinking himself, a smile playing on his thin pale lips.

"What about us?" Rodney nodded his head over to Sharky and Mould, both of whom were now lolling sleepily in their seats. Rodney looked at them and envied their ability to sleep whenever they could. He felt drowsy himself; strange... Then horror and realization set in, the wine was drugged. He struggled to curse Tsygankov and to reach for him. For a moment he fought the drug even though he knew he would eventually succumb. His personal discipline made him fight before the blackness took him, he wanted a little longer, he must know what this man was going to do.

Rodney could still see Polyakov through a grey tunnel of light that was collapsing in on itself, growing darker and smaller by the second.

Polyakov was standing, looking at him from the front of the cabin, his head to one side, he half saluted and half waved at Rodney with his wine glass. Rodney had seen that gesture before and his muddled brain fought to remember.

Tsygankov watched him coldly, lips now unsmiling as Rodney struggled to retain the last of his consciousness. Rodney bit his lip and dug his nails into his palms, "What about us, you bastard?" His words were slurring more and his mouth no longer felt controlled; his eyes tried to focus but they couldn't and the lids felt so heavy they would not function.

Far away he heard the Russian say, "As I said earlier, I am taking you home to mother Russia, it's time you saw something of the other side. If it were down to me I would have you thrown out of the plane for this," he waved his scarred hand at Rodney. "Thank your lucky stars, Major, that I am not in charge."

Rodney was slipping away, "Why?" his words trailed off.

Tsygankov looked at him, "Why indeed?"

Was it because he owed the director his freedom after he had rescued him from Rodney on that deserted Oxford road? And because he had told Polyakov that he was not seeking revenge? He now knew that was not true. As he massaged the clawed hand he felt the need to seek revenge overwhelming.

Brown and his aides had fallen into their hands and all they could do was either kill them or take them with them. They couldn't very well leave them in Cuba, could they? So they would have to travel on to Moscow with the Russian contingent.

The only people that knew for sure that they had the device were the people around him on the plane, and the Arab of course, not that that could not easily be denied.

The British were another story; they would be believed. The tall Russian threw the contents of his glass on the floor next to Rodney's inert form and snapped his finger at his aides to get him a fresh one.

The transfer at a remote part of the Cuban airport went smoothly and men and machine were soon on their Russian long-haul aircraft; Rodney and his men slept on.

* * * * *

Before the Russians and their captives were to touch down at Moscow, the South Africans holed up in South America had been freed. With the disturbances in Guatemala now quiescent, the regime carried out two acts aimed to gain the approval of the Americans and their own people. They released a large number of mainly harmless political prisoners, amongst whom were the South Africans. They were, after all, in the eyes of the Guatemalans, important people from a country whose arms could be acquired in times to come.

So, they had murdered an agent of another power, but had not the other side murdered a black man on their team? To release them would cost them nothing, the generals thought that they could only gain.

"Out," a Guatemalan officer entered the urine-stained and stinking gloomy cell into which Wolff and his two men had been thrown. He indicated the door impatiently with his swagger stick and disappeared into the corridor. "Out, out," he continued to shout. Wolff and his men uncurled themselves from the floor, stood stiffly and walked out of the cell; an armed guard waiting outside the cell for them to emerge pushed them up the corridor with the flat butt of his rifle. Other armed men rattled their rifles along the route to the prison gate.

Out of the main prison complex and on to the street, the South Africans blinked at the sunshine and stood about, confused for a moment.

The Land Cruiser stood in front of them. The officer stood behind them talking to the guard. The guard saluted and disappeared into the prison and the heavy metal door slammed, startling them.

The officer grunted, sneering at the men, "Come." The officer pointed to Wolff with his stick. "You, Major, you drive."

"Drive where?" Wolff was not sure what was going on.

"To the airport, I will show the way. Come on, we do not have all day."

"You mean we are to be set free, just like that?" Wolff was still suspicious.

"Just like that." The officer, a rotund, strutting middle-aged captain with much service behind him, exemplified by the medal ribbons on his thick breast, snapped his fat fingers.

His dark eyes bored into Wolff's, "Our president and the generals have seen fit to release you as a sign of goodwill between our countries. The president will be writing to your government in the near future to that effect. You have been very lucky. Had we not been successful in quelling the coup, the generals would surely have had you shot."

Wolff worried about their situation and the loss of the device until he arrived at the airport when other things that had to be done crowded the messy business from his mind.

As the dejected South African party took off from the Guatemala City airport, the Russian airliner was taxiing into the Moscow terminal.

* * * * *

When the Belize intelligence officer had informed London of the Russian plane's escape from Belizean airspace, Brigadier Robinson had been called over into the operations room at MI6, a place where Robinson was revered. The staff of MI6 knew that he could possibly be the new director designate and they paid him all due deference.

Although the brigadier's was a section apart, dealing mainly with the unusual, when it related to the Eastern bloc he was known to all. His responsibilities seemed to encompass the world and he seemed to have priority over even the activities of other intelligence branches these days. They were a little in awe of this tall man. They didn't fully understand his section's remit nor his methods, or even why he should have his own small organization that didn't appear to be either inferior or superior to the others but nevertheless seemed to be something of a law unto itself. That it appeared to be manned by a band of ex-soldiers and policemen was a contradiction to the professional civil servants.

"Well?" The brigadier looked round the room at the duty officers, all of whom were pretending to be working but really wanted to know what the man was doing here.

The senior duty staff officer indicated that the brigadier should follow him into an aluminium framed, double-glazed, soundproofed cubical off the main duty room.

The staff were disappointed, they would have liked to hear what the brigadier was here for; it had to be important for him to be here in person.

"Sir, as you know the background to the Belize Guatemalan operation, I will come to the point."

"Do that, I set up the operation, by the way." It was a concession to the man to warn him and to put him at his ease at the same time.

"Yes, sir, I was told," the staff officer, a commander, ex-Royal Navy Intelligence, didn't mean to sound condescending but he knew that was how it had come over and felt a nervous sweat break out on the palms of his hands as he saw the brigadier flush.

"Sorry, sir, I didn't mean to sound pompous. Uh, please take a seat," the action of pulling out a chair for Robinson calmed the man. He was stout and about 45. A bachelor, heavily married to the service, five eight with blond hair; probably gay, mused Robinson looking at the jutting chin that set hard as he told Robinson about the message he had received. "It seems..."

"Seems?" said Robinson teasing, raising his eyebrows.

"Yes, sir, seems," the commander was not going to be intimidated by the formidable figure of the brigadier. "That when the forces in Belize failed to stop the Learjet containing the Russian party and your men heading out over the sea for Cuba, our man..." he waited for the brigadier to correct him by telling him that the man was not his but military intelligence, but he didn't. "Our man contacted the Americans to ask them to let him know what became of the passengers of the Learjet after it landed in Cuba."

"And what did they report?"

"They were all transferred to the Russian aircraft, destination Moscow."

"God, there will be hell to pay for this," the brigadier swore under his breath and moved to the edge of his seat, his hands on his knees, but the commander heard and was surprised at the depth of reaction from this normally unemotional and taciturn man.

He hadn't a clue who the brigadier was referring to. Did he mean his man would pay, or the Russians, or himself? He waited for the brigadier to bring his attention back.

"Please go on," he snapped.

"The Americans, with their usual attention to detail, also identified the passengers from the descriptions given by their man there. Well, not all, but enough to let us know that your man Brown was there with two others, plus four Russian men and a woman."

"Do we know them?" The brigadier was suddenly very alert and his eyes blazed.

"Yes, three of them quite well at least, Brigadier; first, Colonel Ivanovich, a back-room communication scientist, who has worked in West Germany, so they were able to pull his file and are pretty certain it's him."

Robinson nodded, "Electronics expert?"

"Yes, sir, how did you know?" The brigadier's frown told the commander that he wasn't going to get an answer; he continued, "A Major Valerie Gershuni, very attractive."

"Makes a change," input Robinson lightly, but the humour was lost on the commander.

"Very dangerous woman," the commander continued without a break. "She is an ex-Swallow and must have been good to make the conversion," the commander said testily.

"Or have the right connections."

"Quite," the commander allowed the side of his mouth to curl slightly. "The others, we only have descriptions; strange, one of them was of unusual height." He saw the brigadier stiffen. The commander rushed on, "Rather gaunt, about sixty, but it was difficult to gauge, the man did however appear to have a scarred, clawed hand."

"I'm surprised they didn't recognize that man; who did you use?"

"NSA."

"That would explain it. This man would not be immediately known to them, only their other lot."

"Do you know him then, sir?"

"Yes, I think so, I think I do," the brigadier was lost in thought for a few moments. "My men call him... oh, never mind. He is a gentleman; cold, even ruthless, but a gentleman nevertheless, even if he is Russian; scar on the left hand?"

"According to this report, yes."

"That will be him, then." The brigadier was impatient to get away, "What about the last man?"

"Not much, a bit nondescript, probably of Latin descent."

"Right, thank you, Commander; if I need you I'll contact you. Now, if you would be kind enough to let me use your office for a few minutes."

"Of course, Brigadier; but I did say four men; the last one was a general called Sergei Ivan Polyakov. He was a deputy director in the KGB, but now heads Directorate 1, as of this week."

Robinson didn't respond but nodded; he had registered this startling news. He rose, thanked the commander and held the door open for the man to leave. The commander left the signals and his notes on the table and almost saluted. "OK, sir; can I get you anything?"

"This phone here got a scrambler?" The commander pointed to a switch box by the side of the phone. "Good, thank you; just a glass of brandy; again, thank you."

The commander was about to say that they didn't keep brandy in the operations room but the brigadier's eyebrows arched in challenge as though he read the man's thoughts; the commander would get some.

"Of course, sir."

"Thank you." Robinson closed the door softly behind the man. His next action was to reach for the phone and he rang his own duty officer.

"Duty Officer."

"That you, Williams?"

"Yes, sir," what good officer didn't know his boss's voice on the phone?

"Pull Tsygankov's file and everything else we have on the man since he left England."

"Anything else, sir?" Williams knew there would be and reached for his pad.

"See if you can get anything on the South Africans and specifically I want to know which of their intelligence service personnel have been out of the country in the last week, particularly those that have been to Latin America."

"That it, then, sir?"

"Yes; no, wait, get a call into the Professor and tell him to be in my office in an hour." Robinson paused, "Carry out the instructions in the order I gave them to you. Get somebody to help you. Get Graham, he's good at this stuff. Tell him I asked him to help you and that it is a priority one. I'll be with you in half an hour or so."

"That it, then, sir?" Williams said hopefully. He had enough to keep him working frantically for an hour.

"One more thing, please." Bloody hell, thought Williams to himself, he's relentless. "When you pull Tsygankov's file, I want you to phone the name and telephone number of his immediate commanding officer to me here," he gave the telephone number to Williams.

The commander knocked on the door, Robinson, smiling, waved him in. The man carried a bottle of five-star cognac and a glass.

"Fetch a glass for yourself."

"Err, sir?"

"Go on man, go on." While he was out, the brigadier poured himself a double and warmed the glass in his hands by twirling it between his palms. He held the glass to his nose and savoured its bouquet as it made his nostrils burn pleasurably. The commander returned. "Hate drinking alone; I thought you might tell me what's going on here and how MI6 is faring; share a bit of the very good brandy you've supplied."

"Certainly, sir," the commander poured himself a drink and took a good pull. "Not bad; where would you like me to begin?"

Robinson put the glass down and smiled at last, "Start with any field operations that you may have going at the moment." The brigadier half closed his eyes as the man started talking and relaxed into his chair. He didn't interrupt, he just let him talk; after a while the brigadier knew why this individual was working the operations room; he was good. The commander's grasp of what was going on in detail was absolute. After the field operations, the commander went on to brief him on staffing and what each section within MI6 was responsible for, key personalities and how they intermeshed with the duty room. Most of the personalities Robinson knew, but it was refreshing for him to hear from another man's point of view what each section was working on.

He then told Robinson of tasks to do with ongoing projects and immediate past achievements that he thought the brigadier would find interesting. In all, the briefing took about 20 minutes.

When he had finished, Robinson asked him if he had to brief often. "No sir, not as much as I'd like. A bit more PR for this department wouldn't go amiss; there's not much that we don't know about or get involved in."

"I'm inclined to agree with you. A little more byplay between us, you and the others, MI5, might be rewarding; I'll see what I can do. Still, we all like to keep our little secrets, don't we?" The commander flushed but didn't have time to reply as the phone rang.

He reached for it. "For me I think," Robinson moved for the phone and the commander withdrew his hand. "Robinson." Williams answered; the brigadier cupped his hand over the mouthpiece and looked at the commander. "One of those little secrets," he said with a smile, and the commander diplomatically withdrew.

"Go on, Williams," the brigadier listened attentively. "Right, patch me through to the man now."

"Now?" repeated Williams, disbelievingly.

"Yes damn it man, now."

"Very good, sir, hang on." Robinson looked at his watch, it should be mid morning in Moscow; Polyakov and the others should have arrived late last night so he expected Polyakov to be in his office by now, with luck he would catch him, if not he would try later.

"Ringing for you now, sir."

The phone rang five times before it was answered, "Polyakov."

"Robinson." The silence at the Moscow end was deafening; it must have been the shock of the unexpected call.

"Robinson? THE Brigadier Robinson?" Polyakov asked, surprised.

"Yes, the Brigadier Robinson," Robinson smiled.

"Ah, one of my opposite numbers, as far as makes no difference," the penny had dropped. The voice spoke tolerably good English, Robinson thought, and Polyakov continued, "What can I do for you? Do you want to defect?" There was a slight chuckle from the other end. Robinson smiled, he had heard that the man had a sense of humour; all the better.

"Not quite, I want my three men back." In his office, Polyakov had risen and motioned the other occupant of the room over; Tsygankov moved to share the telephone so they could both hear what Robinson said; Polyakov played for a little time until he could get his recorder switched on.

"Three men, you say?"

"Yes, my three men that came in with you and your team from Cuba."

"Shall we say in about six weeks?"

"I really want them back here now," Robinson kept his voice cheerful and friendly although he felt anything but.

"My dear Comrade Brigadier Robinson, I don't think that will be possible," Polyakov said apologetically.

Robinson knew he was at a serious disadvantage and he knew Polyakov knew it. He also knew that he mustn't show weakness. "I see. Are they all right?" Robinson kept his voice friendly.

"They are being treated as our guests which is more than they deserve, they did after all enter the Soviet Union without invitation." Robinson noticed a hardening, almost a warning in the general's voice.

"For that, I thank you. Do you have any idea when we can expect to see them?" Robinson already knew in his own mind the answer he would get.

"That, my dear Robinson, is no longer really in my power to answer, although I will undertake to keep you informed on an informal basis. Your men will now be looked after by my people. I'm sure they will soon be contacting your Foreign Office to discuss the terms of their return."

Polyakov became almost friendly and laughed shortly, "I would say that the negotiations will take some six weeks as I said, so I would not expect to see your people for a while."

"Pity you let their arrival go official. It would have been much better if you had turned them round on arrival. We are now going to get into a very messy area indeed." Robinson could just imagine the uproar this was going to create and it would need to be kept quiet, but the price would he high. He tried once more, "Before we terminate this call, are you absolutely sure that the situation is irretrievable and that we can't come to some accommodation ourselves without involving others?" Robinson waited, he felt he could hear the general thinking. He held his breath and unconsciously crossed the fingers of his free hand.

"I don't think there is anything I can think of that would change my mind." Polyakov added thoughtfully, "I don't really think that you have anything that I need desperately enough, at the moment." The last statement was a jibe. They had the device and he knew that Robinson knew it too and now he knew Robinson knew he had it, Robinson knew he was defeated. Polyakov added, "No I don't think there is, but just in case, I will think about it."

"Never mind, I'm certain your people will think of something," Robinson added; he seethed inside, he could bet they would.

He was nevertheless surprised when Polyakov added, "As I said, Brigadier, notwithstanding the efficiency of both our peoples, if I think of something, I will of course let you know. Until then, Comrade, I bid you farewell."

Robinson waited until Polyakov had gently replaced the receiver and then slammed his down.

Polyakov grunted, "Well, my dear Comrade Tsygankov, whether you wanted revenge or not, I think you have gone some way to redressing the balance."

"Yes," was Tsygankov's serious reply.

The general pushed the papers on his desk away in an impatient gesture and then hooked his fingers together before smoothing his thick head of hair back and letting his hands rest on the back of his head. "But the very presence of these men is an issue and does pose a threat. How can we turn that into an advantage?" His heavy hooded lids slid slowly over his eyes, "It's a pity, in retrospect, that we didn't get rid of them en route. Still, what's done is done. They must be kept isolated from everybody."

"They are. Our people have simply been given their names and descriptions and that they are helping us. Gershuni is their captor and in charge of their security," he added with a cough, "and two of my men." The general's eyes snapped open; Tsygankov added, "The men are two of my people from my old London cadre; they know the form."

"Good, now, if there is nothing else to do here, l suggest we go down to the laboratories and see how our people are making out with the device before we go to see the director for lunch."

"Your hat, General." Tsygankov handed the high-peaked cap to his senior officer before carefully placing his own on his tall frame. He held the door open to allow Polyakov to precede him then he ducked under the door frame. With his high-peaked hat Tsygankov's towering height meant there were very few doors he could pass through without stooping.

In the corridor a KGB soldier came to attention. Tsygankov looked down on him. "Like London policemen, they just keep getting younger," he smiled at his private joke. At 66 he was well over retirement age, he often wondered why they kept him on the active list. True, he had skills and he spoke core European languages well. He had long ago decided to keep taking the money until they put him out to grass. He knew the younger ones called him The Skull whilst his opponents called him The Spymaster; his unsmiling bland expression intimidated them. In reality, Tsygankov, thought by his colleagues and others as cold and ruthless in his work, had an excellent sense of humour and was, in his private life, the benign uncle to his family. He had long cultivated his persona for work purposes which served him well when he had to hide his thoughts and feelings.

Chapter 43

MOSCOW RULES

Brigadier Robinson's interview with the professor did not go well. The government adviser was furious. The fact that Rodney and his party were now held in the Soviet Union as bargaining counters meant that the previous ruling on no help if they were caught was, and had to be, negated. Negated simply because, the professor reasoned, the non-interference directive could only be applied when they were in Latin America. Russia was a different situation entirely.

But whether the professor was angrier at the loss of the device or the possible public embarrassment of having to extract the three men, Robinson could not tell.

He was glad to see the back of the man; at one point Robinson had wanted to tell him to get a life, but held his tongue. It would have been immature and a sign of weakness. He had long ago, as a young army officer, learnt that people could rarely keep up an invective for more than three minutes at the most. Still, theorists who had no operational experience set his teeth on edge, anyway, and unelected advisers to the power-hungry politicians, like the professor, raised his hackles on the best of days. Who the hell did this consulting leech think he was? Where was the minister who was supposed to protect the section? Running for cover, probably, in case this debacle reflected badly on him.

The professor gone, he was left to get on with the plan that had been forming in his mind. The professor would see the PM and they would call for Robinson if need be but in the meantime the professor charged the brigadier with reporting every six hours to keep him abreast of the situation.

Once he had left, Robinson called Williams into his office; he entered with a sheaf of papers and files clutched in his arms. "Sir, got what you wanted here. I've got Caroline Webster and Graham Swain outside, just in case," he said almost apologetically. "Err, Miss Webster was on the trip and..."

The brigadier cut him short, "Well done, get her in and bring Graham in too."

The chief watched as Williams laid the papers out in order on the desk. He was nondescript in appearance, of medium height with sandy, thinning hair and a round smooth face; he looked overweight but was very fast on his feet and he had a very sharp brain. The slightly ingratiating manner he effected annoyed the brigadier but he was shrewd enough to know that the man only employed this as a cover.

Robinson believed Williams was reluctant to show up those around him who couldn't think as fast and clearly as he could; in this capacity he was the brigadier's equal but there the similarity stopped. He would never have the director's poise or social graces and that, thought Robinson, would keep this man in the background for his entire service. Williams finished his task, "I'll get Caroline and Graham now," he went to the door and called them.

When Caroline Webster came in, the brigadier felt his pulse race slightly, no wonder Rodney was trying to date this long-legged beauty. She wore her hair loose around her face, little make-up, a black polo-neck jumper and a pencil skirt that emphasized the swell of her hips. The brigadier watched her as she entered the room and bade her sit down. She smoothed her skirt as she sat, crossed her legs and looked attentively at Robinson. Graham crossed the floor and sat next to her. Williams remained in the background. The young woman could see the interest on the brigadier's face and he was a little slow in blinking, causing her to flush red.

Embarrassed, he tore his gaze away from her to Graham and mumbled an apology under his breath, "Sorry everyone, daydreaming of another life, or something like that." He smiled welcomingly before his manner became more businesslike in seconds; silly old fool, he thought to himself, must be going senile. "To the matter in hand. Williams, what have you got on the South Africans?"

"Our intelligence indicates that the key man that was in Guatemala was Major Dieter Wolff."

"Ah yes, I know of him. What happened to him?"

"It's not clear, but it looks as if his party was taken out well before the exchange. He is back in South Africa now, licking his wounds."

"I see," Robinson was thinking and Williams waited dutifully. "Go on."

"I've pulled the files on Tsygankov but there doesn't seem to be much in them that will help."

"Anything else?"

"I took the liberty of booking a call to Major Wolff. The line's open and he is waiting for you to call."

"Well done," Robinson lifted the receiver. "Get him, please," he said, offering the receiver for Williams to take.

"Yes, sir."

The room fell silent except for Williams's crisp instruction he gave over the phone to the service operator. While he waited for the connection, Robinson leafed through the papers he had been given. Miss Webster looked at her nails while Graham simply sat waiting to be tasked.

"Connecting now, sir, it's ringing," he handed the phone back to Robinson.

"Wolff," the line was crystal clear.

"Major Wolff, this is Brigadier Robinson, from the UK."

"Yes, I know of you, we met once. How are you, sir?" Wolff was intrigued.

"Could be better; you know why I am calling?" Robinson was fishing.

"I could probably hazard a guess," Wolff was defensive.

"I am in trouble too; I wondered if you would consider a mutual pact which would be to our common advantage."

The silence from the other end of the line told Robinson that Wolff was considering the proposition.

At last Wolff said, "What do you propose?"

"Initially that you come over here and we talk."

"I think I could do that. It is above my pay grade but I think my boss would sanction it. Do I come alone? I have been working with a trusted police colleague and I would like to bring him," Wolff really wanted Vintner to be in on this.

"That is up to you. It's you that I want to talk to," Robinson's voice was neutral.

"Point taken, Brigadier, in that case, do I bring anything with me or the authority to act on anything that might arise, if you see what I mean?" Wolff was trying to clarify the situation so that he had something he could tell his boss.

"I really don't think so. Whatever we do now will be on our own initiative," the brigadier emphasized 'own initiative'. Whatever happened was unlikely to have the blessing of officialdom.

Wolff chuckled, "I see; your proposition interests me. What do I tell my people?"

"I would be prepared to say I asked to see you and that I may have a promising lead on the device. Suffice to say, I know where it is now even if I can't actually get at it immediately," Robinson proffered.

"You're on, sir. I'll be there on the next available plane. I know where you lot hang out but I would like a few useful telephone numbers to call if I should arrive at some ungodly hour." His South African accent was heavy but he seemed enthusiastic and this cheered the brigadier.

"So be it. I'll hand you over to Williams now and he will take care of the admin. Until we meet..." he handed the phone back to Williams and nodded.

When Williams had finished, the brigadier turned to the room again. "Graham, brief me on what you have and then you lot can take me to lunch." Graham's briefing didn't take long.

Robinson smiled at the trio, "Right, off to lunch, where are we going?"

Miss Webster flushed again. "What, now?" This was not normal, the boss never went to lunch with the team.

"Yes, right now. Italian, I think, is on the menu at the Duke of York's. Graham please get my car round, we go in style." He collected his coat and umbrella. "Williams, please tell the Guardian to meet me in the computer centre at two this afternoon and to please bring the Chekhov files with him. Tell him it is important."

Accompanied by his team, he marched into the Duke of York's. Robinson hated the place but at least they were screened from the tourists and Joe Public. The place was full of civil servants and members of the three services; it was inexpensive and service was swift.

The brigadier swept into the dining room bringing in the red-haired beauty on his arm and flanked by two of his men. The other patrons, who knew who he was, knew well enough to keep their counsel. He grunted a few words to those that acknowledged him. He ordered a red wine for himself and the two men and a martini for Miss Webster.

He ordered four plates of spaghetti bolognese and the food arrived promptly. The meal was eaten in almost complete silence. Surprisingly, all but Robinson felt at ease in the others' company. The silence gave Miss Webster, in particular, time to study the man before her. Tall, and despite the fact the man was around 68, 20 plus years her senior, he still retained the upright stance of a much younger man. His shock of silver hair, slightly too long, framed a strong face. The features that held her attention were his eyes. They were well spaced and the palest blue she had ever seen, set either side of a long hooked nose; they seemed to mesmerize the young woman.

She had difficulty withdrawing her gaze. Once he caught her looking at him and held her glance for a second and then smiled. He knew. The heavy lids drooped to cover the irises and the spell was broken. "Penny for your thoughts, Miss Webster?" he said kindly.

"I was just thinking, staring at you really," she laughed lightly and without embarrassment. "What do you want with me? I would have thought my usefulness to you was over now," it was more a question than a statement.

"You would but you would be wrong. You are involved, along with these two officers, and you know what's going on. I believe you still have a major part to play and an important one. Make sure you have an overnight bag packed and be in the office first thing tomorrow."

She was still puzzled and he saw the questions forming in her mind. He put out his left hand and squeezed her arm gently, "Trust me, I need you and these two at this time, more than you all think."

She leant forward, almost putting her nose close enough to touch his, and opening her eyes wide and staring into his, said, "OK, but only if you call me Caroline." Graham and Williams laughed, enjoying the lightened atmosphere the brigadier had created and the sparkle that Miss Webster had bought to the table. The other near-silent diners looked up from their plates before returning to their meals.

The brigadier stared back at her, "OK, but only if you call me Sir." Both grinned and pulled apart which had all at the table laughing loudly enough for some of the other occupants in the bar to half turn round again and notice them.

* * * * *

At two o'clock a small dapper gentleman in city dress, complete with bowler, waited quietly in the reception area of the central secret service computer centre while the staff tiptoed around him. They knew him as the guardian. Nothing else was known about him.

They only knew that when he appeared, they would be quietly and discreetly excused and herded upstairs, leaving the man alone or with a high-ranking member of the service. When they returned, he and the officer would be gone.

The brigadier arrived with Williams shortly after two and the men shook hands warmly. Robinson nodded to the computer suite manager and the staff were cleared out. Only the manager and two armed guards remained.

"Open the computer to level six, if you please, Jeff." The manager did as Robinson requested. It took seconds, with the man's expert fingers playing on the input console. The levels of security flashed up on the VDU screen only to be replaced by others as the man fed keywords and passwords into the central processor. The machine flashed the final clearance on the screen: Level Six access required. It kept flashing, "Leave us now, Jeff and lock us in. Williams, pass me the files and take Jeff for a coffee. We will be here for some time, so I suggest you and your people disperse round the departments and carry on your work with the desk consoles there."

When they had left, Robinson moved quickly to the command console. He entered his identity and the guardian followed with another string of data. On the far wall a panel opened and the men moved over to it. They placed their hands on it together, the machine read their palms, literally, and steel shutters rolled over the access doors so they were completely shut in, both outside and in. The master console stopped flashing Level Six and the message was replaced by the message: You are now about to access code Level Red.

"Now, Brigadier, what do you want?" the little man looked at Robinson questioningly.

"I want to see Major Brown's controller's file."

The guardian shrugged. The man had authority. He turned and worked at the control console while Robinson waited out of sight of the man's movements on the keyboard. "There you are; I can afford you half an hour."

"That should he ample." Robinson took his place at the keyboard and began to scan page after page of Rodney's carefully kept secrets as they flashed up on the screen, some of the entries made him chuckle.

His second in command had a sense of humour, he could see how his man had developed over the years; and humorous entries began to be replaced by cryptic, serious notes as he sorted through the agent's records. Finally, suddenly there on the screen was the code name Chekhov, followed by entries of intelligence passed, dates and times and then suddenly there it was, 'Chekhov (two) equals Gipsy'. The brigadier was taken aback, he let the breath escape from him in a whistle.

He went back to the screen. "I want to erase a sentence."

The guardian came over to him. "Are you sure you really want to do that?"

"I think that it would be sensible."

The guardian punched a code into the machine. "What page?"

"The next one to that being displayed," the guardian entered the page number.

"Put the screen you want back. Put the flashing dot over the letters you want blocked out and then press the erase button for each letter of the sentence." He looked at the brigadier.

When the man nodded, he moved out of viewing range again; the brigadier quickly completed his task.

"I have finished, let's close down."

"Very well, but don't you think you ought to complete your scan of his file? You may see something else you wish to erase."

Robinson grunted and began to flick through the remaining screens. There were only a few; his man had grown more and more careful over the last two years which he noted with pleasure; "All done; close up please." Robinson felt chilled; the air conditioning in the centre was very efficient, he would be glad to get out of here. How people spent their working lives in this environment was past his understanding.

Robinson went to the rear of the suite and gazed round at all the technology while the guardian returned the system to normal. "All done, we can let the staff return to their normal work stations now." He placed his bowler on his head and held out his hand.

"Thank you so much for doing this, it really was very important to us."

"Anytime, Brigadier, however, notice is always appreciated." As the guardian left, the centre team filed into the room. The throwaway remark, the brigadier realized, was the guardian's way of delivering a mild rebuke to him.

Back in his office, the brigadier's fertile brain was already working. Characteristically, he leaned back in his chair and put his feet on the desk.

So the facts are, he thought, Gipsy is Chekhov (two). His thoughts came fast. He flashed the endgame first. Get the Russian traitor to meet Major Wolff. But where was the trail to achieve that? Fact, he knew Gipsy was a friend of the director of the Russian State Circus. Fact, Gipsy was a member of the touring State Ballet. Fact, the previous Soviet leader's daughter was linked by marriage to the Circus and Gipsy. Fact, the previous Soviet leader himself had a supposed secret or at least ultra private hunting lodge just north of South Africa in Tanzania.

How could he use the Soviet leader's reported almost pathological hatred of the KGB's Chief Director of Directorate Number One? He pondered for a moment about South Africa not being particularly friendly, nevertheless their service was good, almost equal to many in the West, not including the UK and the Israelis. The problem was that the whole country was leaking like a sieve. Any secrets that were fed to the South Africans through normal channels would soon be out and certainly the Russians would probably hear first.

No wonder Wolff and his team were picked up in Guatemala. They may have had Wolff tagged at an early stage.

He scratched his long nose and smiled to himself. There may just be a way to get his people out; Rodney, Mould and Sharky. He had had an idea and he knitted his brows as he focused on the options. Now he knew who Chekhov was, he felt for the first time that day that all was not hopeless. He needed to check out one fact. The final piece of the jigsaw revolved around Gipsy and Gipsy's daughter. He had a pretty good idea who the daughter was but it needed to be confirmed. He mumbled to himself, "Must check out that last fact and then I really think we may get at the device too."

He positively beamed and reached out for his phone to call the PM's adviser, the professor.

Chapter 44

THE GUARDIAN

Rodney lay on an old single iron bed looking at the room's high ceiling with its heavy, ornate coving that ran around the room between the ceiling and the walls. The walls were whitewashed and apart from a few cobwebs were immaculate. The accommodation was spacious, even luxurious; clearly they were being softened up. However, their luxurious accommodation was still a prison; Rodney had no doubts about that. For a moment he felt helpless and was frustrated at their capture. He searched his mind for how they could have done things differently but soon gave that up as a negative exercise. Go forward not back, he thought.

His main puzzlement and concern, however, was that they had not been moved out of Moscow and, from the look of things, as their guards came and went, they were here for the duration; how long would that be, he hadn't the slightest idea. The first order of things was to escape, but how and where to?

They appeared to be in an apartment block close to the centre of Moscow. They had been taken there directly from the airport and finally located in a flat at the top of the building. The three men had immediately looked for a possible means of escape but there were was nothing obvious. The apartment was heavily guarded with a double-entry system. They had worked out from glimpses as the doors opened and closed that the door out of the flat led into a boxed corridor that had a door at the other end of it. Anyone entering the flat was locked into this box before the apartment door was unlocked. Still, they were grateful they had room to move about. They even had the facility of a rooftop and a caged exercise area. Mould and Sharky spent a lot of their time in the cage looking at the city, a city they never expected to visit. The apartment block was much higher than its neighbours, so not overlooked. They soon worked out that they were too far away from the next block for anyone to jump, even if they could defeat the security of the cage. The only way for anyone to get off the roof was straight down the smooth sides of the building, to certain death. So, even though they had been given the complete freedom of the flat and the roof, they were not going anywhere and the Russians knew it. The guards remained outside the flat, only entering through the double-entry system to bring in food and other necessities.

Rodney and his men were only too aware that the apartment would have been bugged for sound and that hidden cameras watched their every movement.

Each day, a man dressed in civilian clothes, dark wool suit, white shirt and old college tie, speaking precise Oxford English would appear and question them. He was so English in his diction, they found it quite disorientating. Middle-aged, in fact middle everything, except the team knew he was very fit. His movements were quick and decisive.

He would accuse them of spying and threaten them with a trial if they would not cooperate. His mantra was well rehearsed and repetitious and their silence never deterred him. His routine included extracts of each man's history and family life or lack of it. He would probe and threaten. The men did admit to themselves that it was, above all, simply wearing. Then he would just nod, adjust his tie, pick up his papers and, without a word of farewell, leave. In some ways this was the most disconcerting part of the interviews and they expected him to be replaced with a team of baseball wielding thugs. So far this hadn't happened.

Now and then the beautiful Major Gershuni visited them on some pretext or other; they were never quite sure why she did this. Rodney would play a game of chess with her; he found it difficult to concentrate. She would ask him seemingly innocent questions and he had to be careful not to answer them directly. He always lost the games. He did feel that there was a relationship between them but he had yet to work out what it was. Certainly he felt that they were inexplicably drawn to each other. Or was he simply imagining it?

Once, Brigadier Tsygankov looked in on them and joined them for their midday meal. He, too, probed but seemed to be more interested in what was going on in England. It was as though he was asking about his own country. Before he left, he made them sit up when he casually announced that their head of operations, the brigadier, had been on the telephone, asking about their welfare and when they would be released. He didn't elaborate but added that, of course, there would be a price to pay. He held up his scarred hand to Rodney, "For you, very expensive."

Their meals arrived promptly at seven every morning, then noon, and six at night. They lingered over their meal in the evening, there was nothing else to do. They had a chess set and a TV but for the most part, as none of them could speak much Russian except Sharky, they simply went to bed early. They could do little but wait and watch for a break. And wait and watch they did, they were model prisoners. They were not idle, however; they casually searched for audio bugs and hidden cameras.

All the cameras they found by the third day but not all the audio bugs except the ones they were supposed to find. And dutifully, as they were expected to, they destroyed them. Rodney reasoned that the ones they had not found were integral to the cameras or within the plaster of the walls. The cameras were more difficult; they would have to wait. They covered every yard of the flat roof. The lights in the apartment were never turned off so they were under constant surveillance. This irked the team more than anything.

As Rodney got up from the bed and went for a shower that afternoon, Wolff was arriving at London airport.

Wolff was alone; Vintner couldn't come as he was still working on the case from the other end. Wolff didn't mind, he thought it would be an education to work alongside the British; Her Majesty's most secret service, he thought with a grimace. Not necessarily the upfront members of MI5 and MI6 but the shadowy figures in the background. He wondered what Robinson would be like. True, he had seen him once and shaken his hand at a meeting they had both attended. He was not sure what reception he would get as the two countries, the United Kingdom and South Africa, were not, in public, great friends. There was certainly no special relationship at this time.

Chapter 45

THE DIRECTOR AND HIS DEPUTY

General Polyakov sat in his director's office listening intently to what the director was telling him. "General Polyakov, my dear Comrade, the sad truth is that our beloved leader is not expected to last the night."

The director had difficulty keeping his voice on an even timbre. Polyakov could sense excitement in the man or perhaps it was naked ambition he was sensing.

It was reported that the director had not been in the department at all this week, even the news of the device and the captured British agents had not brought him back to the directorate and now Polyakov knew why. He had guessed that something momentous was going on, as all the principals of the Soviet Union had been closeted in the Kremlin for the past few days and had been unavailable.

As always, this was a time of danger for them all. Who would emerge as the new leader and who would in consequence fall from grace? Carefully and calmly Polyakov put the question that was expected from him to the director, "Sir, what does this mean for you and the directorate?"

Behind his glasses the director's eyes glinted. Polyakov felt a moment of hesitation; he focused his eyes on the director's broad forehead with its silver-grey hair that swept back. "It will mean, Comrade General, a new director."

Polyakov furrowed his brow in concentration, "Are you to move then, sir?"

"Yes," the director smiled at last. "It may well be that I shall take over the leadership, perhaps only for the time being until things settle, maybe for good; it is really too early to say."

Polyakov was stunned. This certainly was not expected as most knew the premier and the director were often at loggerheads. "May I then now offer you my best wishes and good luck," Polyakov was sincere. The task ahead for the leader would not be easy and Polyakov was only too aware that his director's recurring heart condition would make his task even more difficult. "Is it too early to ask you who will be sitting in your chair?"

"No, it is not. After we part today, I do not expect to return to it. I have engagements and meetings for the foreseeable future. You, General Polyakov, despite your lack of seniority, will fill it; it is up to you to keep it. No one is better qualified. Should matters not work out, I would expect you to give it back to me to pass on, but I don't think that will be the case."

"But what of the other directorate directors, surely one of them would have had reasonable expectations to move into this chair?" Polyakov indicated the director's seat. It was important he knew the politics. Even though he would be almost unassailable in this directorate.

"Yes, they may have, but that has already been taken care of. Now you must show them that we made the right choice, must you not?" The director held the eyes of his deputy, "Don't let me down. In these early days I do not want to have to worry about bruised personalities and any muddled thinking in the KGB. All have to function as before. Can you do it?"

"I shall endeavour to see the confidence that has been afforded me is not misplaced," answered the general seriously.

"Good, but bullshit; you know you can do it and probably make a better job of it than I did. Now, any points before I leave you?"

"Yes, but only two that need concern you, and for which I need a decision before you leave. I take it that I now have the full powers that you exercised?" The director nodded. "Who is to be my deputy?" Polyakov hesitated, "And," he added, "what about the project, sir?"

"Project, what project?" queried the director.

"The project involving the device we took from the South Africans to use on the West," Polyakov said blandly.

"Device, what device?" the director's voice was icy but a smile played on his lips.

"Surely, sir, you remember?" Polyakov tried for one last time but he already had an inkling of the answer he would get.

"I don't think you quite understand. Let me put it plainly. There was never such an outrageous project that I could possibly be involved in or wish to be associated with in my new capacity. It is the sort of thing that might be expected to be hatched and executed by a directorate..." he paused. "Only by a directorate that wanted to embarrass the leader in peace time or as a way of bringing something out of the woodwork."

"In that case, sir, clearly if there were anything like that and I were to stumble on it, I would certainly put it on ice until such time as directed to do otherwise."

"In a word, yes," the director chuckled. "Should that be the case, I suppose so, but only, I suggest, if it's possible to complete the preparations quickly, so that all that has to be done is to plug such a device in. Should it ever be needed on my say-so; if there were such a device, of course."

"Who would share the secret of this hypothetical device, apart from me?"

"Why, your new deputy of course; he already knows enough to make the thing operate, if I ever need it."

The reference to the 'if I ever need it' did not go unnoticed by Polyakov. He cleared his throat, "I take it that my deputy is to be Brigadier Tsygankov?"

"Definitely, and the man I would choose every time! I know he had a supposed failure in England but I think he is the ideal man for you. You will make a great team. His knowledge of the West, coupled with yours, is as good as we have ever had. Add to this your knowledge of the organization, its resources and capabilities."

"Has his appointment also been given the green light by those who support me?" Polyakov questioned.

"Yes," the director put his hands on the arms of the chair indicating he was about to rise. "There is something else you should know; something I will deal with personally using my own private Kremlin guard. If all goes well, a mole will be flushed in the next few days, maybe longer. He has plagued me since the traitor Chekhov attempted to defect and died for his pains and when Tsygankov was forced to flee England as a result. Bringing the British SIS men at this time has guaranteed it. Had it been the device alone we had in our hands," he shrugged, "I would not be so certain but now, who knows?"

"What of this traitor, in general terms?"

"I think he is important and has been closely connected to the leadership over many years. I have never been able to trip him despite many attempts to do so. I have to catch him red-handed; if I don't, my own credibility will be questioned and at a time like this, I can't afford allegations of rigged evidence. Now, is there anything else?" Polyakov shook his head. "Good, then it only remains for me to wish you good luck, not that I believe you will need it." He got up and shook the general's hand, then hugged him and whispered in his ear, "You are now the second most important man in the Soviet Union whether you like it or not. Be fair but hard. I rely on you completely. Come and see me at least once a week; the week you miss, I will know that you no longer need my support and that I am in danger. An old friend gave me that warning."

Polyakov was shocked; the director was telling him that he now feared him. He pushed the director away but held him by the arms at arm's length. "Have no doubts, I am your man as I ever was. Your deputy I was, and will still be; I am happy in that role." He released the director.

The man stood before Polyakov for a few moments and then smiled, slapping Polyakov on the arms, "So be it."

He left then, leaving Polyakov to survey his new surroundings. After a while he pressed for the secretary. He was surprised that the old director's secretary did not appear; instead it was his own. "Where is the director's secretary?" he felt a little annoyed.

"I am now the director's secretary. He has taken his with him; it was his wish that you continue to employ me," she stood steadily in front of him.

He turned his back on her and strode to the window to look out over Moscow and to hide a trace of frustration. So, he thought, I am your friend? Your loyal deputy? But you didn't even have enough faith to leave me to choose my own immediate staff? If he had craned his head out of the window he would have seen Mould and Sharky on their rooftop, looking his way, but he didn't, his eyes were shut tight. He should be delighted with his new found power but instead he felt helplessly engineered. She was still waiting for him. He swung round on her and held out his arms, smiling, "Congratulations to us both I think, what times we will have. Now, fetch my deputy."

She brightened, matching his mood, "Yes, General, but, he doesn't know yet."

"I see," this news somehow made him feel better. At least he and his tall gaunt gangling deputy were together in this. Perhaps, he thought, that is what the director had wanted. Polyakov laughed suddenly, causing his secretary to scuttle away. Damn them all! He rationalized, with a good deputy he could fix anything. The first priority was to get his deputy to close down the decoder project as quickly as possible. It was now an embarrassment and it was about time his man had a little blood on his hands. Polyakov frowned at the thought, there is nothing like a little blood to tie people together.

* * * * *

Back in London, Wolff was being ushered into Brigadier Robinson's office to a warm reception. "Welcome, Major," Robinson shook his hand warmly. "Let me introduce Miss Caroline Webster to you. She will look after you while you are here."

"A pleasure," Wolff shook her hand a little longer than was necessary, or so the brigadier thought.

"Likewise," responded Miss Webster, liking the blond South African immediately; she still held his hand.

"When you two have quite finished," the brigadier said impatiently.

"Sorry," they both said together, amused.

"Right then, let's start shall we?" Wolff and Miss Webster sat up and looked attentive. They both had a smile playing on their lips which the brigadier chose to ignore. In truth he felt a little miffed but shook the feeling away; how could he be jealous at his age?

Clasping his hands behind him he paced slowly across the office, "What I am about to tell you and to ask you to do is against my better judgement but, in the situation I consider it to be expedient. I believe time is of the essence to prevent a catastrophe not only for us but for the Russians as well." He paused, "Your government has unwittingly created, potentially, the most dangerous situation since the Cuban crisis; potentially far worse."

Wolff looked puzzled and was angered that his country should be maligned by this English gentleman. Wolff, no respecter of protocol and suddenly very serious, said, "Sir, I don't see what you mean." His face was flushed and his voice tight.

"Then, Major Wolff, I will explain," the brigadier snapped. "You developed a machine that we in the West and, we know, those in the East, have been working on for years. Didn't your people realize that whoever held the secret of a machine that could communicate with any computer in the world would have a weapon as important as any in our arsenal today? Suppose you hooked your machine into our communications system. The NATO alliance, for example, or even worse, a weapon control system?"

"But surely the machine we are talking about is only of use in plain language? Most important systems are coded."

"Any code can be broken if you have the key. And what if you picked up the intelligence before it got encoded, what then?" The brigadier was unnecessarily brusque and he knew it, he softened, "My dear Dieter, what I am saying is that if they have it, we must have it too, or nobody has it, do you see?"

"Stalemate," said Miss Webster confidently.

"Exactly," Robinson pointed a long finger at her reinforcing the point.

"I see what you are getting at," Wolff indicated his understanding. "We get my government to build another and give it to you."

"I don't see how that is possible; didn't they take everything, the machine, the drawings, or were they destroyed?" the brigadier said doubtfully.

"Yes, but we have the men to rebuild; I think," Wolff was suddenly doubtful that this was the case.

"Yes, you may or may not have. But, as they intend to hold our people for a period, I suggest to you that they may be going to use the one they hold soon. In other words, we simply don't have time to wait. What if your people can't replicate it? We can't wait to find out, we need to do something about it now."

He sat down facing the two of them, "My staff and some analysts have considered what they might use the machine for and frankly it's so horrendous that it doesn't bear thinking about. The use mostly breaks down into three types and, as you might expect, they are the classic trio. Consider its use on the industrial base of a country or continent. Or consider its use to undermine the social fabric of society; imagine a gremlin in our computer that deals with health, pensions, etc. in that last category, let's include politics. Finally, military; it could create havoc in the logistic machines; it could cause chaos in the communications network. But all that pales into insignificance if it was let loose on the strategic weapon control system and I believe that is what they will go for. They want something to counter the cruise missile deployment and they want it badly. How badly, we will see when we actually deploy."

Wolff was impressed; what the man said made sense. He was not sure he could buy it all, but enough to know that whatever he was going to be asked to do, he would probable agree to. "Before I change my mind and get the next plane out of here back to the safety of South Africa, you had better tell me why I am here."

"Well, you are here because you are good at what you do. You are also involved up to the eyeballs and with my three best men locked up in the USSR I have no one else immediately up to speed who can do what you are about to."

"And what about me?" Caroline Webster enquired. She had had a feeling of uselessness ever since Belize when she had been powerless to do anything.

"Well, one of the languages you mastered is Russian, I understand?"

"You know I have, sir. I've only been working on the Latin desk to improve my other languages."

The brigadier smiled, "Yes, indeed, and how else is Major Wolff going to manage in Russia without a good interpreter on the mission I am about to outline to you both?"

She smiled and curled her arm round Wolff's possessively; the brigadier raised his eyes, "Yes, you will have to go as husband and wife."

"Oh good," she said teasingly, looking at Wolff. Wolff looked, or tried to look, embarrassed and wiped his finger round his collar awkwardly.

The brigadier wanted to laugh but the seriousness of the situation and what he was proposing stopped him. Instead he said blandly, "You will make a fine couple. But let's not overdo it. I don't want you two deported as undesirables before you have a chance to complete the mission."

The mood had changed. "No, sir," said Miss Webster, acknowledging the brigadier, and untangled her arm from Wolff's.

Robinson glanced at his watch. "Go and tell my secretary to bring some coffee while I have a talk to the Major and then when we are refreshed we will get down to the meat of the matter."

"Before we do, a question; what makes you think the Russians will not duplicate the machine in their hundreds?" she asked, rising to leave.

"Two reasons; we are talking about microtechnology; it would mean that they would have to take the machine down to its very last component and risk breaking something, or even just scratching a microchip that might render the machine useless. Even if they did, it would take an army of photographers to photograph each microchip and blow it up so that their people could draw the circuitry to use as a template in order to build a new machine. No, I don't think they will risk re-engineering it and, as I hinted before, they will want a quick result. I also don't believe that many people know what's going on or we would have heard about it. Now, get that coffee please."

"Yes sir." She was gone.

Wolff had been watching the brigadier with increasing respect; after the young woman had left, he asked respectfully what the brigadier really thought the Russians would use the machine for.

The brigadier seemed to shrink within himself for a moment, "I wish to God I knew; I have been over every possibility in my mind but I am blessed if I can spot the one most likely. I tell you in all honesty that if I could pinpoint it then I would not be asking you to go." Then forcefully he added, almost in desperation, "We simply must find out what they are going to do with it, or destroy it, or recover it, whatever; at the same time, my people must be got out of Russia or they will surely die there, of that I have never been more certain."

"I see. It looks as though you were right and were not exaggerating when you said we had created a monster."

"I am horribly afraid that is exactly what your countrymen have done. My God, when I think of the uses they could put the device to, my blood runs cold," he shivered involuntarily.

Wolff said determinedly, "Sir, leave the fieldwork to me. Just tell me what to do."

"I'm going to have to; I just wish you had a little more experience in the territory you will be covering. It's not going to resemble the African veldt at all but it is nevertheless a jungle."

"I'm not completely bush," replied Wolff lightly.

Robinson smiled slightly, "No I expect you're not, and you will have help over there, that has all been arranged."

"Trustworthy, I hope."

"The best, the very best."

Wolff shrugged, "Let's get to it then; the sooner we start, the happier I will be."

* * * * *

General Polyakov sat at his new desk with Brigadier Tsygankov standing in front of him. "So Carl, do you accept the appointment and, of course, the promotion?"

Brigadier Carl Tsygankov knew that he had to; he bowed his head to Polyakov, it was a sign of complete acceptance and, for Tsygankov, a sign that the Kremlin had forgiven his failure in England and no longer blamed him for the loss of Lawson.

He was delighted and he said so, "It will be a pleasure to work for you."

"Good, no doubt you will have a great deal to do so I will not keep you tonight, it is very late. But there is one task that will not wait, however this is not currently the place to discuss it," Polyakov cocked his head as though listening.

Tsygankov nodded understanding, placing his high-peaked hat on his head.

His director would want his room checked before any serious business could be discussed. The whole of the building was awash with news of the moves upstairs; there were very few disgruntled officers and most of its occupants had taken the news calmly. To all, it meant a new broom and probably extra work. They had done it before and they would no doubt do it again. A few, the ambitious, waited expectantly to hear if they too had been moved upwards. They would be disappointed.

"I'm going over to the main building; please accompany me, we can talk on the way."

"Of course," Tsygankov hesitated. "But why me? I thought the loss of Lawson would have disbarred me from high office." He faced the general, "Ten years ago, in England, I lost all I'd worked for; that is not so long ago, memories in the KGB are longer."

Polyakov snorted and dismissed what his deputy had said with a wave of his hand. "That was another time; people have shorter memories these days, they can't afford not to. You were not to blame, it was that stupid man Lawson; all you worked for, up in smoke." He smiled, wagging a finger at his deputy, "Let it be a lesson to you that when choosing a man, make sure he always remains beholden to you and does as he is told."

"That, Director, includes me?" Tsygankov twisted his face into a grin of sorts, but his eyes gave him away, they were puzzled, questioning.

"You are my deputy and we must act as one. To the outside world you must appear to support me totally in my policies and whims; privately, in this office, we can discuss anything. Your advice will always be welcome."

"As a working arrangement, that is very acceptable to me and one I welcome. Now, sir, you said we were going for a walk. By tomorrow, your lair will be, shall we say, cleaned."

Despite the fact that they wanted to get outside quickly, they were delayed several minutes by well-wishers or simply by people who wanted to be noticed by the new masters as they made their way through the corridors of KGB power to the exit. Once outside in the cool air they walked quickly from the building. Polyakov spurned the use of his personal staff car and waved the chauffeur away impatiently. The hapless man just stood there for a moment and then got in and followed, crawling along the pavement at a discreet distance from the two officers who stepped out briskly and it was all the director's guards could do to keep up with them.

"Now, Carl..." Polyakov hesitated, then said quickly, "The machine. Once the Colonel confirms that it is ready for deployment, which should be any day now, and you can tell me that hopefully tomorrow, everyone associated with this project, except him and his man in the West, is to be silenced." He let the word 'silenced' hang in the cool air.

Tsygankov stopped in his tracks and Polyakov had to turn and grab the man by his coat sleeve to get him moving again. "Come on man, you don't have to do it yourself, you know."

They resumed their walk in silence, the snow crunching under their boots. There had been a fresh fall and the trees and pavements were carpeted in white.

Tsygankov broke the silence as Polyakov knew he would. "Does that include Major Brown and his people?"

"Particularly Major Brown and his party."

"I see. Is that wise? Has this really been thought through?" Tsygankov questioned.

Polyakov was not in this instance going to discuss the matter. "You don't think that they expect to live once this project is underway, do you?"

"Probably not; but they don't know anything, do they? Even I don't know what it is intended for. They may have value in other ways."

"Include those we took with us. That is the way it will be." Polyakov stopped walking. "Until tomorrow," it was a dismissal.

"Until then, General," Tsygankov saluted and watched the director impatiently wave his car up and get in without a backward glance.

The director's bodyguards poured into another car that drew up.

The brigadier was left in the wide deserted street. He felt alone, old and vulnerable. The cold of the night cut into his tall thin frame and, despite the layers of clothing he had put on, he shuddered. Whether it was from the cold or his state of mind at the time, he didn't know why. He hurried back to the office. It would be a long night for him. He was now the executive officer of the directive; quite apart from Colonel Ivanovich, who he must sort out tonight, he had a feeling that the files were piling up in the director's office and his own office and had been since his master had launched himself into this crazy dangerous project.

As he hurried back towards the building, his shadow was thrown on to the wall by the street lights behind him; he watched it grow as he approached the entrance hall. His shadow reminded him of a huge spider, supernatural, all powerful. He hunched his shoulders, distorting the shape, and the power radiated back at him. As he entered the building, he was filled with an unreasoning sense of his new powers, bestowed on him by his new appointment.

He smiled inwardly, it was only just dawning on him that this directorate was his. Polyakov was now the political head and like the man before him would only have the time and energy to manage the high-level strategic matters.

He now appreciated Polyakov's action, leaving him standing alone in the street; it was to remind him that no one was there to hold his hand. Tsygankov must succeed or fail on his own.

Chapter 46

LONDON MAKES PLANS

"All set?" Robinson enquired as his secretary showed Wolff and Caroline into the room; he stopped writing and smiled at the pair.

"Yes, sir," replied Wolff, "Your men down in the basement have been very helpful; they have given me a few tricks to take with our luggage, flight tickets, the lot. Oh yes and a passport for Valeria."

"Impressed, he was," said Miss Webster in a mock cockney voice.

The brigadier grunted.

"Yes, I was; I could do with some of your facilities and some of the gadgets back home. It would certainly make my job easier." He hesitated, "I suppose I was meant to see what I did?"

"Yes, you were allowed to see what I intended you to see," the brigadier's voice had a touch of humour in it. "Now we have a few hours before you fly early tomorrow morning so I've ordered a meal for us, to be eaten here." His voice was firm; any idea the other two had of sneaking off was clearly not on, they would be alone soon enough. The brigadier just hoped that they would keep their minds on the job. They had obviously taken to each other the moment they had met and the four hours they had been away preparing for the mission had only reinforced that feeling. The brigadier was a pretty shrewd judge of character and he could see plainly that Rodney would have his nose put out. God willing, they would all come back safely.

"Caroline," she started; it was the first time that the brigadier had called her by her first name. "Clear all the papers off my desk and put them on the leather chair over there. My secretary can clear them up later." In a few moments the room was rearranged; not for three people but for five.

"Guests?" Wolff asked.

"Yes, the PM's adviser and her first secretary. You'll find them interesting," he saw Wolff frown.

Wolff shook his head, "I wasn't thinking of that. Embarrassed to say this, but don't you think it a little unwise for me to meet them? I am here under rather strange circumstances; even my own people don't know where I have gone, save one."

"Think nothing of it; I can assure you that the gentlemen will be the soul of discretion," he waved his hand dismissively. "Caroline, please do the honours and pour us some drinks; it's time I told Wolff how we operate here in Britain."

"What would you both like to drink?" she asked.

"Oh, just pour sherries all round from the decanter in the tall cupboard to your left."

She opened the doors to reveal a bar so well stocked that it would have done justice to a small private London club bar. She let out an involuntary, "Whoa." Both men just raised their eyebrows to the ceiling.

"Get on with it," Robinson chided. "Wolff, settle down now, I will be brief," the brigadier poured facts about the service into Wolff for the next half hour. The sherry glasses were refilled more than once; it just seemed to be one of those occasions.

Wolff recognized that he was only being told what was already public knowledge, for those who cared to trouble themselves to read the various parliamentary papers, press releases, books on the subject and the like, but the way the brigadier put it all together fascinated him.

There was so much detail that when he tried to recall the knowledge he had been given as the briefing went along, he could only remember the principles and philosophy behind the way the secret services and guiding agencies worked.

In some ways, to him, it seemed amateurish, but the reputation and success of the organization, plus what he had seen earlier in the day, dispelled any thoughts in that direction. What was it the brigadier had said? The basic principle was to only let the individual know what he needed to know to carry out his task; and, unlike the KGB and CIA with their massive organizations, the British were not so fragmented into departments that they would otherwise jealously guard their activity.

Wolff pondered this, for the British were to a degree compartmentalized, or else why would they need bridging organizations like the brigadier's military intelligence and the like? Whatever the British were doing, it kept everybody on their toes. Perhaps it was the way they shared resources. He considered the reputation of these people; they were highly regarded and rated in his world; that they were successful was a given, perhaps not all the time but they would be high up on any scale of success. What impressed him most was that the British were subtle; he almost smiled at this. Had Robinson brought him in, after all, simply to do the dirty work? They only had to risk a low staffer of a girl to help him.

The brigadier was talking again. "Obviously we can't have all these people running round like headless chickens," at this Wolff did laugh. "So we have a supreme coordinating committee where the heads of our respective organizations discuss ours and their bits." He put his head to one side, "Discuss is too polite a phrase but you get the general idea. We are a little over protective of our own areas of operation at times; it's a sort of fail-safe that has been inbuilt to stop the service and its associated organizations from getting too big, too important and, consequently, too much of a threat. This country, as you probably know, has an ingrained phobia about the police state. It's got to be a hang-up that has been handed down since the days of Cromwell."

"What?" Wolff asked, "Oliver Cromwell? Oh yes, of course, he got rid of the king and made the parliament all powerful."

"Something like that, wrong Cromwell though. It was King Henry the Eighth's minister that was the one." Robinson continued, "You see vestiges all about you in this land. The army for instance has to be approved every year by passing the Army Act. Naturally this goes through on a nod. Same thing applies to the police and the antiterror laws. With us, it is a different story. Because we are secret, they don't understand us and are nervous about what we get up to. We mitigate it with briefing regularly and we have our own ministers. The ministers generally act as a brake on us, more a hindrance than an asset, in practice. But quite rightly so," he concluded as his secretary knocked to tell them the others had arrived.

"Please show them in and fill two more glasses. I'll leave you for a minute or two to introduce yourselves while I get the secretary to send down for the food." He glanced at Wolff, "You are not vegetarian or anything, are you?"

"No, sir."

"Good."

Wolff watched the new arrivals enter the room. He quickly assessed them. The tall, smartly dressed one with the old school tie had to be the first secretary. A competent man who knew he was at the top of his game. Snooty, certainly, good front man, of that Wolff was certain. Dedicated and loyal to the PM, always, but I bet he's murder to work for, Dieter thought to himself. Best to play this one straight, doesn't look as though he could take a joke or would appreciate clever humour.

Wolff switched his attention to the other man. Shorter than Wolff and more running to fat than stocky. Bit country set, could have been Boer back home. He watched the man's eyes take in at a glance the sherry glasses, the scattered papers on the chair and both Wolff and Caroline Webster. This one is clever, Wolff thought; he would describe him as smiling death.

As the evening wore on Wolff was proved right about his initial assessments time and again.

Sir Peter Gray, First Secretary, moved the conversation on whenever it lapsed but, on balance, the professor out-talked everyone. He took them on a tour round the world, the trouble spots, what was going on and what he foresaw.

Wolff asked him what he saw happening in South Africa and the professor's answer startled him.

"In a word I would say trouble!" He paused, smiled and added, "Not necessarily for you but for your neighbours. I also think the world is moving on and I foresee the ending of your segregated black and white society. The more materialistic we become and the smaller the world gets, the more the blacks will want their share in everything; it is inevitable I am afraid."

Wolff could only agree with him in general and asked him if there was any way of avoiding this.

"Dieter, I would not dream of telling you how to run your own country, it would be bad manners. But, as you ask, how could I put it? If I were being facetious, I might have questioned why you don't invite us back over!"

Wolff laughed and the room followed.

Brigadier Robinson began to make moves that indicated the meal was over. Dutifully, the guests made their excuses and left.

Once they were alone, Robinson went to the window, drew the curtain back and looked down on the busy London street below. He grunted, remembering the elegance of the old headquarters in Curzon Street and the rooms in the Boot and Flogger public house, round the corner in Borough High Street, where sustenance could always be found. Many a night he and other young officers, some no longer serving, some now dead, had played poker in the pub's back room. He wondered what the new generation of poker players were like. Many, he knew, were happy to move from the old building but Robinson was not one of them. But as he stared down from Northumberland House, he didn't think his section had done too badly, conveniently located close to one of the capital's principal stations but, he thought to himself, the world seem so much simpler in the old days, just as troublesome, but there was clarity somehow. He was aware that the other two were waiting for him but he continued to contemplate the past for a further minute. There used to be rules, well, sort of rules; now it seemed to him that neither side seemed quite in control. The events all seemed to run into one another; there were no clear-cut lines to a job anymore. The Firm, as he liked to call it, seemed to be forever running to stand still; fuzzy, that was the adjective he had been looking for. Now he had to send two junior operatives into a dangerous situation from which they and his imprisoned trusted team may not return.

He had hinted to Wolff that Rodney and the others were in danger, despite assurances of an exchange when the price was right. His opposite number had been too casual; he felt in the pit of his stomach that their fate had already been determined. His lifetime's experience had taught him that you don't deal in facts and facts alone, you have to add the feel for the situation and whether that was right or wrong, only time would tell.

From this experience, he judged the situation as desperate; logic told him he should abort any rescue and recovery attempt but he was loath to give in without a fight. Rodney and his team had been with him a long time and the device was probably important. He shrugged; he had an ace up his sleeve. At this, he allowed himself a half smile as he turned back to Wolff.

"Sir?" Wolff had risen.

"Yes, you two need to go and get ready and get some rest."

"Have to admit it has been a long and very full day."

"Of course; I'll see you both in the morning before you fly off to Moscow, just in case there is any news."

After they left, Robinson went back to the window; the lights in the street and the passing cars were in full flow. He reflected that, despite the protestations of tiredness from Wolff, he and Webster would be among the throng of people looking for nightlife in the city for a few hours before they crashed for the night. So what, who could know what tomorrow may bring? With a swish he pulled the curtains closed again with a purpose and finality that rattled the pelmet.

His own work for the night was just about to begin. Shortly, in the cellars of the British embassy on the Maurice Thorez Embankment in Moscow, a startled radio operator was talking to the brigadier on the secure scrambler line; Robinson was demanding that he get the junior attaché to the phone.

When the man eventually arrived, considerably miffed at being hauled out of bed but at the same time intrigued at the summons, he received a series of short instructions that left him puzzled but resigned to carrying them out... It was going to be a long night.

First, he phoned the telephone number the brigadier had given him; he waited until the man identified himself and then said quickly in good Moscow Russian, "Sorry, I thought that was number three Chekhov Avenue."

The attaché could hear the sharp intake of breath from the other end. "I see," the voice was deep and slow as though the man was thinking fast. "I understand, but you have the wrong number." The phone was gently cradled and the man from the embassy heard the soft click as the line was disconnected.

He shrugged now to see if the next stage worked. Early morning, the embassy man was out jogging along the Embankment. A few miles into his run, he passed the Ukraine Hotel and saw a dark stocky figure emerge.

He stopped and bent down to retie his trainer shoelace; as he bent down he saw the stocky figure remove and replace his hat as though adjusting it; that was the recognition signal. He let the man get a few hundred yards down the wide tree-strewn Kutuzovsky Prospekt and jogged slowly after him. He passed the man, without recognition, ten minutes later. The second sign that they were not being followed. After he passed the man, he speeded up. The man stretched his arms out windmilling them as though to keep warm in the cold snowy atmosphere and retraced his steps to the hotel.

The runner stopped and did some warming down exercises and jogged slowly back. He passed the man as he was about to re-enter the hotel.

"Uspenskoye Bridge, 7pm." The runner made it seem as though he was saying, "Good morning," and that is what the porter of the hotel would report.

The man half turned, raising a hand, "Keep training; it is the Olympics soon and we must beat the Americans."

The porter would report that the Gipsy had encouraged a Russian athlete to train hard to beat the Americans. Another casual watcher, a Kremlin guard from a window across the street, would report something similar.

The runner, on the other hand, had got his signal that all was well and a meet was to take place. He jogged for another 20 minutes through the backstreets. He had to ensure that he was not followed. He had to be certain. Once he confirmed that he was clear, his tired legs moving without enthusiasm, he made the run for home, not a sprint, just enough activity to stop the sweat freezing. It was not that he was not fit, it was just that a jog at this time was not on his itinerary and mentally his body was rebelling.

Ten minutes later, still in his running kit, he was speaking to Robinson. The time in the UK was ten to seven. Robinson had been up most of the night waiting for this call but had lounged in his chair for a few hours. When the junior attaché confirmed that the meet was on, any tiredness he had felt dropped from his body like a released cloak. He had his ace and it was primed for use.

Chapter 47

MOSCOW

Brigadier Tsygankov was in early that morning, about the time that Brigadier Robinson had received his message from Moscow. Tsygankov's elation of the night before had all but vanished; he had slept badly for a few hours and had given up and returned to his office. The pile of work, interviews and meetings that had to be tackled that day did nothing to improve his mood. He had to take steps to sort out the prisoners and others once the technology colonel confirmed all was ready.

His first action when his secretary arrived and welcomed him was to ask her to get through to Colonel Ivanovich and see how he was getting on.

His secretary buzzed that Ivanovich was on the line; the colonel told Tsygankov that he needed another few days to confirm that everything was going to work as planned. Could the colonel call him again then when he hoped to confirm full compliance?

Tsygankov was taking no prisoners this morning, "Ivanovich, what was the purpose of all that testing we went through in Guatemala if you have to recheck it again here?"

"Sir, yes, we are going over some of the same ground but we have mocked up the actual installation and environment that the device and its peripherals will operate in, including its thermal environment. We are almost there, just need to see it operate for a few days without glitches. Could probably say yes now but..." he left the sentence unfinished.

Tsygankov could do with some breathing space, so he was not too put out; it gave him valuable time to get to grips with other matters. "No, let's be certain, Colonel. Only call me when you are 100 per cent happy or, worst case, there is a problem. Go with that," he replaced the phone.

Chapter 48

LAST CALL

Dieter and Caroline arrived in the middle of the afternoon. They looked out of the window as the aircraft circled Moscow airport before it lined up for its run in. What they saw impressed them; first of all was the size of the airport. Its footprint was larger than that of London's Heathrow Airport and still seemed to be sprawling outwards. On their arrival, the unsmiling silent immigration officer took his time scrutinizing their passports. It was a game, they knew that, but their heart rates were naturally elevated. As they waited for their luggage at the carousel they observed the people around them, 99 per cent of whom were smoking strong cigarettes and not a few were unsteady on their feet; they must have taken the vodka offered freely on the Russian flights intravenously, Wolff thought to himself.

A taxi was organized quick time for them by what appeared to be an ageing gangmaster figure. It was the first visit to Moscow for both of them and everything they saw held them spellbound during the long ride into the centre of the city. The driver was uncommunicative, when Wolff asked him if he spoke English he replied aggressively, "Ruski, ruski!" which Wolff took to mean he only spoke Russian. It had been agreed that Caroline would not show her Russian language skills unless it was an emergency. Her job was to listen and to brief Wolff as needs be.

They booked into the hotel, handed over their passports for safekeeping and filled out the register. They dumped their bags in the room, only staying long enough for Wolff to ferret out a tourist guidebook with a good street map section before they were in the lift, going back down to reception. They made some show of looking at postcards and flyers before consulting the receptionist for a good restaurant. Arm in arm they left the hotel and were soon lost in a maze of streets and shops. Stopping for coffee and cake more than once, they made absolutely sure they were not being followed. Their warm clothing and coats were ambiguous enough to be local Moscow Russian and gradually they faded into the background. They had decided not to loiter long enough in any one location to be spotted or to raise suspicion but to keep moving until the meet. They both felt, by the very nature of their positions, training and background that, after a day of moving round Moscow, they knew the city. By the time evening threatened, they felt that they had an acute sense of the Russian capital and its teeming eight million inhabitants who flooded into the city in the day, and who withdrew to the warmth of their flats at night, leaving the streets, for the most part, deserted, cold and silent.

Approaching seven, refreshed, fed and invigorated in the cold air, they approached the bridge to meet their target. The man they had come to meet was already there, smoking quietly, almost half hidden in a recess at the southern end of the bridge, out of sight to the casual observer, in this case mainly drivers that drove at speed, whipping up dirty snow slush that threatened to swamp Wolff and Webster but which always fell short. Seemingly for their own protection, they moved into the recess behind the man to seek shelter. Exchanges were made. The man in his middle fifties radiated strength. Wolff guessed he had had a very physical life. He was right.

There was a conversation. The man had a surprise for them; he wanted them back to the UK on the eleven thirty flight via a stopover in Berlin. Wolff protested but the man was insistent. He explained that their extended presence put not only him and themselves in danger but also everybody else involved. If Rodney got away then they could compromise everything.

"But will the authorities not be suspicious if, having just arrived, we suddenly leave the same day?" Miss Webster pushed back.

"Send yourselves a telegram, phone call or whatever, something about a death in the family. We Russians are suckers for family tragedies," he explained sardonically in a slow, heavily accented American drawl.

"What are we to do till then, kick our heels?"

"Passports, I take it you have them?"

"Yes, plus one extra," Wolff said.

"For me? No, I will not be coming; I am too well known." It was an unequivocal statement. He added, "I have long ago planned my exit, one way or the other, so don't worry; too old to travel."

"Not for you, for your daughter, Valeria," Wolff said quietly.

The man sagged for an instant then brightened, "You know?"

"Our boss worked it out."

He had recovered from his shock and grunted, drawing deeply on his cigarette before blowing out acrid smoke, throwing the remains to the pavement and stamping it into the slush. "Yes, it's time I think. I feel them close to me sometimes. It could not go on forever, could it?" It was not a question he needed answered.

"Why you?" it was a direct question from Wolff.

"Me?" he hunched his shoulders forward. "I knew Chekhov well, we were great comrades together. I was not political and I supported his ideas. I didn't report him. When they killed him, I think he always knew I would take over. Around the same time they hurt a lot of people close to me. So, revenge is my motivation. Revenge is a fairly strong emotion that has to be satisfied." He paused, "Bringing my daughter's passport is a bonus."

"Now, the plan; you," he indicated Caroline, "are to get back to the hotel collect your gear and then get yourself to the airport." He reached into his coat and brought out two tickets for the flight at eleven thirty to Berlin. "You, Wolff, are going to help my daughter. It is going to happen now, the rescue of the British and the destruction of the device." Wolff did not push back at that remark. He would wait to see how matters developed.

Both visitors, despite their training, had felt their stomachs contract, flutter and their breath shorten; they had been simply unprepared for the idea that they would be involved so quickly.

The Russian looked up and down the bridge, "We don't have much time; what we are about to do is unprecedented. Let's get off this bridge to a more private place and I will explain the plan to you. Come on now, quick, follow me." He clasped them both to him in a bear hug and hurried away. They followed him at a distance to a car a few streets away and got into the back of the car.

In the car was Gipsy's daughter, Valeria. A few hours earlier Gipsy had called her with the code phrase they both hoped they would never have to use, "Valeria, it's your father; it's time we had a holiday together, so come now and discuss it." It was time, because of their family connection to the past Khrushchev elite, they had accepted long ago that they may have to flee one day. Gipsy clasped the British passport in his breast pocket as though it were the most precious item in the world and passed it to his daughter.

Fifteen minutes later they were all ensconced in a dingy flat somewhere at the back of the Kremlin, only a half mile from where Rodney was being held and a mile from where the colonel poured over the device in his laboratory. The laboratory was on a lower cellar floor, just one of the many cellars at the KGB headquarters.

An hour later, the old KGB general sitting as the interim leader of the Soviet Union, sat at his desk, bored to the back teeth, thumbing through uninteresting paperwork when the report of the meeting came through to him. He sat upright in the high-backed chair, smiling to himself, after all these years, it is payback time, he thought. In the small hours he would roll up the traitor but this evening he had to host some bureaucrats from the Russian satellite states.

In his London office, as was his way, Brigadier Robinson settled himself down in his high-backed leather chair and swung it round to look out of the window at the nearby London streets swarming with people. He wondered how many of them ever gave a moment's thought to what the security services did and the dangers they faced on their behalf. He would not leave his headquarters now until this operation was ended, successful or not but, in any event, concluded.

In Moscow, in the Russian agent's flat, Gipsy held his audience captivated as he described the plan and by eight thirty he was summing up as Wolff struggled into the uniform of a captain in the KGB.

The plan that Gipsy had outlined was simple and daring; if it worked, in just over three hours all would be well. The plan was predicated on confidence. If you are self-assured you can get away with many things; few challenge the person who knows or appears to know exactly what they are doing.

At a quarter to ten that night, Valeria Gershuni in the full dress uniform of a KGB staff major let herself into the KGB headquarters by the side entrance leading to the First Directorate. The guard acknowledged the major. Always striking, she looked impressive and haughtily brought her companion in with her. The guard attempted to pull himself to his full height to match hers but failed miserably, knew it and flushed angrily to himself, cursing his lack of stature and his lowly rank that would all his life bar him from winning a woman like that.

He wondered who her companion was; he looked tanned and fit, and very unlike the winter-paled Muscovites. What the hell, in another eight hours he would be warm and tucked up with his woman. She may not be a sleek major but she was his and she was comfortable. He watched Gershuni and her companion step out down the corridor. His woman may not compare with the major in the beauty stakes but she made him feel like a king. Hadn't his father always told him that one day he would come to realize beauty was only skin-deep. Happy at that thought, he settled down to await his next visitor. Still it doesn't hurt to dream, he chuckled to himself and straightened his tie.

Valeria led Wolff swiftly through the building. She moved positively along the maze of high-ceilinged corridors; for himself, his eyes were everywhere. They saw a few other occupants of the building but none of them even acknowledged them; they all seemed too busy buried in their own world and troubles.

They arrived at an old scissor-gated service lift at the end of a dimly-lit passageway. The lift was small with just enough room for them both. He could feel her sensuality in the confined space. It was a physical thing. Valeria sensed his awaking and calmed him by kissing him on the cheek and giving his arm a sisterly squeeze. Wolff coloured a little but smiled and, feeling more at ease, returned the gesture.

Settled now, they were ready, alert for what was to come. The lift descended deep into the bowels of the earth; it stopped suddenly with a jolt. They stood listening for a moment. Valeria pulled back the doors and they stepped into a brightly-lit corridor. A hurried glance down the passage, which seemed to stretch to infinity, showed Wolff that caution was required. Ceiling-mounted cameras monitored the comings and goings in this part of the building. The high peak of Wolff's uniform hat hid all but his chin to them. A few yards from the lift was a grilled barrier manned by a soldier reading a book. He saw the two officers and stood up; his machine gun hung loose by its shoulder strap pointing down to his side.

"Good evening," Valeria offered softly.

The soldier smiled, "Major Gershuni, what can I do for you?" Wolff studied the man; he was late twenties, stocky and solid, only of average height but would be difficult to overpower if that proved necessary.

But without hesitation the soldier opened the grill. Valeria simply beamed at him and beckoned Wolff through with her, "He is with me." The soldier knew the major and that was good enough for him.

"Can I have the key for Colonel Ivanovich's laboratory?" she held out her hand.

For a moment the soldier's brows knitted, "But Comrade Major, the Colonel is working, did not you know?"

Valeria's response was flawless, "Oh, good, that saves us much time and trouble. I was hoping he might be here, there is a rush job on." She looked at Wolff and, for the soldier's benefit, said in Russian, "Just as well or you might have had a wasted journey," she winked; Wolff looked at the soldier and shrugged.

Wolff had no idea what was being said but he picked up the inflections and guessed that all appeared well.

The soldier made a face of sympathy back at Wolff. He was forever being asked to perform tasks of no consequence for officers. He nodded, suddenly gloomy, and turned back to his desk where he sat down and returned to his book. In front of him was a bank of screens showing the far reaches of the passageway and other entrances. Main rooms were also monitored but not the smaller ones. Colonel Ivanovich's personal chemical and electronic laboratory was normally monitored but the colonel had blanked off his cameras a week ago for a reason that was not his concern. What they were doing was their business, although out of his peripheral vision he saw them on a monitor turn off into the narrow corridor leading to the colonel's room.

Just before Gershuni turned into the corridor she looked back at the soldier and smiled. "God, she is beautiful," the soldier relaxed.

As they entered the laboratory, the colonel turned, clearly annoyed at the interruption, "What are you doing here, Valeria, and who is this Comrade Captain?" As he turned, he exposed the device; it sat humming on the bench. To it were connected row after row of oscilloscopes each showing a dancing wave or multiples of waves. Other digital meters and counters were as active as the scopes. In the corner, sat a squat, powerful computer opposite which were shelves of chemicals.

Every few seconds the computer would click and a large printer spewed lines of data. Gershuni registered the mass of paper in a nanosecond, she would use it.

"It seems we are disturbing you at an inopportune moment, I'm so sorry. However, first, you simply must meet..." Gershuni stepped forward to introduce Wolff who advanced, his hand outstretched. The colonel's natural reaction was to move to offer his hand and with the left to remove his glasses. He was about to use them, forcefully, to make a point and to ask his question again. However, Wolff gripped the outstretched hand smiling; he pulled the colonel forward, whipping his arm outwards, then forward and down and as the colonel leaned forward, spun him round to face the other way. Wolff chopped down with all his might with his other clenched fist at the colonel's exposed neck and throat. The colonel collapsed to his knees and Wolff pulled back his head by grabbing his hair, chopped down on the voice box and then, with lightning speed, chopped the colonel under the nose. The senseless colonel lolled as Wolff picked him up from the floor and sat him back on to his stool so that the colonel's arms wrapped themselves around and embraced the device.

"Quickly, now, stay by the door," Valeria ordered. For a moment they both looked at the machine they had come to destroy and briefly contemplated taking it. "Too risky, better nobody has it," Gershuni said, expressing both their thoughts.

She worked furiously for a minute. First she took a bottle of ether from the shelf and, taking out the stopper, poured some of it over the colonel's face. Then she grabbed the stream of computer printout and pulled it around the laboratory. Grabbing a heavy instrument she smashed it down on the device. Her next action was to locate bottles of flammable liquids from the shelves of the laboratory. There were two bottles of alcohol and another of benzene. She worked frantically with the paper and a few rags she had garnered from various part of the laboratory and then poured the alcohol and benzene on to them, placing them on the device bench.

Her final act was to go to the bottle of phosphorous she had spotted and carefully shook the contents out next to the device and around the benches. Already the phosphorous sticks were smoking. In a minute or so the laboratory would be on fire. She and Wolff moved quickly out of the room, closing the door and taking care to close the sprinkler valve before they left. In the corridor they sauntered back to the grill which the soldier already held open for them and stepped into the lift. They left the building as they had come. In the distance from deep within the building they heard the faint sound of a fire alarm.

Walking away from the building, they went to a car that had pulled up a hundred metres from the building. They got into the back.

"All OK so far?" Gipsy wanted to know.

"Yeah, OK," Valeria's eyes were sparking; she was buoyant, times like these were like a drug to her.

"Settle down now, Valeria. Phase two in five minutes, fail, and in six you will be dead," Gipsy warned; his words cooled her. "Wolff, get out of the uniform and into your civilian kit. Your task is done. You need to get out and get a taxi to the airport to meet Miss Webster. Whether we succeed or fail, you and she must be on the plane."

"You sure about that?" Wolff was also ready for more; the recklessness of action had gripped him.

"Yes, we stick to the plan. Cool it; now go, go!" Gipsy turned in his seat and glared at Wolff, "Valeria knows what to do."

The heat and hum of the powerful car engine threatened to lull and relax them. Moments later the tower block they needed came into view. It was like many in the area; only the height and its isolation from the others marked it out and gave it any prominence.

The KGB's First Directive had all the suites on the last five floors, including the penthouse where Rodney and his colleagues were held prisoner. The rest of the building fronted as a state workers' staff hostel.

The reception area would pass for a hotel's with its easy chairs and coffee tables. Few were occupied. The receptionist didn't give Gershuni a glance; people were in and out all the time. She went to the internal phone booths and buzzed the guards on the penthouse floor; only they could send and release the lift that fed the top five floors.

When it arrived, she took the lift to the top and knocked on the door sheltering the two duty guards guarding the British team, they let her in. It was late but she was accredited and a frequent visitor, so their suspicions were not aroused; quite the contrary, they would have the chance to flirt with the major to break the boredom of their watch.

"How are our prisoners?" she asked, stepping out of the elevator and taking off her outer coat before leaning over to see the bank of screens showing the prison suite.

"Good, Major, no trouble. They have eaten and are just watching TV, as you can see."

"Coffee?" it was a command but delivered without demand.

"No problem, Major," the junior of the two guards went into a small kitchen off the guardroom and poured her a coffee from a percolator.

"Join me, you two?" Valeria took out a small flask. "Drink to the new director?"

"Neat for me, please," the guard who had poured the coffee said holding out a mug.

"Me too please, Major," the other guard rummaged for his mug and also held it out.

She poured out the vodka for the two guards and then into her coffee. "Drink," she said as she made a mess of getting the top back on to the flask. Putting the container away at last, she lifted her mug to watch the two guards quickly down their drinks before grasping their throats. They died quickly in an adagio of pain and spasm. She poured her mug of coffee into the sink, stepped over the dead guards and then unlocked the doors into the prison. She felt a great calm overwhelm her. The delayed shock, she knew, would come later.

"You three, we are moving now." Startled though Rodney and the other two were, they grasped the situation immediately. Rodney donned an old Russian overcoat.

She inspected them. "You have Russian clothing, at least, thank God, but you two don't look Russian," she pointed at Mould and Sharky. "Quick, behind the door, bring in the two dead guards' fur hats and coats and put them on."

The atmosphere was electric as they busied about disguising themselves as Russians. Valeria stopped Mould rummaging for the guards' weapons with a hand on his arm. "Stop, what good will they do you?" Mould shrugged, putting his finds back on the floor.

"Come on with me. Mould, when we get to the door, laugh when I wink. You two flash the guards' identities and I will flash mine. It should be enough, the guards know me and they are not expecting trouble from within." The three men looked at each other; crazy, but they had no choice in the matter. There were two dead men upstairs which would not help their cause.

Rodney thought he could smell the tension as they passed easily through the checkpoint and out into the street.

Valeria rushed them round the corner to a waiting car. She organized the three British men into the back of the car and then moved into the front seat with her father.

"Where are we going?" Rodney asked his head still reeling at the speed at which it had all happened.

"Home, I hope," the driver drawled.

"Who are you, American?"

"Chekhov, to you," Gipsy laughed.

"But how...?" Rodney was incredulous.

"Never mind that now, there is no time; Valeria will tell you all later, if you get away, that is." Chekhov was handling the car roughly through the streets but not so fast that it would call attention to itself. The last thing he wanted was to be stopped now.

In the front seat, Valeria struggled out of her uniform and into civilian clothes. Chekhov, in the meantime, passed over three passports. "Get changed into the clothes in the back and for fuck sake learn your new names."

Rodney and the others fumbled into the clothes and then held the passports up so they could read them by the light of passing cars and street lamps.

They made the airport at twelve minutes past eleven. Chekhov was out of the car in a shot and round to the boot, followed by the rest of the occupants. He roughly shoved small overnight bags at them with enough contents not to give rise to suspicion.

He had been busy while his daughter had been destroying the device and rescuing the captives. They were given tickets for the flight at eleven thirty to Berlin, the same flight that Wolff and Caroline were on.

Chapter 49

GIPSY

Near midnight, inside the Kremlin, in the anteroom to his sleeping chamber, the interim leader of the Soviet who was now, to all intents and purposes, the leader of the Soviet Union sat calm and immobile in his high-backed chair as he listened to the call from the airport.

He thanked the caller and gently cradled the phone back on its rest. In front of him, in the other high-backed chairs, sat two men, one rigid, the other relaxed. Separating them was a large round brass-topped coffee table, beautifully carved and inlaid with gold and silver to depict the geographic features of the Afghanistan lands, a gift from a friendly Afghan warlord. The table, protected by thick glass, was high enough to use as a desk, and now supported several open files, a bottle of the leader's favourite liqueur, Drambuie, and glasses for all three. The room itself, on that cold night, was warm and comfortable, the dark rosewood panelling, its Persian carpets and heavy velvet drapes gave the room a Middle Eastern feeling. The quietness of the room bordered on a physical presence. Ghosts of wars, past great deeds, good and foul, seemed to fill the air.

"I think, gentlemen," the leader began, "I owe you some sort of explanation as to recent events. However, you are intelligent men and I expect that you may well have pieced together most, if not all, of the events that have led up to tonight."

The leader poured the two men a tot of liqueur. "In a way, Carl," Brigadier Tsygankov seemed to become even taller and more rigid in his seat than ever. "You started the whole thing ten years ago." He noticed the concern in Tsygankov's face, "No! No! Nothing to worry about, nothing you could have done anyway and that goes for tonight's events, too. So relax and enjoy the Drambuie and listen to my story."

He raised his glass, drained it, and poured himself a second before he sat back, lovingly warming the fiery liqueur by twirling the glass as though it were a brandy goblet in the palms of his hands. "You see, almost immediately Chekhov was killed, the flow of secret information from the highest levels again began to find its way into England. Perhaps it was not so frequent or great in volume and probably not so critical, but still, over time it could have damaged us further, he may have got lucky, one day and sent them the mother lode." He sipped his drink. "We know this from the various false trails and other techniques we used, as well as our sources in the English secret service, civil service, armed forces, government etc." he reeled off the list of organizations with a chuckle. "The intelligence was authentic, except what we fed in for damage limitation purposes but as I hinted, at intervals, as the years progressed, we discerned a rather clever mole, one that could and probably was going to hurt us seriously, eventually. There are always moles of one degree of importance or another, petty leaks etc. but this one was a little special, he or she had to be. Try as I could I could not catch him. I say him because I know him now. I had worked out for myself half a dozen game plans that I would put into operation if enough positive factors came together. Well, they eventually did, in a way. I confess I was a little concerned because I was up against a time constraint. This appointment was coming up and I wanted to be sure I'd got the man before I sat here and could no longer play with all the toys now at your command. Gentlemen, cheers!"

He put his glass out to the others who clicked theirs against his. "Success," they drained their glasses and he refilled them. "It was purely coincidental that we had been working on our own device. It was not coincidental, when the possibility of a similar device from South Africa, offered by the man Hough, that I should be involved. It fitted one of my game plans. It was something the English would give their eye teeth for, it was important enough to interest Robinson's people; although we couldn't pinpoint the source in Russia, we could pinpoint the recipient in England. It was Major Rodney Brown, in Robinson's section. Why Brown? Well, I reasoned soundly that as Brown had been central to Lawson's demise, that Chekhov's replacement would pick Robinson's crew rather than any other. Robinson is our generation, Tsygankov, so it was likely he would appoint Brown, his second in command, as the handler.

The old general sighed, "My problem was that I soon discovered that the contact was one way. In other words, our mole had chosen Brown and simply passed our secrets to him, unsolicited. I could not disabuse myself of the belief that, most likely, Major Brown, at least, knows who the man is. If Brown knows, likely Robinson does or could find out. Tonight proves I was correct. As for Brown, he would simply pass what he received to the various spymasters, but he would have kept the tops and tails etc. to himself; and so, over time, he would know who was sending him the data, of that I became sure."

"Did you ever think of lifting Brown?" Polyakov questioned.

"Hmm, yes and no; you see, although we are talking some years, I would say it's only in the last two that I have had even what was, at best, a somewhat cloudy view of most of the picture and, well, I have been hoping to turn the knowledge to some advantage. Again, until six months ago there was not the pressure for me to eradicate the mole personally. As you know, others in the directorate were working on leaks."

He paused, "But, as I said, with the possibility of this job, the pressure increased." He paused again and then added enthusiastically, "Suddenly, here we were with something the English wanted, and Brown in our hands." He leant forward, his large peasant face lit up.

"Thank you, Carl. And, I confess, I played a little game through you by getting General Polyakov to order you to eliminate the English agents but not allowing you to carry out the deed until the device had been declared compliant and, knowing the nature of our technical colonel, I judged it would be a few days before he satisfied himself that the device was everything we were hoping for. A gamble, but well... that would have given enough time for the elimination order to leak to the British. But in the event, as we know, it wasn't necessary. They appear to have been ahead of my game plan, even before I'd set the pieces up, and every time, it seems." He frowned, pursing his lips, "Brigadier at the helm, I suppose. I would like to meet him some day."

"But," Polyakov questioned when he saw the leader pause again, "it was a little costly." He was thinking of the price in time, money and in human life.

The leader hesitated again, "The price of doing business; but some success I think, you have the mole's name now, do you not?"

Tsygankov interjected, adding, "A shame, all the same, about the loss of the device and our man. Someone once told me, as you just reminded me, in such matters it is simply the cost of doing business, when I questioned a particularly expensive event."

The leader smiled, "I believed in the device, don't get me wrong, but the implementation phase was, in reality, far too dangerous, I think, and perhaps a pipe dream. I wouldn't admit that to anyone else, so don't quote me. As for the men, I am sorry that they and the Colonel should have lost their lives so horrifically."

Polyakov uncrossed his legs and sat up. It was an offer to the leader to dismiss them if he wanted to. "Relax, my dear General, the night is young and I have two more events for you to enjoy before the day is out. First, let's recharge our glasses, smoke if you want to, I'm going to have a cigar," he pressed a button on the chair and one of his green-uniformed aides arrived immediately.

"Bring another bottle, another glass, some cigars and sandwiches. Then have the prisoner brought in."

As the men waited for the aide to bring the refreshments to comply with their leader's wishes, Rodney and his party were landing in Berlin to be met by embassy staff and whisked away to freedom.

The three men in the Kremlin ate, smoked and drank expectantly. Initially under guard, but not restrained, Gipsy was brought into the room and waved to the fourth chair. The Soviet leader dismissed the guards who initially protested but had to concede.

The leader offered Gipsy a cigar and poured him a liqueur. Gipsy thanked him and sat back in the easy chair, content but curious.

The leader toasted the others and then Gipsy, "Got you!"

"Yes, it seems you have," Gipsy's deep rasping voice showed he was unafraid and relaxed, even relieved, although somewhat puzzled.

"The thing is, what do we do with you?" the leader looked to his two men, questioningly.

Both men knew Gipsy, they had met him and seen him often, especially during the Khrushchev era. It was probably true he was Khrushchev's daughter's friend and possibly her lover. The man had influence and friends that still wielded power.

"If we were to do a cost-benefit analysis, would we make a profit out of you at this stage?" Polyakov half smiled and lifted his glass to Gipsy.

Gipsy hesitantly picked his up and sipped the liqueur. "Could we use Gipsy to pass disinformation?" Tsygankov suggested, adding, "But only after his credibility had once more been established." He shrugged, "After all, after tonight it would be reasonable for them to suspect that he had been compromised or at least under surveillance since his daughter escaped."

"Suppose," Gipsy put in wearily, "I just chose death to welcome me."

"Not possible. As long as you remain alive, your daughter will too." The leader put in quickly, "You hear me well, Gipsy. There is nowhere safe for her if I say so," he wagged his finger at Gipsy as a warning.

Gipsy swung his heavy head and shoulders to squarely face the leader. "You leave me little choice," his eyes were steady, giving nothing away.

"None, from now on you will be shepherded by two of my faithful guards for as long as you live. Life will not be bad, but you will have to do as you are told. But finish your drink first and tell us why in hell's name you of all people played such a stupid game. You have everything you need, friends, money and influence."

Half an hour later Gipsy made his excuses; the leader pressed the button on his chair once more for the guards to collect him.

When the three were once more alone, the leader addressed them again, "I want that man used initially for about three to four months, after that we will see. I want, say, three or four valuable pieces of intelligence passed by him, and then I want to stir up the Middle East using the Americans in some way, possibly over the hostages. Illegal arms deals generally create so much trouble that the few remaining US dependent Arab states will prefer to deal with us; my political staff are working out a number of scenarios."

He paused for a moment to gather his thoughts, "When the time comes we will use our Gipsy to sow the seeds of mistrust and such like." He smiled at Polyakov, "Thank you, my friend, for your help tonight and you, Tsygankov, if you had not stepped down security before and after the incidents tonight, I'm not sure Brown and his party would have got away. After all, what is the point of having a mole for us to use if he's got nobody to send his information to, eh?"

The three men laughed and the glasses clashed again and again well into the night. Later, as they parted, Polyakov and Tsygankov were each given a final task to perform.

Chapter 50

LONDON RULES

In the aftermath of the destruction of the device and the return to England of the agents with Valeria Gershuni, life readjusted itself for the participants as it does with guaranteed rapidity as new issues and new crises filled their days.

Rodney and his men settled back into their supposed routines. Sharky was back after a month, wounds treated and sense of humour intact.

The South African, Wolff, went home and it didn't surprise anyone when Caroline Webster followed a few months later to be with him.

Valeria was debriefed for a full two months, then given a new identity and she disappeared into the English countryside. Her only visitor was Rodney who, over time, became her constant companion and lover, whenever he was free. Valeria, talented like her father, spent her time painting and writing her book.

As for Gipsy, nothing was heard for a while and it was assumed by all and his daughter that he had been silenced.

To the surprise of Robinson's people, they were notified that Gipsy had appeared at his hotel and in public after a month. He seemed to be carrying on his life as normal. Four weeks after the affair, the first dispatch arrived at Rodney's home address. The intelligence was consistent with previous dispatches and Rodney, suspicious, as he should be, was nevertheless interested to see if the information purporting to be from Gipsy would prove accurate.

He called Valeria and with her he went over the dispatch carefully. She was very excited and clearly emotional. It meant that her father was not only alive but, it would seem, free.

Only Rodney knew how vulnerable she could be and had seen that side of her. His first indication that the hard lady had a soft centre was on the plane from Moscow to Tempelhof Airport in Berlin. She had trembled violently and tears had welled up in her eyes during the flight. Rodney's comforting arm and gentle way could do little to soothe the distressed Russian woman. On a night, weeks later, over dinner with Rodney, she confessed the tears were as much for the three dead men she had left behind as they were for her father.

Although convinced that the letter was from her father, Rodney urged caution, at least for a while. His six senses were warning him that it was all a little too simple. In the weeks that followed new information was received; its quality and content were checked and found accurate; as time went on the quality and importance of the intelligence continued to increase.

Robinson, as a precaution, had had Gipsy checked out by the men in Moscow and no discernible change in the agent's lifestyle could be seen except that he was almost always accompanied when he left his residence.

Robinson's scepticism, like Rodney's, gradually waned as the months went on. Four months later disturbing information was transmitted to Rodney even though it at first made him smile.

It seemed the Americans had let a contract for ball bearings for the rotor gearbox of their heavy-lift military helicopter. The firm it seemed had been unable to complete the order and had bought bearings from another supplier. The new product, whilst meeting their specification, had been made in Russia, a delicate matter as the Americans were as oblivious to the facts, as was the contractor.

The next dispatch from Gipsy arrived with disturbing information about a number of people who had been compromised. The people concerned were in authority and had been hooked by the KGB when they were either visiting Russia or had been exposed in the UK. The report concerned a minor clerical officer in MI5, a colonel in the MOD, a sprinkling of middle-ranking civil servants spread from GCHQ to Whitehall and two air force officers.

In the following week the intelligence sent by Gipsy moved swiftly and subtly to the Middle East, touching Cyprus briefly. There were transcripts between the Arabs and an unknown American colonel; the theme seemed to be a deal over American hostages held in Beirut.

The warning bells sounded in Rodney's mind as Gipsy's information now seemed to be fixated on outing and embarrassing the West. Curiosity got the better of him. With each dispatch, more and more detail was added about the Middle East deal. From the American side emerged a desperation to get the hostages free at any price. The colonel appeared to be acting for a political group that had an irrational fear that the media would use the hostages to get at the Democratic ruling party's inability to free their fellow Americans. An Arab called Saied seemed to be the driving force; the man had set the negotiations up in the first place. He never admitted he worked for the Iranians but it soon became obvious he was their third party agent and the Iranians held the key.

The moral dilemma faced by the British was how to pass to the Americans the knowledge that their secret negotiations were not secret. If the Russians and the British knew, who else did? Further, how could the small group of Americans prostitute themselves to the Iranian regime while America was supporting Saddam in Iraq at the same time? The problem was the British didn't know how far up the establishment the deal was being negotiated. Did it reach to the White House itself? Rodney and Robinson watched the situation develop.

The brigadier kept the prime minister fully conversant with what was going on and, at one meeting with her advisers, it was decided to tell the American president what they knew and to tell the South Africans that the Arab they sought for the murders at their computer centre had surfaced in Cyprus.

The reaction in both camps was explosive and instant. The South Africans went to terminate Saied the following day.

The Americans asked the prime minister for help; they wanted a neutral figure to negotiate openly for them. This would satisfy the Iranians and allow the real deal in weapons and spares for the Iranian's war machine in exchange for the hostages to go on unabated. The deals were made and shortly afterwards the final hostages were freed. Inevitably it became public knowledge and the world press took up the mantle of the global conscience.

The question on everybody's mind was would the president be the second Democratic president to be ousted by the media this century?

In Russia, when the news broke, the leader thanked his KGB chief and his spymaster for creating the situation. The turmoil for the American president was, he thought, almost as good as the device might have given. The use of the Arab was a master stroke. Before they left him in his gloomy study, surrounded by files and paperwork, the leader reminded General Polyakov and Tsygankov that it was time to perform the final act to enable him to close the file forever.

Chapter 51

END GAME SOUTH AFRICA

The following day Rodney received a message from Gipsy by the agreed channels he had put in place, telling him he was going hunting and that his daughter should meet him at the lodge on the last day of the month.

Rodney stared at the message, it meant nothing to him but he suspected Valeria would be able to decode her father's cryptic message. After sitting for a few moments thinking over the wording, he slowly got up from his desk; he needed to discuss this with the boss. It simply felt wrong to him; Gipsy knew the pipeline was secure and yet he had chosen to disguise the destination. An hour later, after he and the brigadier had considered all the implications, it was decided that Rodney would go with Valeria and if, after his discussion with her, he could, if he needed to, take a few of the team with him. He collected his car from the secure underground car park and swung it into the London traffic. He was relaxed, untroubled, looking forward to seeing Valeria. He imagined her welcoming greeting and grinned to himself. He hadn't warned her he was coming – he didn't need to. After an hour escaping the London crush and a fast run up the motorway he hit the country roads, arriving shortly after noon. He found her in the garden, painting. The old farmworker's cottage that the organization had found for her was down a quiet narrow tree-lined lane, hidden from the public on a large estate of a Duke who was a member of the Service Central Intelligence Committee.

The cottage had had a wild overgrown garden when they first placed Valeria there, but over the months Valeria had tamed her environment and it was a picture at this time of the year with its views from the rear kitchen garden over the Downs.

Valeria gave a whoop of joy as Rodney bounded into the garden. He held out his arms as she ran into them and he clasped her tightly before lifting and swinging her into the air. Rodney, at 45, was eight years older than Valeria but it didn't seem to matter to them. Their relationship had developed quickly after they had returned to England. In truth both knew from their first meeting that it would, if only they had a chance. Each satisfied the other's needs of a life partner.

Whilst the relationship between a serving SIS officer and an ex-KGB major would have been frowned upon by many and, for Rodney, as he well knew, possibly career limiting, in truth he did not care; he was happier now than he had been for many years. He had taken the decision to tell the brigadier when matters had become serious.

The brigadier had nodded sagely but then smiling had said, "Rodney, you're not the first to fall..." he had hesitated, "to fall for, shall we say, a victim." He concluded that the matter was for them alone and wished them happiness. He had no objections.

As Valeria read the message from her father, it was difficult for her to hide her excitement. "Is this possible? Why don't you see! This is wonderful," and she threw her arms round his neck. They made love. Afterwards Valeria lay in bed beside him, smiling to herself.

"Penny for your thoughts," Rodney said gently.

"I was thinking of my father," she said seriously.

"I should have guessed," he grinned. "Exciting eh? Like some wine?"

"Yes, please."

Rodney slid out of bed and went to the kitchen, bringing back a bottle of white wine and two glasses. He slipped back into the bed and poured them a glass each.

"It could be dangerous for you. What if it's a trap?" Rodney took a sip of the wine, "Now I understand where the meeting is it doesn't change things and I still have a niggling concern. I will go and get him myself, if you like, and I'm sure Dieter would help me." Rodney put the glass to his lips, again he was thoughtful. It never occurred to him till then that all may not be as it seemed.

"No, I'm coming; he asked for me." There was something in her eyes that Rodney recognized as defiance. Like her father, she was not one who understood the word can't.

Rodney tried one last time to point out the danger, "If you do that you risk exposure. You know the KGB are not fools and they have observers that will be looking for you to break out of the UK. You're bound to be seen. It is a risky course, although I understand your feeling, but I ask you again to reconsider. Let me go for him."

"So what, to the danger, eh?" She leant over to him and tapped Rodney's chest with a finger lightly, her blond hair falling around him. "What's life without a little risk?" she coiled two long chest hairs round her finger, trapping the hairs with her thumb and her finger, and pulled.

Rodney yelped and the wine spilt over the cover. It really didn't matter, Rodney thought, this is why I love her; she's fun to be with.

The week before they were due to fly to South Africa, Rodney and Valeria made contact with Dieter, to alert him to their visit and to ask for his help to move freely around the border area. Rodney's department was interested in the trip when they knew about it. He had had to inform them and get sanction for it. Rodney and the brigadier had several discussions on what actions they might consider if indeed Gipsy did show and was free to either come over to them or to return to his life in Russia.

In the run-up to the visit, Valeria got more and more excited and it was all Rodney could do to keep her feet on the ground. Valeria and Rodney arrived in South Africa a few days ahead of the meeting and were met at airport arrivals by Caroline and Dieter. It was a happy reunion of four people who had shared experiences.

Wolff told them of the reception he had received from his boss when he had returned from his jaunt. It wasn't all bad. He related his debrief interview to them, grinning, "I was marched in to the boss by the Colonel's executive officer who was his right-hand man. I really thought I was in the mire good and proper."

"And what happened?" Rodney asked with concern in his voice.

"The boss had his back to me when I was marched in but only because his bulky body was hiding glasses and a couple of bottles of champagne. I found out soon enough that they been called by the Brigadier and they had had a great time discussing all our exploits. They were simply delighted that the device had been destroyed. After that initial surprise the boss dragged in Paul Vintner and the rest of the crew. The only person really pissed off was a civilian who had lost his device."

Then, before first light in the cool of predawn the next day and after a night of good food and wine, the four flew up to the border in a

Beechcraft. At the landing strip, a member of Wolff's organization had a dusty 4x4 waiting for them to use on the final leg of their journey. As the instructions were for Valeria to meet her father at three that afternoon at the hunting lodge, Wolff discussed the route and time to the target rendezvous with the local man; Valeria was so excited, they all caught her mood.

Wolff had been thinking about the meet and the location and on balance thought it would be all right. The South African security force controlled the border and the land on the other side to a considerable depth and this part of the border was considered safe. Wolff checked out the old stripped-down Land Rover for fuel, oil and water and with a satisfied grunt slammed down the bonnet and waved the party forward. The day was now hot and flies buzzed around them; in the absence of air conditioning, only the breeze from the slipstream as they drove along, streaming over the passengers, made it bearable.

They had stopped at a shanty town store at the edge of the airfield and bought a few cans of drinks and fruit for the two-hour trip to the lodge and Rodney reached for a bottle of water. He watched the heat haze in front of them as they bounced along the track.

The landscape they passed through was flat, rising to a small range of hills to the north, which were jungle covered. At the rest stop, the two women went off to take some pictures, leaving Rodney with Wolff. Wolff shook out a crude map and aligned his compass. Rodney looked at him questioningly, Dieter laughed, "Just checking. There is a good dirt road to the lodge, but you never know, it's a big country. Is this the lodge that really belonged to Khrushchev's daughter?"

"As far as we know it still does," Rodney said quietly. "What I don't know, but I have thought about, is if the lodge has armed security or worse, KGB presence."

"I just hope we know what we are doing. This has all the hallmarks of turning into a disaster. But you know that, don't you Rodney?"

"Are you armed?" Rodney asked hoping he was.

Wolff shook his head, "Wish I was, but they vetoed my request." It was well out of his jurisdiction.

"Oh well, I'm probably seeing problems that are not there," Rodney slapped him on the shoulder. "Come, let's get the ladies and be off, we've still got a half hour to go."

The next half hour had a tension to it that Rodney found hard to explain. He tried to lighten the mood with observations on the wildlife and birds, of which there were fleeting glimpses.

When the lodge did appear out of the sparse bush, it seemed to dominate the area. They saw its sweeping drive approach, and they drove the last few hundred yards with caution, even though Valeria could hardly contain herself and was pushing for them to go faster.

They pulled up in front of the lodge just before lunch and it seemed largely deserted. A few tame animals padded round and nosed up to the vehicle. The African staff were mostly at their chores. A steward appeared and invited them in. The dining room was large and comfortable and displayed trophies on the walls around a large open stone fireplace.

At one end of the room that led to the veranda was the bar. "Drinks?" the waiter led them on to the veranda and sat them down.

"Please bring a jug of Pimm's and some groundnuts," Wolff said, adding, "And the menu; we will eat lunch while we are here," Wolff instructed the steward with a smile.

The view from the veranda was stunning and the nearby acacia trees in full bloom wafted their perfume down at them; the aroma was so akin to orange blossom that it reminded Rodney of the Cyprus orange orchards in the spring. But that was a lifetime away now, he thought. No regrets, he was with Valeria now. He allowed himself a private smile.

Under the shade of the veranda roof, the temperature was pleasant enough and after a meal of rice and a large shared platter of fish, they settled down to wait for Gipsy.

Even Valeria, who had been very excited, relaxed; she, like the others, had not realized that the lodge was also a commercial establishment; very enterprising of Khrushchev, they all thought.

Just before three that afternoon they heard the unmistakable thumping sound of a helicopter. Valeria stirred and moved to the edge of the veranda to lean against one of the wooden roof supports.

It came in low and overshot the lodge once, then came round in a tight circle and landed on the other side of a clump of trees, 150 metres from the lodge.

Valeria walked down the veranda steps and craned her eyes, shading them from the bright sunlight; Wolff, Rodney and Caroline sat up in their chairs. Rodney had a growing sense of foreboding. Why had the helicopter not landed closer, he wondered.

From behind the trees appeared a man running. He was large and heavy, even at this distance they could recognize the outline of Gipsy. He was waving, gesturing. Valeria was off the veranda in the next moment and running to meet her father.

Rodney interpreted the signals first, it was a warning. He was out of his chair racing after Valeria as fast as his gammy leg would allow, a warning growl formed in his throat. Too late he watched in horror as Valeria fell, followed immediately by her father. Both crumpled like rag dolls. For a moment the shock of the situation held him. Then he was running again to the prone form of the only woman he had ever wanted to spend his life with.

He felt Wolff catching him up and he was suddenly at his side, grabbing his arm, dragging him back. Rodney was only half conscious of Wolff, pulling him away from the lifeless form of Valeria as he strove to get to her.

"It is too late, Rodney, come back!" Rodney stopped, started off again and finally gave in, letting his gaze alternate between the two lifeless figures and the tall figure that emerged from the edge of the bush. It was Tsygankov.

Rodney and Wolff saw two other men emerge from the trees, both cradled rifles, barrels pointing at the ground but the butts in their shoulders. Rodney recognized them as professional soldiers. They stood alert beside the tall gaunt figure, their gaze never wavering from Rodney.

The distance between them was less than a hundred meters. Rodney stared at the Russian spymaster and shook off Wolff. "Tsygankov, you bastard!" Rodney bellowed angrily. "Why? Why?" His voice carried easily to Tsygankov.

Tsygankov shrugged his thin shoulders. "Because, Rodney, Major Rodney Brown," he shouted back, his voice carrying clearly, "it is the business you and I have chosen to work in. It is a game, but there are checks and balances and always consequences. Today is a reminder that for you it is not yet over." He slowly raised his left arm and held his scarred hand palm forward so Rodney could see it, "Oh no, Major Brown, we will meet again. I think now we are even. Next time, it is every man for himself. But not today; revenge, Major, is a dish that should always be served cold, don't you think?"

With that gesture, the Russian turned and indicated that the gunmen should follow. A minute later the helicopter engine noise increased and it took off swinging north.

Rodney watched it go; in his heart he felt only resignation and defeat. He knew he would recover but he didn't know when or how. All he knew now was a surge of red-hot anger and an unquenchable desire for vengeance. Somebody would pay for the deaths of Valeria and her father he promised himself; when that would be and where, he had no idea.

END

Lightning Source UK Ltd.
Milton Keynes UK
UKOW06f0806260615

254165UK00001B/1/P